OTHER BOOKS YOU MAY ENJOY

DAVID ARNOLD

THE STRANGE FASCINATIONS OF NOAH HYPNOTIK

PENGUIN BOOKS

PENGUIN BOOKS
An imprint of Penguin Random House LLC, New York

First published in the United States of America by Viking,
an imprint of Penguin Random House LLC, 2018
Published by Penguin Books, an imprint of Penguin Random House LLC, 2019

Visit us online at penguinrandomhouse.com

THE LIBRARY OF CONGRESS HAS CATALOGED THE VIKING EDITION AS FOLLOWS:
Names: Arnold, David, 1981– author.
Title: The strange fascinations of Noah Hypnotik / David Arnold.
Description: New York : Viking Books for Young Readers, [2018] | Summary:
"This is Noah Oakman, sixteen, Bowie believer, concise historian, disillusioned
swimmer, son, brother, friend. Then Noah gets hypnotized. Now Noah sees
changes—inexplicable scars, odd behaviors, rewritten histories—in all those
around him. All except his Strange Fascinations" —Provided by publisher.
Identifiers: LCCN 2017038030 | ISBN 9780425288863 (hardcover)
Subjects: | CYAC: Best friends—Fiction. | Friendship—Fiction. |
Brothers and sisters—Fiction. | Twins—Fiction. | Hypnotism—Fiction. |
Family life—Illinois—Fiction. | Illinois—Fiction.
Classification: LCC PZ7.A7349 Str 2018 | DDC [Fic]—dc23
LC record available at https://lccn.loc.gov/2017038030

Penguin Books ISBN 9780425288870

Printed in the United States of America
Set in New Aster Lt Std   Book design by Kate Renner

10   9   8   7   6   5   4   3   2   1

To Mom and Dad,
for helping me through the maze

THIS IS ➤ PART ONE

"It's not enough to put myself into my art — I have to die to it. And that's how I know it's something."

—Mila Henry,
excerpt from the Portland Press Herald *interview, 1959*

1 ➜ *that sadness feels heavier underwater*

I'll hold my breath and tell you what I mean: I first discovered the Fading Girl two months and two days ago, soon after summer began dripping its smugly sunny smile all over the place. I was with Alan, per usual. We had fallen down the YouTube rabbit hole, which was a thing we did from time to time. Generally speaking, I hate YouTube, mostly because Alan is all, *I just have to show you this* one *thing, yo,* but inevitably one thing becomes seventeen things, and before I know it, I'm watching a sea otter operate a vending machine, thinking, *Where the fuck did I go wrong?* And look: I am not immune to the allure of the sea otter, but at a certain point a guy has to wonder about all the life decisions he's made that have landed him on a couch, watching a glorified weasel press H9 for a bag of SunChips.

Quiet, and a little sad, but in a real way, drifting through the Rosa-Haas pool—I fucking love it here.

I would live here.

For the sake of precision: the Fading Girl video is a rapid time-lapse compilation of photographs clocking in at just over twelve minutes. It's entitled *One Face, Forty Years: An Examination of the Aging Process*, and underneath it a caption reads: "Daily self-portraits from 1977 to 2015. I got tired." (I love that last part, as if the Fading Girl felt the need to explain why she hadn't quite made it the full forty years.) In the beginning, she's probably in her early twenties, with blonde hair, long and shimmery, and bright eyes like a sunrise through a waterfall. At about the halfway mark the room changes, which I can only assume means she moved, but in the background, her possessions remain the same: a framed watercolor of mountains, a porcelain Chewbacca figurine, and elephants everywhere. Statues, posters, T-shirts—the Fading Girl had an elephant obsession, safe to say. She's always indoors, always alone, and—other than the move, and a variety of haircuts—she looks the same in every photo: no smile, staring straight into the camera, *every day for forty years*.

Always the same, until: changes.

Okay, I have to breathe now.

◀▮▮▮▮▶

I love this moment: breaking the surface, inhale, wet hair in the hot sun.

Alan is all, "Dude."

The moment would be better alone, to be honest.

"That was like a record," says Val. "You okay?"

A few more deep breaths, a quick smile, and . . .

I love this moment even more: dipping beneath the surface. Something about being underwater allows me to feel at a higher capacity—the silence and weightlessness, I think.

It's my favorite thing about swimming.

◀▮▮▮▮▶

The earlier shots are scanned-in Polaroids, but as the time lapse progresses and the resolution of the photos increases, the brightness of the Fading Girl begins to diminish: little by little, the hair thins; little by little, the eyes dim; little by little, the face withers, the skin droops, the bright young waterfall becomes a darkened millpond, one more victim in the septic tank of aging. And it doesn't make me sad so much as leave an impression of sadness, like watching a stone sink but never hit bottom.

Every day for forty years.

I've watched the video hundreds of times now: at night before bed, in the morning before school, in the library during lunch, on my phone during class, in my head during the in-betweens, I hum the Fading Girl like a song over and over again, and every time it ends I swear I'll never watch it again. But like the saddest human boomerang, I always come back.

Twelve minutes of staring at your screen and watching a person die. It's not violent. It's not immoral or shameful; nothing is done to her that isn't done to all of us, in turn. It's called *An Examination of the Aging Process*, but I call bullshit. That girl isn't aging; she's fading. And I can't look away.

There it is, the inevitable shoulder tap.

Time to join the land of the breathing.

"The fuck, Noah? You trying to drown yourself?" Val is on a float in the middle of the pool, wearing these giant sunglasses, sipping some kind of homemade daiquiri.

"For real," says Alan, popping a handful of caramel corn into his mouth. He's been working on this giant tin can (the kind with forests and snow and frolicking deer painted on the side) most of the afternoon. "Ours is a delicate triangle, yo. You drowning fucks up the whole system."

Val and Alan Rosa-Haas are twins. The Rosa-Haas house is a quick walk from my own, plus it has this amazing in-ground pool and Mr. and Mrs. Rosa-Haas are rarely around, so you tell me.

Alan was the first kid I met when my family moved to Iverton. We were twelve and he came over to my house and we read in my room, and he told me he thought he was gay, and I was like, "Uh, okay," and he was all, "Um, uh," and it was totally squirrely. And then he said not to tell anyone, and I said I wouldn't. And he said, "If you do tell, I'll whiz on your hamster." Back then I had this arthritic hamster called Goliath, and I didn't want some kid whizzing on him, so I assured Alan that my lips were pretty much sealed. Later I found out I was the first person Alan had come out to, and, at twelve, I had no idea how important a step this was. All I knew was my hamster was in dangerous proximity to a person threatening whiz. I asked Alan why he didn't want me to say anything, and he told me I wouldn't understand. A couple years later he came out publicly—and kids called him terrible names, and kids jumped a mile in the air when he bumped into them in the halls, and kids moved tables when he sat with them at lunch, not all kids, but so many kids—and I found out just how right he'd been. "I hadn't planned to tell you," he'd said in my room that day when we were twelve. And he told me how he felt like a shaken-up can of Coke, and how I just happened to be around when the lid blew off. I told him I was fine with that. So long as he didn't whiz on Goliath.

We made a pact.

And then we whizzed out the window together.

Truth is, from the moment I met Alan, I knew I loved him. He loves me a lot too. When we were younger, we talked about what it would be like if I were gay, to which he always said, "As if I'd even be into you, Oakman," to which I usually flexed a budding bicep, raised a single eyebrow, and nodded in slo-mo, as if to say, *How could anyone* not *be into* this?, and we laughed and imagined it was so. We imagined how we'd get married and buy a cabin in the mountains somewhere and just spend our days weaving baskets and eating out of iron skillets and talking about deep things.

But that was a long time ago.

"Who gave us this, anyway?" asks Alan, perched out on the edge of the diving board, swinging his pruned feet over the water.

"Who gave us what?" asks Val.

"*This* piece of shit." He holds the now-empty tin above his head.

"Okay, you basically just made love to that caramel corn," says Val. "Now you're done with it, you're calling it names?"

"That's not his point," I say, treading water by the edge of the pool.

"Exactly. No one buys these things for themselves," says Alan. "It's a blow-off gift, an afterthought. Should come with a card that says, *You mean next to nothing to me*."

Val is all, "Well, I think it's a nice gesture, but I'll be sure to express your displeasure with the Lovelocks next time I see them."

"Wait, like, *the* Lovelocks? Up on Piedmont?"

"They were over for dinner the other night. You were at practice."

Alan tosses the empty tin into the swimming pool, all, "A pox on the Lovelocks!" and dives in with a yell.

Val rolls her eyes, lays her head back on the float. Unlike Alan—who is pale year-round, taking after his father in what he calls the "perpetual Haas hue"—Val is always the first of us to tan. When we were young, she was just my best friend's annoying sister, a constant unwanted presence like a gnat buzzing our faces. Cut to the summer before high school, and one day she opens the door and I'm all, *Uh, hey, Val, uh, um, like, uh*. It's a deafening finality, getting smacked in the face with that first notion that perhaps sex isn't gross after all.

Like a two-by-four, really.

I don't know if it happened slowly, right under my nose, or if it was an overnight thing, but I suddenly found Val's presence far less annoying. That year I asked her to homecoming, and she said yes, and it was a little weird because we'd known each other so long, but it also felt like one of those things that needed trying. So we tried it. And here's what that looked like: me holding Val's hand in the hallway for all of two minutes before Alan sees us; thinking it's a joke, Alan busts a gut laughing; realizing it's not, he swings into complete and utter berserkery.

That was the last time we held hands, and the first time Alan referred to us as "the delicate triangle."

Still, I'd be lying if I said I didn't occasionally think about her like that. Val has this charm about her, smart without being arrogant, funny without taking over the room. She makes little comments under her breath as if annotating the situation, and you get the feeling she'd do this whether anyone was within earshot or not, which makes you feel lucky just being in her orbit.

Also, she has perfect breasts.

Alan backstrokes the length of the pool. He's getting faster, which I almost say out loud, but I know where that will lead: *The team misses you, Noah. We need you, No. How's the back, No? You okay, No?*

"You okay, No?" asks Val, like out of nowhere, too. A by-product of the triangle, I guess: near telepathy.

"It's fine," I say. "Doing better, I think."

She pushes those huge sunglasses up her forehead. "What?"

Shit. "Sorry," I say. "I thought you meant my back."

"I meant you zoned out. But . . . now you bring it up, how *is* your back?"

"It's fine."

"Doing better, you think?" She lets her sunglasses fall back into place, sips her daiquiri, and stares at me. No one does unnerving like Val.

I climb out of the pool, head toward the diving board.

"Dr. Kirby said to take it easy, right?" she says, but it's a big pool, and she's drifted near the opposite end, so I pretend not to hear. And maybe I can escape Val's stare, but her first question climbs right out of the pool and follows me like a dripping shadow: *You okay, No?*

Up on the diving board now, right out on the edge. The sun is almost down, and there's that warm kind of dimness that only late summer can bring, when the air feels milky, and it's beautiful but kind of sad watching the day die right in front of you like that, knowing there's nothing you can do for it. I guess the sun and the Fading Girl are a lot alike.

You okay, No?

It's like this: one summer, when I was eight (pre-Iverton days), I went to this camp where I made a bunch of new friends who taught me how to make slingshots, and that's where I had my first (and only) cigarette, and this one kid even had a picture of a lady in her underwear, which prompted an eye-opener of a talk, and that was when I learned sex was more than just naked kissing. Then, after camp was over and I came home, I went back to playing with my old friends and realized they knew nothing of slingshots and cigarettes. They did not know sex was more than naked kissing.

Much as I love Val and Alan—and it's a lot—it sometimes feels like they know nothing of slingshots and cigarettes. Like they still think sex is just naked kissing.

Across the pool, Val slides off the float, grabs one of those long foam noodles, and whales on Alan's head; he splashes her back, and they laugh carelessly in that summer way people do.

I close my eyes, dive, give myself over completely to the

water, and there, submerged in its slumber, I imagine a diagram of my heart:

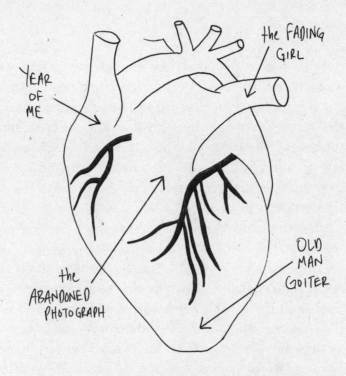

Whatever portions were once filled by the people I cared about most have been transplanted with Old Man Goiter, the Abandoned Photograph, Mila Henry's *Year of Me*, and the Fading Girl. I do not know how or why this happened.

I call them my Strange Fascinations.

3 ➜ *some thoughts on Iverton and home and walking while walking home through Iverton*

Iverton, Illinois, is the personification of its resident youth: someone gave it the keys, a credit card, and no curfew, and now it thinks its shit doesn't stink. The suburb is populated by these gaudy, homogeneous brick houses, each a clone of the one next to it; driveways and garages are stocked with a variety of shiny SUVs, lawns are pushed to the greenest of greens, and trees grow in suspiciously symmetrical fashion.

"How white is Iverton?" Alan would ask.

"How white?" I would respond.

"So white, the snow doesn't show."

Val and Alan's mom is from San Juan, Puerto Rico, their father of Dutch descent. ("Rosas come second to none," was all Mrs. Rosa-Haas would say anytime someone asked about their last name. Apparently it was the only way she would agree to marry Mr. Rosa-Haas.) In a town like Iverton, being half Puerto Rican means half the people assume Val and Alan are white, and the other half ask questions like, "No, really, where are you *from*?"

Last year this kid on the swim team asked Alan that question, to which Alan said, "Iverton," to which the kid said, "No, I mean, *from* from," to which Alan said, "Ohhhhh, I thought you meant from *from* from-from-from *frooooooooooooooom*," to which the kid turned every shade of red, pretended to hear his cell ring, and walked away.

Val and Alan get this shit all the time, and they pretend it doesn't bother them—and maybe it doesn't, what do I know.

But I'll never forget something Alan said once. "It's like this town wants me to be Rosa *or* Haas. Like it can't deal with me being both at the same time."

So, yes, Iverton may have the keys, the credit card, and no curfew, but me-oh-my, does its shit stink.

◀━▌▌▌▌▌━▶

Halfway home now, and I will give it this: after dark, on a clean summer night, Iverton is highly walkable.

Some might argue that walking is the slowest method of getting from point A to point B, and fair enough, but for me, getting from points A to B is only an ancillary benefit. I find inherent value in the steps themselves. This is exponentially true of my walks to and from the Rosa-Haas house, as if I'm closest to my true self when I am somewhere between my friends and family.

I walk up our driveway, past the assortment of Oakman automobiles: my Hyundai hatchback (which Alan refers to as my *fun guy ballsack*), Dad's Pontiac station wagon (complete with wood paneling and a backward-facing trunk seat), and Mom's ancient Land Rover. If you listen closely, you can actually hear the neighborhood's collective sigh of disapproval.

We bought this house shortly after the passing of Papa Oak, who lived his final years as a semi-reclusive widower, and who, upon his death, confirmed suspicions regarding his net worth. Everyone in the family got a sizeable chunk, at which point I learned something: if nothing reveals the deepest desire of one's heart like a windfall, my father's deepest desire had less to do with torque and German engines, and more to do with suburban bliss. Dad is a vegan chef, and he does okay for himself: weddings, bar mitzvahs, and bat mitzvahs, mostly. And while Mom is an attorney, she works for the state government, which means we basically owe our house to Papa Oak (RIP).

I'm hardly through the front door when I hear Mom from the living room, all, "Hey, honey." It's her knee-jerk response to the two-beep alarm anytime a door in the house opens.

Beep-beep-hey-honey.

I could swear I hear them whispering, but when I round the corner into the living room, they're all smiles, snuggled up on the couch, watching an episode of *Friends*.

"How was the pool?" asks Dad, pushing pause.

"Fine," I say, imagining myself pausing them.

My parents are basically super in love, which, kudos to them, but it's a bit much sometimes. Take this ritual with *Friends*, for example. They watch at least one episode a night from their prized DVD collection. Dad with his bourbon, Mom with her wine, they sing, "I'll Be There for You" in unison and recite all of Joey's lines right along with Matt LeBlanc.

"How's your back?" asks Mom. "Any developments?"

Developments. Like my back is a riveting television miniseries.

"It's okay," I say, careful to keep the descriptive language as vague as possible lest Mom put on her cross-examination hat. "A little tight, but okay."

Our half-dead Shar-Pei hijacks the conversation by walking into a wall. Dad scoops him up, all, "Poor Fluff," gently settling the dog onto his lap. Fluffenburger the Freaking Useless limps around the house, generally owning the crap out of his name, and while he is most definitely not a lapdog, try telling that to my dad. Ever since last year's incident, in which Fluff yapped himself permanently hoarse, my parents seem to think of our ancient dog as more of a human toddler.

"Dinner?" I ask.

Mom sips her wine. "It was my turn to cook," she says, which means chicken cordon bleu. Dad calls it his "vegan cheat night," and he pretends to love it, but I know the truth: he loves her, and it's all she can make. "Penny got hungry, so we ate already, but I put a plate in the microwave. Just push start, should be good to go."

I head toward the kitchen, and again, just out of earshot—I hear some whispering. Probably sweet nothings. Probably I don't want to know.

I connect my phone to the Bluetooth speaker in the kitchen, play Bowie's *Hunky Dory*, press start on the microwave, and stare at the spinning plate. My hunger has decreased significantly since I stopped swimming competitively, and during that time the idea of food has become kind of weird to me, animalistic even. The tearing, the chewing, the crunching, even the word—*masticate*—suggests some wildly carnal activity.

I mean, we're basically a bunch of wolves.

The microwave beeps, the plate stops spinning, my prey awaits. I carry it over to the bar counter where Mom has a napkin and a drink and silverware all set out for me. And right there beside it is a Post-it with my name on it (in Mom's handwriting) followed by five exclamation points and an arrow pointing to the voicemail light on the home telephone. Dad insists we keep a landline as "home base" for his business calls, and while we mostly end up with one sales pitch after another, there is one other thing this phone is designated for, my only personal experience using it: recruiting calls.

In the background Bowie sings of lawmen and cavemen, sailors fighting in dance halls, and I wish he were here now, in this kitchen with me, and I would hold his hand and together we would talk of life—on Mars, or otherwise.

4 ➜ *a concise history of me, part nineteen*

On January 8, 1947, David Robert Jones was born in London. It was a Wednesday. It was snowy. Somewhere across the Atlantic, a little boy named Elvis celebrated his twelfth birthday. Neither was considered a musical prodigy, though both would go on to shake music to its core, shaping and reshaping it until the word itself—*music*—was hardly recognizable.

When baby David was born, legend has it the midwife claimed, "This child has been on Earth before." Years later, David Robert Jones became David Bowie, and people speculated that perhaps he'd spent time on other planets too.

When Elvis was born—January 8, twelve years prior—his twin brother was stillborn. Gladys Presley would go on to tell friends that her son Elvis "had the energy of two." For much of his life, Elvis was haunted by his twin brother's death and by his own seemingly random survival.

Some people have been on Earth before and some people never get the chance.

On January 8, 1973, an unmanned spacecraft called *Luna 21* successfully launched into orbit. After landing on the moon, *Luna 21* deployed a Soviet robotic lunar rover called the *Lunokhod 2*, which took over 80,000 TV pictures and 86 panoramic images.

Little David grew up, wrote songs about astronauts and space, and released a record the same month *Apollo 11* landed on the moon. (Apollo being, among other things, the god of music.)

Years later, David Bowie's son would make a movie called *Moon*.

Little Elvis grew up and joined a band called the Blue Moon Boys. He had a daughter who would go on to marry an iconic musician known for a dance move called the moonwalk.

Later, Elvis would strike out on his own, eventually hiring a man named Thomas Parker as his manager. About Parker, Elvis would say, "I don't think I'd have ever been very big if it wasn't for him."

Thomas Parker's nickname was Colonel Tom. Colonel Tom made Elvis a star.

David Bowie wrote a song about Major Tom, who was left to float among the stars.

Luna 21 and the *Lunokhod 2* are no longer on the moon. Little David and Little Elvis and the moonwalk dancer are also out of commission. Their music is alive, though. I've heard it, I know.

And so are those pictures from the *Lunokhod 2*. I've seen them, I know.

I often wonder about the subtle connectors of the universe stretching through time and space, some skipping from one star to the next like smooth stones across a pond, some left to float through the wide, aimless infinite. I wonder about words like *reincarnation* and *relativity* and *parallel*. And I wonder if any of those stones ever land in the same place twice.

I was born on January 8.

5 ➡ I am thinking about wolves again

It started freshman year. Alan said, "We should join the swim team," and so we did. For as many hours as we spent in the Rosa-Haas pool, and for as many races as I'd won, I figured why not. Turned out I was pretty good—fast, not the fastest. Then, sophomore year, I grew into my limbs or something, because suddenly my times were ridiculous. Not Olympic ridiculous, but good enough to get early interest from a few lower-level D1 schools like Saint Louis, Manhattan State University, Eastern Michigan, and University of Milwaukee. (My parents were especially excited about the prospect of UM, as Milwaukee was just a couple hours from Iverton.) Junior year my times continued to improve, interest escalated, and by July 1 of this year—the first day a college coach can call a recruit—I got two phone calls: one from Coach Tao at Manhattan State and one from Coach Stevens at Milwaukee, both indicating a potential full ride. These weren't elite schools with deep pockets, so full scholarships were few and far between, a fact made abundantly clear to me on the regular.

The great secret: I don't love it. Swimming was just this thing I enjoyed, this thing I was pretty good at, and before I knew it, a thing I was *really* good at, and then everyone was all, *Welp, I guess this is the path for you, young man*, talking about swimming with a gleam in their eyes so bright, they never noticed I didn't have one for myself.

And then this summer happened. Long-course training (Olympic fifty-meter), I'm in the middle of the pool, when I start cramping and my whole body clams up. Someone pulls me out, and Coach Kel is all, "You okay, Oak? What's wrong? What hurts?" And without even thinking, I say, "My back."

That's it. All it took. I wasn't off the team, I didn't have to quit—I just didn't have to swim anymore.

As it turns out, back injuries aren't always straightforward, so it's not terribly difficult to perpetuate the lie as long as I keep it vague. I have regular appointments with a chiropractor, Dr. Kirby; most mornings I have physical fitness drills with Coach Kel, who assures me this will go a long way not only toward keeping me in shape, but also toward showing college coaches I'm serious about rehab. Mom and Dad and Coach tag-team calls with the schools, and right off the bat, Saint Louis and Eastern Michigan drop out. I don't know if it's Mom's courtroom prowess or what, but both Coach Stevens at Milwaukee and Coach Tao at Manhattan State agree to stick it out for a while.

The last few weeks have been full of played-out hypothetical situations. Mom or Dad go on about the importance of acting with urgency at the first sign of an offer, to which I remind them that most swimmers don't commit until spring. "Yes,"

Mom says, "but most swimmers haven't missed weeks of practice with a back injury." Then Dad says something along the lines of striking while the iron is hot, to which Mom says, "If you're lucky enough to get an offer this fall, you really want to wait and see if it's still there in the spring?"

I never said much at this point. There was no real offer on the table, so I didn't see that it mattered much.

But now: a voicemail on the landline, and a Post-it with exclamation points.

I look at the plate of chicken in front of me and envy the wolf its simplicity. I imagine it spending hours tracking its prey, chasing it, the violent takedown—and in the end, dropping it from its jowls, leaving it uneaten, and calmly walking away.

I pick up the phone, press the voicemail button: *"Hi, guys, Coach Stevens here. I've got some good news. . . ."*

6 ➞ *the further away, the stronger the urge*

"You *have* to come, No. Everyone is going to be there."

Val should know better than to think that last part was sweetening the deal, especially given the portrait of my life at this moment: sprawled in bed, laptop on stomach, Coke in hand, halfway through my third *Gilmore Girls* episode of the afternoon.

"Which one is this?" she asks, plopping down next to me. Before I can answer, she's all, "Ohhh, right." Val is a *Gilmore* junkie. She's seen every episode, including the reboot season, like, a half dozen times.

"Wait, don't tell me," says Alan, perusing my bookshelves like he hasn't done it a hundred times before. "Luke and Lorelai flirt, sexual tension meets butter knife, nothing happens, the end."

"*Alan*," says Val. "You have zero romantic wherewithal."

"*Valeria*. I have no idea what that means."

On-screen, Lorelai walks into Luke's for something like her fourth coffee of the afternoon.

"Do they ever drink water in Stars Hollow?" I ask.

"Only when filtered through a bean." Alan likes to dump on *Gilmore Girls*, but on more than one occasion, Val and I have overheard him belting the opening theme song from his room with all the off-key gusto of the Lollipop Guild. "However," he says, "I have to admit, Stars Hollow in the winter is dope as fuck."

I nod from my little pillow nest. "Wish they'd capitalize the *g* in *girls* during the opening credits, though."

"Right?" he says. "What is that?"

"It's completely asymmetrical, is what it is."

"Okay." Val pushes the space bar to pause, sits up, crosses her legs and arms. "Noah. I want you to come to this party tonight. For me. Please."

I don't move a muscle. Stasis, inertia, the complete physical atrophy of a morning and early afternoon spent on nothing but Netflix: these are the things I will miss most about summer. "You know how I feel about people making me do things," I say.

"I'm not *making you*. God. I'm asking."

"And I'm saying I can feel summer slipping through the hourglass like the sands of time, and a night at the Longmires' isn't how I'd like to spend, you know . . . my sand."

"It's cool, we get it," says Alan, standing over my desk, tapping the stack of facedown papers. "Award-winning writer such as yourself—might be uncouth to show your face at a lowly high school party."

Last year, AP English, Mr. Tuttle instructed us to write a "concise history," wherein we explored something specific from our own lives that intersected with a piece of world history. A vague assignment, maybe, but I latched on to it, and when it was over, I didn't let go, just kept writing all these historical vignettes. Eventually, I combined what I had into a single project entitled "A Concise History of Me" and entered it into a national contest hosted by the *New Voices Teen Lit Journal*. I didn't tell anyone, because of course I wouldn't win.

And then I won.

"You're becoming a hermit," says Val. "You know that, right?"

"I am not."

"You never go out."

"I go out."

"The Rosa-Haas pool doesn't count, No."

"I go . . . other places."

"What other places?"

"I don't know," I say. "Places."

"You know Bowie died the same year as Prince *and* Muhammad Ali?" says Alan, holding my copy of David Bowie's biography. "That shit always happens in threes."

"George Michael died that year too," I say.

"Oh. Fours, then."

"And I'd like to know what's so bad about becoming a hermit," I say. "Hermits get a bad rap, now that I think of it. All they want is to stay home and be left alone. What's wrong with that?"

Alan is all, "Hermits don't get laid, bro."

At that exact moment, Mom pokes her head in the open doorway. "Who's not getting laid?"

"Mrs. O!" Alan rushes over for a hug. The two of them have this weird sort of connection where Alan flirts with her in exaggerated and inappropriate ways, and my mom pretends she doesn't like it. She is fooling exactly no one.

"I thought you guys were out hiking for the day," says Alan.

Mom, blushing like crazy: "Just Todd. He has this little posse that goes up to Starved Rock every few months, try to prove they haven't aged."

Alan gives Mom—my *mother*, understand, the one who brought me into this world and has repeatedly threatened to take me out of it—an exaggerated up-and-down, a look only he can get away with. "Well, I don't know about your husband, Mrs. O, but I think you're aging backward."

Val says, "Okay, Alan."

"Seriously, we may have a Benjamin Button situation on our hands here."

"That's enough now."

"Noah, tell me your mom isn't smoking hot."

"Alan, God."

"I'm sorry, Mrs. Oakman," says Val. "My brother was dropped on his head many, many times as a child."

Alan winks at my mom, gives her that winning Rosa-Haas

➡ 23

smile. "Don't listen to her, Mrs. O. You're looking good today. Extra crispy."

"Well, I'm not sure what that means," says Mom, just eating it up, totally pretending this isn't exactly why she came in the room to begin with. Actually . . .

"Mom, you need something?"

I can tell she wants to ask about Coach Stevens's voicemail but is unsure whether to bring it up around Alan and Val.

"I just wanted to see if you guys wanted . . . some snacks or something."

"Some snacks?"

She nods. "Or something."

"We're not seven, Mom."

"Neither am I," she says, "and I *love* snacks."

"You got any Cheetos?" asks Alan.

Mom scrunches her nose. "Rice cakes?"

I jump in before Alan can pretend he loves rice cakes. "Thank you, Mom. We're good, though."

After Mom leaves, I scroll to an old Radiohead playlist. Val sets the laptop on the floor, lies down on the opposite end of the bed so we're foot to head, and then Alan flops next to me, and the three of us stare up at the ceiling, listening to music. Sometimes simple things and complicated things are the same things, and the three of us moving as one, listening to music in the same bed is like that, intimacy dialed into some strange underground frequency.

"Think of Iverton as a stage," Val says, almost in a whisper. "The show is almost over, and this party is our final bow."

"Rather dramatic of you," I say. "Plus, senior year hasn't even started. Plus *plus*, who says we'll be separated after high school?"

Alan has his eye on DePaul's animation program; Val, with her ever-expanding photography portfolio, has talked about the School of the Art Institute of Chicago the way Rory Gilmore talked about Harvard. Recent frustrations aside, the knowledge that my best friends aren't moving across the country next year is hugely comforting.

"Any word on scholarships?" asks Val.

I could tell them about the voicemail, but I know what they'd say. The only people more excited than my parents about the potential of my attending Milwaukee next year are Val and Alan. Assuming they land at DePaul and SAIC, the quick drive to UM would keep the triangle intact.

But there are other ways to make that happen.

"Maybe I'll just get a job in the city," I say, ignoring Val's question. "Do the whole college thing later."

"Noah."

"Val."

"Be serious."

"I am."

"What would you even do?"

"The world is wide, Val. I'm sure there are plenty of opportunities for a strapping young lad such as myself."

"You say that, but you know you'd end up at Starbucks."

Alan says, "I hear they have great benefits," to which Val sticks her foot in his face. He swats it away, and for a second we just lie there listening to "Everything in Its Right Place," which I often think of as my own personal anthem: the unadorned walls, the alphabetized bookshelves, everything white or pastel, my desk with its perfectly angled stacks of paper, and I say, "You know what it is?"

"What," says Val.

I remember when Penny was younger, but growing fast, there were times I'd see this idea dawn on her that she wouldn't always be a kid, and in those moments she regressed—she'd talk like a baby or cling to my mom in ways she'd long since abandoned.

The further away I felt from my friends, the stronger the urge to draw them in.

"I love you guys." I wrap one arm around Alan's neck, the other around Val's ankles. "I love you guys, and I love our summer, and I just—don't want to be with other people right now."

The song ends and a different one begins, "Daydreaming," which is the kind of song that seeps melancholy into the air like a sinking oil tanker.

Val sits up, claps her hands. "Okay, boys. We're not spending the entire day in this sterilized bedroom, listening to sad bastard music like . . ."

"Sad bastards?" says Alan.

"Exactly. We are not sad bastards. We are young and vigorous and thirsty, and we have, you know . . ."

"Thirst?"

"Unquenchable thirst is what I'm saying. Luckily, I know just the party for kids like us."

I grab my laptop off the floor, plop it back onto my chest, and pick up where I left off with *Gilmore Girls*. "You can't make me go."

Val leans over, positions her head so her eyes barely peek over the top of the screen. "Noah."

"I have rights."

"It would be a pity if I accidentally ruined the ending for you."

I look up a few inches, slowly meet Val's gaze. "You wouldn't."

If eyebrows could shrug, Val's just did. "You'll never guess who runs off to California."

"Not funny."

"Or who gets married on a cruise ship."

"You actually think I'd go to some dumb party to avoid *Gilmore Girls* spoilers?"

"Or who *doesn't* get into Harvard."

7 ➜ I go to some dumb party

Will and Jake Longmire fell out of the douche tree and hit every nozzle on the way down. Also, and not entirely unrelated, they're really good-looking, but in the same way Lochte or the Hemsworth brothers might be called good-looking, by which I mean, when one sees them, one senses the overwhelming urge to punch them in the face. And I'd feel bad thinking it, only I've seen the way they treat their girlfriends, and I've heard the "jokes" they toss at Alan, so I don't punch them, but I'm fine with wanting to.

The Longmire house sits a solid football field off the curb, and if there's one residence in Iverton that stands out as bigger, flashier, more Ivertonian than all the rest, it's theirs. Val parks her black BMW between two other BMWs, and the three of us climb out. Alan pulls a case of something out of the trunk, and it looks like beer, but seems a touch too—I don't know—bedazzled? Against my better judgment, I ask what it is.

"Case of Hurricanes," says Alan.

"Case of what?"

"Mixx Tail Hurricanes."

"Sounds . . . catastrophic."

"Only around bottle number four, dude."

I'm not much of a drinker. I mean, I drink on occasion, but being a "drinker" conjures images of sweaty foreheads and glazed eyes, and I don't know—I prefer my forehead dry and my eyes clear.

"And that?" I point to the plastic takeout bag in Alan's other hand.

"Bulgogi," he says. "Korean barbecue. But not barbecue like you think of barbecue. Bulgogi has its own thing going on."

We cut through the front yard, the lawn composed of the most perfect blades known to man, and suddenly I feel like the collar on my T-shirt is strangling me.

"You okay, No?" Val throws an arm over my shoulder. "You seem a little tweaked, or something."

"I'm fine. Just wish I'd known to bring a dish."

Alan chuckles. "It's not a fucking potluck, son. This isn't to share."

"Okay, well, also, I really don't want to be here right now, so there's that."

"Calm your bones, man," Val says. "We'll get inside, get you a drink—you'll be glad you came, I promise."

"And who knows," Alan says. "Maybe we can prove wrong that age-old proverb about celibate hermits."

No matter how many times I tell Alan I'm not interested in having sex yet, he doesn't believe me. And okay, over the years I've gotten close. Probably thrown away a half dozen pairs of underwear just to keep my parents from asking too many questions on laundry days. (I know. But it's easier to play dumb about one's curiously dwindling underwear supply than to explain *that*.) And I mean, look: my decision to not have sex isn't for lack of abilities or urges. I know what a dad thing this is to say, but it's more like—I've always felt this potential for real depth in a relationship. I know what sex *can* mean, and how it would most certainly affect that depth one way or the other, and for me that's a weighty scale, too precarious to fuck with (so to speak). It's a modest and oft misunderstood outfit, we Virgins by Choice, but I'm okay with that.

Val stops us for a selfie in front of the Longmire house, and because I'm fairly certain my mood is showing, I hope she doesn't post it anywhere. A year ago I wouldn't have cared, but a year ago Val didn't have over 100k followers.

Valeria Rosa-Haas has become something of a social media sensation. Which I guess plenty of people aspire to, but for her it's the medium that matters: photography. It started with the usual buffet of street signs through grainy filters, sunrise walks, cool shoes at dusk. Eventually she shifted into what is now her trademark, these elaborate prop photos from her favorite movies: recognizable items or outfits the characters wore, books they discussed, records they listened to, geographical references, thematic colors. It's all very artistic and tasteful, and if her follower count is any indication, I'm not the only one who thinks so.

She supplements these posts with the occasional social commentary photo, my favorite of which is a shot of a man at the zoo, head down, on his phone, while on the other side of a thick glass pane, a gorilla watches him. Val captioned the photo, simply: "Cages."

She is going to kill it at SAIC next year.

The closer we get to the front door, the more the ground shakes: a pounding bass, a rumble of chatter and laughter, the house is absolutely bouncing, all systems go. Val leads the way, pushing the door open without ringing the bell, and Alan and I follow. Kids are everywhere, drinking and laughing, groping, talking, like that. We walk through the front hallway and pass four grandfather clocks, two on either side of the entry. There's a massive chandelier hanging over our heads and a wide, winding staircase going up the left side of the wall. It's all very modern Gatsby, and Val, in true East Egg fashion, takes subtle command of the room, never once being too loud, never once too demanding, but somehow more present than the rest of us.

"Hey, No," says Alan, pointing to the chandelier. "You could probably park your fun guy ballsack in that chandelier," and that's about the time I make a very important decision: I will get drunk this evening. Sweaty forehead and all, eyes glazed as a doughnut. It is my only hope of survival.

◆━━━━▶

The kitchen isn't so much a kitchen as a Food and Beverage Atrium: a double-wide refrigerator, vaulted ceilings, hanging pots and pans, exposed brick. It would really be a sight to see if it weren't currently littered with cans and bottles, bags of chips, and takeout boxes that appear to have undergone a variety of experimental surgeries.

The whole thing makes me want to go ape with a DustBuster and a pair of industrial rubber gloves.

"Just FYI," says Alan as I tear into the case of Hurricanes, "those things are eight percent by volume," and since I'm not a big drinker, I have no clue what he's babbling about, so I guzzle the thing. It's cherry red and tastes like a Jolly Rancher, and before I know it, it's gone, so I grab a second one, and as I drink, I begin to feel the possibility of having an actual conversation with another person without the overwhelming desire to slowly insert my fist into my mouth. Or their mouth. Or anyone's mouth, really.

Just sip my Hurricane, walk around the house without any real plan.

There's an enormous pool out back that makes the Rosa-Haas pool look like a moderately portioned appetizer. It's packed, of course—kids drinking, climbing up the slide, making out on a giant swan float, doing pull-ups off the edge of the diving board, splashing, screaming, all very *Lord of the Flies* and whatnot.

Hurricane gone.

Back to the kitchen for number three, and there are just so many rooms in this house, most of them filled with kids I recognize from school, though a few faces are new. Eventually I wind up in a roomful of people dancing, ground zero for the booming stereo, let the music take over, and before I know it, I'm dancing with some girl whose name I haven't caught yet. She's hot, so I'm not sweating it, but I'm sweating because it's hot, and also this Hurricane is posing an interesting question: Was I actually born this awesome? I mean, right? Or was it more of a nurtured thing?

"So you wore that yesterday?" asks the girl.

We're up against a wall now, on the perimeter of the action. At some point we decided to take a break (*from dancing, I assure myself, not from being innately awesome*), and I'm explaining my love of Henry David Thoreau and how he inspired me to wear the same clothes every day.

"Yes, I wore this outfit yesterday. Also the day before that, and the day before that, and so on and so forth."

"So then . . ." The girl takes a single step back, eyebrows raised.

"No, I mean—I have, like, ten pairs of the same pants and shirt. Just put it on rotation, like that."

She nods slowly, sips her beer, looks around.

I'm all, "So my clothes are super-clean, is what I'm saying." *Attaboy, Oakman, keep talking about those freshly washed linens, you're doing great.* I don't know why I listen to myself, but I do. "Decision fatigue is a real thing, though," and like the party animal I am, I'm telling this girl about how I went to the mall with my mom, chose my favorite outfit—slim-fitting cuffed navy pants and a white David Bowie T-shirt (a picture of him smoking, and across the top in bold letters: BOWIE)— and bought ten of each. I round it off with my favorite pair of brown lace-up boots, and that's that. Val calls the ensemble my "Navy Bowie."

"It helps with daily efficiency," I continue, "but like I said, Thoreau was the real catalyst. 'Our life is frittered away by detail,' he said, which I think is true, don't you? And I know what you're thinking."

The girl says, "Bet you don't," but I go on.

"You're thinking, most people go through a Thoreau phase and grow out of it, and then they're all, *Oh, how cute, those days when I was young and thought Thoreau was so fancy*, but fuck that. I love Thoreau and his fucking righteous philosophy of simplicity. *Walden* especially, am I right? Have you read that?" Gulp the Hurricane. "The idea that we strip away the clutter, just go live by a lake somewhere and write? That's essentially what Mila Henry did too, you know." Essence of cherry-flavored malt liquor goodness is dropping some knowledge tonight! "And I guarantee you, neither of them ever labored over whether or not the requisite amount of days had passed between wearing their favorite ironic T-shirt. 'Simplify, simplify.' I try, I really do. Anyway."

Only now do I notice the girl in front of me is not the girl I was originally talking to. This new girl is chugging something that smells like straight whiskey out of a Solo cup. She laughs, all, "You're *so funny*, Jared."

"Who's Jared?"

The girl laughs hysterically. "See? *Who's Jared?*" she says, waving her arms around in the air, some of her drink splashing onto the floor. "Uh, *fuck*, I'm gonna throw up . . . Not really, I mean, but. What?"

The room is at a fever pitch, so it's possible I missed something. "What?"

"What'd you say?" she asks.

"I didn't say anything!"

Again with the lilting laugh, the waving of the arms in the air, the drink spillage: this girl is thoroughly drunk. Speaking of which, I should really just grab two of these things next time; this cherry shit is the shit.

"Come on, Jared!" Apparently done with talking, the girl drags me out to the middle of the floor, backs into my crotch, dances off tempo, and proceeds to raise her Solo cup into the air slowly and purposefully, draining its contents into a circle on the floor around us.

I scan faces in the crowd for Val or Alan, just some viable backup. Val is nowhere to be found. There's Alan, leaning against a stack of subwoofers, making out with Len Kowalski, the tennis jock who used to egg my house every other weekend.

From the opposite corner of the room, a girl smiles in my direction. She's unfamiliar, pretty, and hard to miss with a bright blue bandanna tying her hair back.

"Jared!"

I look back at the girl in front of me. "What?"

Guess I'm Jared now.

"Come to Vancouver with me," she slurs, close enough for me to smell her breath, a strangely intoxicating combination of sweet corn and wood fire.

I pull her hand off the back of my neck, while speculating how her hand came to be there in the first place. "What's in Vancouver?"

She laughs like it's just the funniest joke, then screams, "Weed, man!" at which point she slips in her own puddle of liquor and—okay, she's down.

The song changes to the latest from Pontius Pilot, and the room amps into a frenzy. I try to block out the song while helping this poor girl to her feet, walking her to the next room over and onto a couch. "You're jusss—so fucking *nice*," she says, poking a finger in my chest. "The world is a terrible place, Jared. Terrible and shitty. But not you. *You're* nice!"

I get her settled on the couch, arrange her head on a pillow, and say the first words that come to mind, a favorite passage from *Year of Me*. "'Perhaps the world was not so giant a shitball after all.'"

She chuckles, all, "Shitball," and like that, she's asleep. I wait around for a few minutes, make sure she's breathing okay, then it's off to the Food and Beverage Atrium to test Alan's theory about the catastrophic effects of a fourth Hurricane.

8 → *the sunlit narrative of Philip Parish*

Pontius Pilot is a Chicago-based recording artist who performed in the Iverton High School auditorium last year as a reward for our junior class having a decent magazine fundraiser. Nothing takes the wind out of a concert's sails like a Tuesday morning billing; even so, the student council dubbed the event the Magazine Mega Gala, and, like that, Pontius Pilot became a legend. Though collectively, the Iverton High populace felt about his music the way one feels about their fourth-grade soccer trophy, or the crinkle-cut fries in the cafeteria: it's a nostalgic love, weak at the root.

In the hour following his performance, Pontius Pilot had agreed to speak about his creative process to my AP English Lit class.

"Is that your real name?" some kid asked.

Pontius Pilot said, "My name is Philip Parish, but having

a pseudonym helps your brand. And as a musician, brand is everything."

"Care to delve into that a bit more?" Mr. Tuttle had checked out long ago, his physical body replaced with an automaton doomed to an eternal loop of overanalyzing the ending of *The Grapes of Wrath*, reciting *Macbeth*, and asking questions like, "Care to delve into that a bit more?"

Parish shrugged. "Brand tells people who you are, makes you stand out from the crowd. Eventually, hopefully, people hear your name and associate that with your thing." He pointed to the school-issued computer on Mr. Tuttle's desk. "An apple with a bite taken out of it." Shifted his finger to Mr. Tuttle's Pepsi can. "Blue can with the red, white, and blue circle."

"But those are objects," Alan said. "Not people."

Parish pointed right at me. "That guy understood brand."

"Noah?" asked some kid.

"He means Bowie," said Val. (AP English was the only class all three of us had together last year. The front offices were sure not to make that mistake again.)

Parish nodded at me. "Tell me you're not just wearing the shirt, kid. You know what I'm talking about, right?"

"David Robert Jones," I said.

Parish said, "Anyone in here think they would have remembered the name *David Robert Jones*? Maybe. The man revolutionized music, revolutionized a *lot* of things, really, so maybe. But *man*—just look at that shirt."

The whole class shifted until everyone was staring at my chest, the bold type BOWIE across the top, and under it, the man himself with a cigarette hanging out of his mouth.

"The music, the sexuality, the image," Parish said. "All

of it comprised in a single, universally understood word—
Bowie."

Some other kid raised his hand. "So your pseudonym is inspired by that dude in the Bible?"

"Something like that," Parish said, suddenly fidgety.

"But he spelled it differently, right?"

Parish shrugged. "Purposeful misspellings can help your brand."

Val raised her hand. "Would you say you put a lot of yourself into your songs?"

If Parish had looked uncomfortable before, watching him try to answer Val's question made him look downright wounded. He mumbled something like, "That's a tricky question," and when Mr. Tuttle said, "Care to delve into that a bit more?" he cleared his throat and stood up.

And this was where things got weird. When he'd first entered the classroom, Parish had carried a small notebook. I'd assumed it had samples of his work, something he could use to exemplify the evolution of his writing.

"Every song is personal." Parish clutched the notebook to his chest. "Most of my lyrics are based on the mood of a thing, not the thing itself. I make up a story, write myself into it. I call it the shaded narrative." And then his voice changed, sounded like it was coming from under a mask. "But sometimes . . . something else comes out of me, a song I didn't know was there. Those are more personal. Those are the sunlit narratives. Sorry, I'm not . . ." He shook his head, looked at Mr. Tuttle, then back at the class like he'd forgotten we were there. "I'm sorry."

And then he left—walked right out of the room, dropping an item from his notebook as he went. So far as we knew, it was the first time a guest speaker had up and left right in the middle of their thing. "Guess he didn't care to delve into it a bit more," someone said, and the class laughed in that relieved way you do when normalcy is restored. And then Mr. Tuttle instructed us to open our Steinbeck tomes, and our laughs were replaced with visions of dust and booze and haggard tires on the road west, where the busty, analogous milky white breasts of rural America patiently awaited our arrival.

After class had ended, I stalled until I was the last one in the room; on my way out I grabbed the item Parish had dropped, slipped it into my pocket, then locked myself in the nearest bathroom stall.

It was a photograph: a simple portrait of a young guy looking slightly off camera with not so much a smile on his face as the idea of one. On the back I found the inscription, *The sun is too bright. Love, A.* Later that night, after dinner, I searched the Google jungle for the phrase (vague as it was), or any sign of this guy on Pontius Pilot's Facebook page, but nothing. Something about the inscription seemed familiar, and at first I'd thought maybe it was related to Parish's talk of the "sunlit narrative," but that wasn't it. There was something else; I just couldn't place what.

That's how it goes with my Strange Fascinations.

9 → they are talking about Tweedy and college and things of that nature

Jake Longmire returns from the bathroom. "Hey," he says, all, *Hey*, like the whole world has just been sitting around twiddling its thumbs in anticipation of his arrival. "I forget what we were talking about."

"The massive suckage that is the band Wilco," says Alan.

"Come on, bruh," says Jake. "Gotta respect the pride of Chicago."

"I do not."

I'm in the corner of the Food and Beverage Atrium, halfway through my fifth Hurricane. (Number four went down like a champ, no trouble.) There's a bunch of people in the room, lots of chatter and laughter, but all eyes are on Jake. He is the sun around which the room of lonely stars rotates.

Alan is smoking weed. I have no idea where it came from. "I just don't get why everyone has auditory orgasms over Tweedy," he says. "Dude cannot sing."

Jake polishes off a Natty Ice, crushes the can in one hand while simultaneously grabbing another. "You think Van Morrison could sing, or *Jim* Morrison? What makes them great is that they sound like no one else. Take your boy's guy"—Jake points to my T-shirt—"Bowie. You think *he* could sing?"

Hard swig. Hurricane, don't fail me now.

"What is that?" Jake asks, pointing to my bottle.

"Hurricane." Swig, like that, and then: "It's delicious."

"Oh right, the girly drink." Jake laughs in a grunt. "Think Alan's rubbing off on you, bruh."

Before Alan can toss an empty beer can, Jake raises his Natty Ice in salute, and Alan pretends he's fine, and I'd like to rescind my earlier ruling about not sticking my fist into anyone's mouth, and not only that, I'd like to pass a decree that blatant homophobes not be rewarded with such fantastic fucking kitchens.

"What about you, Oakman?"

Alan and Jake are looking at me. It was Jake's question, so really the whole room has at least a peripheral eye on my response.

"What?"

"Collegiate athletics. You gonna swim?"

"Oh. I don't know yet."

"You should. You're fast." Jake points at Alan. "Unlike this little bitch," and the room laughs; Alan proceeds to toss that beer can at Jake's head.

"I'm fast," says Alan.

"Yeah?" says Jake. "Prove it."

"What?"

"Race me."

Alan coughs on the weed. "I'm not doing that."

"Tell you what. You beat me, and I'll let you see it." Jake points to his crotch. "Like the *Titanic*, bruh."

The whole room laughs, and suddenly all I can see is twelve-year-old Alan making me swear not to tell anyone he's gay.

And I wondered why.

"First off, gross," says Alan. "And second, I'm not putting

you to shame on your own turf. Would be highly unsports-manlike."

"I grew up in that pool. Plus, I'm in this new rec league in Elgin? Yeah, you're not putting me to shame."

Alan asks what Jake swims, to which Jake says, "Five-hundred fly."

There is no five-hundred fly, but I guess when you have a kitchen this incredible, and all these stars in your orbit, you raise a beer and say what you want.

Jake asks, "Noah, what do you swim again?"

"Middle distance." I barely get the words out. "Two-hundred backstroke, five-hundred freestyle."

Jake raises a Natty Ice. "Michael fucking Phelps in the house."

People chuckle, and I begin to feel a new side effect of these Hurricanes. "Actually, Phelps is known for the butter-fly. I mean, he swam backstroke, but his only medal there was silver in the Pan Pacific Championships. He did free-style, but so far as I know, he never won a medal for the five hundred, which is what I swim. So it's really not an accurate comparison."

The room stares me down.

"Dude," says Alan. "Why so salty?"

"Nah, it's cool," says Jake. "Man of principle. I can respect that." Jake gulps his beer, wipes his mouth with the back of his hand. "So how's your back, bruh?"

I shrug. It's all I have in me.

"My cousin had a herniated disc or some shit," says Jake. "Laid him up for weeks. You seem pretty okay to me, broski."

"You seem like a titanic dickhead."

Alan hops down off the counter. "Come on, Noah. Let's take a walk or something."

"Alan," I say, but nothing else comes out, and he doesn't say anything, just looks at me like I'm the one who's been crushing him like an empty can of Natty.

"Know what?" I say. "I'll go. You stay here and get high with your friends."

I leave the kitchen before the look on Alan's face makes me cry in front of everyone.

10 → exit the robot

I love the way my boots sound on hardwood floors, the ultimate walking value, each step a statement, and I have to wonder: Does alcohol make us say things we don't mean, say things we really mean, or just say really mean things?

Swigging of Hurricane, clunking of boots, this is my life now I guess.

"You can go ahead of me," says this girl in line at the bathroom door. "I'm waiting for a friend."

I've seen her before, but I'm not sure where. "I'm not here for the bathroom."

"You waiting for someone too?"

"Nope."

Blue bandanna. It's the girl from earlier, the one who

was smiling at me from across the dance floor. She's pretty, but not in the same way as Val. This girl has wavy dark hair under the bandanna, pale skin, and freckles around her nose and eyes.

She's all, "You're just a fan of standing in lines, then."

"More aimless roaming, I guess. But also I needed a way out of a room."

"Well, I would be careful where you aimlessly roam." She motions at the doors lining the hallway. "Someone is having sex."

"Really?"

"Oh yeah. It's quiet now, but a second ago it was full-on Animal Planet."

"Good to know."

"I'm Sara Lovelock, by the way. Sara without an *h*."

"Noah Oakman. With one."

She smiles, nods toward my Hurricane. "Hurricane, huh?"

"Yep." I take a swig like I'm proving it. "Also, I like your bandanna."

"Do you? I was trying it out, but I don't know. Feels staged or something. Not sure it's me, you know?"

"I wear the same clothes every day, so."

My head is swimmy, but not so swimmy that I don't realize that this night has been full of me being on the non-sober side of conversations. And yeah, the kitchen fiasco sucked, but I'm feeling fairly awesome at the moment.

"You wear the same clothes every day," Sara says, all freaking smiles.

"Decision fatigue. I'm kind of complex, just warning you."

Another swig to prove that shit. Don't call it a comeback.

"You're kind of adorable."

Choke on the Hurricane. The Hurricane has betrayed me. "Thanks, um. You too."

You too? What is even happening right now.

Sara's friend emerges from the bathroom, we say good-bye, and I mentally replay the conversation. *I'm kind of complex?* What in the world.

She did say I was adorable, though.

Out of nowhere, a moan. Yeah. Someone's definitely having sex in one of these rooms. I feel like an intruder, or one of those guys who never moved out of his mom's basement. A basement dweller, like that.

The sounds are coming in swells now, and it reminds me of this conversation I once had with Val: *People are like songs,* she said, *ups and downs, swells and beats, happys and sads,* and I said, *That's true,* but I didn't say what I was really thinking, which was, *Sometimes I feel all those things at once.*

I set my bottle on the floor in the hallway, stare at it, and here it comes: the tears, that high voltage unleashed, out of nowhere, too. Mila Henry called it "exiting the robot," the idea that our physical bodies are constructs, ones we can exit at will. She warned against it, saying once you got out, it was tough luck finding your way back inside, and maybe it gave you a sort of spiritual bird's-eye view, but it was dangerous, the toxicity of things outside the robot. It happens like this: I feel too much, eat too little, want to go places I've never been, feel those swells and beats inside, the happys and sads, too, and for once I'd like to feel a single thing for what it is, just the *one* fucking thing, but it's never like that. It's everything all at once, and no matter how organized I get my room, my records, my books, no matter how precisely I communicate a thing, or how many arrows point to how many objects, in the end I'm floating through space in a most peculiar way.

Okay.

Everything is swimming underwater.

Okay.

"There you are." Val comes out of nowhere. "The fuck did you say to Alan?"

"Nothing."

Now that she's closer, her demeanor softens. "You okay, No?"

"I'm fine."

She eyes the empty bottle on the ground. "How many of those have you had?"

"I don't know. Five. I think."

"Okay, well—tell me you're done."

"I'm done."

"And you'll find me when you're ready to go," says Val. "I'm not drinking, so I can drive."

"Okay."

"And you'll apologize for whatever you said to Alan."

"Val—"

"I'm serious, Noah. I don't want to know a world where you and Alan aren't hopelessly and semi-romantically in love with each other."

A smile seeps through, but it melts as quickly as it comes.

"Listen," says Val. "I know you didn't wanna come tonight. And I'm sorry if you haven't had a good time. Gimme, like, an hour, and I can go. In the meantime, why don't you hang in the library."

"Library?"

Val nods. "Straight out of *Beauty and the Beast*. Honestly, I'm shocked you haven't pitched a tent in there yet."

"Where?"

She points to the end of the hall where the ceilings curve into a high-arched doorway and a dimly lit room within. "Knock yourself out," she says, heading toward the bathroom. "I'll come find you in a bit."

Alone again, I walk to the end of the hallway, peer into a cavernous room of books, every wall filled with them, old and new. And sitting in a leather armchair beside an unlit fireplace in the corner—either a captive to the army of books, or their captain—a boy I've never met sings a song I know well.

11 ➡ *Circuit, a conversation*

"Hey."

"Shit, dude. You scared me."

"Sorry, I just— You were singing."

"Ha. Yeah. My mom says I do it without thinking, like a tic or something. What was it this time?"

"'Space Oddity.'"

"Fellow Bowie fan, I see?"

"What?"

"Your shirt."

"Oh right. Yeah. Okay, then. Sorry I scared you."

"You're Noah, right? One third of Valanoah?"

"One third of what?"

"Did you guys become friends because your names mash up like that?"

"I'm not sure—"

"Oh, come on. Val. Alan. Noah. *Valanoah*. Sounds like a fucking ski resort."

"Do I know you from school, or . . . ?"

"Nah, I'm homeschooled. But I've seen you guys around the neighborhood. You okay? You look like you've been crying."

"So you live around here, then?"

"Yeah, just up on Piedmont. I'm Circuit."

"You're what?"

"Circuit Lovelock."

"Oh."

"What?"

"I think I just met your sister? Sara?"

"That's her."

"Cool. I wasn't lurking out here, just so you know."

"I didn't think you were. Here, you want some?"

"Oh, thanks, no. I don't really smoke weed."

"Suit yourself."

"Okay. Well, nice meeting you."

"Can I be real with you for a second, Noah? You seem like the kind of person I can be real with."

"Um. Sure?"

"For the last hour or so, I've been in here contemplating the Middle English origins of the word *conversation*."

"Really?"

"When I get nervous, I look up the origins of words in the dictionary. Calms me down. Anyway, being in this house—

out there with all the drunken buffoons—I got to thinking about the word *conversation*, which, according to this dictionary, means . . . Okay, where'd it go? Here it is. . . . 'Oral exchange of sentiments, observations, opinions, or ideas,' and do you know what occurred to me?"

"I do not."

"We have monologues, make-outs, drinks, dancing, shooting of shits, plenty of socialization going on, but in the entirety of this enormous fucking house, there isn't a single conversation happening. Without *exchange*, there is no conversation. And then do you know what I realized?"

"No."

"I can't remember the last time I had a real conversation, as defined here in this dictionary. So I promised myself the next person I saw who wasn't a colossal douche, I would initiate one. And lo and behold, you show up."

"Oh."

"You're not a colossal douche, are you, Noah?"

"I like to think not."

"So. Shall we converse?"

"We sort of are, aren't we?"

"Nah, I'm basically whining, which doesn't count. Here, join me in one of these ridiculous chairs. You want scotch? Longmires keep the good stuff. Looks like we have . . . Springbank ten-year-old? Something called . . . Glenmorangie? Not sure I'm saying that right. Oh wow, this one's twenty-six years old. Single malt, what do you say?"

"I say you know a lot about scotch for a non-dad."

"Here, try this one."

"What is it?"

"Laphroaig fifteen-year-old. This was Dad's favorite."

"*Shit.*"

"Right? Puts hair on your chest."

"Tastes like fishy lava."

"Okay. We are sitting, we are drinking, we are speaking as adults. Tell me something about yourself. Something real, though. And then I'll tell you something about me. Remember—exchange of ideas."

"Circuit. Look, this is weird. Don't you think this is weird?"

"If it is, it's only because authentic conversation has been programmed out of us."

"Okay, well. Fine. My friend Alan."

"Yes."

"In the kitchen just now, we had an argument. Or not really an argument, so much as . . . I don't know. I said something."

"Go on."

"Alan's my best friend, and I love him, but sometimes his bullshit is tiring. And sometimes it's just little stuff, like they were just talking about Wilco—"

"The band."

"Yeah. And Jake *fucking loves* Wilco, and Alan *fucking hates* Wilco, and they just went on like that for a while."

"So what, then. You like Wilco?"

"I'm indifferent, actually. I don't feel strongly one way or the other, which is like a lost art. It's like, if you don't love something or hate something, your opinion doesn't count. But not everything boils down to the best and the worst. Not everything *fucking rules* or *fucking sucks*, some things are just a little okay, or a little not okay, and that's that. But it's like, with Alan . . ."

"What?"

"Nothing. Never mind."

"It's okay, Noah. You can trust me."

"I've heard about you, you know? There aren't a lot of Lovelocks on the block."

"But that's not why you've heard of me. Is it?"

"Your dad, he's like . . . I mean, he *was* . . . this famous inventor, right?"

"You know—the important thing about true conversation as I see it is willing vulnerability. Letting the ideas flow in whatever direction they see fit, no matter how uncomfortable. If you'd like to discuss my father, we can. I'm happy to do that, Noah, happy to be vulnerable with you."

"Thanks?"

"You're welcome."

"So . . . your dad."

"Not yet."

"Sorry, I thought you just said—"

"Oh, we'll talk about my father. But you're avoiding the bigger issue."

"I am?"

"We were discussing your issues with Alan, and then— *bam*—we're talking about my dad. Part of the human condition, we get too close to the truth and it scares us. But let's try to stick to the spirit of things."

"Which is what, exactly?"

"Truth. Consequence. *Exchange*. Noah—this is the only real conversation happening in this house right now. What we say here can *matter*, you understand? We don't have to cluck like a bunch of fucking chickens, or talk about favorite bands or shit movies, or will-they-won't-they on TV, or will-they-won't-they IRL, LOL, SM-fucking-H. We're not debating the inherent value of a like over a favorite, or how the

Clarendon filter really brings out the blue in my eyes."

"Is that hydroponic weed?"

"We don't have to talk about one hundred and one ways to succeed in life. I've done that, you've done that, and I think we're both done with that."

"The spirit of the thing."

"The spirit of the motherfucking thing."

"I'm afraid I've outgrown my life, Circuit."

"*Now* we're getting somewhere."

"I mean—I hear myself say it, and I can't . . . I don't know."

"It's okay."

"Last night I found out I got a swimming scholarship to University of Milwaukee, which I know I should be silly jazzed about, but it's like we start these trajectories when we're twelve, or worse, the trajectories are started *for* us, and then we're expected to stay on that trajectory for the rest of our lives? Fuck that. I'm done swimming. And I don't want to go to college. I want a new trajectory. Everything—*everyone*—in my life is stagnant. I'm not saying I'm better than anyone. For all I know, everyone else is growing too, just in different ways, but—it's like my life is this old sweater. And I've outgrown it. Doesn't mean I don't like that particular sweater, or I don't see the value of the sweater. It just means I can't wear it anymore."

"You need a new sweater."

"I need a new sweater."

"Noah?"

"What."

"I think you should come with me."

Begonias, as it happens, are not especially fragrant. Or maybe these used to be, who knows. I do wonder if the Ivertonians who live here knew what they were getting into when they planted their flowers so near the sidewalk, that one day some kid would consume his weight in Jolly Rancher beer, top that off with some fishy lava juice, have a bizarre conversation with a total stranger in a huge library, and agree to walk home with that stranger at the drop of a hat, at which point this kid would need a convenient and timely spot to blow Jolly Rancher lava chunks.

I should send a thank-you note. Just to let them know their begonias were used exactly as they'd imagined.

"You okay, dude?" Circuit keeps his distance behind me.

"Define *okay*."

"Ha. Right."

"I mean I drowned myself in a sea of cherry beer, so you tell me."

"Sounds . . ."

"Catastrophic?"

"I was going to say *spectacular*. But then I'm not the measure of restraint."

We resume walking, and I can't speak for Circuit, but it takes most of my concentration just to keep one foot in front of the other. I don't know if he drove to the party or not, but Piedmont is only six blocks over, which is great because there's no way I'm getting in a car with this kid.

"I would kill for a coffee," I say.

"Oh, dude. No doubt. What I would do for immediate transportation to the Wormhole right now."

"The Wormhole?"

"Don't tell me you've never been to the Wormhole." He pulls out his phone and a minute later hands it over. "Check this out."

I scroll through pictures of a coffee shop decked out in eighties paraphernalia—everything from ancient computers to classic movie posters to . . . "Is that—"

"Yep. A DeLorean."

Being drunk is weird. Like a coffee shop with a DeLorean doesn't sound all that strange now, but I'm guessing at some point tomorrow it'll hit me, and I'll be all, *WTF?*

I hand the phone back and only now realize how tall Circuit is. I never got a great look at him back in the library, other than the horn-rimmed glasses and shaggy hair. His skin is even paler than his sister's, translucent almost. Like a ghost. Who doesn't get out much.

A hermit ghost.

"Truth be told," Circuit says, "I never really understood its value."

"I forget what the— Hmmm . . ." God. I am never drinking again. "I forget what we're talking about."

"Restraint, and how I have none. *Restraint!*" he yells; the word echoes through the neighborhood, and I feel a little better knowing I'm not the only one losing my shit. "I just always felt like—you know, why wouldn't you want *more*?" he says.

I know exactly what he means. "I sometimes think"— swallow, shake my head, get it together—"I think my appetite for life exceeds that of a normal human, like I'm about to run out, so I'd better live it all, feel it all, do it all now before it's gone."

"My dad once said he wasn't built for long-term maintenance. Which now seems eerily premonitory."

Earlier this year an article about groundbreaking inventions ran in *Time* or *Newsweek* or something, and Dr. Lovelock's name was mentioned as one of the year's true tragedies. Bullet to the head, as I remember, which culminated in perverse levels of curiosity throughout the neighborhood. The Iverton hive mind isn't exactly forgiving of those who seek privacy, a by-product of being wealthy and bored at the same time.

"So your dad," I say, every bit a part of the curious hive.

Luckily, Circuit doesn't seem to mind. He says his dad preferred the term *cognition architect* to *inventor*, as people generally associated the latter with middle-school science fairs. "He was always a little strange, though. Hence my first name." Apparently Circuit's parents couldn't agree on a name, so they flipped a coin to see who chose the first and who chose the middle. "And that's how one winds up with the name Circuit Patrick."

He starts whistling "Space Oddity" again.

"That your favorite Bowie?"

"I think so."

"Alan's too. Whenever we debate superior Bowie songs, he always says, 'It literally opens with a launch countdown, No. The future of space exploration hangs in the balance.'"

"So what did you argue was the superior Bowie song?" asks Circuit.

"I like 'Changes.'"

"Ha. Appropriate."

Circuit doesn't really laugh, I've noticed. He says *ha*, like it's any other word, which ends up sounding scripted, like we're in a stage play and he's regurgitating memorized lines.

"Favorite Bowie album?" I ask.

"Hmm, that's tough," says Circuit. "I mean, I know it sounds like a cop-out, but all of them, really. Impossible to pick just one."

Okay, look: no one loves Bowie as much as I do, and not even I like *all* his stuff. From first album to last, the man evolved maybe more than anybody, so unless you're the kind of listener who really does like everything (I've never understood these people), it's difficult to imagine a person truly loving all his records.

My phone buzzes in my pocket before I can challenge Circuit on it: five unread messages from Alan, one from Val.

Alan: Dude. Did you seriously leave???

Alan: WTF is going on with you right now?

Alan: OK we're talking later. Jake just challenged me to a "25 freestyle swim race" whatever the fuck that is

Alan: Imma put him in his place

Alan: You're not off the hook with me, No

The one from Val was a single word. . . .

"This is me," says Circuit, pointing to a house three doors down.

My phone buzzes again; I switch it to silent and stick it back in my pocket as we walk through a yard to a house that looks, unsurprisingly, like a cookie-cut version of my own. Next door, an old man sits on a porch, smoking a cigar. At his feet a longhaired collie stands at attention, watching our every move with a certain gleam of human awareness. The dog is quiet, calm, seems old.

"My dog would be walking in circles about now," I say, and it's true; he always does when strangers walk by the house. And God forbid someone ring the doorbell. *Pandemonium pissing*, that's what Mom called it once, a pretty accurate description of events.

"That's Abraham," says Circuit. "The dog, I mean. Been around since I was little." Circuit waves at the old man, raises his voice a little. "Hey, Kurt. You're out late."

"I was just thinking the same thing about you, Young Master Lovelock."

"Ha. You got me there, man." Circuit unlocks his front door, swings it open. "Well, see you around."

The old man blows a ring of smoke into the night sky. "Not if I see you first."

13 ➜ *a concise history of me, part twenty-two*

The road to Fluffenburger the Freaking Useless is paved with many Jacks.

But here, I should start at the beginning:

Twenty-six thousand years ago, a boy walked through a cave. The cave was in France, and it was called Chauvet Cave. The boy carried a torch. A dog walked by his side. There were, most likely, torch-bearing boys walking beside dogs long before this one, boys and dogs and torches aplenty. But this particular boy's footprints and this particular dog's paw prints were captured in time, and the ashes from that particular torch fell to the ground in Chauvet Cave where they survived far longer than that boy could have imagined. Eventually, science did what science does: it caught up to them. It caught that boy, but more important, science caught his dog, the grandfather of dogs the world over, its paw prints the earliest evidence of man and wolf in like mind, walking side by side, cohabiting.

Man's first best friend.

Twenty-five thousand, nine hundred some-odd years after that boy and that dog walked in a glimmering flicker through Chauvet Cave, I read *The Call of the Wild* in the glimmering flicker of a T. rex night-light. I was only ten, but I remember a chapter called "The Dominant Primordial Beast," in which two dogs fight to the death to prove their own supremacy, and thinking at the time, *The Yukon really isn't all that different from the playground.*

I was never very tough.

The book was a Christmas present from my uncle Jack, who was the worst. Noogies, wedgies, titty twisters, wet willies: Uncle Jack belonged to that peculiar subgroup of individuals who found pleasure in the obnoxious, but he liked dogs, had a big one named Kennedy, which looked like a wolf. And, that curious Christmas, as I pulled back my uncle's musty-scented camouflaged wrapping paper to reveal *The Call of the Wild*, Uncle Jack produced a low-pitched growl from deep within his belly, let it build a bit, and then . . . barked. Like a dog.

Uncle Jack: ever the dominant primordial beast.

A man named Jack London wrote *The Call of the Wild* while living in what is now Piedmont, California. He wrote other books too—his words and stories would go on to influence the likes of Aldous Huxley's *Brave New World*, but more than anything, he is remembered for the dogs he created: White Fang and Buck.

And so began my righteous plotting for a dog, that joyous, age-old process of wearing down one's parents until they are but a ghost of their former selves. The result? A family trip to a local breeder, where we found a cute little Shar-Pei with rolls upon rolls of coarse skin, who was not at all fluffy, but come hell or high water, I'd decided my dog would be named after the three-headed mutt in *Harry Potter and the Sorcerer's Stone*, and so it was. Fluffy the Shar-Pei. (He would not become Fluffenburger the Freaking Useless until years later, after commanding his true potential as the most useless animal the universe had yet sprouted from its perplexing loins.) And for a while we were thick as thieves, Fluff and me, all because my crazy uncle Jack gave me a book wrapped in camouflage.

Three days before the following Thanksgiving, Uncle Jack was shot and killed in a hunting accident. It was November 22.

Jack London died on November 22, 1916.

November 22, 1963, Aldous Huxley died of laryngeal cancer.

C. S. Lewis, who wrote about a different kind of primordial beast, and whose friends called him "Jack," died that same day too.

Huxley and Lewis are remembered for their work, their words. But neither is remembered for the day they died. That day is overshadowed by a different death.

John F. Kennedy, sometimes called Jack, was killed on November 22, 1963. Kennedy is best known as being the President of the United States. He is also known as being the namesake of my uncle's wolf-dog.

For all I know, he was my uncle Jack's namesake too.

The Kennedy family had a dog, given to them by a Soviet leader. (The Soviets are known more for their robotic lunar rovers than their gift giving, but hey.) That dog was called Pushinka.

Pushinka is Russian for "Fluffy."

I sometimes picture myself in a cave, late at night, in the glimmering light of a torch. I feel its ashes brush my shoulder on their glided-fall to the ground, and I wonder if someone, twenty-six thousand years from now, some Person of the Future with capabilities beyond my imaginings, might find those ashes.

And I wonder what those ashes will say.

Circuit says his mom is at some convention, and all his sister's friends were at the party too, so she won't be home for hours. "Just ignore Nike," he says on the way up the stairs. "She's a little pissant." A cat (presumably Nike) is perched on the top stoop, calmly and quietly watching us as we approach. From a couple steps away, Circuit bends down and literally roars—like a lion—in her face. The cat scampers down the stairs, brushing my leg as she passes. Clearly I'm not the only one who has a complicated relationship with the family pet.

"I need to urinate," I say; Circuit points to a room down the hall, and when I come out of the bathroom, he's literally standing there waiting for me.

"Ready?" he asks, and I think, *Ready for what, weirdo?*

All that comes out is, "Okay."

Inside Circuit's bedroom there's a full bed, a couple of half-empty bookshelves, a dusty electric guitar in the corner, and a desk, at which Circuit has already taken a seat, pulled himself up, and opened his laptop. The desk is a scrambled mess, which I'd pay a solid twenty bucks to clean: stacks of papers in no apparent order; textbooks on top of textbooks, all of which have the word *psychology* somewhere on the spine; a few mad-scientist-type devices, one of which appears to be a pair of binoculars welded to a large pair of goggles; and, buried among the rubble, a small framed photograph of Circuit and Sara standing in front of the White House with their parents.

"Dude." From his seat, Circuit is staring at me staring at the picture. "Tell me you're checking out my sister and not me."

Considering Sara's first name, I'm guessing their mom won that coin toss. "So what's her middle name?"

"Ha. Flux."

"Circuit Patrick and Sara Flux."

"Sara always joked that together we make one normal human and one cyborg."

"Speaking of cyborgs." I point to the hybrid binocular-goggles on his desk, where a bunch of wires run from the contraption to his laptop.

"We call that the Oracle," says Circuit.

"You and Sara?"

"No, I meant—never mind." He points to the edge of the bed. "Have a seat."

I sit, catch a glimpse of a document on his computer with the heading *Catalepsy and Chaining Anchors*. Circuit swivels in his chair to face me, and suddenly I feel like I'm in a doctor's office, like he's about to tell me to open my mouth and say *ahhh*.

"You want a new trajectory," he says.

"What?" I try to stand up, but my legs aren't cooperating and everything feels heavier—my eyelids, my head, my arms—like I've been an empty vessel my whole life and someone just filled me with rocks and sand. "I should go." But my lips are heavy too, and I'm not sure I said anything at all.

"It's simple, Noah. Trust me."

LOOK, IT'S ➥ PART TWO

Henry: . . . which is probably why I'm so dead set on writing real people. Because of the minutiae.

Mod: The minutiae?

Henry: Yes, I prefer minutiae.

Partial transcript from "A Conversation with Mila Henry"
Harvard, 1969
(Henry's last known public appearance)

Two summers ago my family took a Caribbean cruise, and one of the many lavish evening performances was a hypnotist. I remember watching in curious horror as he told a volunteer to close her eyes, imagine she was at the top of a long, beautiful staircase with a hundred steps down. He told her that the further down she went, the more relaxed she would become. Eventually, this woman was under to the point she was basically a human marionette subjected to the whims of her puppeteer. And while this was disturbing enough, what happened after is what really stuck with me. I saw this woman around the boat a few times that week, and I saw her face in the crowd of the other evening shows—the magician, the comedian, the feathery dance troupe—and not once did she smile. She just sat there, eyes glazed, every bit the stringed puppet.

━━▮▮▮▮▮━➤

Nike won't budge. She guards the door like a sentry, blocking my exit, calmly looking around like I'm not standing one foot away. I pick up the cat and expect a fight, but instead she nuzzles my arm and purrs. Set her at the bottom of the stairs, glance up the way I came—Circuit's room looms at the top of the staircase, a soft glow seeping through the bottom of his closed door. He didn't say a word when I said I was done, not a word when I forced open my eyes, stood up, walked out of his room.

It's simple, Noah. Trust me. Close your eyes. Breathe deeply, in and out, there you go. Now. You're standing at the top of a staircase. . . .

With a pounding headache and a solemn swear never to return to Piedmont Drive, I'm out the front door and through the yard, boots on pavement, hitting the streets in the direction of home.

Kurt, the old neighbor, nods as I pass. He's in the same spot on the porch next door, his cigar now a stub.

His dog barks. Abraham, Circuit called him.

I stop. Everything goes slightly numb, hazy; I look back at Circuit's house, an odd sensation of having been there before tonight.

Abraham whines, staring at me with those glowing eyes, all-knowing and diligent. Kurt pets his head and talks so quietly, I can hardly hear. "So last spring I'm hiking out near Starved Rock, and it's pretty regulated, you know, with guides and horseback riding and a winery, but I'm not interested in all that, am I, Abe? No, sir, nothing worse than manufactured nature."

I stand motionless on the curb in front of this stranger's house, listening to him tell a story to his dog.

"So I go off grid, opt for the *un*guided tour, when I come upon a cave. Not one of those protected caves with the cascading waterfalls and touristy shit, just a natural cave. Dark, dank, mysterious as the depths of hell. Well, you know better than anyone what a curious old cur I am. I set my walking stick a-straight and strode on inside. Way I see it, what good is the life untested, what value in nary a risk taken? I intended to risk and test, and I reckon that's exactly what I did. And you know who I met in that cave? A mystery, and that's a fact. God Almighty! Iffin' that don't beat all. And you know what God told me?" Slowly, intentionally, Kurt takes a final puff of his cigar, crushes it beneath his boot, and his eyes land on me. "She told me to come into the light."

The walk home is foggy, inside my head and out, and there is no joy or inherent value in these steps, only distraction.

When I walked into Circuit's house, Abraham was a collie.

When I walked out, he was a Labrador.

16 → that night in a dream I am suspended from the ceiling

Just hovering up here, a spirit of myself, looking down at my sleeping body in someone else's bed. Beside the bed Abraham the Labrador barks constantly, but it's silent, a rhythmic, mute bark. There's someone else in the room too, standing in the opposite corner, facing the wall, dripping wet like he just climbed out of a pool. A puddle of water gathers around his feet, and I only see the back of his head: dark hair, and every time he turns around, time speeds up until he turns back to face the wall. The air swirls like an invisible tornado, and then—colors everywhere. Big colors, colors so bright, it's hard to look at them: blinding shades of pink-heavy fuchsia, turquoise, lavender, vivid greens and blues and yellows.

And in the brilliant swirling colors, letters begin oozing from the walls: the *A*s come first, then *T*s, then *N*s, then a whole pack of random letters of all shapes and fonts, floating and churning through the room in chaotic disarray until, eventually, they take shape, one letter in front of the other, and two words form, float right up to the ceiling, and stop just in front of my face: STRANGE FASCINATION.

In the bed below, my eyelids flutter, and suddenly I'm in my body again, conscious and unconscious, aware of my own sleep and of an urgent desire to wake up.

⬅||||||➡

5:37 a.m.

Shit.

My head is absolute murder. Like with knives and guns and some unidentifiable infectious disease.

I grab my phone off the floor (nightstands are glorified clutter), to find twenty-three unread messages from Alan.

> Alan: OK I've decided wild hearts can't be broken

> Alan: Which is to say our love soars on eagle's wings

> Alan: Which is to say I love you a TUN and tonight sucked

> Alan: And jake is, in fact, a Titanic Dickhead

Alan: (who btw got his ass handed to him in the pool by yours truly)

Alan: Also I'm pretty high right now

Alan: Yo, remember that time we rolled your mom's basil?? That was funny AF

Alan: Yo gabba gabba!

Alan: WTF is a gabba anyway???

Alan: The Flintstones were dope

Alan: I AM FLINT-STONED!

Alan: Heyyyyy kites

Alan: I want CHICKEN

Alan: Give me chicken an no one gets hurt!!

Alan: 24 hour KFC drive-thru FTW!!!!!!!!

Alan: Think outside the motherfucking bun!!!!

Alan: Shit that's taco bell ˉ_(ツ)_/ˉ

Alan: Wait. Check this out . . .

Alan: o— ˉ_(ツ)_/ˉ

Alan: it's a mic drop, haha

Alan: Rosa-Haas OUT

Alan: o— ¯_(ツ)_/¯

Alan: Night night bae

Reading this thread from my best friend in the sober, albeit early light of morning at least answers one question from last night: I was wrong to say what I said to Alan. And even though the pendulum can swing hard the other way too, I really do love him.

Me: Alan, I am so sorry.

Me: I was an asshole x 407,000. Please forgive me.

Me: Whenever you see this (assuming that won't happen for a while) I want you to say the following words out loud: "Noah Oakman loves me a great deal."

I swipe over to Val's thread just to make sure I didn't miss a follow-up to her one-word text.

Val: Noah

Nope. That's it. Just *Noah*. Time-stamped 1:01 a.m.

Best I can tell, I have the internal workings of a forty-year-old man: once I'm up, I'm up. After a long, thorough shower, I pull on some fresh Navy Bowie, sit in my ergonomic swivel, scoot up beneath my desk, open my laptop, open YouTube, find the Fading Girl, find solace.

I love my room.

17 ➡ *passage of time (I)*

The rest of the day is like one of those chapters in a book where the author jumps ahead in time because I guess nothing interesting happened to the character. Henry called them "passage of time chapters," and while she wasn't a fan, sometimes nothing happens worth mentioning. Sometimes you sit in your room, recovering from a shitty party where you had way too much to drink and followed some kid home when you should have apologized to your best friend. Sometimes you overanalyze a one-word text because the more you think on it, the more you realize texting a person's name usually precedes something more substantial, like *We need to talk*, or *I have a confession*, but you never respond, and that person never follows up. Sometimes you take a day to toggle between episodes of *Gilmore Girls* and the Fading Girl until you decide to write a little, and then, after an hour of getting nowhere, you get mad at your writing for masquerading as Important Work when it is, in actuality, a waste of fucking time, so you move on to something that knows exactly what a waste of time it is. . . .

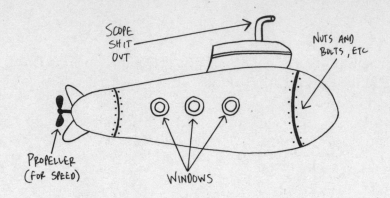

SCOPE SHIT OUT

NUTS AND BOLTS, ETC

PROPELLER (FOR SPEED)

WINDOWS

Sometimes you finish the drawing and feel entirely relaxed, taking comfort in the knowledge that a submarine diagram will never hurt you. And you find yourself wondering if you'll ever have the opportunity to ride in a submarine, which leads you to other modes of transportation you've yet to experience. . . .

HOT AIR BALLOON

Sometimes you get meta and think, *If all I want to do is sit in my room and draw, I might as well draw my room. . . .*

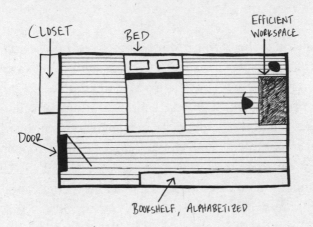

Sometimes you wonder if there's a career in drawing diagrams with little arrows, but then you think, *What possible job would require this particular skill set?* And you think, *I should really do something more productive.* So you imagine two of your drawings procreating and producing a child. . . .

And sometimes that's your day.

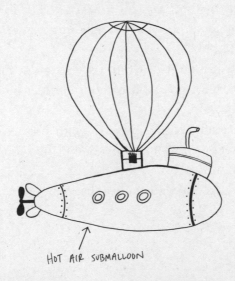

HOT AIR SUBMALLOON

Next morning, the same dream wakes me before the sun again. I shower, get dressed, brush my teeth, and once I'm done stuffing my backpack with new textbooks, I start an episode of *Freaks and Geeks* for some first-day-of-school inspiration. As it plays, I can't help wondering how many nights in a row constitute a "recurring" dream. I can't help wondering about the dripping wet guy in the corner and the letters coming out of the walls. But also, I can't help wondering how NBC could have canceled *Freaks and Geeks* midway through Season One when it was so utterly brilliant.

Mysteries of the universe abound!

A knock on my door, immediately followed by its opening. "Hey," says Mom. She always knocks, but it's less a request, more a heads-up. "I was going to tell you it's time to get up for school, but . . . I see you're ready to go."

"Yep."

She smiles in that sort of concerned but loving way, a look moms in general, but especially mine, own. "So. Coach Stevens's voicemail."

It was only a matter of time, I guess. Honestly, I have to give them credit for not asking about it yesterday.

"Yes."

"So not a full ride like we'd hoped, but, Noah—*fifteen thousand*. That's *great*. That's huge, all things considered."

"I know, Mom."

"You know, it's not really about the money, but about being at—"

"Being at the place that values me most. I know."

This has been my parents' catchphrase from the beginning. And I know they want to mean it, and part of them probably does, but when *budget meeting* and *kind of a tight week* are part of your family's vernacular, and someone puts fifteen thousand dollars on a table, you do more than stare at it.

"And with your back, there are no guarantees of—"

"Can we talk about this later?" I ask.

A beat; Mom's disappointed I'm not more excited. "Sure. I'll call Coach Stevens tonight," she says. "Tell him we're considering. That okay?"

The subtext: *Are* we considering?

"Sure," I say. "Yes."

She nods once. "You look terrible, honey."

"Thanks, Mom."

"You know what I mean. Tired, I guess. Are you getting enough sleep?"

"Mom? I'm good."

She's about to leave when I notice a scar on her left cheek. "Hey, what happened?"

"What?"

"The scar." I point to hers, then motion on my own cheek. "What happened here?"

She catches her breath—like, I actually hear her catch a breath. "Noah, do me a favor. Go to bed early tonight. You clearly need some rest." She backs out of the room, closes the door behind her.

Before I can figure out what just happened, there's another knock on my door, only this time it stays shut.

"Come in, Penny."

I swear, every time my sister opens a door, an angel gets its wings. She always cracks it open by inches, like she's afraid it might fly off its hinges if she's not careful, and I don't know—it's about the cutest thing I've ever seen, one of the few holdovers from when she was little.

"Hey," she says, poking her head into the room like a tentative groundhog emerging from its hole. Fluff whines in the hallway behind her. "Hush now," says Penn. "The grown-ups are talking." Then, to me: "Have you noticed Fluff acting strange lately?"

"Not unless you count walking into walls as strange."

"That's the thing. He doesn't really do that anymore."

"He just did it, like, a couple nights ago."

Penny rolls her eyes. "Well, *I* haven't seen him do it, darling."

My sister goes through these phases where she gets completely obsessed with a thing, and when she's in one of those phases, *that thing is the only thing*. Currently, that thing is Audrey Hepburn movies, which means she won't quit bugging me to watch *Breakfast at Tiffany's* with her, and she's always walking around the house, calling everyone *darling*.

"He's barking again," she says. "Have you noticed?"

Fluff yaps from the hallway like he's showing me what she means.

"I'm afraid things are beginning to weirden for him."

"I don't think *weirden* is a word, Penn."

"Well, it should be. And doesn't he seem a little, I don't know—*better*?"

"Better how?"

"More agile, I suppose."

"Penny, even when Fluff was agile, he wasn't very agile."

She still lingers in the doorway, her head in my room, the rest of her in the hallway with Fluff. "Anyway, the real reason I popped in was to check on our appointment tonight."

"Ah. You've found a new way of putting it, I see."

"I assure you, Noah, I haven't the faintest idea what you're referring to."

"Not even the faintest?"

"Noah. *Darling.* Listen. You don't know what you're talking about. Now, I can't help you if you're not going to be reasonable."

"Okay."

"As it is, your position on *Breakfast* is entirely *un*reasonable."

"I love breakfast."

"You know what I mean."

"I do."

Penny clears her throat, and when she finally steps fully into the bedroom, I can almost feel a hiccup in the floor, as if my minimalistic decor is unable to digest the colors and quirks of Penny Oakman. Today she's wearing old black high-tops, bright pink tights embroidered with both skulls and hearts, a skirt whose color might best be described as "in the fuchsia family," an I HEART NYC T-shirt, and a black mess of hair that looks like she went to a salon and asked for the Bellatrix Lestrange.

"Stay," she says into the hallway. (Cue Fluff's *Where'd Penny go?* whine.) She walks across the room and hands me an envelope with my first *and* last name inscribed on the front, her stature and movements indicating the officialness of the gesture. "Here. I've composed a list of reasons why you should reconsider your position on *Breakfast at Tiffany's* and, in particular, why you should watch the movie with me. Feel free to read it at your leisure, darling, though sooner rather than later would be preferable."

She pronounces *leisure* like *le-zure*, and *rather* like *rotha*, because of course she does.

I stick the envelope in my pocket, try my best to keep a straight face. "I'll take it into consideration."

"Wait, what are you doing?"

"What do you mean?"

"You just put it in your pocket." Penny eyes the side of my pants as if the pocket ate her letter whole.

"Where *should* I keep it?"

"You'll forget about it in there," she says.

"I will not."

"Oh, really?" Penny taps her foot in a perfect Mom-mimic. "Remember that time you put a Kit Kat in your pocket, and then forgot about it—"

"Okay."

"And a couple hours later everyone thought you shit your pants?"

"Don't say *shit*, Penn. And seriously, I won't forget. Here, look. I'll set the timer on my phone, okay? As a backup."

"So when the timer goes off, you'll read the letter?"

"Absolutely. I will read it and consider all the wisdom contained therein."

Penny nods curtly. "That's all I ask." Fluff barks out in the hallway, to which Penny says, "All *we* ask, that is. Now, if you'll excuse me, I have an important engagement to attend to."

"Just so you know, eighth grade is a little less important than one might think."

"Maybe for *you*, it was," she says on her way out the door. "But I plan on being an absolute smash, darling."

19 ➝ *OMG*

Taking the long way to school means catching Old Man Goiter on his route. I slow down just a little between Mill Grove and Ashbrook, and there he is: the cane, the fedora, the potato-sized goiter on the left side of his neck, the man himself. *Who are you, OMG? A retired shepherd? A war hero? A fast-food tycoon?* Today I imagine him in his youth, an up-and-coming restaurateur in Paris, American expat from Alabama made good in haute société, all *voulez-vous coucher avec moi?* I approach slowly, try not to crane my neck as I pass. There's that grim look, as always, God love him. OMG definitely understands the inherent value of walking. He never takes his eyes off the sidewalk, resolute in his decision to walk at this time, in this place, every—single—day.

Nothing cheers me up like OMG.

By the time I pull into the Iverton High parking lot, I'm barely even depressed about the beginning of the school year.

"Noah!"

Tyler Massey, one of those kids whose popularity is a mind-boggling mystery, as it sure seems no one likes him. I almost pretend not to hear, but you have to keep guys like

Tyler fed or they'll follow you around all day, taking little bites, just nibbling you down to the bone without you even knowing. Best to give him the entire helping up front.

"Hey, Tyler," I say, climbing from my car, but I can tell how this is going to go, and suddenly I wish I could go back in time, pull over, and walk with OMG, ask him where he's really from and why he does what he does, and we could chat about my Strange Fascinations, and I could finally tell someone the truth, how I think he and the Fading Girl probably understand the dangers of living outside the robot, and OMG listens, and lo! the world emerges a beautiful and glorious place.

Tyler Massey grabs his crotch, jiggles it around. "How they hanging, dickwad? You pop your cherry this summer or what?"

I fucking hate high school.

20 → one school is like the other

If one followed the branches of the Oakman family tree (or the "Oak Tree," as my dad once called it), one might stumble across my mother's brother, Orville O'Neill, proud owner of Orlando Orville's School of Human Flight.

Uncle Orville and Uncle Jack were identical twins, best friends, and pretty much operated in all the same ways. Mom was a mess when Jack died, but Orville took it the hardest. We only see him once a year now, at Thanksgiving, and even though it always falls right around the anniversary of Jack's death, we never talk about him. (Or maybe we never talk about him *because* it falls around the anniversary, what do I know.) But for someone like Uncle Orville—whose favorite topic of conversation is the human free fall, who lives alone, and who sends VHS tapes of his company's regional commercials to the people in his life who are obligated to at least pretend to like them (aka his family)—it's safe to assume Orville sees the Thanksgiving table as offering more than one kind of feast.

"People think skydiving is just jumping out of a plane," he said last year between bites of cranberry sauce. "There's a lot more to it than that." Uncle Orville went on to talk about "static-line jumps," which, as I understood it, was the equivalent of skydiving with training wheels. Basically, a cord called the "static line" was connected from the plane to the jumper's parachute deployment bag (or, as Uncle Orville referred to it, "the d-bag," because of course). The jumper had a very limited free fall before the parachute's rip cord was automatically pulled by the static line.

I'd remained silent for most of the meal, but I had a question. So when talk at the other end of the table turned to the state of the Bears' season, I knew I'd found my moment. "Uncle Orville," I said, tapping him on the shoulder.

"What's up, slugger?"

Uncle Orville, in keeping with that constitutional amendment dictating that all kids have no fewer than one uncle refer to them in athletic terminology, snubbed the usual suspects of *sport* and *big guy* and chose the dark horse, the far more eloquent *slugger*.

"Well, I was wondering—"

"You want a *splat* story," he said.

"Um. What?"

My uncle held his left palm up, then raised his right hand and slowly let it fall until one met the other, at which point he made an explosion sound. "A *splat* story."

Much as I hated to admit it, in that moment Orville got me.

He took a sip of iced tea, shrugged. "Had this student on his second static-line jump whose parachute didn't open. Now, if he'd been in an accelerated free fall . . . *major* splat. Lucky for him, the static line turned out to be more of a lifeline. When the cord reached its end—*phhht*. It caught him. He just hung there, getting dragged by the plane. Actually, it reminded me a little of waterskiing, only, you know, in the sky."

Waterskiing in the sky. I couldn't make this shit up.

"Sounds dangerous," I said.

"Oh, it was. Took nine guys to pull him back in. Dude was in shock, spent a bunch of time in the hospital, his back never was the same. He tried suing, but you basically sign away your life when you dive, so that went nowhere fast."

The other end of the table was still talking Bears football, while our little corner was silent for a second. And then . . .

"Wakes me up in the middle of the night," said Uncle Orville.

"It was a close call."

"Well, yeah, that . . . but also . . ."

"What."

"Nothing," he said. "It's just—sometimes I dream I'm him. Dangling thousands of feet aboveground, gripping my bag, just hanging on for dear life."

And I realized: that was high school.

21 → joyous virgins

I grip my bag, hold on for dear life as masses of kids zip through the hallway.

"I've decided to bring back *duh*," says Alan, handing me a breakfast burrito. Breakfast at the Oakman household usually consists of the latest in flaxseed technology, some new concoction for which Dad needs a family of guinea pigs before officially introducing it on his menu. Most mornings my stomach is growling like a grizzly by the time I receive the text from Alan. *Sonic order, yo! Burrito or sammy?*

"What do you mean, you're bringing back *duh*?" asks Val.

Alan is all, "Which part requires explanation?" to which Val says, "You can't bring back a word that was never in to begin with."

Alan sighs dramatically. "Come on, Val. *Duh* was in big-time."

It started freshman year: we'd meet by the front doors, walk to the opposite end of the school where the unused lockers came together in this little pocket of semi-seclusion we dubbed "the Alcove." The three of us would sit on the hallway floor, backs against the wall, legs outstretched mere inches from the rushing current of shoes, excited discussions of who was supposedly with whom, and what so-and-so said or did, or what they *didn't* say or do, and God, can you believe this or that, and oh me-oh-my, I know, isn't it all just hilarious or awful or unfair or boring?

Mostly, the three of us sat in the Alcove united in our belief that we were, in fact, living our best lives.

"Okay, then," says Val as we plop down our bags and claim our spot on the floor. "If you're bringing back *duh*, I'm bringing back *rad*."

"News flash," says Alan. "*Rad* was never out."

"The fact that you just used *news flash* in a sentence negates your opinion on the subject of what's in and what's out."

I chew my breakfast burrito, staring blankly into the raging current, grateful for the mindless discussion. It makes things feel normal, or if not normal, it at least distracts from the elephant in the room: how each of us had gone our separate ways from the Longmire party two nights ago and how we hadn't spoken of it since.

Val nudges my arm. "Are you still hungover or something?"

"Um, no."

"You're, like—totally zoned right now."

"Sorry," I say. "End-of-summer blues, I guess. Plus, I ran into Tyler this morning, so my day was pretty much shot before it even started."

"Tyler Walker?"

"Massey."

"Oh God," says Val. "Yeah, that's rough."

"Let me guess," says Alan. "He made some crude sexual

remark? Something about you being a flamer or popping cherries or having a small wiener."

"He did, actually," I say.

Val scrunches her face. "Don't say *wiener.*"

"Tyler's a chronic turd," says Alan. Then, through a mouthful of egg and cheese: "Which is a shame, 'cause otherwise, he's kind of cute."

Val says, "Yeah, you're a real catch yourself," to which Alan kisses a bicep and belches.

"Seriously, though," he says. "Do you know anyone who talks about sex more frequently or with less personal knowledge than Tyler Massey? He's one of the world's more tragic virgins."

"Which would make people like Noah what?" says Val, winking at me. "*Joyous* virgins?"

Alan stops chewing mid-bite. "Why does that sound familiar?"

I stare at my boots and wonder if it's possible for my feet to blush. "Um, ninth grade. Your parents' basement."

Alan ramps into uncontrolled laughter, and Val is all, "What's funny?" and Alan explains a particular hiccup in ninth grade when he'd had an especially bad day at school where he'd been called some especially cruel names, and so, upon arriving home, decided to dedicate the weekend to turning himself straight.

"Yeah, you can't do that," says Val.

Alan brushes crumbs off his shirt. "Duh, Val. *Duh.*"

"So what did you do?"

Alan can't stop chuckling, so I take over. "Alan thought maybe if he watched, you know . . . straight . . . *porn* . . ."

Call me a prude, but I'm uncomfortable with the word almost

as much as I am the thing itself. "Anyway. As you probably know, your parents get Cinemax."

"Cinemax, seriously?" says Val. "Ever heard of the Interwebs?"

"Ever heard of parental controls?" says Alan. "Search histories, Net Nanny, et cetera?"

"Not to mention malware," I say.

Val shakes her head. "You guys are cute in, like, the saddest way possible. Wait, what does this have to do with *joyous virgins*?"

Back to staring at my boots. "It was the title of the late-night special that evening."

Val loses it, joining Alan in his already-lost-it, at which point I can't help losing it too. "So some bullies call you names," says Val, "and you decide you're all in for conversion therapy."

"Okay, first off," says Alan, "I was a freshman. And second, it wasn't *just* name-calling. Remember how obsessed I was with Iron Man?"

"How obsessed you *were* with Iron Man?"

"Tony Stark is the man, Val. Always with a different girl, and, I don't know, it's not like there was some kick-ass gay superhero I could look up to."

Jackson, this six-foot-something teammate of ours, walks up and asks how my back is doing. "Better, I think," and I throw in a "We'll see," for good measure. He gives a fist bump to Alan, then to me. "Praying for you, dude," and he's gone, taking our lighthearted laughter right along with him.

There are times when I wonder if Val and Alan know about my back being fine. We've been friends so long, it's like lying into a mirror and expecting myself to buy it. If they do know, they haven't said a thing about it.

A song plays over the loudspeaker—two minutes until homeroom. We gather our things, walk in silence, and I imagine what it was like before the Powers That Be switched scheduling to A Day and B Day, back when everyone had to use lockers because they had more than four classes a day. (If I think about it too much, it makes me sad. Just these empty, useless metal boxes. I can't really explain it.)

Alan bends down to tie his shoe, glances over his shoulder at his own ass, then at me, all, "See something there you like?" and I'm all, "You wish," and, "Oh my God," says Val, "you guys are children."

"*Please,*" says Alan. He stands, and we resume walking. "Noah and I are giants among men. Isn't that right, No?"

"You are really tall."

"Stalwart citizens of a more refined age."

Val points to Alan's mouth. "You've got green pepper in your teeth."

Alan puts his head down, scrapes his teeth with his fingernail, and peels off into their classroom. Before walking in behind him, Val says, "Your best friend's a moron, you know that, right?"

"Duh."

"Rad."

It was one of those things that didn't register at the time, but as the day wore on, and homeroom became first block, then second and third, the more I thought about it, the less it made sense.

Remember how obsessed I was with Iron Man?

How obsessed you were *with Iron Man?*

It was like someone planted those two lines in my head this morning, and now here I was in AP German with an oak in my brain.

"Bratwurst, poltergeist, pretzel, blitzkrieg." Herr Weingarten is in the middle of his annual first-day-of-the-year speech, which inevitably outlines all ways the German language is superior to English. As the fourth year of an elective, it's a tight-knit group; other than one new kid, we've all been here from the beginning. "Bildungsroman, sauerkraut, schadenfreude—just a few examples of commonly used words the English language jacked from Deutsch."

Danny Dingledine raises a hand. The class giggles, which is what we do whenever Danny Dingledine does anything. Danny is hilarious even when he doesn't try to be, which I'm guessing has saved him many an ass-kicking through the years.

"Yes, Mr. Dingledine," says Herr Weingarten.

We giggle.

"Hi, yes, hello," says Danny Dingledine. (More giggling.) "I don't know what *schadenfreude* means."

The new kid raises his hand but doesn't wait to be called

on. "It's when someone derives great pleasure from another person's misfortune. Literally translates to 'harmjoy.'"

Mayday, mayday, competence in the air. The rest of us look at each other, knowing what's at stake. For three years, we'd worked hard to curate a space in which the minimum amount of work was required, collectively lowering standards until low standards were the norm.

And now here's this new kid all knowing shit and stuff.

Herr Weingarten looks about as shocked as a teacher who hasn't had a student voluntarily provide a correct answer in over a decade. He commends the new kid and tells him, as a reward, he can have first pick at his German name for the year.

"I'll take Norbert," says the new kid. The entire class, Herr Weingarten included, turns their eyes to me. Thing is, I've been Norbert for three years. No one is more Norbert than me.

I *am* Norbert.

Herr Weingarten is all, "Um, well, as it happens," and stumbles through a lengthy explanation as to why this kid can't be Norbert, the gist of which is *Noah has dibs*.

"Herr Weingarten," I say. "It's okay. I can just be, um . . . Klaus."

Based on the class's response, you'd think I'd just stripped down to socks only, propped my feet on my desk, and lit up a doobie.

Herr Weingarten, very quietly: "But you're Norbert."

Yes, I think. *I am Norbert.*

The new kid, having now recognized his misstep, speaks up. "It's fine, Herr Weingarten. I can be Klaus."

A collective sigh sweeps through the classroom.

I smile at the new kid. *"Danke, meine neue Freundin."*

Herr Weingarten clears his throat, but before he can say anything, the new kid—*Klaus*—jumps in. "Actually," he says, all *ac-tually*, which is just so Klaus, "you called me your new girlfriend. I think what you meant was, *Danke, mein neuer Bekannter*, or, 'Thank you, my new acquaintance,' which seems more appropriate."

Actually, Klaus, what I meant was I would derive great pleasure from your misfortune.

"*Thank you*, Klaus," I say, teeth gritted.

"*Bitte*, Norbert."

Herr Weingarten's customary lecturing process includes long tangents that do not require the presence or participation of other humans, namely us, his students; later in the year this class will morph into more of a study hall, but for now I let my mind wander back to the first time I ever walked into Alan Rosa-Haas's bedroom.

The kid had more comic books than I'd ever seen in one place. Shelves upon shelves of them, piles on the floor, posters, bedsheets, you name it. I've never really known much about comics, but I spotted a few familiar names—Batman, Catwoman, Wonder Woman, Superman, Aquaman, Green Lantern—and eventually I learned the name of Alan's preferred niche: DC Comics. I learned other things too, things Alan wouldn't shut up about, and even though I usually zoned out during his little rants, some of the information seeped its way into my brain. Like the fact that most (though not all) superheroes were divided between DC Comics and Marvel Comics, and that there were factions who bought wholeheartedly into one or the other, and if you went deeper into those factions, you might find individuals who, on the Spectrum of Fandom, fell less on the side of "casual hobby" and more on the side of "religious fanaticism." Alan wasn't religiously fanatic about DC Comics, but he wasn't far off, which is to say, the Alan I know would never sing the praises of Tony Stark, because the Alan I know was never obsessed with Iron Man, because Iron Man is *not* a DC character.

"Herr Norbert?"

Herr Weingarten stares at me in anticipation.

"Yes?" I say. "I mean—um—*ja?*"

He sighs heavily, pulls off his glasses, and rubs a temple. "Just a sentence," Herr Weingarten mumbles. "That's all I ask. One sentence describing your day."

I have this theory about teachers, and what separates the good ones from the bad: it's not that good teachers don't think about quitting; it's that they never look like they've already quit.

"Um, well," I say. "It's been okay so far, I guess. Sort of a rocky start, but—"

"*Auf Deutsch, bitte, bitte,*" says Weingarten, temple rubbing with increased velocity.

"Right. Okay, so . . ." My phone vibrates in my pocket, the alarm reminding me to read Penny's letter from this morning. "*Dinge beginnen, für Norbert . . .* um, *weirden zu bekommen.*"

Herr Weingarten rubs those temples, plops backward into his desk chair.

"*Weirden* isn't a word," says Klaus the new kid. "In German *or* English."

"Hey, Klaus," says Danny Dingledine, "what's German for butt-for?"

"What's a butt for?" says Klaus, and the class loses it, but all I can do is count down the minutes to the end of the day. Between Mom's scar and the shape-shifting dog from the other night, I don't need another looming question mark. One look in Alan's room, and I'll know if he's mysteriously switched comic allegiances.

23 → the pros and cons of Penny Oakman

My darling brother,

Due to your irrational apathy in regard to the very brilliant film Breakfast at Tiffany's, I am compelled to make a list of pros and cons for you. (Do you know about "pros and cons," darling? It's when you write down all the reasons you should do something [pros] and all the reasons you shouldn't [cons], and then compare those reasons side by side.) I believe when you see the overwhelming evidence in the PROS section, you will have no choice but to agree. Now pay attention!

Should Noah Watch
Breakfast at Tiffany's
with Penny?

reasons for (pros) and against (cons)

Pros:

1. It's a really good movie

2. Audrey Hepburn

3. Quality time with Penny

4. Audrey Hepburn

5. The fashion, darling

6. Audrey Hepburn

7. Based on a novel by Truman Capote

8. Audrey Hepburn

9. Good music (well, decent anyway)

10. Audrey Hepburn

Cons:

1. The racist depiction of Holly Golightly's
   neighbor, Mr. Yunioshi. No doubt, this is an
   absolute con, and a total drag on the movie.
   But you're in luck! Your terribly clever and
   resourceful sister (that's me!) long ago took
   the liberty of jotting down the time stamps of
   every scene that includes Mr. Yunioshi, and can

happily report her ability to fast-forward said scenes with her eyes closed.

So. Will you watch Breakfast at Tiffany's with your darling sister? Please check one:

Yes, of course I will ☐

No, I never will ☐

I'm still considering ☐

Love always
(and I do, even when you're being ridiculous),

Penelope

24 → the arpanet, the golden age, and an exclusive look inside the first celebrity canine wedding!

I stand on the front porch of the Rosa-Haas house, somewhat apprehensive, gripping my sister's letter in my pocket like a charm, imagining two scenarios: Alan's room is the same as it ever was, like DC vomited comics everywhere; Alan's room now rotates in the Marvel universe.

Before I can build up the courage to ring the bell, the door swings open.

"Noah?"

"Oh. Hey, Val."

She's changed into cutoff shorts and that AC/DC tee with the ripped-wide collar. No one scrubs like Val.

"You just standing out here?" she asks.

"Uh, yeah."

"Care to accompany me to the mailbox?"

We walk down to the end of the drive, where Val pulls out a small stack of mail and a *People* magazine. "So you were standing on the porch, what—hoping I'd intuit your presence?"

I shrug. "It worked, didn't it?"

Back on the porch, Val says, "I'm making pegao if you want some."

"Sure."

Inside, she walks down the hallway, leaving the door open for me to follow. It's a very familiar move, very Val, very East Egg. In the kitchen, she tosses the mail onto the counter, adjusts the temperature on the stove.

"Alan around?" I ask.

"Seriously, No?"

"What."

"He has practice."

"Oh. Right."

I sit at the counter and watch Val stir the pegao with one hand while navigating her phone with the other.

"Shit."

"You okay?" I ask.

"Yeah, I'm just—not supposed to disturb the rice at the

bottom." She puts a lid on the pan, adjusts the temperature again. "It'll be fine."

"Your mom usually uses a different pot, I think."

The look she gives me—my God. "First off, it's a caldero, not a *pot*. Second, you can't even say pegao, what makes you think you know how to cook it?"

I should have lied. Rung the doorbell, said I'd forgotten something in Alan's room; that would have gotten me up there, no questions asked. Now I'm committed to this pegao and hanging with Val until it's ready.

On the counter, one of the Kardashian sisters smiles up at me from the cover of *People* magazine. I pick it up, read the subtitle: AN EXCLUSIVE LOOK INSIDE THE FIRST CELEBRITY CANINE WEDDING!

"This is ridiculous."

"What?" Val looks up from her phone. "Oh yeah. Clearly a slow week."

"Remind me why she's famous?"

"Sex tape, I think? Went viral?"

"Freaking Internet." I thumb through the first few pages. "Should be called something else. *Internet* sounds too harmless."

"I don't think it was called that in the beginning, was it?"

"Wasn't it?"

"Here, I'll google it," Val says.

"How very meta of you."

She pushes herself up onto the counter by the stove, and a second later she's got it. "Okay, looks like its original name was the Arpanet."

"That's not better at all."

"Invented by Robert E. Kahn and Vinton Cerf."

"Way to ruin everything, Bobby and Vint. Couldn't even get the name right."

"You do know people fall in love online, right? Form life-long friendships, find jobs, houses. It's a place where the marginalized have a voice, where we can all gain a broader worldview—"

I hold up the magazine. "Where we can become famous for nothing?"

"Like everything else, Noah. You take the good with the bad."

I toss aside Kardashian as if that'll show her a thing or two. "I bet the nineties were great. Nirvana, Pearl Jam, no smartphones, flannel far as the eye could see."

"I think we need to cool it with the *Gilmore Girls* binging for a bit."

"You know what I miss most, though?"

"You can't miss it, No, you weren't alive."

"The part where not everyone in the known universe knew everything about everyone else in the known universe."

"You're hopeless, you know that, right?"

"Just a sliver of anonymity is all I'm asking. Like, if I could take a trip to the fucking bathroom without my second cousin in North Carolina liking it, that would be great."

"If they're liking it, you're posting it, which in this case raises some questions."

"And it's not like *I* need to know when everyone *else* goes to the bathroom. Or like, you had stewed rabbit with fresh rosemary for breakfast."

"So quit," says Val.

"What?"

"I'm sick of people shitting on social media like they don't have a choice. This isn't mandatory participation. If you hate it, quit. No one cares."

"That's just it," I say. "The act of quitting is itself a statement. Like slamming the door on your way out of a party or ending a text with a period."

"Noah, your online presence is roughly the equivalent of a silent fart in the middle of an empty field. I think the world will keep spinning should you go gentle into that good night."

"Very poetic of you."

"Also, you end texts with periods all the time."

"Yeah, I feel bad about that."

Val slams her phone on the counter. "Four hours."

"What?"

"Four hours. That's how long I spent on my last post. It was Nico with the Velvet Underground, and it was fucking awesome."

"Val."

"I know social media sucks sometimes. But it's also a gathering of minds. You know how hard I work on my art, how important it is to me. The *Arpanet* is my gallery, Noah."

"I hadn't thought of it that way. You're right. I'm sorry."

Val swivels on the counter to face the stove, pulls the lid off the caldero. "Son of a bitch, the pegao is toasted." She slides down onto the floor, turns off the stove, and pushes the caldero to the back burner.

"I thought it was supposed to be that way."

"It's supposed to be crispy, not . . . like this." For a second Val just stands there staring at the stove.

"Val, I'm really sorry."

She turns toward the hallway. "I'm going for a swim. You can use that moral compass of yours to find your way out."

25 → monsters

But I don't leave, not yet.

Upstairs, outside Alan's bedroom door, I think of how often I still look under the bed for monsters. I know nothing will be there, but I also know that at some point later that night my arm will be hanging off the edge of the bed, and I'll imagine some scaly-skinned hand reaching up, coiling around my wrist, and I'll imagine the monster pulling me out, pulling me under into darkness, and so I get down on the floor and look first because I know I'll need the proof later.

I turn the knob and push the door open just wide enough to get my head through.

"I'll call him later," I say out loud. No one hears me, or I don't think they do, which is another reason I love walking: very conducive to thinking out loud. "I'll call him and ask him," I say, but no, this needs to be in person. I need to see his face when I ask, see how absurd a question he thinks it is; and I need him to see mine, see that I'm being real with him. "I'll talk to him tomorrow," and—as if my mind is playing out the afternoon in reverse—I hear Val say, *It was Nico with the Velvet Underground, and it was fucking awesome.* I pull out my phone in a sudden panic. "No-no-no-no-no-no-no," but yes, there it is, the monster under the bed. Scroll, scroll, checking, double-checking date stamps, maybe she's just changed courses, but no, "No, no, no . . ."

I remember the day Val told me her idea about movie-related photos, how she'd labored over which film to start with, ultimately landing on her favorite movie of all time: *Kill Bill*. And I remember, more recently, how excited she'd been when her *Star Wars: The Last Jedi* Rey-themed post put her over 100k followers.

I remember these things because they happened.

Phone in pocket now, I spend the rest of the walk home trying not to be sick. Through the front door, *beep-beep-hey-honey*, and Fluffenburger the Freaking Useless is jumping and yapping at my heels, and Penny whispers, "See? He's *changed*," and Mom is in the kitchen with her hair pulled back, that scar more visible than ever, and all I can do is go to my room, shut the door, shut out the world. All I can do is wish I'd never looked under the bed.

Val's feed is all music now.

And Alan's room is filled with Marvel.

26 ➜ *a concise history of me, part twenty-six*

350 B.C.E.

Aristotle writes *Parva Naturalia*, a seven-piece collection on the body and soul, including a treatise called *De Insomniis*—or, *On Dreams*—in which he analyzes the toll imagination takes on our dreams, and the way our waking brains process afterimages in order to differentiate between reality and unreality.

Our sleeping brains do no such thing.

It goes like this: You see an animated movie containing a dragon in tights. You walk outside and imagine that same dragon in tights flying through the sky. Having just seen this image in a movie, you can picture it easily, and depending how imaginative a person you are, it may be a fairly strong rendering. But you are a reasonable individual, able to distinguish those things that are externally present from those that are imagined. Dragons do not exist. And even if they did, they would not wear tights. (Of this, you are relatively certain.)

Later that night, however, in a dream, you see that dragon in tights again, only now the sucker really exists, or at least you *could swear it does*, because it's just so real, and *of course* it wears tights, what else would a dragon wear to cover its legs and hindquarters and, moreover, you just heard that dragon declare an affinity for *The Nutcracker*, which, as it so happens, was produced by your uncle Orville's mechanic's pet gerbil, a real go-getter named Rodney. Whatever piece of your brain had so easily distinguished external reality from perceived unreality was no longer in use during sleep.

1899. (Or 1900, depending on the source.) Sigmund Freud publishes a book called *The Interpretation of Dreams*, in which he refers to this effect as hallucinatory. His book touches on other topics such as condensation (when a single object within a dream represents multiple ideas or feelings), displacement (when the dreamer substitutes one thing in their dream for another), and wish fulfillment.

Freud began his clinical work as a hypnotist, until one day a patient just wouldn't shut the fuck up long enough to be hypnotized.

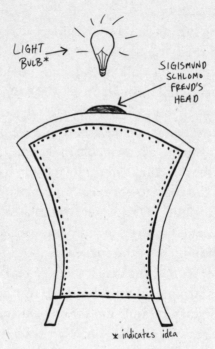

LIGHT BULB*

SIGISMUND SCHLOMO FREUD'S HEAD

* indicates idea

Freud realizes that if you let the patient talk, uninterrupted, there is no need to induce a complex state of consciousness in which the individual morphs into a very compliant puppet. Just talk. Eventually, those talking will let down their guard and raise the curtain on the unconscious self.

Freud would go on to abandon hypnosis for psychoanalysis.

Dreams remind me of being underwater, how everything close to me slows down while the world above continues its frenetic trajectory. And when I swim, I think of words like *inwardness* and *peace* and *solitary*, and in this place it doesn't matter if the population of the world is seven billion or seven; I am free to start my own trajectory.

I don't really miss swimming. But I do miss that.

27 → application

The cover of David Bowie's biography is a barrage of bright pinks and blues, like a rainbow having an orgasm, and I think, *Here is a cover befitting the man himself.* I've read it a few times. Some books are songs like that, the ones you go back to, make playlists of, put on repeat. And then sometimes I just pull the book off the shelf and hold it, knowing that's as close as I'll ever get to Bowie himself.

I bring the book to bed with me, crawl under my covers with all my clothes on, burrow into those white sheets and blankets, shut down power, and imagine the mute bark of a dog, the soaked person in the corner, the blinding tornado of colors. And while I can write about dream theories until I'm blue in the face, the truth is, I don't feel much like falling asleep tonight. Because I don't know how many nights in a row constitute a recurring dream, and I don't care to find out.

NOW FOR ➥ PART THREE

Mod: During an interview with the Portland Press Herald, you're quoted as saying, "Sometimes writing is quitting. You know how many times I've quit? Thousands, just for the good of my own soul."

Henry: Yeah.

Mod: For someone who so clearly believes in the magic of writing, the magic of storytelling, I wonder if you might explain what you mean by that.

Henry: That was what—a decade ago?

Mod: So you don't think it anymore?

Henry: I don't know.

Mod: Come on.

Henry: Saying I don't know isn't a non-answer. I don't really know how I feel about writing. It's like . . . any other love.

Mod: In what way?

Henry: It's like a pendulum, I guess. If the bob swings hard one way, it's going to swing hard the other eventually. Now, if it's just barely swaying, sort of caught in the middle, it doesn't go very far in one direction or the other. This is why a casual acquaintance might cause only minor irritation, while someone we truly love can induce murderous rage. Do I want to quit writing? Absolutely. Do I fucking hate my life some days? Sure. But that's because I love it. And I trust the pendulum.

Mod: So when the pendulum swings the other way, when it's not about quitting—when it's something you love—what is writing?

Henry: I think . . .

(Silence)

Mod: Yes?

Partial transcript from "A Conversation with Mila Henry"
Harvard, 1969
(Henry's last known public appearance)

28 → *I think writing is less about the words and more about the silence between them*

Over the next couple of weeks, I saw changes everywhere I went—understated, yet undeniable—and it reminded me of something Henry said in one of her final public appearances about words being less important than the silence between them. And in some cases my changes were like that, like the silence between the words: like how Christa and Carla now chatted up study hall with their dreams of a Venice honeymoon, whereas before it had always been Paris; or how Rawlings the quarterback (I never knew if Rawlings was his first or last name) now greeted me daily with a "'Sup, dude?" in the hallways between third and fourth block; and some were more physical, like I could swear Benji Larkin had *never* been that tall, and Rachel Dillard had *never* worn glasses, and so on, like that.

I sent Circuit a quick Facebook message (apparently we're "friends," though I have no memory of this happening) asking for his phone number. I didn't want written documentation of this conversation. I'd considered walking over to Piedmont, confronting him in person, but that house loomed too large in my mind.

The first time I called, I was keyed up, and he answered on the first ring, which just keyed me up even more.

"What the fuck did you do to my head, Circuit?"

"What?"

"You heard me, motherfucker."

And that was about the extent of things.

I kept calling, one day after the next. He never answered after that first time, but I liked the thought of him feeling his phone ring and hoping it wasn't me again. I liked the thought of his face when he saw my name on his screen, and I liked him knowing I was present. And maybe because the changes were more trivial than monumental, these unanswered phone calls were enough.

For a while.

29 ➜ *ch-ch-ch-ch-ch-ch-changes*

"You ever notice how artificial peach flavoring tastes like how earwax smells?" asks Alan, contemplating the lollipop in his hands.

"What?"

"You know, peach candy," he says. "It tastes like how earwax smells. That can't just be me."

"It can just be you."

We came to the library this morning instead of the Alcove. Alan's idea. He said it was best if I avoided Val for a day or two. Apparently she was still stewing over our argument in the kitchen yesterday.

Alan bites into the hard candy and stares at the little white stick all pulpy from having been in his mouth so long. "But I prefer peach, which seems . . . disturbing. Like, I *choose* it over, say, lime, which actually tastes like limes."

"Feels like we've talked about this before," I say.

"Now, obviously I'd choose to eat a real lime over earwax, but in candy world I choose peach—which tastes like earwax— over lime, which tastes like limes."

"Who can explain the curiosities of the human body, Alan?"

"We are a weirdo species, yo."

"So when did you sell your comic collection?"

Alan looks at me like this is the strangest part of our conversation thus far. "What?"

"You sold them, right?" I ask. "Or traded them for another collection?"

"Dude."

"So that's a no, then."

Alan, distracted, looks around the library. "Listen, let's keep this whole thing under wraps. I don't like all the whispering in here—too many suspicious ears, you never know who's listening."

"So you did sell them?"

"What? No. I mean about the earwax thing. Last thing I need is something like that getting around school."

I briefly consider the possibility that I was wrong in the first place, that Alan has *always* loved Marvel, *always* hated DC. But we've gone to all the Batman movies, debated the better Joker; we saw the latest Superman only to walk out of the theater with a pound of kryptonite dangling from our necks; and we even saw the *Batman v Superman* bullshit cash cow, which we agreed was worse than the Superman reboots.

I'm not wrong about this.

Alan points to the next table, where a couple is hunched over a textbook, clearly flirting. "What do you think's going on there?"

"Probably one of them prefers booger-flavored potato chips."

Alan shakes his head. "Weirdo species, yo."

◀▌▌▌▌▶

I eat lunch in my car for a few days, and it's peaceful, the solitude of the school parking lot; I listen to music, revel in the sameness of everything. Third day in, I have the Beatles on shuffle when "Across the Universe" comes on and, like a flashback, the snap of a finger, I'm transported to a snow day last winter when Val had braved the elements to come over for a movie in our basement. Alan was sick, or something, so it was just the two of us.

"Oh, let's watch that," she said.

The icon for the movie showed a couple about to kiss in the middle of a heart-shaped apple. "Val. Come on."

"Uh-uh, wait. Read the synopsis. The whole movie revolves around Beatles songs. You love the Beatles."

"Of course I love the Beatles. Who doesn't love the Beatles?"

"People who hate music, I guess."

"I'm just not sure I love the Beatles enough to watch a romcom."

The movie was called *Across the Universe*, and we ended up watching it, and it wasn't a romcom at all, and I loved it. Val too. And when it was over, we just sat there on the couch in the basement, Val's legs propped up on my lap, and I listened to her amazing insights on cinematography, the different shots and lighting, and as always, I felt lucky to be in her orbit.

"It could be like a movie-music crossover post," she said, talking about her plans for an *Across the Universe* photo. She was wide-eyed and keyed up, and I loved when she got this way. "Who do we know who has a vinyl collection?"

"My dad," I said.

"Really? You think he has the White Album?"

"Probably. Is 'Across the Universe' on the White Album, though?"

Val said it didn't matter which album that particular song was on, since the whole movie was filled with Beatles songs. She was more concerned with the artistic direction of the shot, how the colors of the DVD cover (which she'd already ordered on her phone) would need to pop against a stark white background. "Will you find out if he has that record? I'll need to buy it otherwise."

Dad was away for work, so I texted him.

Me: Do you have the White Album on vinyl?

Dad: Does Harry Connick Jr. have one luscious head of hair?

Me: Um.

Dad: Is nutritional yeast the secret
   ingredient in vegan mac and cheese?

Me: Dad.

Dad: Yes. He does, and it is. And I have all the
   Beatles' records on vinyl. (Except Magical
   Mystery Tour, which doesn't count.)

Val was glowing. "It'll be *perfect*."

In the car now, I turn off the song, stick a half-eaten sand-wich in my lunch bag, and pull up her Instagram—scroll through hundreds of photos of records and bands, think-ing maybe *this* one will still be there. It is relevant to both music *and* movies, so it's possible. And maybe more than any other photo Val took, this one made an impression on me. I'd witnessed its conception, watched the seed of her idea germi-nate and ultimately blossom. Whatever the case, I remember the post well and Val was right: it was perfect.

I stop scrolling, click on a photo, and there it is, her *Across the Universe* post complete with DVD and vinyl.

But it's not the White Album. It's *Magical Mystery Tour*.

That's the last day I eat lunch in the car.

◄▐▐▐▐▐►

I'd pretty much ignored Penny back on the first day of school when she'd commented on Fluff's newfound agility, but as the days wore on, I couldn't help noticing it myself. Before, if there'd been some rando pit to fall into, or wet cement to get stuck in, or a banana peel to slip on, that dog had been sure to find it. But recently there was an undeniable sense of *cool* about him, like he'd been injected with a B12 shot or discovered the fountain of youth.

"I think he needs a new name," says Penn. We're in the backyard, watching him defend a small nest of baby birds against a stray cat.

"You can't just rename a dog, Penn. Especially not one as old as Fluff."

"He just doesn't seem like a *Fluff* anymore."

She's right. He seems different, like a pup again. "Okay," I say. "How about Hepburn? Heppy, for short."

"Doesn't fit. But that reminds me—did you read my letter yet?"

"What?"

"The pros and cons list." Penny sighs dramatically. "You didn't read it."

"I did, actually. Just sort of forgot about it."

"Well, I didn't want to bug you."

"That's very generous, Penn."

Penny looks up at me, unwavering. "And?"

"You *just* said you didn't want to bug me about it."

"And *you* just said you read it. But hey, far be it from me to act the part of the annoying little sister. Forget I asked." And then, a minute later: "So what should we call him?"

"Who?"

"*Our dog?*"

"You really want to change his name?"

Penny taps her chin. "Who's your favorite actor? And don't say Bowie."

I have to give Penny credit for even knowing David Bowie was an actor, too. "Okay, well, if not Bowie . . ." *Boogie Nights* was one of the older movies Val insisted I watch, and one of my favorites. "Mark Wahlberg."

Fluff abandons the baby birds, runs straight for me, sits on his hind legs, and gazes lovingly into my eyes.

"Mark Wahlberg," I say just to see what will happen.

Fluff barks once.

"Mark Wahlberg."

Fluff barks again.

"Well," says Penny. "Guess we found the name."

<hr />

My parents: Mom's scar was still a mystery, and at first I thought maybe Dad was off the hook, that for whatever reason he'd proven immune to this epidemic of subtle modifications.

But then, two nights ago, on my way to the bathroom in the hallway, I heard that nineties sitcom canned laughter coming from inside my parents' bedroom. Single episodes of *Friends* often turned into late-night marathons, but something sounded different. I tiptoed up to their door until I was close enough to hear clearly. It wasn't Joey making them laugh, or Phoebe, or Chandler. I'd never actually sat down and watched a full episode, but I'd been around the show so long, heard it in the background, seen clips while walking through rooms, that I was pretty familiar with it.

And this sounded new. Some guy talking about how he liked sports, how he thought maybe he could be a professional color commentator, when someone else explains to him that those jobs are usually given to people in broadcasting.

I knocked lightly on the door.

"Come in," said Dad between laughs.

"Hey," I said, a prolonged glance at the TV.

Mom paused the episode. "You heading to bed?"

I nodded. "Just wanted to say good night."

"Noah," said Dad, clearing his throat. "We wanted to give you some time with the offer. But have you had a chance to consider?"

"Hmm?"

"Coach Stevens's voicemail. It's huge news, bud. Just wondering what you think about it all."

I nodded toward the TV. "What're you guys watching?"

They gave each other a quick look like I was playing a prank or something. "It's *Seinfeld*, Noah."

"Oh, okay. You taking a *Friends* breather?"

Mom said, "What's a friends breather?"

"No, I mean—you're taking a break from watching *Friends*."

"The TV show?" asked Mom.

I tried to read her eyes. In addition to the scar she wouldn't talk about, lately it seemed she was avoiding me. I'd walk into a room just as she was walking out of it, and I don't know—we'd always been friends, ever since I was a little kid. She'd sit on the edge of my bed at night and tell these amazing stories, and when I found out later she hadn't actually made them up, but had just regurgitated the synopses of her favorite movies, I never called her on it. Because I didn't want the stories to end, and because I've never been the kind of person to care where stories came from so long as they kept coming.

"Noah?" said Dad, but that's when I saw it: on the dresser,

next to their trusty old DVD player, there was no *Friends* DVD box set; in its place, there was *Seinfeld: The Complete Series*.

"You okay, bud?"

I said I was, but I wasn't, walked back to my room where it was okay to not be okay, crashed in bed with my laptop, clicked play on the Fading Girl video.

A knock on my door, a muffled, "Noah?"

"Not now, Penn," and I felt like shit, just watched the video until I began to feel I *was* the Fading Girl: my face became hers, and I stared into the camera *every day for forty years* while the world around me revolved and evolved, revolved and evolved.

30 ➔ *between my sixth viewing and falling asleep*

I realize Penny still wears the same brightly colored out-fits, maintains an unnatural obsession with *Breakfast at Tiffany's*, carries around the same ten-pound persona in the same five-pound sack: so far as I can tell, my sister hasn't changed at all.

"You know how people use putting a man on the moon as their benchmark for what's possible?" asks Alan. He's holding up his rectangle pizza, staring at it like he's about to make out with it.

"Sure," I say.

"I don't," says Val.

"Actually, yeah, me either. Alan, we don't know what you're talking about."

The three of us are in our usual spot with the swim team in the cafeteria. Ever since my failed lunch-in-the-car experiment, I notice the guys have stopped asking about my back, and I can't help wondering if Alan convinced them to drop it.

"We can put a man on the moon," he says, "but we can't keep cereal from getting soggy. We can put a man on the moon, but we can't adequately reheat fries."

"Sounds like you just use it as a benchmark for what's possible with food," says Val.

Alan takes a huge bite from the corner of his slice, clearly savoring the process, and then, shaking his head: "We can put a man on the moon, but we can't make every pizza rectangular."

Under her breath, Val says, "Chocolate milk on me if you can change the subject in five seconds."

"Alan," I say, "I couldn't help noticing that you're wearing some pretty short shorts today."

"Well played," says Val, dipping a fry in ranch dressing.

Alan stands, turns in a full circle. "I'm bringing back

Umbros. If you got it, flaunt it, amarite?" He slaps his bare legs. "Gotta let these suckers breathe."

Val reaches for another fry. "They're called Umbros because it's what you say when you see a guy wearing them."

At some point last week, Val lifted her shun on me, which, thank God. Things just weren't the same without her running commentaries.

"Nice legs, douchebox." Tyler Massey stands behind us, holding a stack of red note cards. I sometimes think Tyler shares genetic makeup with a shark, only instead of smelling blood from miles away, he smells the opportunity to be a dick. "Got a question for you," he says to Alan. "Could you possibly be more gay?"

Smile intact, Alan pulls up the legs of his Umbros by a few inches, circles the table until he's right up in Tyler's space. "I don't know, Tyler. Wanna find out?"

Tyler Massey's face goes dark red. "I just came over to give you guys your invite." He pulls a note card from a stack, hands it to Val, and he's gone, off to harass the next table.

"'You are cordially invited,'" reads Val, "'to participate in the highly anticipated cinematic experience from acclaimed director Tyler Massey.'"

Alan dips a fry in Val's ranch. "'Acclaimed'? Is he for real with this?"

"'A *Sex, Lies, and Videotape* for the new generation,'" reads Val, "'*The Vagina Dialogues* is a harrowing tale of lust and intrigue, love and friendship gone awry, a luscious thriller that brings new meaning to the term *coming-of-age*.'"

"It does *not* say that," says Alan.

Val laughs to the point of shaking, turns the invite around for us to read, and we pretty much lose our shit.

"Oh, hey." I turn to Val and sing, "Chocolate milk," like a song. She hands over money, and I head to the line for three milks, and when I get back, I overhear the tail end of a conversation in which Alan says, "Like, how is that even possible? How could I prefer *that* to artificial lime flavoring?"

"Really, Alan?" I pass around the chocolate milks. "With the earwax thing again?"

Alan mumbles something, and Val tosses a fry at his head. "What, you're giving me recycled material now? You gotta run conversations through him first?"

"You guys weren't speaking at the time," says Alan. "You missed good material, he missed good material. What do you want me to say?"

"Like what?" I ask.

Alan takes a huge bite of pizza. "Hmm?"

"You said I missed good material. What did I miss?"

He nods as he chews, holds up one finger to indicate we should wait, and then wipes grease from his mouth. "Bloody hell, that's delicious. Okay, so. Your fun guy ballsack? Yeah, we can't call it that anymore."

"Okeydokey."

"I know this comes as quite a blow."

"I'm okay with it."

"And you're probably wondering, *What's it all mean?*"

"Nah, I'm good."

"Thing is, I saw a Hyundai commercial the other day, and guess what?" says Alan. "It's pronounced *hun-day*, not *hun-dye*, which means fun guy ballsack does not, in fact, rhyme with Hyundai hatchback, and if it doesn't rhyme, what's the point?"

"Indeed."

"Which is why I shall now be referring to your Hyun*dai* hatchback as your fun *gay* ballsack. Rhyme intact. Plus it's better, I think. Logical, anyway."

"I believe we've long abandoned the realms of logic."

"I think we should go," says Val.

"Go where?" asks Alan.

Val smiles, points to Tyler's invitation. "*The Vagina Dialogues* premier."

"Uh, no thanks."

"Come on. Remember his movie last year? *Harken the Dream*, or whatever? It was hilarious."

"Unintentionally."

"Still hilarious," says Val. "Plus, we need to stock up our memory reserves, take advantage of what little time we have left, you know?"

"Please," says Alan. "You really want to subject yourself to a Tyler Massey movie mere months before heading to the film capital of the world? Talk about tainting the well."

Sometimes words are spoken that seem to match the tenor and frequency of the words around them, until closer inspection reveals otherwise.

"Wait, what?"

Val's eyes dart to Alan, then to her plate. "Look, I know we don't talk about it, and I get it. I'm sad too. But I refuse to mope through my entire senior year."

"What are you talking about?"

Alan pops the last corner of pizza into his mouth. "It'll suck, but it'll work, remember? Global village and whatnot."

"*If* we get in," says Val.

"We'll get in. And wherever Noah lands, LAX is an easy flight."

"*If* we get in."

Alan rolls his eyes. "Val, please. You were born for UCLA. And once they get a look at these Umbros, I'm as good as blue and gold."

"UCLA," I whisper, and for some reason I'm thinking of how my eighth-grade girlfriend dumped me via Facebook Messenger—that little blue note with the *it's-been-great-but*, and the *not-ready-for-a-commitment*—and feeling the bottom drop out of my gut. All that time I was the only one living our shared history.

"You okay?"

I look up at Val. "What?"

Alan puts a hand on my shoulder. "Noah, I'm telling you this as your friend? You need to take a nap, yo. You've got these bags under your eyes, like—"

"Big ones," says Val.

"You spend too much time watching that YouTube video we found of the lady who ages in slo-mo," says Alan. I had totally forgotten he was with me when I discovered the Fading Girl video, and I guess the look on my face indicates as much. "What, you think I don't notice you watching it all the time?"

I stand up and wonder: What happens when the keepers of your shared history no longer recognize that history? "I have to go now," I say, and without another word, I walk out of the cafeteria, through the parking lot to my car, and all I can think of is that woman from the cruise ship who'd been hypnotized, made into a human marionette, and the look on her face in the days following, that blank stare she'd carried with her around the boat. I don't know what's going on, but if I have strings attached to my arms and legs, I know who put them there.

32 → Sara, a regrettably brief conversation

"Noah-with-an-*H*, I was wondering if I would see you again."

"Yeah, me too. I mean—wondering if I would see you. I see me, like, every day."

"Oh good. You're squirrely when you're sober, too."

"Sorry about that. I don't usually drink."

"Wait, did you back into our driveway?"

"Um, yes. Yeah, that's me."

"Very efficient of you. Sure you're not a dad?"

"I know, right?"

"You want a grilled cheese? It's grilled cheese day."

"Grilled cheese day."

"Yeah, pretty sure we're the only homeschooled kids with a monthly lunch calendar."

"Actually, thanks—but I need to talk to your brother for a second."

"Oh. Okay. You wanna come inside?"

"I'll wait here, thanks."

"What do you want?"

"Can you step outside a sec?"

"Can I *step outside*? What, are you gonna hit me?"

"I'm not going to hit you."

"Calling me five times a day isn't enough, you gotta come harass me at my place of residence?"

"Okay, listen. Whatever you did, I'm done being mad about it. I just need you to undo it. Just fix me, or whatever."

"I didn't *do* anything."

"Circuit, I'm serious. My brain is fucked up."

"In what way?"

"Everybody's . . . different."

"Ha."

"What?"

"Don't look now, dude, but sounds like you got exactly what you asked for."

"This isn't funny."

"I didn't say it was."

"I'm having these dreams, Circuit, these weird dreams like every night. And now my best friends are leaving. And my mom has this scar on her face, and I'm just . . . I can't . . . I can't breathe."

"Okay. Noah, calm down. All right, look. Cards on the table. I *tried* to hypnotize you. It would have worked if you'd given me a minute, but once you saw what was happening, you were gone."

"You're lying."

"I'm not. So unless you wanna come inside and finish what we started—"

"I'm not going in there."

"Okay, then. My grilled cheese is getting cold. Oh, and, Noah?"

"What."

"I know you have friends, and I know I'm not one of them. So maybe instead of calling me every day, you should try calling one of them."

34 ➜ *the vase*

Me: Dean and Carlo. Your house. Pronto.

I send the text before pulling out of Circuit's driveway, and it's a testament to Alan's loyalty that he responds immediately with On my way, even though it means skipping class and most likely practice, too.

"Good pizza today," Alan says. "Extra rectangular."

We're in his room now. *The Matrix* is on in the background, and even though we're not really watching, the movie accompanies our session appropriately. I sit at the foot of his bed, he sits at the head, and both of us stare straight into the eyes of the other. The deal is: we talk. Honestly and openly. We got the idea last year when our class was supposed to read *On the Road*, by Jack Kerouac, until a few parents got wind of the assignment and put the kibosh on the whole thing. They said it wasn't age appropriate and had the book banned from Iverton High. Thing is, none of us had planned to read that shit originally, but as it turns out, telling a bunch of kids not to read a certain book is a highly effective way to get them to read that book. Within days the halls were filled with kids bumping into each other, everyone's head stuck inside *On the Road*.

Alan and I read it together. He had the idea we should "do it up right," like a book club, so that's what we did. We took notes, baked some brownies, and discussed the book's haphazard sentences, the overall get-up-and-go tone like it had legs of its own. It wasn't until near the end that we both admitted we actually didn't like it all that much.

Except one scene.

In it, two of the main characters, Dean and Carlo, sit on a bed and talk through the night—just talk, openly and honestly about anything and everything, so long as it's real.

"It was fine pizza," I say. "But what's with the rectangles?"

"Makes it taste better."

"I think you're the only one who thinks that."

"I am misunderstood in my time."

"You're misunderstood in every time, Alan."

"It is as you say."

We're not whispering, but it's close, a very serene state, almost meditational, which was our mutual interpretation of Kerouac's characters in that scene.

"You don't have to talk so quietly," says Alan.

I swear sometimes he can read my mind. "Talking quietly was our mutual interpretation."

"Oh."

"Plus, you're talking that way too."

"Okay."

"Okay."

"Stop saying *okay*."

"I like saying *okay*."

"Okay."

In the background, Neo meets the Oracle for the first time. She tells him not to worry about the vase, and he says, "What vase?" and then promptly knocks over a vase, which shatters on the floor.

"Okay, rapid-fire," I say. "Just answer, don't think."

"Hit me."

"One thing that happened today that you loved."

"Rectangle pizza," says Alan. "Killed it in my Umbros."

"Um, bro? That's two things."

"You said don't think."

"Fair," I say. "Okay, one thing that happened today that made you sad. Or mad."

"Someone put a note in my backpack that said, 'Go back to Mexico.'"

A beat. "Shit. Again?"

He shrugs.

"Was it signed this time?" I ask.

"What do you think?"

"Alan, that's twice now. You should report it."

"First of all, no. Actually, that's it. Just no."

"Why not?"

"Because I refuse to waste my time on douchesacks who have zero-percent clue what they're talking about. Of course, I can't *go back* to someplace I've never been, but I do find some comfort in imagining how that sentence would proba-bly tie the culprit's brain in knots."

"I'm staking out your bag tomorrow."

"Actually, we should go to Mexico, like, for real."

"We're talking full-on martial law," I say. "Skull cracking, the works."

"Mexico City especially sounds dope. The food and all. Get a couple cervezas. And they're big into wrestling, right?"

"Noah the Skull Cracker, that's me."

"God, I love wrestling. Watching it, primarily. Never ac-tually wrestled myself. Well, I've *wrestled myself*, if you catch my drift."

"Alan, I'm serious."

"I know you are, yo. But this isn't up to you, okay? I deal with this shit in my own way. By mocking the intelligence of the perpetrators."

For all the ways Alan can be a child—and they are legion—there are times when his maturity knocks me on my ass.

"But thanks for having my back," he says.

"I really do. I know we haven't Dean and Carlo'd in a while. I've been a little distant, probably. But I do have your back."

"I know. And you're hella cute when you're incensed."

"It really is sad how much you love me."

"Please," Alan says. "That shit is *extra*-requited."

"You're right."

"Oh, I know. I've seen the way you look at me from 'cross yonder room."

"What yonder room?" I ask.

"Every yonder room. Whichever yonder room I happen to be in at the time."

"I don't make a habit of looking at people 'cross yonder

rooms. And even if I did, it wouldn't mean what you seem to think it means."

"Oh really?"

"Yes, Alan. Because I can acknowledge someone as attractive without wanting to have sex with that person."

"You are a Zen master, bro. An example for us all."

"It is as you say."

More staring, more not listening to *The Matrix*, all while I try to bring up what needs bringing up.

Alan says, "Remember when we were kids? And we used to talk about getting married?"

"Basket weaving in the mountains."

"Eating from iron skillets."

"Skillet eating and basket weaving," I say. "That was the dream."

"Such lofty aspirations."

Silence again. Thinking, et cetera, very Dean and Carlo. Alan asks what I want out of life, and I say, "Other than basket weaving in the mountains?"

"Obvs."

I shrug. "You'll laugh."

Alan puts his right hand on his shorts. "I swear on my Umbros, I will not laugh at your dreams."

"I would like to make a living by living."

"So like a hunter-and-gatherer-type situation?" asks Alan.

"No, like—I just want a job I don't hate, and family and friends to love. Be less concerned with what I do, more concerned with who I am."

Alan nods. "Sometimes I worry those are the same things."

"Yeah."

"Noah?"

"Yeah."

"What's going on with you?"

I take a breath. "UCLA."

"Yes."

"You're both going?"

Alan hesitates, then: "We've talked about this, like, a thousand times, No. You don't remember?"

"When was this decided?"

"I mean, Val's wanted to go for forever. UCLA has one of the top photography departments. She read some thing about how they value the narrative of photography over technical aspects, and she was sold. Plus, LA's live music scene is second to none, which sort of combines Val's biggest interests."

"And you?"

"You really don't remember?"

When you've known someone as long as I've known Alan, you can spot a lot of punch in few words.

"I'm sorry, Alan. I don't."

He nods, but I know disappointment when I see it. "Marvel has offices in LA," he says. "There's an internship I want, but I have to be eighteen and a student at an accredited university. Figured UCLA was the perfect scenario. It puts me out there, plus Val is going. Just made sense."

I climb out of his bed, sit on the floor in front of the TV; Alan follows suit.

"Noah."

"I'm going to say some things now. And they're going to sound weird, but I really need you to listen," and Alan says, "Okay," and I dive in. I start with the Longmire party, my conversation with Circuit, and the ensuing trek to his house where he may or may not have hypnotized me, and how everything went to shit from there: his neighbor's bizarre story about finding God in a cave, the shape-shifting dog, the recurring dream, Mom's scar, the *Friends*-to-*Seinfeld* thing, Val's social-media switchover, and eventually I get to Alan's own shift in allegiance from DC to Marvel.

He doesn't say anything at first, which I appreciate. No platitudes, no false comforts, just the two of us sitting on the floor of his bedroom surrounded by Marvel, listening to Agent Smith explain the history of the Matrix to a bound-up Morpheus.

"Too bad they butchered two and three," says Alan.

"What?"

He points to the TV. "*Reloaded* and *Revolutions*. Talk about anticlimactic."

"Yeah."

"Trinity's fucking badass, though."

"Yeah."

"Have you told Val?"

"No."

Alan runs both hands across his face, sort of gives his whole head a shake. I've seen this move before, usually when we're doing homework together and he's trying to figure out how an airplane traveling from point A to point B in eight hours can travel from B to A in seven.

"Okay," he says. "My thirteenth birthday."

"What about it?"

"Let's figure this shit out. Where were we on my thirteenth birthday?"

Every year since I moved to Iverton, Alan and I have spent our birthdays together. I go through a revolving door of themed parties and trips to the zoo and trips to . . . "The Discount."

"And what movie did we see?" asks Alan.

That night was etched in my brain because Alan literally walked into the theater in a Batman costume. He'd wanted me to go as Robin, but I didn't because I was worried we'd see someone we knew. I remember getting there and regretting how much I cared what other people thought.

"*Dark Knight Rises*."

Alan's eyes change, but I can't tell if he's surprised or what. "Okay, follow-up. After the movie, we walked outside and you said . . . what?"

That day was the beginning of our Joker Debate Camp, and who we believed was the better Joker. "I said I liked the movie, but it wasn't my favorite, because I liked the Joker. You said something about Heath Ledger's performance, I said, *Yeah, but I meant Jack Nicholson*, at which point we started, you know . . . *that* argument."

"Noah."

"What."

"The only Batman I've seen is the one with George Clooney. Put me off all the others, actually."

In the silence between us, Neo and Trinity are in the middle of rescuing Morpheus from the clutches of Agent Smith.

I look right at Alan, and I'm almost afraid to ask. "Your thirteenth birthday. Where were we?"

"We went to the theater, but . . ."

"What?"

"It was for *The Amazing Spider-Man*. My second time seeing it, your first."

"And after we walked out of the theater, what did I say?"

"Some bullshit about Garfield's Spidey being superior to Tobey Maguire's."

"Alan."

"What."

"The only Spider-Man I've seen was animated."

It's quiet for a second, and then a thought occurs to me. "The scar on my mom's face. Do you know where it came from? Or how she got it?"

"No," says Alan. "She's had it for years. I just figured . . . I don't know, like an accident in her youth or something."

Neo and Agent Smith and Trinity and tons of topflight sequences I normally love but currently don't give two shits about.

"This is weird," says Alan.

"*Weird* is a word, I guess."

"Look. Okay. Okay, look. Everything's going to be okay."

"Yeah? Do you possess magical powers of which I'm unaware, something to rearrange the order of the universe so everything makes sense?"

"Let's try looking at this a different way."

"Which way is that?"

"Instead of focusing on what's changed," says Alan, "let's look at what *hasn't*, and figure out why."

"Okay."

"So what's the same?"

"Nothing."

"Noah."

"Actually—okay, yeah. My sister." And so far, it's true. Since the party, she's literally the only person in my life who is exactly the same.

"Okay, good."

"Steady as ever," I say. "Obsessed with Audrey Hepburn, talks like a middle-aged socialite, dresses like a cracked-out American Girl doll."

"Okay, what else?"

I try to think, but all I can see is the room in my dreams: the person in the corner, the colors, the letters coming out of the walls . . .

"My Strange Fascinations," I say.

"Your what?"

"You mentioned that video where the lady ages in slow motion."

"What about it?" asks Alan.

"So I have these . . . mild . . . obsessions, I guess. Like, a list of things I can't explain but can't stop thinking about. There are four of them, and that video is one."

"What are the other three?"

"There's this photograph of a guy. I found it on the floor at school."

"Oh, cool, you have one of those too?"

"But for real. Remember last year when Pontius Pilot performed after our magazine fundraiser?"

"The Magazine Mega Gala."

"Right. And then after, Parish came and spoke to our—"

"Who?"

"Philip Parish. Pontius Pilot's real name."

Alan chuckles. "I forgot that was his name."

"Right, but you remember him speaking to our class?"

"Yeah," says Alan, but he can't stop giggling. "I don't know why it's so funny. I just don't see him as a Philip."

"What can I do to help get you past this?"

He shakes his head, takes a breath. "Continue."

"So anyway, he's in our classroom, talking about his writing process, when he kind of freaks out a little."

"I remember this. He walked out of class right in the middle of his thing."

"Right. But not before dropping a photo out of his notebook, which I picked up on my way out."

"What's the photo?"

"It's just this guy—sort of smiling, maybe? But on the back there's this inscription that says, *The sun is too bright. Love, A.*"

"Who's A?"

"No idea. But that's my second Strange Fascination. Then there's Old Man Goiter, this old man with—"

"Let me guess."

"Right. But he walks the same stretch of road every day, and there's just something about him, like in a previous life we were friends or something. Or no, you know what it's like? It's like a time-travel movie, where you see a person who feels familiar, and then at the end of the movie you find out you *are* that person."

"You do like to walk."

"That's what I'm saying."

"So what's the fourth one?" asks Alan.

"Okay, so you've read Mila Henry—"

"I mean, not like you, but like a normal person."

"But you know her trademark sketches, right? At the top of each chapter?"

"I love those."

I nod. "So this one sketch in *Year of Me*, Chapter Seventeen, is different from the others."

"In what way?"

"I don't know, it's, like, a different style or something. But *how* it differs really isn't the point. The point is, *why?* Just that one out of all those sketches? Seems like it must mean something. Anyway, that's it. Those are my Strange Fascinations."

"That phrase sounds familiar."

"It's Bowie," I say. "A lyric in 'Changes.' Also the name of his biography."

"Well, if I'm in your shoes, I go that way."

"What do you mean?"

Alan watches *The Matrix* while he talks. "It's like variables and constants, right? You've got a million things changing, and you can't chase them all. But you just listed five things that haven't changed."

"Four."

"Plus your sister. If I'm you, I investigate that shit if for no other reason than because it's *doable*."

Every once in a while Alan offers these little nuggets of wisdom, which inevitably leads me to think: Perhaps I don't give him enough credit. Perhaps Alan is more of a subtle sage, a man whose acumen only *masquerades* as nonsense and is not itself nonsensical.

"You think Neo and Agent Smith ever get it on?" he asks.

Then again, perhaps not.

I say, "I don't see Agent Smith having much of a sexual appetite. Not sure how he'd have time, what with practicing his enunciation."

"Bet he gets plenty of action as Elrond, Lord of Rivendell."

"Your brain is literally in your balls, isn't it?"

"I guess some of us can't acknowledge something as being hot without wanting to have sex with it," says Alan.

"Elrond is an elf, you know."

"Correction. He's a *lord* elf. Plus, the ears."

We watch the movie in silence for a second; Trinity kisses Neo, which, naturally, brings him back to life. Been a while since I've seen the movie. Sort of forgot he died.

Alan reaches over to his nightstand, opens the drawer, and pulls out a sketch pad and pencil.

"What are you drawing?"

"You'll see," he says.

Alan's sketches put mine to shame, but then I'm not really an artist so much as a diagram enthusiast. He works fast, and a couple of minutes later, he hands over the sketch pad. At first glance I think it must be some superhero from a comic I haven't heard of—the character is muscly in that prototypical caped-crusader way—but he's dressed like me, full-on Navy Bowie, and he has my hair and eyes. In big block letters across the top of the page, it reads HYPNOTIK.

"All these characters have kick-ass names," says Alan, pointing to the TV. "Neo, Trinity, Morpheus, Tank. They're not superheroes, exactly, but they have heightened awareness, special abilities, and whatnot."

I stare at his sketch and try to think of something to say, but all I can come up with is, "It's good. You misspelled *hypnotic*."

Alan smiles. "Like Philip said, purposeful misspellings help your brand."

I hand the sketch pad back, all, "It's really good," while avoiding eye contact by pretending to watch the movie.

"Noah."

"What do you want me to say, Alan. I appreciate your trying to help." I leave it at that, and because I do appreciate him, I don't say the rest of what I'm thinking: *I don't need a*

*brand. I don't have heightened awareness, and I don't have spe-
cial abilities.*

"Hey," he says, and as so often happens, I could swear he's reading my mind. "Most people feel stuck in the world, Noah. You're the only one I know who came unstuck."

In *On the Road*, near the end of the chapter where Dean and Carlo sit on a bed and talk through the night, the narrator, a guy named Sal, tells them to "stop the machine." I can't be sure what Kerouac meant by that, if maybe Sal just wanted his friends to shut up already and go to sleep. But it sure reminded me of exiting the robot. Either way, I couldn't help thinking Dean and Carlo were lucky to have a friend like that.

35 ➜ *that sadness feels heavier suspended in midair*

All the mighty colors of creation now, my dream: the luminous prism. It's like the room is a petri dish, and the colors are bacteria, and I hang there helplessly watching them join and multiply, join and multiply, breeding as greedily as their colors are bright. And then come the letters, and Abraham with his silent barking by the bed, and the person in the corner who is soaked to the bone, whose face I will never know, and the letters take shape, the unconscious and conscious in harmony, a total cluster of oblivion.

Come into the light, She said.

And for a fraction of a second I do. I open my eyes, see a room, a blurry figure—and it's over.

I wake up in a cold sweat, the first inkling of a morning sun through my window.

Every night for over two weeks, the same dream, the same sweat. You'd think I'd be used to it by now, but each time feels newer than the one before, as if the dream is rendered in reverse, its resolution sharper and more radiant with each passing night.

A list. That's what I need.

Something about making lists, ranking things from start to finish in alphabetical order, chronological order, auto-biographical, topical, logical order is, for me, as endorphin-producing as a good run for most people, borderline orgasmic, which I know how that sounds, but look: I like lists, and I don't care what anyone thinks about it.

I roll out of bed, sit at my desk in boxer briefs only, open my computer, and go.

WTF HAPPENED.

An Elegant List of Theories, by Noah Oakman

1. My brain is broken. (Simultaneously explains everything and nothing at all.)

2. My life is reality TV, and I am its unsuspecting star.

3. I've never existed as anything other than a character in a novel. (See #1.)

4. Without knowing it, I have stumbled into a black hole and am living in a parallel universe.

Thing is, I can juggle a thousand theories as to how I got here, but figuring that out won't keep Val and Alan from LA. Alan was right: there are too many variables to go chasing every possibility. I need to focus on the constants right now: my Strange Fascinations, and Penny.

So, a new list:

WTF DO I DO NOW.

An Elegant List of Action Items, by Noah Oakman

1. Make contact with the Fading Girl.

2. Make contact with OMG.

3. Confront Philip Parish about the photograph.

4. Google the shit out of Mila Henry's sketches.

5. Consider spending time with Penny.

Investigate that shit, Alan said yesterday.
Okay, then.
Start from the top.

There are over eight thousand comments under the Fading Girl video. Mostly, it's mild stuff like, lady has a lot of time on her hands, ha. Or this one from a user named SquareRootOfBro_6 (because apparently five other bros had already square-rooted themselves): WTF LMFAO SMH.

SquareRootOfBro_6 is capable of feeling many abbreviated sentiments at once.

And, of course, scatterings of bitterness pepper the comments section with that special brand of enthusiastic vitriol only the anonymity of the Internet provides. For example: Someone tell this ugly bitch no one cares about her fucking life.

I once heard someone compare the Internet to a playground, which seems pretty accurate. Go there in the light of day. Hang with your friends for a while, learn some shit, and go home. Much as you might want to, you can't cook or work or go to the bathroom on the playground. Inevitably, someone else is going to do some cool trick that you can't, and so now you feel like shit; or worse, they try to do a cool trick, fail, and you feel better about yourself. And really, there are only so many times you can swing a swing or go down the same slide before you start looking for ways to fuck it all up.

I know what Val said about the benefits of the Internet, and she's right. All I'm saying is, I could do with a little less *schaden* and a little more *freude*.

I scroll the cursor over the box that says Add a public comment, and my heart picks up. I've never written in the comments section of anything, so this is a big moment for me. I begin a message, then get scared I might accidentally hit enter before I'm done, at which point I close out the browser altogether, open up a Word document, and draft away.

Think concise, effective, friendly. . . .

> Hi there. I'm Noah. I'm not a stalker or anything, but I've watched your video a few hundred times and was wondering where you live.

Delete. Start over.

> Hi-ya!

Nope.

> Every night before I fall asleep . . .

Delete, start over, delete, until I come up with something I don't hate: Hi! Really enjoyed your video. I have a quick question. If you get a moment, would you mind emailing me at twobytwooak@gmail.com? Thanks!

It's a little more exclamatory than I like, but such is the way of society.

Five minutes later I have a twobytwooak@gmail.com account, and I'm back on YouTube, having copied my draft over from Word. I hold my breath as I post the comment, stare at its place under the Fading Girl video the way I imagine a parent might watch their young kid on the playground: proud, excited, scared shitless.

A quick knock on the door, and Mom is inside, all, "Noah!

You need to get dressed pronto if you expect to be at school on time."

Thing is, I don't expect to be at school on time. Or even close, really.

37 ➜ *action item number two*

From the hood of my Hyundai hatchback, I stare at a dick-and-balls-shaped pool of grease in the gas station parking lot and try not to read too much into things. Alan would certainly have a thing or two to say on the reading of this Rorschach test.

If this works, I'll probably miss first block today, but all in the name of investigation.

And, like clockwork, a few minutes later, there he is. The fedora, the cane, the goiter; the myth, man, and legend: OMG himself. I hop off the hood, cross the parking lot as casually as possible. I've imagined this moment many times, tried to think of the perfect opener, an introduction to charm-and-disarm. I'm about to start in, something like, "Hi, I'm Noah," when out of the blue, and without looking at me, OMG says, "Well, kid, don't just stand there," and walks right by me.

I don't know how much time passes, but walk we do. No talking, just two people basking in the inherent value of one foot in front of the other. A casual stroll.

We take a right on Ashbrook, and it occurs to me I have no idea what I've signed up for here, having never actually seen where OMG begins or ends these walks, and just when I start thinking things like maybe he doesn't actually *live* anywhere but just *walks* for days, circling the city like the world's most peculiar guardian angel, he turns onto a quaint little stone pathway, which leads to a quaint little stone house with a quaint little stone sign that reads AMBROSIA'S BED & BREAKFAST. Ever so slowly, OMG climbs these quaint little stone steps to the front door, where he keys a code into a lock above the knob, opens the door, and disappears inside.

And as mysteriously as it began—it's over.

I try the door. Locked. There's a doorbell, but what in the world would I say? *Uh, hey, I just took a walk with one of your elderly guests. Wondering if I can have a quick peek inside?*

On my way back to the gas station I get a text from Alan: Fool! Got your Sonic bfast goodness. WHERE YO FINE ASS AT?

The whole thing lasted less than fifteen minutes, which means if I hustle, I can make this work on school days without being inordinately tardy.

On the drive to school, I imagine my relationship with OMG in the coming days, weeks, months, the two of us owning the streets of Iverton.

Well, kid, don't just stand there.

Something tells me those six words are just the beginning.

Chiropractor visits, physical fitness drills with Coach Kel, homework, school, recurring dream, scour the Internet for information on Mila Henry sketches, *Well, kid, don't just stand there*, says OMG, and I walk with him from the gas station to the bed-and-breakfast where, every day, he shuts the door in my face.

No leads on Philip Parish. I've googled "the sun is too bright," until I can google no more, memorized his Wikipedia page, and studied every Pontius Pilot image I can find to see if the guy from the photo shows up, but nothing.

No response from the Fading Girl. Twice more, I posted on her YouTube page in the hopes a nudge might do some good, but the only emails sitting in my new Gmail inbox are Google welcomes and ALL-CAPS advertisements for risk-free ways to lengthen my penis.

At some point Mom and Dad decided family dinners were their opportunity to corner me about the offer from UM. Once I detected this strategy, however, I countered it with a pretty brilliant strategy of my own: every afternoon, after studying Pontius Pilot's Wikipedia page, I would hop over to Audrey Hepburn's page and memorize a minor piece of trivia; then, like tossing a slab of meat to a starving dog, I would casually mention this trivia at the dinner table and watch Penny go to town.

This worked until it didn't.

One day in mid-October, right when the leaves started turning colors, Mom knocked on my bedroom door. "Your father and I would like to speak to you in the kitchen."

This didn't bode well. "Okay," I said. "Well, I'm sort of swamped with—"

"Nope. You'll be downstairs in five minutes." Mom gently closed the door behind her, and I knew—the time had come.

Downstairs, Mom and Dad sat at the kitchen table over coffee. Mom pushed out a chair with her foot, while Dad poured me a mug. "Have a seat."

I sat, watched Mom sip her coffee. It was sad, but her scar had become a physical representation of our relationship these past couple months. Secretive, cagey, drawn across her skin like a line in the sand: Mom on one side, me on the other.

"Noah, would you agree that your father and I have been exceedingly patient about the UM offer?"

Mom with the classic lawyer move. She was good, I had to give it to her. If I agreed—*yes, you guys have been patient*—it presupposed an end to that patience. If I disagreed, she'd ask for a specific example, of which I had none. Because the truth was . . .

"Yes," I said. "I agree."

She nodded. "We felt it was important that you have space to make a decision. And maybe you're still considering options, and that's fine. But it's time to talk solid timelines."

"Timelines," I said.

She looked to Dad for help. He cleared his throat, nodded. "That's right. Timelines," he said, sipping his coffee.

Attaboy, Dad. Get in, get out.

Mom glared at him, looked back at me. "I spoke with both coaches yesterday. Your drills with Coach Kel have helped. The UM offer stands, but I'm not sure how long we can assume that will be true. Coach Tao, as you know, has made no offer at all, but she's still interested. Obviously, we'd love Milwaukee because we want you close, and because an offer is on the table. But if Manhattan State is something you'd like to consider, I think that's still a possibility."

"You do remember we're not behind schedule with this," I said; part of this was my fault, but nothing was more exhausting than having the same conversation over and over again.

"Noah—"

"I just don't understand the rush."

"We're not rushing. We're trying to be smart here."

"You've missed months," Dad said. "Coach Kel says your junior year was strong, and your workouts have improved, but at this point you're running on fumes, bud."

"You have to see how lucky we are to even have interest from colleges at this point," said Mom. "Maybe most swimmers wait, but you don't have that luxury. There's a moment here, and we think it's best to jump on it."

"What about my back?" I asked, barely able to get the words out.

I could almost feel the weight of prior conversations in the room. Dad said, "Dr. Kirby doesn't anticipate this being a permanent injury. So I have to ask, Noah. Do you?"

I searched their eyes, tried to pick up on any clues that might suggest they knew, but nothing. "No, I don't."

Mom said, "Okay. So. Forward motion, right?"

Dad nodded. "Right."

I got out a weak, "Right," and thought about number four on my WTF HAPPENED list. Honestly, if this wasn't a parallel universe, I wouldn't mind finding one about now.

"So, a timeline," said Mom. "What do we think is reasonable?"

"December twenty-first," I said.

The look on Mom's face was comical.

"Noah," said Dad. "Come on."

"You guys have always said 'a fall decision.' December twenty-first is the last day of fall."

"Actually, I think it's the first day of winter," said Dad.

"Guys? Doesn't really matter," said Mom. "Because we're not waiting that long."

"So what'd you have in mind?" I asked.

"I was thinking two weeks."

Growing up, I got pretty good at knowing when the time had come to shift the conversation from Mom the Mother to Mom the Attorney. I also got pretty good at playing my parents off each other.

"Okay," I said, really counting on Dad to come through here. "I said two months, you said two weeks. . . . I don't know, is there like a benchmark date we could use somewhere in the middle?"

I could see Mom trying to follow my thread. "A benchmark date?" she said. "I mean—we'll just pick a day and that—"

"Ooh," said Dad, and like that, I knew I had him. "Thanksgiving. Perfect."

Dad *loved* Thanksgiving.

"Oh," I said, a slight smile at Mom. "Good idea, Dad."

He rubbed his hands together—like he'd just mediated the entire agreement—and then set to work cooking dinner for the night.

Mom sipped her coffee, smiled at me over the rim. "Well played, counselor."

39 ➡ *a concise history of me, part twenty-nine*

August 1949. Mila Henry publishes her first novel, *Babies on Bombs*. In it an aspiring poet named William von Rudolf uses the word *absquatulate*, only to discover the word is all but dead. He then ponders the life of a word, its birth and death, and eventually arrives at the conclusion that words are simply people in hiding.

William von Rudolf writes the following rhyme:

> *People on a page, people on a page*
> *Words are people on a page, it seems*
> *Hiding in mouths and lurking in scenes*
> *Muddied on signs, waiting in the wings*
> *Some wear glasses, some a hat*
> *Some are round, some lie flat*
> *Some contort this way and that*
> *Disguise all they want, those slippery fiends*
> *They don't fool me by any means*

William von Rudolf spends the rest of the novel trying to give birth to new words. With the exception of *umyumtopia* (*noun*: a society that subsists entirely on a pancake-and-whiskey diet), his efforts are deemed unsuccessful.

Umyumtopians beg to differ.

October 1895. A different William (William James, who was an actual person and not a character in a book) puts pen to paper and writes the word *multiverse*.

No one had ever done that before.

1935. A different Rudolf—Erwin Rudolf Josef Alexander Schrödinger (whose parents presumably had a difficult time making decisions)—devises a thought experiment, which would come to be known as Schrödinger's cat. *Very* boiled down: a cat is in a box with a radioactive source that may or may not decay and trigger a poisonous gas that will kill the cat. By quantum mechanic principals, until one opens the box and observes the radioactive substance, it exists in a superposition. It both has decayed and has not decayed—or, more simply, the cat is both alive *and* dead.

On the one hand, this seems utterly senseless. Impossible, even.

On the other:

Yesterday I got online and looked at pictures of New Zealand, imagined myself among the mountains, and it was easy to do so—they were right there on the screen. I thought, *Maybe I'll go there someday.*

Not long ago, someone somewhere wanted to look at pictures of New Zealand, so they went to the library and pulled a book off a shelf. This person imagined themselves among the mountains, and it was easy to do so—the mountains were right there on the page. This person thought, *Maybe I'll go there someday.*

Some time before that, someone somewhere had heard of New Zealand, in school maybe, or from a family friend. *Sounds exotic,* they thought, and then moved on about their day.

Not too long before that, someone somewhere barely thought of the world at all. It was simply too big a place.

I often consider the timeline of the world, and my place on it. And when I look into the past and see all the things humanity so drastically misunderstood, assumed impossible—

ideas once shelved under science fiction now housed in science—how ignorant would it be for me to turn around and, facing the future, say, "Impossible."

More and more experiments seem to verify the possibility of a single particle existing in multiple spaces simultaneously until observation causes them to collapse into one. And because all matter is made of particles, theoretically, why couldn't this apply to a cat? Or a person? Or a universe? And if the cat's fate is not determined until observed, when we consider the outcomes of our own fates, it does raise the question: Who is observing us?

I do not understand these things. But that's okay. Not understanding isn't the same as misunderstanding. And maybe one day, not long from now, a new word will be born, and a book will be moved from science fiction to science, and we can turn to face the future—perhaps even the multiverse— and say, "Maybe I'll go there someday."

40 → senioritis

Halloween approached as it did every year, with the same forewarnings. Penny cleaned out the top drawer of her dresser for the bountiful quantity of Snickers and Milky Ways to come. (Full-sized of course, because nothing is more déclassé to the true Ivertonian than to seem apologetically small; and let's face it: nothing says *I'm sorry* like a "fun-sized" candy bar.) Mom and Dad watched *The Nightmare Before Christmas* no fewer than a half dozen times. And Val was devising her yearly scheme to suck as much candy as possible from the neighborhood.

"The way I figure," she says, "if we really hustle, we *might* be able to fit in three rounds this year. First round with *Scream* masks, second round as Bears players—the helmets should effectively disguise our faces—and third round as hobos, by far the quickest change."

A few years ago, Val worked out a foolproof trick-or-treat system: we'd get dressed up in Costume A, which required a mask or head covering of some kind, hit the streets for round one, then reconvene at the Rosa-Haas house to change into Costume B (no masks this time) and hit up the same houses again. Apparently this year, she's going for the trifecta.

Alan is all, "Very ambitious. I like it."

The entire senior class is in the school theater, a giant screen onstage; behind us a projector flips from an image of class rings to a pair of graduating class sweatpants.

Val pulls out her phone, snaps a photo of the screen. "Nothing immortalizes like a quality pair of sweatpants," she says under her breath while typing up a post.

"I'm holding out for the fanny pack," says Alan.

Some guy from a company called Zalsten's is giving his sales pitch, trying to squeeze every last drop from the Iverton High trust-fund crowd. He passes around yet another form, this one for something called the Mascot Package, which is basically a bundle offer including cap, gown, tassel, announcement cards, thank-you notes, a T-shirt, and, yes, sweatpants, all for the low, low price of $296.90.

"That's a pretty huge package," says Alan, far louder than necessary, to which Val elbows him. "What?" he says. "I'm just saying the Mascot Package is a great deal. Way more bang for your buck than some smaller packages."

"Such a child," says Val, putting her phone away.

Principal Neusome takes the microphone from the Zalsten's guy, puts on that stern voice of his, and threatens to take away our senior trip if we don't quiet down.

No one is listening.

Some teachers pass out stacks of FAFSA forms for loans and grants, and someone from some agency is talking about how if we don't fill out these forms properly, we won't be eligible for "any monies for any colleges, at all, period," to which Alan whispers, "What do you think she *really* means, though?"

"This part is of actual importance," says Val, leaning over one of the forms with a pen. "As opposed to sweatpants."

All these color-coded forms are giving me a familiar sense of dread. Mom helps out with the senior advisory board, so I knew most of this stuff was coming, but seeing the actual words on the actual pages in my actual hands—

"Speaking of college," says Val, "you talk to Coach Stevens lately? Or who was the other one? At Manhattan State?"

All air in my body rushes for the exit.

"Coach Tao," I say.

Ever since the incident in the cafeteria when I first learned of Val and Alan's plans to attend UCLA, they've altogether avoided the topic of college—until now.

"Right, Coach Tao. You talk to either of them recently?"

Principal Neusome has the mic again; he's going through

a list of certain dooms for those who haven't properly filled out their FAFSA, and I just let loose: "Why is college a given? I mean, I'm not saying I don't want to go, like, *ever*, just that I'd like a choice in the matter. Like, let's all calm down and realize a person's life doesn't expire the day they decide maybe they won't go to college."

"Can't blame people for looking out for your future," says Val.

"Yeah, but it's like everyone in my life thinks they know what's best for me, but how can they when they're *not* me? Like, if only we knew someone who *was* me, maybe that person could tell us what *I* think. Oh, wait."

"Okay, Noah."

"I'm just saying."

"And I'm just saying college is a huge privilege, and maybe it's not for everyone, maybe it's not for you, but also maybe keep the whining to a minimum. You don't know everyone's situation."

Alan says, "Titi Rosie would murder us if we talked like Noah."

"Murder us good and dead," says Val.

Every couple summers, the Rosa-Haas family visits Mrs. Rosa-Haas's mother and sisters in San Juan. During their last trip, Alan took the opportunity to come out to everyone, including his beloved Lita, who was bordering on a hundred. Before they left, Alan told me he was afraid his announcement might do her in, but as it turned out Lita's only concern was that Alan do his part in carrying on the Rosa name. This apparently led to quite the conversation about surrogacy and adoption, which led Alan to confess his reluctance to ever have kids in the first place, which produced the wailing and gnashing of teeth he'd assumed would accompany his initial announcement.

It was quite the trip, from what I understand.

"After I came out," says Alan, "Titi Rosie said it was none of her business who I dated, so long as I finished college. Said she'd move out here and walk my ass to class."

I've met their aunt a few times when she's come to visit, and it's not hard for me to hear this going down. "I still love that her name is Rosie Rosa."

"We have a cousin named Rosemarie Rosa."

"That's amazing," I say.

"Oh, Puerto Ricans know what's up."

Val is all, "You do get our point, though, yes? College, no college, different strokes, et cetera, fine. Just—"

"Keep the whining to a minimum," I say.

"Well, yeah, but also remember that where you come from, figuratively and literally, isn't the same as everyone around you. And then speak accordingly. Cool?"

"Cool."

"So have you talked to them? The coaches?"

I tell them about my parents' Thanksgiving timeline for a decision, to which they both yell at me for not having told them about the Milwaukee offer in the first place.

"I don't really want to talk about it," I say. "You guys are supposed to be my safe place."

"I never agreed to that," says Val.

"Me either, yo." Alan punches his fists into the air like a boxer getting geared up for the big fight. "Ain't nothin' safe about *deez nuts*!"

Val sighs. "Just once I'd like to not feel like the babysitter."

"Yeah, you're right," says Alan, suddenly serious. "And I'm

sure responsible babysitters everywhere are currently plotting ways to con people out of twice the usual Halloween candy."

"Three times, actually. Speaking of which"—Val throws her legs up on the chair in front of her, flips over the FAFSA form, and diagrams our neighborhood—"I figure we'll start here tonight." She points to their next-door neighbor's house.

"Don't you guys think we might be a little—"

Alan throws a hand over my mouth. "Don't say it."

I pull my head away. "Too old for trick-or-treating?"

Alan pretends to faint into Val's lap.

"We've been over this," says Val. "Sixth through ninth grade, it's awkward and weird for everyone. But tenth through twelfth? That's the trick-or-treating sweet spot."

"Okay, well. I can't go."

Val and Alan give me the exact same look, and okay: I've known them so well for so long, at some point I stopped thinking they looked alike, but in this moment, with this look on their faces . . .

"You guys are freaking me out a little."

"Why?" says Val.

"The way you're looking at me. Since you're twins, it sort of—"

"Not that. Why aren't you coming with?"

A beat, then: "Homework?"

They aren't buying it.

"Look, I have . . . plans. Let's leave it at that."

"Who is she?" asks Val, half smiling.

"It's not a girl."

Val raises her eyebrows, looks at her brother.

"Please," says Alan. "If Noah wasn't tragically straight, he'd be all over me right now."

I kiss a bicep. "You wish."

"Oh my God," says Val. "You guys with that joke. It's like a hundred years old."

Principal Neusome dismisses us, and the entire senior class stumbles to their feet, zombie-eyed from all things FAFSA, and right there in the middle of the commotion, Val says, "Where were you this morning?"

"What do you mean?" I ask.

Alan clears his throat in a not at all subtle way, stares daggers at his sister as we walk out of the auditorium.

Val acts like she doesn't notice. "Every morning since freshman year we sit in the Alcove and shoot the shit before class, but okay, go ahead and pretend like your ongoing absence is totally low-key, Noah." She walks ahead of us, disappears into the flow of staggering seniors.

"What'd you tell her?" I ask.

"Nothing."

"From our Dean and Carlo session? You didn't say anything?"

Alan looks at me, suddenly serious. It's eerie how quickly he can change masks like that. "Noah, who's the smartest person you know?"

All the classroom doors open at once, freshmen through juniors flood the hallway, and Alan gives me a sort of nod before peeling off toward his next block. I follow the current's flow and consider all the things Alan just said without saying much of anything.

Maybe conversations are more about the silence between the words too.

Penny and I sit in the backward-facing trunk seat of Dad's Pontiac, sunglasses on, stone-faced staring down this couple in the car behind us.

When they first pulled up they were jamming to some song, but it's a pretty long stoplight, so that's all over now.

"So," says Penny.

"Yes?"

"I assume you're still considering."

"Considering?"

Penny pushes her sunglasses up her forehead, turns to me. "The pros and cons list, darling. *Breakfast at Tiffany's?*"

"Oh. Um."

She lets her sunglasses fall back into place. "You know, I think Mark Wahlberg was right about you."

It takes me a solid five seconds to realize she's referring to our dog and not the actor. "Really committed to that name change, huh?"

"When I asked him if he thought you would ever watch *Breakfast at Tiffany's* with me, he said I shouldn't count on it, because I can't count on you."

"Is that so?"

"Mmhmm. And then, when I asked Mark Wahlberg if he had any insight as to why you refused, he said it's because you're a perpetual child."

I couldn't help laughing at Penny's portrayal of our dog as something between a Magic 8-Ball and a therapist.

"You guys excited for tonight?" asks Mom from the front seat, which from here may as well be Detroit.

Penny sighs, all, "Can't wait!" in an overtly bogus voice, and it occurs to me: not only is our dog *not* a therapist or a Magic 8-Ball, he is also incapable of speech. *I can't count on you. You're a perpetual child.* Someone thinks these things, and that someone is not Mark Wahlberg.

You have to respect the level of commitment it takes to combine five words—*that's, book, boo, spook, fantastic!*—into one. A portmanteau for the ages, *s'BOOk-tastic!* is billed by the Iverton Public Library as a "trick-or-treating alternative" for those parents who question the long-established system of strangers handing candy to small children in costumes. (There was a time when my parents made fun of *s'BOOk-*

tastic!, but then last year a bunch of teenagers in hockey masks stole Penny's candy, so yeah—that time had passed.)

"Thanks for being here," says Dad, putting an arm around me. We watch Penny accept candy from a librarian dressed as a clown. So far every librarian has complimented Penny on her "costume," not knowing they've been duped: she literally walked out of the house in the same thing she'd been wearing to school today.

"Wouldn't miss it," I say.

Truth is, I didn't feel like trick-or-treating with Val and Alan.

Also, I just really like being inside libraries.

Most of the *s'BOOk-tastic!* participants are between the ages of zero and seven, though a few stragglers attend, older kids whose parents can't cope with the fact that their little tike's all grown up. When we first walked in, I overheard a dad say, "Man, I wish I had *s'BOOk-tastic!* when I was a kid. *This* is totally *awesome!*"

So like—when you become a parent, evidently you forget the pungency of bullshit? Apparently this is like a prerequisite for raising a kid? The stork drops it off on your porch, all, *Here you go, one fresh . . . little . . . sort of human thing. Cool, now I'm going to need your ability to smell bullshit. Thanks. What? Oh, no, you can keep the ability to* produce *bullshit, you just won't smell it anymore. Hey, check it out, I can fly.*

"Who are you?" asks a librarian.

"What?"

She motions to my outfit. "What are you supposed to be?"

"Bowie fan," I say.

Her eyes well up, she slow claps, and then hands me a shit-ton of candy.

I do wonder how my parents feel knowing they can take their kids trick-or-treating at the drop of a hat, no costume changes required.

"Hey, Mom." I unwrap a Bit-O-Honey, pop it into my mouth. "I'm gonna wander for a bit."

"Okay." Mom looks at her watch, hair falling across her face in a way that somehow highlights her scar. "Leaving in twenty."

42 ➜ *the tender arms of madness*

I love the intentional, aimless wander that comes from years of experience roaming the aisles of libraries, imagining all those who have tread before—some at a casual saunter, hands in pockets maybe, taking it all in; some frantically scanning the spines for that *one* book that might save their lives—and letting the mind delve the depths of a proper vanishing among books, just really good and fucking turned around.

There is no kind of lost like library lost.

Fiction, aisle G–I—scanning, scanning, there: *Henry, Mila*. She only published four novels (all of which, I own) before retreating to the wilds of Montana. Still, I have this compulsion. Every time I'm in a library I look for her. It's like if you're in an airport, and you find out your friend is in the same airport. You already know all about them, see them regularly, but you still sprint to their gate before their flight leaves.

I stare at her shelf—with its multiple copies of all four novels—and feel comfort in the presence of a friend.

"Rank them."

Turn around, and there's Sara Lovelock, just standing there looking up at the Henry shelf.

"Oh hey," I say, and, in the most classic move ever, choke on the Bit-O-Honey.

"You okay?"

I nod, pull myself together, and can almost hear Alan's voice in my head. *Play it cool, yo. Don't be a chump.* "Yes," I say. "Yes, I'm okay. Hi."

"Hey." She nods in a super-chill way, but not *overly* chill like her brother. She's wearing the hell out of this red-and-navy-checkered flannel shirt, oversized like a tunic.

"Hello," I say for like the fourth time, all kinds of mad fucking chill up in here, just layer upon layer of the stuff. Sara purses her lips, says, "Hi," in a smile, and if I had to guess, I'd say she was thinking something along the lines of, *This guy struggles with where to go after the initial greeting.*

"Well, now we've got salutations out of the way"—she points at the shelf of books behind me—"you can tell a lot about a person from their favorite Henry books. So let's hear yours, Noah-with-an-*H*. Rank them."

Good thing about crashing and burning right up front, there's nowhere to go but up. I hold up four fingers, tick them off as I go. "Number four, *This Is Not a Memoir*. Three, *Babies on Bombs*. Two is *Augustus Third*, and my favorite is *Year of Me*."

"You don't like *This Is Not a Memoir*?"

"It's my least favorite book from my most favorite author. I adore *This Is Not a Memoir*."

"So who else do you like?"

"Hmm?"

"What other authors?"

"Um, okay, after Henry—Vonnegut, obviously. Thoreau and Salinger, unapologetically. David James Duncan, Munro Leaf—"

"I haven't heard of him."

"He wrote that kids' book, *The Story of Ferdinand*?"

"Oh yeah, the bull who won't fight. Sits just quietly—"

"And smells the flowers," I say.

"Nice. Shitty movie, if I remember."

"Isn't it always?"

"True."

"Also, Murakami," I say. "You read *1Q84*?"

"Meh. It was okay. But I adore *Tsukuru Tazaki*."

"That's on my list."

"Well bump it up, dude."

"Done. What about you?" I ask.

"What about me?"

"Favorite authors?"

"Okay, well, other than Henry," Sara says. "Virginia Woolf, for sure. I love Jesmyn Ward, Meg Wolitzer, David Mitchell, Zadie Smith, and recently I've gotten into Donna Tartt. *The Secret History* sheds a whole new light on Henry's idea of exiting the robot."

"I'll put it on the list," I say. "Surprised you didn't mention Vonnegut. I mean, considering how much you like Mila Henry."

Sara slaps a palm against her forehead. "Oh right, I forgot, because we need a dude to put her work into context."

"Wait, what? No, that's not . . . what I—"

"You know what I don't understand?" asks Sara; she digs through a messenger bag with a patch on the side that reads MELVILLE ROCKS, MOBY DICK SUCKS. "Why anyone is put off by feminism. I'm sorry, but if you can't get your mind around equal rights for women, I have to assume you've lost it."

Pretty sure the entire library just felt the rumbling bob of my Adam's apple. Like, it definitely registered on the Richter scale.

"*I'm* a feminist," I say, a rather feeble attempt even to my own ears.

"I'm sure you are, Noah-with-an-*H*. Given the many women on your list of favorite authors."

There's this feeling—when you've been owned—which I've recently become acquainted with. I swallow hard again, watch Sara as she texts.

"You here for the kiddie trick-or-treat thing?" I ask, regretting the words even as I speak them.

"No, I had a book on hold. But I'm guessing you are?"

"What? No. Ha. Of course not."

Mom pokes her head around the corner. "Here you are. Trick-or-treating's over, sweetie. Time to go, okay?" She shoots a quick smile at Sara—who is clearly trying not to laugh—and Mom's gone.

"Well," says Sara.

"We're here for my little sister."

Sara nods, all, "Sure thing," and then points to my mouth. "What you got there, Bit-O-Honey?"

I am thoroughly defeated. "I gotta go. It was nice seeing you again, Sara."

She drops her phone into her bag, and I catch a glimpse of a book with library binding. "Nice seeing you too, Noah."

Sara turns to leave, and just before disappearing from the aisle, I watch a small slip of paper fall from her purse to the floor. I open my mouth to tell her she dropped something, but instead what comes out is, "What can you tell about me?"

"What?" she asks.

"Before. You said you could tell a lot about a person from their favorite Henry books. What can you tell about me?"

Sara's eyes move from my boots, to my shirt, to my hair. "You're scared of something," she says, and just when I think that's that, she adds, "just like Cletus."

◀▬▬▶

Year of Me is my favorite Henry, and while *June First, July Second, Augustus Third* is widely recognized as her magnum opus, I prefer the borderline fantasy settings and bizarre characterization that *Year of Me* is so well known for.

Cletus Foot is the tragic hero in *Year of Me*, an aspiring writer who, after receiving multiple rejections for publication in a sci-fi magazine, travels around America in a stolen clown car, pilfering people's mail. This goes on for a while until a chapter called "The Light," in which Cletus is driving down the road in his "truncated auto," minding his own business, when the clouds (literally) part and a woman's voice, claiming to be God Herself, speaks to Cletus, urging him to return the clown car, stop stealing people's mail, and, for the love of Herself, do what Cletus was created to do: join the Marines. And so Cletus does. In the end, he survives the war only to be shot and killed by the very clown whose car he'd stolen those many years ago. (He'd forgotten to return the truncated auto, see, which, due to the cutthroat nature of the clownery business, had driven that particular clown right out of the industry and into the "tender arms of madness.")

Chapter 17 is the focus of much speculation. Some critics point to this particular chapter as the perfect example of Henry's stubborn nature when it came to editing her own work, and I get that. The chapter does seem a little *wedged in* or something—it has very little to do with what comes before or after, but I like it.

Mostly conversation, the whole scene takes place in a diner where Cletus discusses the nature of art with a painter named Nathan. It begins with their mutual longing to create for a living and ends with them deciding the world is a "shitball" that wouldn't know what to do with their art anyway.

They leave the diner without paying.

Henry's books are known for their unique sketches at the top of each chapter, original drawings by the author herself. The artwork parallels the content of its respective chapter and is *always* done in the same signature style: a fine-point pen in a cross-hatch pattern.

The single exception to this rule is *Year of Me*, Chapter 17.

The sketch at the top of Chapter 17 is simple: two men, on either side of a booth in a diner. One has pancakes. One has a burger. It looks very similar to Henry's other trademark drawings, identical almost. Except no cross-hatch. I've studied it under a magnifying glass to see if I'm missing something, if maybe the pattern *used* to be there but got changed somehow. I've scoured the Internet, but like the only forgery expert to spot some famous painting as fake, it seems I'm the only person in the wide universe to detect the stylistic departure of the sketch. Which leads me to wonder many things: Did Henry purposefully draw this *one* sketch differently? If so, why? And what, if anything, does it indicate about the chapter? Did Henry even draw it? If not, who did? And why?

I have a lot of questions, but no answers, which I guess is what places it squarely in the camp of strangely fascinating.

I pretend not to see my family waiting for me by the front door of the library.

At the help desk, I nod at a librarian, who is, quite possibly, typing at the actual speed of light.

"May I help you?" he asks.

More out of curiosity than anything, I picked up that slip of paper Sara had dropped. To anyone else, what was scribbled on it—*TINAM, Coll ed.*—might have seemed random and inconsequential. "I'm looking for the collector's edition of *This Is Not a Memoir*, by Mila Henry," I say. "I didn't see it on the shelf."

The librarian gives me a look like I'm trying to pull one over on him. He leans across the counter, whispers, "Is there, like, a Mila Henry scavenger hunt I should know about? Because I want in on that shiznit."

"What?"

"All right then, play it cool. But somebody's one step ahead of you."

"What do you mean?"

"I've worked here four years, kid. Until today, no one has asked *specifically* about the collector's edition of that book.

And now two requests in the span of ten minutes. Anyway. It's gone. She got it."

"Who?"

The librarian's face turns suddenly serious. "I can't tell you that. Breach of policy." He turns back to his computer, types like the wind, points to the screen. "There's one at the Harold Washington Library—it's the central Chicago branch. Want me to put a hold on it?"

I've read *This Is Not a Memoir* a couple times, have a copy of it on my shelf at home. The story recounts, in first-person, Bigfoot's battle with loneliness and depression. Given Henry's subsequent reclusiveness, some speculate it may be more of a memoir than first believed. I remember hearing about a collector's edition once, but it was either super rare or super expensive or both.

So I say yes, and decide I'll drive into the city on Saturday.

On the ride home I opt out of the rear-facing bench seat, choose instead the privacy of the middle row, pull out my phone, and do some research. A couple rabbit holes later, and I find an expired sale on eBay with a slight description at the bottom:

> MILA HENRY'S FINEST—*This Is Not a Memoir: A Memoir*, COLLECTOR'S EDITION. Fringe imprint, only a few thousand published. 40+ page appendix. Never-before-seen pics of Henry and family. Beaucoup BONUS MATERIALS.

Saturday can't come fast enough.

PRESENTING ➛ PART FOUR

Mod: You certainly have a way with words, Ms. Henry, silent or otherwise. In fact, some have called you the "female Kurt Vonnegut." How do you like that title?

Henry: Probably about as much as Kurt would if you called him the "male Mila Henry."

Partial transcript from "A Conversation with Mila Henry"
Harvard, 1969
(Henry's last known public appearance)

"Do you have any idea how ridiculous you sound saying that?"

"It's true, though. Remember, he used to eat anything? Even his own"—Penny scrunches up her nose and mouths, *Poo*. Then she grabs a piece of bacon off her plate. "Mostly fat, see? Here you go, Mark Wahlberg." Penn drops the bacon onto the floor, where our dog sniffs it, tilts his head, and looks back up at Penny, leaving the bacon untouched.

"Okay," I say. "Yeah, that's weird."

"Now watch," says Penny, grabbing another piece of bacon, this time an especially meaty bite. She drops it onto the ground, where Fluff—or Mark freaking Wahlberg (what is my life)—gobbles it up immediately. "Crazy, right?"

Mom joins us in the kitchen, pulls OJ out of the fridge, and pours herself a glass.

"Mom, watch this," says Penny. She does the bacon thing again, and the three of us watch Mark Wahlberg turn his nose up at the fatty piece and then eat the meaty piece. Mom seems more perplexed by Penny than anything, though.

"Why are you calling him Mark Wahlberg?" she asks.

"You know," says Penny. "He just doesn't seem like a 'Fluff' anymore, what with him not limping around and stuff."

"He has a limp?" asks Mom.

"Well, no," I say, eyeing Penny. "Not anymore."

Mom nods, clearly not on the same page. "So what're you guys doing with your Saturday?"

Penny stuffs the rest of the bacon into her mouth, talks through it. "'I'm writing a check. You must have seen me write checks before.'"

Mom looks at me for help; I shrug and shake my head, and she's all, "Okay then. What about you?"

"Driving to the city. I have a book on hold at the main library."

Penny's eyes light up. "Can I come?"

"No," I say.

Mom gives me that classic Mom look, the one that says, *We know how this ends, don't we?* Thing is, I've genuinely been looking forward to the solitude. It would give me anywhere from forty-five minutes to an hour and a half (one way, depending on traffic) of solid think-time. Throw Penny in the mix and that's out the window.

"What about all those checks?" I say. "Those things don't write themselves, you know."

"It's a line from *Breakfast at Tiffany's,* which you wouldn't know anything about."

"Fine," I say. "You can come."

Penny jumps out of her chair, does this series of windmill motions where both arms simultaneously spin in opposite directions, the whole thing wildly out of control, until she brings her fists together by her chin and says, "*Yaaaaasssssssssssssssssssss.*"

I honestly don't know how my sister survives middle school.

⬛️▶️

Penny insists on bringing Mark Wahlberg, and while I feign reluctance, I'm actually fine with it. Even before morphing into Fluff 2.0, he was too senile to really know what was going on when we put him in a car.

"What's that for?" I ask, watching Penny toss a suitcase into the trunk. It's bright pink and has a giant skull on the front.

"Nothing," she says, climbing in the passenger seat. "You'll see."

"Penny."

"What."

"Need I remind you of the last time you attempted a Mrs. Basil E. Frankfurter? When you tried to move into the skating rink?"

"Frank*weiler*, darling. And no, you needn't. That's not what the suitcase is for."

A few minutes into the drive, when Penny mentions how weird it was that Mom didn't remember Mark Wahlberg's limp, it occurs to me that if Penny notices changes in our dog when no one else does, there's a chance she's noticed other stuff too. It would only make sense: if she is a constant, then it stands to reason she might recognize the variables.

"So, Penn. What do you know about the scar on Mom's face?"

Penny calmly turns from the dog to me. "What do you mean?"

"Well, like—has she told you about it?"

"Uh. *Right*."

"What?"

"Like anyone ever tells me anything."

"Okay, well. Do you know how long she's had it?"

"I don't know. Not long, like . . . a month? Two, maybe?"

Even though Penny can't say how the scar came to be, the fact that it's a new development to her is huge. That, plus her recognition of Mark Wahlberg's miraculous evolution, has to mean something.

"Have you noticed anything different lately, like sudden changes with your friends, or . . . stuff like that?" I ask.

Penny doesn't answer, just shifts in her seat to look out the window. "What's going on with you?"

"What do you mean?"

"I mean you're asking some freaky questions, dude." From the backseat Mark Wahlberg gives a yip, to which Penny nods and says, "Took the words right out of my mouth, Mark Wahlberg."

"You know, we don't always have to use his full name."

"What—we should call him *Mark*?" Penny giggles.

"You're right. I don't know what I was thinking."

Penny rolls down her window, stretches her arm into the rushing air outside, lets the wind push it back and forth, up and down. "Strange weather," she says. "You ever remember a November this warm?"

I say, "I don't, actually," and then roll down my own window, stick my left arm out, and it's like we're little kids again, pretending our arms are wings, propelling our vehicle skyward.

We don't talk the rest of the flight into the city.

44 ➜ *to the Wormhole, through the Wormhole*

The exterior of the Harold Washington Library is the opposite of the Iverton branch in almost every conceivable way.
Namely, it looks less like a library and more like the architectural love child of an old museum and a maximum-security
prison; I could see someone thinking it's ugly, but I love it.
And the inside is even better, with its Thoreau and Eliot
quotes on the wall, its ten stories of bookshelves, nooks, and
offices, and massive windows bathing the floors in natural
light. And the rooftop terrace garden, my God, the rooftop
terrace garden!

Talk about getting library lost.

We park a couple of blocks away and walk the distance in
no time, which is good because it's suddenly freezing outside.
Seriously, like that—one minute we're talking how strangely
warm it is; the next it's balls-to-the-wall cold, as if the weather
gods simply needed a reminder.

Penny waits outside with Mark Wahlberg while I run in to
pick up the collector's edition of *This Is Not a Memoir*. It takes
a little longer than expected, because for some reason I get
turned around. I've been here before, but when I go in what I
thought was the front entrance, I find myself in the back hallway. Through the window I see traffic on State Street, which
I could have sworn the library *faced*, but I must've been mistaken. I get straightened out, and five minutes later I'm back
outside, book in hand.

And now it's snowing. Like, seriously.

We hustle back to the car, where I crank the heat.

"Confession," Penny says, holding her hands up to the vents. "I had ulterior motives for wanting to come today."

"Okay."

"So there's this coffee shop called—"

"Penny."

"It has rave reviews, darling. Check your phone if you don't believe me, and you know you love a good macchiato as much as the next guy."

"I don't know what a macchiato *is*, Penn."

"*Plus*. Are you ready for this?"

"I'm very sure I'm not."

"It has a DeLorean."

The déjà vu hits hard, followed by that flush-faced rush when reminded of something best forgotten.

"It's the car from *Back to the Future*," says Penny, and I tell her I know, and she says something else, but Penny's words swirl into the air, and it's that peculiar sensation that so often accompanies me when I exit the robot, and the thing is: I am *sure* I walked in the front entrance of the Harold Washington Library.

"Noah," says Penny, her voice soft and here again, and now her tiny cold hand is on mine. "You okay?"

I fold myself up like a piece of paper, edges and corners properly aligned, now back inside you go. "The Wormhole, right?"

"Yeah," Penn says. "You've heard of it?"

I pull up the address on my phone, start driving in that direction, and try to block out the voice of an inebriated kid I met, a kid I foolishly followed home, a kid responsible for the ever-widening chasm in my brain. *What I would do*, the voice says, *for immediate transportation to the Wormhole right now.*

So as it turns out, the coffee shop does not allow dogs inside, which of course Penny already knew, because she'd called ahead.

Enter: the pink skull suitcase.

"No way," I say. Penny unzips her suitcase and ushers Mark Wahlberg into it. "Penn, you can't walk around with a dog in your suitcase."

As if to prove me wrong, Mark Wahlberg hops inside. I found street parking; we're currently on the sidewalk a few doors down from the Wormhole.

"Now take a nap, Mark Wahlberg," Penn says. "We won't be long."

He's small, so there's actually plenty of room, but that's not my primary concern. "Can he even breathe in that thing?"

"Don't be dramatic, Noah."

"I doubt Mark Wahlberg would consider it a dramatic question."

She zips up the sides of the suitcase, leaving the top part open. "You good in there?" she asks, peering down inside.

A little yip.

"Okay, let's go."

And so my twelve-year-old sister wheels our dog into a coffee shop where she orders a quad Cuban-shot espresso macchiato like it's nothing, all while wearing a pink Marilyn Monroe tee and mismatched Toms, and I'd say the look on the barista's face sums up my own feelings at the moment: *Where did this girl come from?*

I order a cold brew, and we sit on a green leather couch. The Wormhole is easily the coolest coffee shop I've ever seen, like the eighties exploded and landed in little pieces everywhere: it's all *Ghostbusters* and *Beetlejuice* posters, Millennium Falcons and time-travel paraphernalia, a wood-paneled TV with a Nintendo game menu on the screen, an ancient boxy computer next to the sugar, a catalog of floppy disks next to the half-and-half, and yes—an actual DeLorean. I'd had a hard time envisioning a car—*any* car—inside a coffee shop. But there it is, parked on top of a high platform right next to our couch like it owns the place.

"I was born in the wrong decade," says Penny.

"You may have been born in the wrong dimension, Penn."

"Appropriate you should bring that up here."

"Appropriate how?"

She sips her macchiato from a tiny mug. "We are *in* the Wormhole."

"Of course you know about wormholes."

"Noah. *Darling*. I'm not a complete barbarian. I've read *A Wrinkle in Time*."

"Well, I'm a complete barbarian, then."

"Wait, you mean . . ."

"Never read the book. Never saw the movie."

"You are *shitting* me."

"Don't say *shitting*, Penn."

She sets her mug on the coffee table by our couch. "Okay, so I'll just explain wormholes the way they explain it to Meg in *A Wrinkle in Time*."

You have to love a kid who shrugs off someone's understanding of a concept if that understanding doesn't come from their favorite book.

"In the book they call it a tesseract, but it's really just a wormhole." Penny points to a little square napkin on the table. "If a bug was at one end of the napkin and wanted to get to the other end"—she points to the opposite corner—"in three dimensions, it would have to walk the length of the napkin. But if you do this"—Penn picks up the napkin, folds the two corners together—"suddenly he's there. It's way more complex than all that, though. Einstein and some other guy came up with it. It's just a theory, completely impractical, obviously."

I sip my iced coffee to hide the smile on my face. "Can I ask you a question?"

"Shoot."

"Why do you like Audrey Hepburn so much?"

She thinks on it for a second. "Why do you like David Bowie so much?"

"He was completely fine being himself no matter what." What a rarity that a knee-jerk response would also be the truest. "Musicians evolve, but no one evolved like Bowie. Don't get me wrong—not all his evolutions were for the better. He had some terrible phases, but they're forgivable because *that's* who he was at the time. And I think people are drawn to that. True Bowie fans aren't really fans— they're believers."

"So you're a believer?"

"Yeah, I am. The man was a walking revolution, decades ahead of his time on things like gender identity and sexual identity and just general *identity*, which is probably why that's the first thing I thought when you asked the question."

"He was fine being whoever he was."

"Pathological authenticity. That's the goal. And I mean, the music was just . . . When Bowie was good, he was better than everyone else."

Penny nods, a loose strand of wild hair falling in her face. "Do you think I'm . . . pathologically authentic?"

That smile breaks through, and strangely, I feel the impulsive urge to cry. "Penn, any more authentic and you'd be too real to handle."

And now she can't stop her smile. She polishes off the last of her macchiato and then checks on Mark Wahlberg, who is, apparently, napping happily. "I think I like Audrey Hepburn because of what I said before about being born in the wrong decade. I don't know if life was like that, like in her movies. I don't know if people really talked that way. Or dressed like that. But I like to think so. Because if things *were* like that then, maybe they can be like that again."

Sometimes talking with a sibling is like hiking in a foreign country only to round a corner and find your house. Penny and I are so different in so many ways—and yet, I know this place well.

"How do you do it?" she asks.

"Do what?"

She clears her throat. "Never mind."

"Come on."

"I don't really know what I mean. School, I guess? I don't know. Everything is just so hard."

If Penny really believes I know what I'm doing, I'm every shade a fraud. And just when I'm about to tell her exactly that—that I can't get it together long enough to decide what I want to do, when I want to do it, or who I'd like to do it with—I open my mouth and say, "It's about finding the right friends." I don't know where it came from, but it keeps coming. "School is like—those white-water rapids, you know?"

"You've never been white-water rafting," says Penn.

"You know what I mean. Like in the movies, a group of people in a canoe or something, and the water suddenly gets faster, and they panic and scream, and then there's a waterfall—"

"And they all die a horrible death."

"Okay, so not the right metaphor. But you get it, right? I'm still trying to get through too, so it's not like I have all the answers. But I know one thing. You need friends in that canoe, Penn. Friends you can count on. The right friends will save your life. The wrong ones will sink you."

"Do Alan and Val save your life?"

"Yeah," I say, and then, thinking of them in LA: "I think so."

Penny shifts sideways on the couch, leans her head back onto my shoulder, and together we stare up at the DeLorean.

"You think they disassembled it to get it through the door?" I ask.

"Maybe."

"Or maybe they took out the windows."

"Yeah."

"So who's in your canoe, Penn?"

She lets out a sort of humming sigh, and then: "'It's useful being top banana in the shock department.'"

"I don't know what that means."

"Means grab a paddle, darling."

45 ➞ *two weeks a tide*

You're reading on a beach, and it's all relaxing and whatnot, the waves crashing onto the sand way up yonder, and you're really into your book, and everything is just perfect, and before you know it, *bam*—you're sitting in water.

And that's isolation.

I spend the next two weeks walking with OMG, scouring the bonus materials in the collector's edition of *This Is Not a Memoir*, reading the inscription on the back of Parish's photograph, waiting for a response from the Fading Girl, and the day is coming, I know, when I'll arrive at Val and Alan's house to find a stack of boxes labeled "LA" in bright red Sharpie, and this thought alone is enough to keep me from going over there, and it is not lost on me that in my attempt to keep them close, I am pushing them away.

Two weeks and it's getting colder. And I'm barely aware of the isolation until I feel it pooling around my feet.

46 ➞ *a concise history of me, part thirty-two*

According to the National Oceanic and Atmospheric Administration (NOAA), water covers just over 70 percent of the earth's surface. NOAA also states that humankind has explored less than 5 percent of the ocean. In their own words, "Ninety-five percent of this realm remains unexplored, unseen by human eyes."

For precision: .95 x .7 (or, 95 percent of 70 percent) = .665.

Over 66 percent of our planet has never been seen by human eyes.

As fascinating a thing as space exploration sounds, it does feel a bit like receiving a puppy for Christmas, deciding it's too much of a hassle, too much upkeep, too little reward—and so asking for a pet elephant instead. Don't get me wrong, I love space, with its infinite incomprehensibility, its scope and mystery. Space is really damn sexy. But when you haven't laid eyes on 66 percent of your own home, maybe consider exploring *that* before moving on to other peoples' houses.

How about we raise the puppy first, is what I'm saying, see how that goes before graduating to an elephant.

A few highlights from the 5 percent of the ocean we *have* seen: Thonis-Heracleion, once a port of entry to Egypt, now buried in the depths of the Mediterranean Sea; the Yonaguni Monument off the southern tip of the eponymous Japanese island, an ancient underwater pyramid; the Stonehenge-like arrangement of rocks at the bottom of Lake Michigan, one of which boasts a very clear drawing of a mastodon. Countless ruins of once-thriving coastal cities now fully submerged in water.

And me-oh-my, how easy it is to imagine future sunken civilizations: the Lost City of Los Angeles, discovered by some unsuspecting clone in the year 8016 who, while diving off the coast of Vegas Province, discovers a mysterious world of silicone, reel-to-reel projectors, and a giant algae-covered HOLLYWOOD sign. Clones the world over would teleport to conferences to study these artifacts, fascinating remnants from days when actual skin-and-bone originals produced other skin-and-bone originals in unspeakably antiquated methods of rhythm and secretion. *Can you imagine*, the clones would think to each other in telepathic whispers, scratching genetically perfect heads at these relics, *what it must have been like to live back then?*

I like to look at photographs of sunken civilizations and mouth words like *graveyard* and *long-forgotten*; I look at godlike statues in stone temples with that greenish-blue hue of underwater submersion, and I think of the people who built those structures. Were they erected in the light of day in sand or snow? Whose sweat is embedded in *that* stone, whose aimless songs ingrained in its memory? Did their makers wish only to finish a good day's work, to be home, to be loved, to be fed? Or did their minds wander to far-off lands, worlds to be conquered, women and men to be laid? Mostly, I imagine one of these laborers, a mere cog in the great wheel of industry, stopping in the middle of their work, taking a step back, and, seeing their creation in a new and premonitory light, whispering, *One day, this will all be at the bottom of the ocean.*

That's usually when I realize I am the cog.

47 ➡ just another yard

This is the first time I've read pages aloud to anyone. It feels like every ounce of my blood is camped out in my ears.

Alan is all, "Damn, yo."

"What do you think?"

"It's good, man. Weirdly depressing. And just straight-up weird, but . . . good." He looks around my room, checks his watch. "I gotta take a leak. I'll be right back."

"Alan."

"Yeah."

"What's up?"

His face, for once, is wholly unreadable. "Hold that thought," he says, and disappears into the hallway.

While he's gone, I look back at my computer screen. In my darkest moments I worry my Histories are total rip-offs. Once, right in the middle of a piece about how everywhere I go I imagine myself living there, I discovered a line in Thoreau's *Walden* that said, "At a certain season of our life we are accustomed to consider every spot as the possible site of a house." I calmly placed *Walden* on my bookshelf, and thought maybe the most sensible thing a writer can think: *Fuck it, I'll write it anyway.*

I can't say for sure, but I suspect large portions of the words I write are really just my favorite books regurgitated.

Alan comes back, but he's not alone—Val is right behind him. "Okay," she says, sitting on the edge of my bed. "You start yet?"

Alan says, "No, waiting on you," and I'm beginning to

wonder if maybe Alan went to the bathroom just to stall until Val got here.

"Start what?" I ask.

Val says, "Alan tells me you're going through some shit right now."

I look at Alan. "The fuck?"

"Be chill, No," says Val. "He won't say what's going on." It's quiet for a second, and when it's clear I'm not going to say anything, she continues. "One of the things I love about us is that we don't bullshit each other. Or at least not until this fall. I don't know what's going on, and I don't have to know, that's fine. But I've seen too many friends drift apart, and they never name it. And then they don't even know each other."

"We never hang anymore," says Alan. It comes out in a rush, like he's nervous, like he's been sitting on it for a while. "You stopped coming over, you're not at practice, I never see you outside school."

"What about our Dean and Carlo session?" I ask.

"You mean when we had *The Matrix* on? Noah, that was, like—two months ago."

It's quiet for a second while I consider the cold isolation that's been gathering around my feet for the last two months.

"So here's the thing," says Val. "We're at a crossroads, I think. If you need space—from us, from the whole—"

"Delicate triangle," says Alan.

Val nods. "Just say so. Or you can clue us into things, and we can help. As it is, we're not what we used to be. So let's name it. Let's call it that instead of watching the whole thing drift away."

They both smile in this nervous way, and I think, *They've*

rehearsed this. I picture them in their house, running through lines. *You say this, then I'll say that, and maybe he won't flip.*

Open my mouth to say something, I honestly don't know what, but all I can hear is Val's voice, *We're not what we used to be*, and I start crying. It's not a sob, just a solid, quiet cry, and they let me have it without platitudes or shoulder pats or quiet *it's okay*s. And when I'm done, Val says, "We love you."

Alan nods. "Love you, yo."

I wipe my eyes, try to let the calm wash over me, but instead: "I can't believe you guys are leaving." I don't know if this is what Val meant by naming it, but there it is. "I can't believe it."

"Come with us," says Alan, and Val nods. "I mean, we may not even get in, but if we do . . . you could come too."

Sometimes I feel like a guest in a house full of loving people I barely know, and I see a wide-open yard out back, and think, *That's where I want to be*, and so I walk outside. But standing alone in the empty yard, I look back inside at a house full of loving people, and I think, *Why did I come out here again?*

Maybe I'll go to LA. But part of me is afraid it's just another yard.

"You're right," I say. "Everything you said. I haven't been around. I've been a shitty friend, and I'm sorry for that."

"Let me in," says Val. "Whatever's going on, we can help."

And looking at her, I have to believe that admitting we aren't what we used to be isn't the same as accepting we won't somehow be more in the future.

Take a deep breath, now go: "So the night of the Longmire party . . ."

Whether it's the promise of a brutal Chicago winter around the corner, or a brutal family Thanksgiving, people suddenly feel the insatiable need to clear the air. "We need to talk," says Mom literally the morning after my sit-down with Alan and Val. Not to mention it's Monday, and the sun is barely up.

"I know, Mom. We said Thanksgiving weekend. I still have, like, a week."

"Not that," she says, pouring herself coffee. "I mean, yes, that's right. But that's not what I meant."

Dad rounds the corner, growls like a bear, all, "Mmmmmm, coffffeeeeeeeeeee." He pours himself a full mug with all the enthusiasm of Augustus Gloop in Wonka's chocolate factory.

"Okay," says Mom. "I assume your room is as spotless as ever?"

"Um, yes?"

"Good. Orville should be getting here late tomorrow night."

"Okay?"

"He'll probably get a cab here," continues Mom, "but it'll be late, after we're in bed. I told him to let himself in. Which reminds me, I should go ahead and disable the alarm."

"Mom?"

"What?"

"Are we getting to the part where you tell me why the cleanliness of my room relates to the impending arrival of Uncle Orville?"

"Oh. I thought I said it already? He's staying in your room."

I have no words, except: "Sorry, what."

"Watch the tone," says Dad, parachuting into the conversation.

"I couldn't very well offer him a guest room, could I?" says Mom, rolling her eyes in Dad's direction. Our house has two guest rooms, both of which have slowly and inadvertently been converted into pantry storage for Dad's catering supplies.

"Where am I supposed to sleep?" I ask.

Mom motions to the couch in the living room, waving her arm like a game show model presenting some fabulous prize. "Or the basement, totally up to you."

"Fine."

She pauses, tilts her head. "Noah. Are you okay?"

"Well, I don't love the idea of Uncle Orville in—"

"No, I mean—" And suddenly Mom is in my space, and now she's hugging me, and now she's all, "Seems like you've been a little . . . I don't know. Off, lately."

I don't say what I'm thinking: *That makes two of us.* Ever since that morning in my bedroom on the first day of school when I asked about her scar, she's basically treated me like a twice-removed cousin.

"If something's wrong, you can always talk to us," she says.

"I know, Mom," and we're still hugging, and I smell her smell, lean in to it, absorb it now while I can.

She pushes my hair back, kisses me on the forehead. "I know your uncle can be sort of . . . eccentric, but—"

Dad laughs a little, realizes his mistake, sticks his head in the fridge. "Oh, boy, looks like we're running out of carrot butter."

"Orville is a *sweet man*," says Mom, full-on death stare at Dad, who is currently heaving an armload of carrots from our industrial vegetable drawer in an effort to restore our dangerously low supply of carrot butter. "And even if he weren't, he's family." She digs through her purse for her keys, finds them, kisses me on the forehead again, then says, "No kisses for the carrot man," and she's out the door.

Dad is all smiles, pulling out the food processor, setting a pot of water to boil, chopping carrots. The man is in his element. "Big plans today, Noah?"

"Not nearly as big as yours, from the looks of it."

"Ah, to be young and smarmy."

"Young and what?"

"How about you play hooky and help your old man? The fun part is about to start."

I grab my jacket off the counter. "I'm more of an apple butter man myself."

"*Apple butter*. Bush league."

I head for the door. "Have fun with your carrots, Dad."

Last thing I hear before closing the front door is a crunch.

48 → *the life and times of Mr. Elam*

After weeks of getting a door shut in my face, I've landed on a new, slightly more aggressive tactic with OMG. It was Val's idea, and no telling if it will work, but I'm about to find out.

OMG rounds the corner right on time; I hop off the hood and approach, only this time, when he's all, "Well, kid, don't just stand there," I respond with, "Just so you know, I'm coming inside today." He says nothing, gives no indication that he even heard me, and our walk continues as always. We make the right on Ashbrook, closer now, and the way my heart is pounding you'd think I was walking home a new crush, debating whether to make a move on the front stoop. A quick glance at his goiter, which seems bigger today, large and in charge—or, larger and in charger—then down the narrow stone path to the front porch of Ambrosia's Bed & Breakfast, now up the steps to the door.

So close.

He keys in the code and opens the door for me. "Ladies first."

After weeks of the same six cold words every morning, it only took these last two to convey the warm complexities of Old Man Goiter.

◀▮▮▮▶

A few years ago we did a home exchange with a family in Boston. It was two weeks in an old brownstone, and this place reminds me of that—like, to a T—and not only for its visual aesthetic, but also the smells (old bookstores and herbal teas) and sounds (creaking wood, a heavy, old silence). If the outside of Ambrosia's Bed & Breakfast is quaint, the inside redefines the word. Dark hardwoods, dusty red rugs, dim lighting, a crackling fire in a sitting room just off the entryway: the whole thing almost feels too B-and-B for its own good.

"Hey there, Mr. George," a woman says from the sitting room.

OMG mumbles incoherently, shakes his head, leads the way upstairs.

The stairwell is just like the Boston brownstone too, but I guess a lot of these old places were designed during the same time, architectural trends and whatnot.

Second floor, at the end of the hall now, last room on the left—OMG pulls out an old skeleton key, inserts it, turns the bolt with a satisfying clunk, and swings open the door. "No shoes," he says, slipping his off.

What with this being a bed-and-breakfast, I'd been expecting a single room, but this is a full-fledged apartment.

"I'll be right back," he says. "Don't touch anything."

OMG shuffles off while I unlace my boots and look around. The smell is wholly different in here, a rich, sugary cedar. A single easy chair faces a fireplace and a small boxy TV; behind the chair is a wet bar and two filled-to-the-brim bookshelves, each spine etched in gold or silver. Other than the bookshelves, the rest of the wall's real estate belongs to photographs: mostly mountains, forests, fields, animals. No people to speak of. One shelf is just sports memorabilia: a number of baseball cards; a framed ticket to a boxing match signed by Muhammad Ali; a basketball card signed by Michael Jordan; and a 1945 Chicago Cubs World Series pennant.

"Whoa."

"You a Cubs fan?" OMG stands over the bar, gazing at a variety of fancy-looking bottles of whiskey. Some are full, most are close to empty, and in that moment it strikes me how defeated the old man appears, as if, like his whiskey bottles, someone has poured out all but a few drops of his insides.

"Yeah," I say. Considering the fever pitch of Dad's Cubbie-love, it was a fandom near impossible to avoid.

"You know what happened in '45, then?"

"Sure. Curse of the Billy Goat."

OMG chooses a bottle, tilts a generous pour into a glass, and hands it to me. "Hadn't won it since 1908, figured the wait was over." After pouring himself one, he shuffles back into his easy chair, its cushiony form enveloping him, appropriately, like a well-worn baseball mitt. "If I'd known then what I know now, just how far from the truth *that* was—how many years I'd have to wait . . ."

I take a labored sip, study a framed baseball card of a youngish kid in a jersey with NY embroidered on the front. The card looks about a hundred years old, and as far as I can tell, it's the only piece of baseball memorabilia that isn't Cubs-related. The name on the bottom reads *Merkle*.

"People think the curse started with that damn goat," says OMG. "But I know the truth." He sips his whiskey, savors it, and seems to lose himself in something. When he looks up, it's like he forgot I was in the room. "Kind of a weird kid, aren't you?"

"I mean . . . I don't think so."

"Follow a lot of strangers home, do you?"

If you only knew, I think. Actually, that was the last time I had liquor, the night I followed Circuit home. Probably not the healthiest habit.

"Never heard of anyone living in a B-and-B," I say.

"Probably a lot of things you've never heard of."

I raise my glass. "Like bourbon before breakfast?"

He downs the rest of his, heads back to the bar. "You can wait till breakfast if you want."

I choke down a sip and notice a small urn on the mantel with a gold-plated plaque reading RIP HERMAN, ONE HELL OF A CAT.

"You a cat person, Mr. George?"

"It's Elam."

"Sorry?"

He tips a bottle over his glass, this pour lasting a little longer than the first. "My name," he says. "I prefer Mr. Elam. And I don't know what that means, *Am I a cat person*. I used to have a cat. Now I don't."

"Okay."

"You doing a report or something?" he asks. "For school?"

"No."

He points to his goiter. "It's this, then, yeah? You noticed it, got curious, maybe even Internetted it. Ultimately, you figured you'd go"—he makes a little clicking noise out of the side of his mouth—"*straight* to the source."

"I'm not—I didn't—"

"You are," he says. "And you did. How you like the bourbon?"

"It's good," I say, and then, "Listen," but how to explain that for the past six months I've concocted a hundred stories of his life, rearranged my own schedule to catch a glimpse of him walking his route, every day, same time, without fail? He's right: I'm curious. But it's not the goiter. It's him. I would like to know who he is: at most, to figure out why he, as a Strange Fascination, hasn't changed; at least, to go back to breathing properly between Mill Grove and Ashbrook. "Mr. Elam, I'd like to hear your story. That's the long and short of it. I don't want anything from you, I just want to hear your story." As an afterthought, I add: "If that's okay."

He opens his mouth and for a second I think it's over, he's kicking me out and that's that, but then he starts talking, and like Penny's wormhole illustration I am an ant on a folded napkin, transported through time and space into a whole other world, one emerging not as a beautiful and glorious place, but as an honest place, a place where wives die young, where wars are hard fought, where life plays out in ways you never imagined. And it's more fantastic than anything I could have concocted not because of *what* happens, but because *it happened*, because it is Mr. Elam's story.

George Elam moved into Ambrosia's Bed & Breakfast after his wife of forty-two years, Barbara, died of cancer. The cancer came as cancer does: out of the blue, leaving a black hole in its wake. George and Barbara Elam had long been friends with the owner of Ambrosia's, and what started as temporary lodging ("I couldn't sleep in that house after she died") ended up a permanent arrangement. The goiter came along shortly after that. His doctor showed concern, expressed interest in various treatments, all of which Mr. Elam declined. "When it's my time, it's my time," he says on more than one occasion, which leads me to wonder, *Does this man hasten his time?*

Mr. Elam fought in World War II, landed on Omaha Beach, pushed through the hedgerows into France, "endured and survived the Battle of the Bulge," and advanced into Germany, where "we woulda shot the little chicken shit had he not done the deed himself," and I imagine Mr. Elam the soldier, blood on his hands and friends, blood on his thoughts and actions, and I am forced to confront that burning question I can only assume all young men of ensuing generations face when presented with an honest-to-God World War II story: *How would you have fared?*

Ten years after Barbara died, Mr. Elam fulfilled a lifelong dream of qualifying for *Wheel of Fortune*. He did well, was up the whole game until the puzzle turned to pop culture, and the *before and after* phrase incorporated a current movie star, and Mr. Elam hasn't "seen a single movie since 1990," because that's when *The Godfather Part III* came out, which put him off movies for the rest of his life.

He lost tens of thousands on that puzzle.

Mr. Elam refills my empty glass, and his own. "Used to go to church," he says, "until they stopped singing the good songs. Still believe in God, even though I don't understand one damn thing He does," and now he's not speaking so much as regurgitating memories, as if his brain is spilling over and the only outlet is his mouth, his words. "My wife loved numbers, but that was a long time ago," he spills, mostly fragments now, "just a baby," and then something about daily walks and a family motto, but I can barely hear. "'One plus one plus one equals one,' she used to say."

It's dead silent for the first time in a while.

One plus one plus one equals one. The family motto.

"So . . . you have a kid, then?" I ask.

Mr. Elam takes a deep breath—it reminds me of the moment my head breaks the surface of water, that very first inhale—and then: "I'm done now."

"Okay," I say, "thank you," and I mean it, and suddenly I feel very foolish to have ever referred to this man as anything other than Mr. Elam. He opens the door, and it's not forceful or rude, but it is final, and now I'm in the hallway lacing up my boots, echoes of other lives ringing in my head, so many silly stories I'd concocted floating away, forever replaced by the true Mr. Elam.

I can't help but smile a little as I walk downstairs, a whiff of Boston brownstone unfolding the napkin, restoring the present timeline, and like an ant confronted with the sudden and daunting distance between corners, I walk out the front door of Ambrosia's Bed & Breakfast, feeling the weight of possibility on my shoulders, the burden of knowledge that comes from having listened to the story of a life well lived.

And in my head, Mr. Elam's voice on a loop . . .

Well, kid, don't just stand there.

49 ➔ *productivity begets productivity*

Today's visit with Mr. Elam ran long, and by the time I arrive at school, I've already missed first block and most of second. I wait it out in the car, then head to third block where I zone to Herr Weingarten's titillating lecture on verb conjugation, instead channeling the commanding baritone of Mr. Elam: *Ultimately, you figured you'd go . . .* straight *to the source.*

I've posted a comment directly on the Fading Girl's YouTube channel. I've walked right up to Mr. Elam. I've scoured the bonus materials of *This Is Not a Memoir*. But instead of directly investigating a local musician, I've been hyperfocused on the identity of some rando guy in a photograph that musician left behind.

A quick Google search under my desk and I have Pontius Pilot's event schedule, which includes a standing gig at a bar in Lincoln Park called the Windy City Limits. He's there every Tuesday night at eleven thirty.

Tomorrow night.

I make a clicking noise out of the side of my mouth. "*Straight* to the source."

"*Ja*, Norbert?" says Herr Weingarten.

I look up to find the entire class looking at me. "What?"

"*Hast du etwas gesagt?*" he asks.

Shit. "Um, *nein. Ich habe . . . nichte . . . sagte . . .* um, *nichte.*"

The class chuckles, and Danny Dingledine raises his hand, which ramps up the chuckling, and then Danny asks for permission to "use the facilities for a big-time *Nummer zwei*," and the class becomes one chuckle united. Even Klaus—who's proven as big a competent turd as we feared—gets in on the action, and Herr Weingarten rubs his temples, and I'd feel bad for the guy, but all this productivity has me feeling a little drunk at the moment.

That, plus Mr. Elam's bourbon.

◀▦▶

That evening after dinner, I receive two emails in my twobytwooak@gmail.com inbox: an exclusive offer from Williams-Sonoma (which, WTF), and a message from

SquareRootOfBro_6 asking if I would like to buy his football cards.

Mysteries of the playground abound!

I climb into bed with the collector's edition of *This Is Not a Memoir*, and the magnifying glass I ordered online, which I've used to study the photographs in the back of the book. It's mostly Mila Henry with her dad, and then with her husband, Thomas Huston, and eventually their son, Jonathan.

Jonathan Henry was an artist and writer primarily known for his very terrible novel, *On Wings of Total Chaos & Destruction*, which was exactly as sad as its sad title insinuated. While reading, one could almost feel the great shadow of Jonathan's mother spread across the page, and I had to think, if ever a writer was doomed from the start, it was the son of Mila Henry.

I stay up late googling Jonathan Henry—his relationship with his mom (a real champion of her son's visual art, in one early interview even going so far as to say, "The world doesn't know what to do with Jonathan yet because it's seen nothing like him before"), his derivative writing, his divisive paintings—and it feels like someone dumped a billion-piece jigsaw puzzle in front of me. I can't be sure where to start, but I tell myself that breakthrough revelations usually arrive with exhaustion, when one's brain is focused on something else entirely—that's when it hits you.

My phone buzzes with a text from Val: How'd it go with OMG today?

Unable to keep my head in an upright position, I fall into bed and text her how it went, thank her for the suggestion, ask if she'll update Alan.

Val: Maybe tomorrow? He had late practice, just
     crashed.

Me: Great. Night Val.

Val: Night, No

Me: Hey

Val: Hey

Me: Thank you

And at some point, just before falling asleep, while focused on something else entirely, the breakthrough revelation: within the name Jonathan lies another name.

YOU GUESSED IT ➳ PART FIVE

—Excerpt from Chapter 17 of Mila Henry's Year of Me

'Nathan.'

Cletus watched his new friend cry. The young man was clearly down on his luck, but there was more to it than that. Truth be told Cletus saw much of himself—much of who he wanted to be, much of who he used to be—in Nathan. For Cletus, the world had stopped letting him down when he'd stopped expecting it not to. But Nathan still felt things & deeply. Nathan still believed in possibility, still believed there was a chance the world was not in fact a smoking shitball of disappointment.

Which it was, of course. One big stinking, smoking shitball.

Cletus opened his mouth to break this news to his friend, when suddenly he glimpsed a small burst of color protruding from the inside pocket of Nathan's blazer. 'What is that?' asked Cletus.

Nathan pulled out a painting about the size of a pocketbook. 'I thought maybe it would impress someone. At the mixer, I mean. Silly of me.'

'May I?' asked Cletus, taking the canvas in his hands. He turned it, then again, trying to decide if he loved or hated it. The painting seemed both loud & soft, a little presumptuous of its virtue, until Cletus looked closer & decided no, it had just the right account of its own virtue. And then Cletus began to cry (a thing he rarely did), & he was dumbfounded (a thing he rarely was), for he understood that what he held was rare magic, that Nathan had harnessed that magic, had completed the unspoken commission of artists the world over: *Create something* new *for godsake.*

Cletus looked from the art to the artist, this shell of a man sitting across from him, & in a blinding revelatory blaze, he understood. To complete the commission—to create something truly new—it was not enough for the artist to put themselves into their work; they must also die to it.

'I just want to create,' said Nathan, as good as dead. 'Just to create.'

Cletus reached his hand across the table, placed it on Nathan's. 'So did She. And here we are. But you know—I'm not sure Her creation would know what to do with yours.'

Nathan was overcome with emotion at these words & the two men wept openly onto the Formica tabletop. Nearby patrons whispered, eyes darting furtively at these strange men who would dare cry & hold hands in so public a place. Cletus did not care. For in one hand he held magic & in the other the magician.

And Cletus Foot wondered if perhaps the world was not so giant a shitball after all.

'I'm sorry, Nathan. I'm just so sorry.'

50 → *omen*

It's Tuesday morning and the gas station parking lot is spotless, not a grease stain to be found.

Mr. Elam never shows.

51 → *fifty shades of beige*

This morning before class, I meet with Coach Kel for physical fitness drills, and to discuss what I'm missing in practice, and eventually that discussion turns to Coach Stevens and the UM offer. "You make a decision yet?" he asks. "Helluva coach, helluva program. They'd be lucky to have you."

Afterward, I see Alan in the hallway. He clearly sees me, sees that I saw him see me, does a ninety-degree turn on a dime, and stares at the blank wall. With his nose mere inches from the beige cement blocks, he tilts his head to one side and scratches his hair like he's admiring a masterpiece at the Guggenheim.

Yesterday after Mr. Elam's, I'd gotten to school so late

I hadn't seen him at all, making this our first encounter since their intervention in my room Sunday night. And as opposed to the many rifts I've had with Val, Alan and I have only ever had one real argument before: the night of the Longmire party this summer, and that was resolved through text, so we have no real protocol for in-person friendship realignment.

"Hey."

He looks at me like he's surprised to see me. "Oh. Hello, Noah Oakman."

I turn sideways so our shoulders almost touch, then stare at the wall right next to him. "This is nice. I can see why you chose this spot. The beige is more, I don't know, beiger than, say, right there." I point a few feet down the wall. It's exactly the same, but I shake my head like that particular section of beige has really let itself go. "It just sucks, 'cause none of the other beiges will tell that beige to its face. They'll just talk about its lackluster beigeness behind its back. I really feel for it, man." Still nothing. "Okay, movie idea. *Fifty Shades of Beige*, starring . . . Steve Buscemi. Costarring Dolores Umbridge. Instead of sex, they're obsessed with a variety of tantalizing board games. Clue. Monopoly. Risk. Tagline . . . *Work hard, play hard*."

"Steve Buscemi's super-talented though."

"Who would you have gone with?"

"What about one of the villains from *Home Alone*?"

"Works for me."

Alan shakes his head. "This conversation, though."

"You know, I just figured—our first post-confrontation in-person talk was bound to be awkward, might as well really go for it."

Alan throws an arm around my shoulders. "I'm glad we got that over with."

"Same."

We part ways for first block, and Alan tells me to text him during the perfect storm to let him know how it went with OMG. I say I will, and on my walk to class I wonder how it's possible talking such stupid shit can make me feel so good. And then I wonder who I'll talk stupid shit with next year.

◀▥▥▥▶

Alan: Dude

Alan: Yo

Alan: OK, like

Alan: Whatever you're working on better be a masterpiece of the utmost import

Alan: Because I'm actually learning shit here

Alan: About American history and whatnot

Alan: For example, did you know Abraham Lincoln didn't have a middle name?

Alan: Ooh, or that he loved chicken casserole? (What even is chicken casserole and can I have some amarite????)

Alan: HOLY SHIT BOOTH WAS AT LINCOLN'S
2ND INAUGURAL AND THERE IS A PHOTO
OF THEM TOGETHER AHHHHHHH

Alan: Noah the learning is real

Alan: Okay

Alan: So what kind of timeline are you thinking?
Like today, or . . . ?

Alan: Should I break out my e-reader?

Alan: (E-reader, that's a thing, right?)

Alan: Do you need another round of revisions
before sending?

Alan: So I'm considering shifting occupational
focus from animation to goat farming.
Your thoughts

Alan and I have always referred to B Day, first block as the "perfect storm." He has American history with Ms. Ray and I have AP psychology with Mr. Armentrout, both of whom are usually too wrapped up in the superiority of their own subjects to notice a little undercover texting. Today, Mr. Armentrout was a little more attentive at first, so Alan had a bit of a head start.

Me: OK, regarding OMG (who I now feel legit bad having ever
even called OMG, bc dude has LIVED A LIFE) there's too

much to text, so I will catch you up later. More recently I have a theory re: Chapter 17 of Henry's Year of Me. Remember how near the end of the chapter Cletus apologizes to Nathan and how that—well, the whole chapter really—has been criticized for being so totally out of the blue? I think I cracked the case wide open.

Alan: You have my attention

Me: If you recall there was never any explanation as to what Cletus was apologizing for.

Alan: Right

Me: I think it's because the entire chapter is written from Mila Henry to her son, Jonathan.

Alan: Fuuuuuu;lksd;lfaj;sl fja jf;;alksnd;lfkna;

Me: First, the name. Nathan is so quintessentially un-Henry. Too common, unlike her other character names. Plus that name is literally inside the name Jonathan.

Alan: FUUUUUUULKJAS;DFJ ;LJ;JF; JS;LKAJDS;LKFJAS!!!

Me: I think Mila Henry was doing in one of her books what she could never do in real life . . . I think she's apologizing to her son.

Alan: For what tho?

Me: Jonathan tried writing

Alan: On Wings of Total Chaos or whatever

Me: & Destruction. And the title was the best thing about it haha.

Alan: Adapted it into a killer bad movie tho

Me: True

Alan: J was a painter too right?

Me: Yeah but never really broke out. Reviews were always "Jonathan, son of . . ."

Me: Mom's shadow loomed LARGE. I think she felt guilty

Alan: None of this answers your initial question. Why is that one sketch different from the rest?

Alan: (I'll give you some time on this one)

Alan: (It's prob a long answer)

Alan: (Me texting would just be annoying)

Alan: (No one wants to be *that guy*)

Alan: (By the way, been meaning to ask: WHATS YOUR FAV COLOR?)

Me: What better way for that particular X to mark the spot than to have it be a discrepancy in the art? If she couldn't tell her son in real life, hard to imagine she would come out and say it in a book. BUT. She might have been able to toss her kid an Easter egg in the hopes Jonathan would find it for himself. Or maybe not. Maybe it's just for her. Like when Catholics give confession. Just getting it off her chest probably helped.

Alan: Freaking Sherlock over there

Me: Still no idea why the SFs haven't changed when MY BEST FRIENDS have.

Alan: You'll get there

Me: In the meantime we'll always have Joe Pesci

Alan: ???

Me: Home Alone villain

Alan: You're a genius

Me: A genius with the IMDB app.

Alan: Hold up, Pesci and Umbridge would actually be a pretty good match

Me: Oh I know. Team Umbsci tearing it up with those board games.

Alan: Team Umbsci!!! You're perfect and I love you

Me: I know

Alan: Don't you Han Solo me

Me: Is that a euphemism?

At which point Mr. Armentrout confiscates my cell phone.

52 ➜ *hypnotik returns*

Class had just let out. Thanksgiving break, finally. Between that and my interaction with Alan, I left school that day with lots of spirit, stepped out into the crisp Iverton air, and truly felt, for the first time in a while (maybe ever), like Hypnotik, Alan's muscly, caped-crusading rendition of me. "Philip Parish," I said, fists on hips, chin to the sky, "I am coming for you," at which point this tiny-kid-with-giant-book-bag, who happened to be passing me just then, broke into a full-on sprint, leading me to assume his name was Milip Garish or something, because the kid just took off, and so what with all that buoy in my step, I ran after him, waving my hands above my head, all, "I'm not just standing here anymore!" and laughing in these rhythmic, maniacal gulps, so.

As far as I know, that kid is still running.

53 ➤ *over one billion served*

That night over dinner we touch on Thanksgiving plans: who is coming, who can't make it, which casseroles which family member is bringing, et cetera. Apparently Dad cleaned out a guest room so Uncle Orville will, in fact, have his own room when he gets here—a relief, needless to say.

My impending timeline for a college decision sits in the middle of the table like Dad's experimental vegan lasagna: no one touches it, we barely look at it for fear of contamination, its very existence boggles the fucking mind. After dinner I hunker down in my room with the bonus materials of *This Is Not a Memoir* and bide my time until the sound of my parents' sustained chuckles from the next room over die down. Around ten p.m. I dig around in the back of my desk drawer for the fake ID Val and Alan's cousin made for me last summer. Keys and wallet now, and last but not least: Parish's Abandoned Photograph.

The hallway is quiet. Now or never. I creep to the top of the stairwell, down the stairs, carefully avoiding that traitorous second-to-last step, with its squeaky floorboard. I considered telling Mom and Dad I was going out with Alan and Val, but inevitably they'd want to know where. And since I wouldn't be with them at all, that stuck me with two lies to land. One was hard enough to get by Mom; two was like infiltrating the CIA, so not mission impossible but damn near close. But really, once Mom mentioned disabling the alarm for Uncle Orville I knew sneaking out would prove far less risky.

"Whatchya up to?"

"*Shit*. Penny. What are you doing down here so late?"

"You know I like to read by the fire," says my sister, fists on hipbones like Pan the Man. At her heels, Mark Wahlberg lets out the quietest of yips, like even he understands the importance of stealth right now. Hell, he probably does, the cheeky little bastard. "What are *you* doing down here so late?"

"I'm not doing anything." I fake yawn. "Just headed to bed, actually."

For a second she stands there in those holey jeans, an old Sammy Sosa T-shirt (with a defaced name on the back so it now reads *Soso*), rain boots, and an eye patch. And then, quietly: "Take me with you."

"What?"

"Wherever you're going, take me with you."

"I'm going to bed is where I'm going."

"I'm not dumb," says Penn.

"Penny—"

"Take me with you, or I'm telling."

Every sibling relationship operates under a certain code: call it the Sibling Bill of Rights. Each bill is different, its principles as varied as the kids themselves. Under ours, Penny is free to annoy the ever-loving bejeezus out of me, and I, in turn, have carte blanche to replace every contact number in her phone with that of Domino's Pizza. (Though admittedly, these antics have recently fallen by the wayside. Who knows, maybe we're growing up.) Point is, our Bill of Rights states in no uncertain terms that there shall be no tattling, not ever, for any reason, under any circumstances, period.

"Be reasonable, darling. Remember our little outing at the Wormhole? That wasn't so bad, was it?"

I don't know which scares me more: Threatening Penny or Cunning Penny.

"It wasn't bad at all, Penn."

"Okay, so where are we going?"

I glance up at my parents' closed bedroom door. "I need to go to this bar—"

The words barely escape my lips before Penn's eyebrows shoot a foot in the air. "A *bar*?" she says.

"Oh boy."

"Like . . . a *bar* bar? Like with a bartender?"

I don't even want to think about how much higher Penn's eyebrows might be if she knew how many times I'd been to a *bar* bar.

"Will you keep it down, please? And yes. Bars usually have bartenders."

"Wow."

"Look, it's not a big deal, Penn. But obviously—"

"I can't believe we're going to a real *bar*."

"Uh, no," I say. "*I* am going to a bar. *We* are not going anywhere."

"Wait, don't we have to be twenty-one? How are we getting in?"

"Penn, read my lips. *You're not going.*"

Her eyes squint, and I can tell she's weighing her earlier threat. Our front hallway suddenly transforms into a dusty scene from the Wild West, the two of us in a showdown, hands at hips, thumbs twitching, waiting for the other to draw.

Penny looks up at my parents' door and says simply, "I'll do it."

"Penny. It's a *bar*."

"*Exactly*, darling."

In the end I have no choice. I agree to let her come if she agrees to remain in the vehicle at all times, text at the slightest hint of trouble, and bring along Mom's pepper spray. I'm buckled in with the engine running before I notice Mark Wahlberg in the backseat. Penn sits next to me, knees tucked under her chin, just staring me down with smiles. I've grown used to her whimsical fashion, but the eye patch is downright distracting.

"You do know *this* is more of a Halloween costume than your *actual* Halloween costume, right? Starting left fielder for the Cubs, Captain Jack Sparrow, and his trusty sidekick, Mark Wahlberg."

Mark Wahlberg barks from the backseat.

"Right field," says Penn.

"Hmmm?"

"Sosa played right field."

"Okay, then."

I start up my car and pull out onto the street. Our subdivision is always empty this time of night, but it feels even more uninhabited than usual, staged almost. Every house light is off, the streetlamps reflecting a light dusty snow on the ground, which seemingly dropped from the sky when no one was looking. (This happens occasionally.) You can almost feel the neighborhood hunkering down, anticipating a few days of holiday hibernation.

"So why don't you want to swim?" asks Penny, and out of nowhere, too.

"What makes you think I don't want to swim?"

"You're not swimming, are you?"

"You know about my back."

The words hang in the car for a bit; Penny stares out the window. "So do you think he'll have one of those little white towels thrown over his shoulder?"

"What are you talking about?" I ask.

"The barkeep."

It's questions like this the rest of the drive into the city, and when we finally pull into the Windy City Limits parking lot, I'm shocked to realize I know the place. It used to be called Shitbucket, and it's where Val and Alan and I first used our fake IDs. Not to rain on the new ownership's parade, but barring some sort of miraculous interior renovation, Shitbucket is a far more appropriate name for this venue than Windy City Limits. If I remember correctly, the walls are covered in Sharpie-drawn expletives, the bathrooms have no doors, and they serve PBR by the trough.

I do notice, however, that they've updated the marquee in the parking lot.

"That," says Penny, "is impressive."

The sign is made from actual repurposed McDonald's arches, the glowing yellow curvatures turned upside down so the very large "M" is now the "W" in "Windy," and where once there might have been something to the effect of *The McRib is back!* there is now just a list of bands and artists performing this week.

TUESDAY-THURSDAY, 9P-1A: OPEN MIC

FRIDAY, 11P: YE REALLY OLDE EGGIES

SATURDAY, 11P: BOGIES ARE PART OF THE HUMAN ANATOMY

SUNDAY, 11P: METALLICAN'T

OVER ONE BILLION SERVED

"So *this*"—Penny has all ten fingers spread out in front of her as if witnessing some historically relevant occurrence—"is the *bar*."

"It is *a* bar, yes."

"I can't believe I'm at the bar."

"You are in the parking lot of a bar."

"It's perfect."

I shift in my seat, run through the set of rules with her again. It's not that I don't trust her, but there's something about that gleam in her eye every time she says the word *bar*, like it's the Great Hall at Hogwarts and we're about to be sorted into houses.

"I'm leaving the keys in the car so you'll have heat. I want to hear the doors lock as soon as I get out, okay? And don't unlock them for anyone, under any circumstances, until I get back."

"What if someone's bleeding out?"

"What?"

"You know, like, if there's a stabbing, and someone's dying on the ground."

"If there's a stabbing, call 911."

"So I should just let the guy die, then?"

"This was a mistake."

"I'm kidding, Noah. Not that stabbing someone is a laughing matter. But I'll be fine. I won't open the door. For anyone. Not even for stabbings."

I remind her I have my phone on, and to call or text if she needs me. Then, just before getting out, something else occurs to me. "Why *did* you want to come tonight?"

She pulls out her own phone, scrolls through God knows what, and says, "'It's useful being top ba—'"

"'It's useful being top banana in the shock department,'" I interrupt. Should have seen that one coming. I climb out of the car, and can't help wondering at the real reason behind Penny's outrageous clothes and her seeming inability to answer simple questions. It's almost like she wears these masks because she doesn't want to face the world as Penelope Oakman. I approach the bar entrance, pull out my fake ID, and push down a small whisper in the back of my mind: *So what's your excuse?*

A look from the bouncer like maybe he suspects something, but I don't open my mouth. Alan and Val's cousin (the procurer of fake IDs) hammered home the necessity of silence. *You will feel the urge to jabber,* he used to say, *to joke about what a baby face you have and how* annoying *it is. I* implore *you—fight those urges. Let the ID do the talking.*

The bouncer stamps my hand ЅНТВСКТ. (Windy City Limit's ink stamps have, apparently, yet to catch up to its new signage.) He then nods toward the entrance with a grunt, and like that, I'm in. And it's exactly as I remember it. Sharpie expletives, doorless bathrooms, horse-sized buckets brimming with yellow beer; the air is sticky, pulsing with grime.

A really great birthday present, for me, would be one hour alone in this place with a pressure washer and microfiber mop.

Onstage, a band is rocking in that balls-to-the-wall way so you can't tell if they're trying to make music, make love, or if they're just super-hungry.

Also, they aren't wearing shirts. So I don't know.

I claim one of the empty tables near the back, text Penn to make sure things are fine. The crowd is sparse, though not as sparse as you'd think given the holiday week. There seem to be quite a few baby faces scattered throughout, eyes darting over gulped beers, spurts of overeager laughter, kids popping French fries with the gusto of a chain smoker on break. (I have no memory of French fries last time, which makes me wonder if the fries came with the repurposed arches outside.) The whole place sort of screams, *We don't give a shit how old you are.*

The shirtless band's song comes to a close. They unplug

guitars and pack up gear while a guy with a ponytail and a shirt that says GO THE F*CK AWAY climbs onstage.

"Okay, uh," he says, consulting a piece of paper in his hands. "Let's hear it for . . . shit, that can't be right. What're you guys called again?" Behind him the shirtless guitar player mumbles something, to which he responds, "Really? Okay." Then, back into the microphone, Ponytail shakes his head. "Let's hear it for Rippd . . . without an *e*." Shirtless Guitar Player mumbles something else. Ponytail is all, "Dude, I'm just relaying information. Rippd without an *e*, that's what you said." Shirtless Guitar Player mumbles again, to which Ponytail lets out a little laugh, turns back to the microphone. "One more time for Rippd-without-an-*E*, who just played their Final-with-a-capital-*F* show at Windy City Limits." Shirtless Guitar Player flips him off; Ponytail turns and points to his shirt.

Doorless bathrooms or no, this place is all right.

"Okay, my name is Dave, and I'm the . . . *events coordinator* here at Windy City Limits." He says this like even he can't believe his ears. "Tuesday is open mic night here at our recently revamped institution. You guys see the new sign outside? Fucking baller, right? We stole it, along with the French fry recipe. Rock 'n' roll."

I don't know if Dave is joking, but I'm starting to think this place is more liable to get busted than a Longmire party.

"Speaking of rock 'n' roll," Dave continues, "next up we have a band guaranteed to knock your socks off, all while keeping *their* shirts on. Give it up for Lenny Lennox and the Xylophone Virtuosos."

A solitary dude with a xylophone climbs onstage, explains to Dave that he is not a band, but an actual xylophone virtuoso. Dave rubs his temples in a circular motion, his ponytail seems to wilt, and for the next twenty-two minutes Lenny Lennox plays the hell out of that xylophone.

All I can think is how much Alan would love this. I pull out my phone to take some video for him, but only have 8 percent battery and decide to save it in case Penny texts.

After Lenny's set, Dave introduces "solo artist Harrison von Valour Jr.," which actually ends up not being the name of a person at all, but a band.

It has been a long night for Dave and his flaccid ponytail.

Harrison von Valour Jr. plays three songs. The music isn't bad, a little reminiscent of early Radiohead. Once done, they pack up their guitars while Dave introduces Pontius Pilot. Some of the kids in the crowd clap a little, and I wonder if Philip Parish performed in their high school gymnasiums too, if he was a guest speaker in their AP English classes, if maybe this is what he does, just scatters photos of people with mysterious inscriptions on the back.

Pontius Pilot starts in on his first song, and some people get up to dance, and that's when I see her. Or I think it's her, hard to say from here. I circle around to the other side of the room, and—yeah. Definitely her. Up by the stage, dancing, singing right along with Pontius Pilot.

Sara knows all the lyrics.

Me: My phone is almost dead so last check in. You ok?

Penny: Nope. Got stabbed

Me: Not funny

Penny: Also mugged. It was your standard
        mugging/stabbing

Penny: Shit night to this point

Me: Don't say shit. And I shouldn't be much longer.

Me: Down to 6% so text for emergencies only.

Penny: I see people eating fries. I'll have some of
        those

Me: I wasn't taking your order. Also what people?

Penny: Chill. Some kids are out here smoking
        and they have fries. Is it McDonald's on
        the inside too?

Me: No

Penny: WAIT. Is this place like an undercover
      McD's???

Me: It is not.

Penny: OK. Mark Wahlberg sends his regards

Me: OMG. Gotta go. Out soon

◄||||||||►

After Pontius Pilot finishes his last song, he disappears backstage through a door labeled MESS/GREENROOM in white stenciling. I'd spent his whole set debating whether to go up to Sara, but at the moment she's nowhere to be found, which is probably for the best. I didn't sneak out of the house and get SHTBCKT stamped on my hand so I could flirt.

The voice of Val and Alan's cousin rings in my ears: *Act bored, like you've done it a thousand times.* I yawn like, *No big deal*, push open the MESS/GREENROOM door, and walk backstage.

For precision: it is immediately clear that the *mess* in MESS/GREENROOM is meant to reflect both a state of disarray and a fully equipped kitchen. In that kitchen now, a man with a mustache stands over a sizzling deep fryer with a metal basket of fries. Behind him are two doors labeled with that same white stencil: BACK ALLEY and PISS CHAMBER. To my left, a lounge, complete with couch and card table, amps and cables, guitars and beer cases. The shirtless guitar player from Rippd is lying on his back on the couch, studying the ceiling, and smoking weed.

From the stage on the other side of the wall, the next act begins. It's a girl's voice, whimsical and weightless, more painting than song, really, and I stand there trying to think of something to say, but all I can do is listen. The song is short, maybe a minute and a half, and for its duration, it's like all three of us in the room are under some enchantment. Before the next one starts, I'm about to ask if they've seen Pontius Pilot, when a toilet flushes from inside the PISS CHAMBER, then a running sink, and then . . . the door swings open.

"Oh," I say. "Hi."

Philip Parish looks at the man with the mustache, who shrugs and shakes his basket of fries. Parish pulls a bottle of water from the fridge, chugs it, wipes his mouth on his sleeve. "You with Harrison von . . . whatever?"

Shirtless Guitar Player pulls the joint out of his mouth, yells at the ceiling, "Harrison von Valour Jr. *sucks giant steaming turd balls!*"

Parish rolls his eyes.

"I'm not with Harrison von Valour Jr.," I say. And even though I thought they were a jillion times better than Rippd, I figure this guy just got his ass handed to him by a cynical MC in front of a bunch of underage kids who didn't really like his set all that much to begin with, so I add, "And I agree they suck giant steaming turd balls," just for an added sprinkle of camaraderie.

Back out onstage, the angelic voice sings, and this new song is even more iridescent than the first, its architect in possession of that rare magic that renders the resonation of melody through air both inevitable and miraculous: this girl sings the way most of us breathe.

"I have something for you." I pull the photo out of my

pocket and hand it to Philip Parish. He takes another chug of water, looks down at the picture for what seems an endless second—and maybe because I'd anticipated some seismic shift in the room where his heartbeat gradually increased, decibel by decibel, as if plugged into one of these old amps until the whole venue shook and rattled, all of us joined together in a communal orgasm of *shit making sense* for once, of *beautiful things happening* for once, of *removing the mask to find the man* for once, instead of it always being the other way around—maybe because of all this, the smoky-rough voice of Shirtless Guitar Player cuts so deep.

"That your boyfriend?" he asks, nudging Parish in the ribs, draped over our shoulders like a soaking wet quilt. I hadn't even heard him get off the couch.

Parish's eyes change, flicker to a fake sort of cheeriness. I could've sworn he was about to reach out and take the photo, but instead he says, "I have no idea who that is."

Slowly, from the bottom up, my legs begin to lose feeling. "AP English, Iverton High. You dropped this in my classroom."

Parish looks at Shirtless Guitar Player like, *Get a load of this kid.* "I did what now?" he says to me.

"Last year. You performed for our Magazine Mega Gala."

Shirtless Guitar Player chuckles, drops back down onto the couch.

Parish laughs too. "Oh, right. I remember that."

"You spoke to my class afterward. You had a notebook, and this fell out of it. I picked it up, and I think maybe—I don't know. I thought maybe it was important."

Philip Parish glances around, chugs the last of his water, tosses the empty bottle into a trash can. "I've never seen that picture in my life." But he doesn't look me in the eye when he says it, just shakes his head and, without even a good-bye, disappears through the door labeled BACK ALLEY.

"You sure you ain't with Harrison von Valour Jr., kid?" says Shirtless Guitar Player from the couch, and there's a loud hiss to my right as the man with the mustache drops another batch of frozen fries into bubbling oil. As if to punctuate the disappointment, the angelic voice onstage has been replaced by the mumblings of Dave, those miraculous (and far too short) songs supplanted by his flaccid ponytail. And my own heartbeat increases in volume now, decibel by decibel, as if plugged into one of these old amps, a cold announcement that shit rarely makes sense, that beautiful things seldom happen, and that, more often than not, what's under the mask is a total letdown.

55 → meanwhile, on my fun gay ballsack

Sara Lovelock is perched, literally, on top of my car. Through the windshield, I see Penny with her pepper spray at the ready, twisted around in an effort to keep both eyes on this perfect stranger sitting atop the vehicle like a sentry on post. I may be wrong, but it appears Mark Wahlberg is taking a nap in the backseat.

Dog has mad chill.

"Nice ride," Sara says, patting the roof.

I zip up my jacket. "My friend Alan calls it . . ."

"What?"

"What."

Sara pulls her hands into her coat sleeves. "You said, 'My friend Alan calls it,' and then you stopped talking."

"I'm afraid it wouldn't be appropriate."

"Noah. I'm literally sitting on top of your car."

"Okay, then. So as you can see, the car is a Hyundai hatch-back, and my very classy, not-at-all-juvenile friend Alan used to call it my 'fun guy ballsack,' until we—"

"*Fungi*? Plural for *fungus*?"

"I always heard, like, a dude who is fun. Either way, he recently discovered Hyundai is pronounced *hun-day* not *hun-dye*, and so then Alan was all, 'Even better!' and that's pretty much the story of how my Hyundai hatchback became known as my fun gay ballsack."

Dog's owner has zero chill.

"Good story," says Sara.

"Well, don't ask me to tell it again. It was just a one-time thing."

Penny's arms wave frantically from the front seat, and I'm about to open the door and tell her not to worry about this random girl on the car, when Sara says, "So you gonna ask me out or what?"

"What?"

"Damn, son."

"No, I didn't mean . . . Sorry, you caught me off guard."

She pops her hands out of her sleeves, slaps them on the hood (causing Penny to jump about a foot in her seat), and pushes herself down off the car. "So we keep running into each other, and I'm not one to tempt fate. Also, I have a thing for guys who wear the same clothes every day."

"I have ten on rotation, FYI. It's not like I wear the same *actual* T-shirt every day."

Behind us, the driver's-side window rolls down a few inches. "Noah?" Penny is holding the pepper spray out, eyeing Sara suspiciously.

"It's fine, Penny. At ease. This is Sara. She's a . . . friend."

"Hi," says Sara, smiling at Penn. "You're Noah's sister?"

Penny glares at her, says nothing, rolls the window back up.

"Sorry about her. She's a little weird."

"I mean, I did climb on top of a car while she was inside."

"True."

"Dog didn't seem to mind, though."

"That's Mark Wahlberg for you."

"You named your dog Mark Wahlberg?"

"I think I've met this evening's quota for stories that make me sound like I have no friends."

"Fair," she says, smiling, like that.

"Okay, well." *Do it. Just do it.* "You wanna go out sometime?"

"No way, dude."

The sudden urge to vomit . . .

"Kidding," she says. "I'd love to. You got your phone?"

I pull it out of my pocket. "Um. It's dead."

"Noah, Noah, Noah." She opens the door of the car next to mine, climbs in, and grabs a pen. Then, from her pocket, she pulls a crumpled piece of paper and starts writing.

"How'd you know it was mine?" I ask. "The car, I mean."

"Oh, I stalk you online? Yeah, I pretty much know everything about you, social security number, felonies, that kind of thing."

"So you probably saw I'm wanted for seventh-degree murder."

Sara smiles, hands me the crumpled paper. "What's that one again?"

"It's when you consider killing your friend's twice-removed cousin's boyfriend."

"Well, I'm sure he had it coming. But seriously. That time you came over to see my brother, you *backed into* our driveway. I could pick that thing out of a hatchback lineup."

I look at the crumpled paper expecting a phone number, only to find something that looks more like a list:

This Can Only Get Better

Moby Dick Sucks

Alone or Lonely

"Are these songs?" I ask.

"The other side. And don't think for a second this is a fool-around invite. It's not."

"It's not."

"I'm a classy girl, Noah. Treat me right, or rue the day you were born."

In her backseat I spot a guitar case, and it hits me. I flip the crumpled paper back over, and the angelic voice rings in my ears, each note a vibrant color floating around like particles of dust in the sunlight. "You sang tonight."

Sara looks in her lap, and I can tell I've changed the tenor of the conversation. She starts the car but doesn't drive off.

"You were amazing," I say.

"Thanks." She doesn't look up. "You know, I never really understood what Henry meant when she talked about exiting the robot. I thought I did, but I didn't. Until I started playing out. When I'm onstage, I don't think about any single person in the audience, or any single person in my life—I just lose myself completely. Go empty. Which is nice. Or not nice, but necessary."

"Sounds exhausting."

"The hard part is finding myself again afterward, filling myself back up with me. Also, the whole music-peer thing."

"Music-peer thing?"

"I've played out enough to know, musicians are all about vulnerability in front of an audience, but put them in front of other musicians, and it's the tight-lipped, stone-cold fucking cool act, a total zero-sum game. God forbid one artist show weakness in front of another."

We say good-bye, I promise to call or text, and as I watch Sara's car disappear into the wintery-dark streets of Chicago, I know exactly what to do.

56 → revolution in their bones

"Five minutes," I say through the window, holding up five fingers. Shrug, hold up the other hand. "Maybe ten."

Penny hasn't moved since Sara left, just sits on her knees

in the driver's seat, staring at me through the window (which she refused to roll down for me). Sara must have really spooked her.

"Sorry, Penn. I'll explain when I get back."

At the main entrance the bouncer takes one look at me and shakes his head. I show him the SHTBCKT stamp on my hand, to which he says, "Nice try."

"I was just here, like, five minutes ago. You don't remember?"

He throws a quick but pointed gaze across the street, where a police cruiser idles silently, parking lights on, cab lights darkened.

Shit's about to go down in this bucket.

The bouncer says, "Beat it, kid," and I head through the side parking lot, down the street a full block until reaching the alley behind Windy City Limits, where I double back behind the buildings. Hustle between dumpsters and fire escapes, avoid puddles of God knows what, and in my head, Parish's words weigh heavily: *I've never seen that picture in my life.*

I think about the masks we wear, who we wear them around; I think about what Sara said, how musicians are vulnerable in front of an audience, but "tight-lipped, stone-cold fucking cool" around other musicians. Say, in the greenroom of a venue at which you regularly perform. Say, in the presence of another fledgling local musician, one who has very clear opinions about his fellow fledgling local musicians.

I find Parish leaning against the dirty brick wall, smoking a cigarette.

"Hey."

"Hey," he says, like we're old friends, like we'd planned to meet back here all along. I hand him the photograph, which he accepts without question. "'When he approaches the light his eyes will be dazzled, and he will not be able to see anything at all, of what are now called realities.'"

"What?"

"'Allegory of the Cave.'" Parish takes a long draw, exhales into the cold air, and then slides down the wall until he's sitting on pavement. "Plato. You know it?"

In ninth grade I'd gone through a bit of a philosophy phase: paradoxes and Nietzsche mostly, but with a soupçon of *Cogito, ergo sum* for good measure. At that age, philosophy is a rite of passage and, like a new photographer taking pictures of dead leaves or books on the beach, my philosophical output was little more than mimicry.

"Picture yourself at the back of a cave," says Parish. "You were born in this cave, it's all you know. You're all tied up so you can't move, not even your head. All you've *ever* seen is the wall in front of you. Behind you is a fire, and between you and that fire is this little path. People walking around, carrying stuff up over their heads. Now, you can't turn around, but because of the fire, you see their flickering shadows on the wall. And since you've never *seen* the people walking, never *seen* those objects they're carrying, never *seen* the fire itself— that shadow on the wall? That's your reality. And those people walking around, free to leave the cave at will, trading in that little fire for the great big sun, they're the enlightened ones. They know true reality." He pauses a moment, smokes, stares at the boy in the photo. "Abraham and I used to talk about Plato's cave all the time."

All my hairs stand on end. "What?"

Parish holds up the photograph, points to the guy in it.

"My little brother, Abe. He was obsessed with the 'Allegory of the Cave.' We used to marvel at those Greek philosophers, man. Aristotle, Plato, Socrates, those guys had entire revolutions in their bones, but they weren't flashy about it. The 'Allegory of the Cave' is a written-out dialogue between two dudes. Just a conversation."

There are times when I wonder if everything that's ever happened in my life right down to the finest seed of minutiae was planted on purpose, in *that exact spot*, and *that one too*, so that one day a tree might grow tall and mighty, affording me a shade of acumen I might otherwise have missed entirely.

"The 'oral exchange of sentiments, observations, opinions, or ideas,'" I say, stepping into that shade, recalling a conversation from so many months ago; and later that night, after Circuit had finished fucking with my brain, an encounter with his neighbor, who talked of God and caves, who lovingly rubbed the ears of a shape-shifter named Abraham.

"What's that?" asks Parish.

"Definition of *conversation*," I say in a breath.

"You know that shit off the top of your head?" Parish doesn't wait for an answer. "Sentiments, observations, and what else?"

"Opinions and ideas."

Parish smiles up at me. "I didn't catch your name."

I step up against the wall, slide down next to him, and offer a handshake.

57 → *Philip Parish, a conversation*

"I'm Noah."

"Philip. You want a cigarette?"

"No thanks."

"Smart man, Noah."

"Yeah, I mean—never really understood smoking, no offense."

"Nah, I mean Noah from the Bible. All buddy-buddy with God, saw clouds no one else saw. Even when everyone laughed at him building that ark, he went on and did it anyway. I do wonder about those animals, though. All cramped up for days on end."

"Penguins and polar bears."

"What now?"

"When I was a kid I went to Sunday school with a friend, and the lesson was Noah's ark. Of course all the other kids think I'm some big expert because *I'm Noah*, so just to push back, I ask the Sunday school teacher if penguins and polar bears were on the ark too. She says, 'Yes, all God's animals were present and accounted for.' So I ask, 'How did they get there?' And she's all, 'Get where?' and I say, 'Look, I can buy the old man single-handedly built a boat the size of a freighter, and I can buy the apocalyptic flood, and I can even buy God's animals-first philosophy, but can you please explain how two representatives from every species, separated by continents, oceans, and ecosystems, all gathered in the same place at the same time?'"

"So what'd she say?"

"She looks me right in the eye and says, 'He picked them up.'"

"She did not."

"I was like, 'Come again?' And she's all, 'Whatever animals weren't already in the vicinity were picked up by Noah later on.' So then she tries to move on to the post-flood rainbow, but I'm like, 'Hold up. Were they on rafts?' And she's like, 'Who?' And I'm like, 'These animals that weren't in Noah's vicinity, did they build rafts?' And she says, 'Now you're being ridiculous,' so I'm like, 'Tell that to those poor animals, just floating along on a wing and a prayer.'"

"The balls on you."

"Anyway, my friend invited me back the following week, I said thanks, but I was busy fishing for hoary marmots."

"What're those?"

"They're like—these giant squirrels that live in Alaska."

"Get the fuck out. Giant Alaskan squirrels?"

"Hoary marmots, look 'em up."

"I'll do that."

"Here's something else weird. The National Oceanic and Atmospheric Administration—the country's leading authority on all things oceanic—goes by the acronym NOAA, pronounced like my name."

"Really?"

"Their entry on Wikipedia actually says, 'NOAA warns of dangerous weather.'"

"How do you know all this?"

"I write these things—Concise Histories. It doesn't matter. It's a long story."

"Which is it?"

"It's a long story that doesn't matter."

"All right then, my turn for a story. Actually, first off . . . how old are you?"

"Sixteen."

"Sixteen, shit. All right, let's start here. When I was your age, I was high *all* the time. Weed mostly, then meth, and eventually heroin. I was a drop-dead junkie. Always high, always alone. And this didn't fly with Abe. He was a year younger than me, a good kid. Only thing he loved more than going to church was bugging me to come with him. I was just like . . . what's the point? But he kept asking, so I finally came up with a solution. Here I had this lonely brother, doing his thing all by himself. And here I was, doing my thing all by myself, both of us lonely as all get-out. Why not—"

"Shit."

"Yeah. So I tell him about my idea to trade time with each other. He gets high with me, I go to church with him. *Just the once*, I told him. Fucking stupider than stupid."

"That's him in the photo?"

"Yeah."

"So what happened?"

"I went to church with him, necktie and all. I remember like it was yesterday. Preacher talked about innocence. You know who Pontius Pilate was, right?"

"Know the name."

"So Jesus is brought to trial, and Pilate, he's basically the judge. But he's conflicted, see, because he thinks Jesus is innocent, but this crowd of people wants him dead—and not just dead, but crucified. That's a brutal death, all manner of ways crucifixion can kill you. Blood loss, shock, organ failure, exhaustion, starvation, even . . . but you know what most books list as the actual cause of death?"

"What?"

"Asphyxiation. You're just hanging there, choking, flat-out unable to breathe, until *phht*—you're dead, man. So here's Pontius Pilate with a decision to make. Go with his gut? Or go with the crowd?"

"I think I know how this story ends."

"Right. But get this. There's this line in Matthew, says just before Pilate hands over Jesus to be crucified, he washes his hands, claiming to be 'innocent of this man's blood.' But I think, deep down, Pilate knew. He didn't kill Jesus with those freshly washed hands of his, but he may as well have."

"You think?"

"Say you're inside a room with a bunch of people. It's dark and there's only one door. Let's say it's your house, even, and you are intimately familiar with the surroundings. And you know that directly on the other side of that single door is a sheer drop off a cliff. But you open it anyway. First person steps through, *phht*, dead. Next person steps through, *phht*, dead. Now, you didn't push them off the cliff, but you knew what would happen when you opened the door. So who do you think is to blame?"

"So, like—were these people blindfolded?"

"Come on."

"Also, if that's the only door, how did we get inside the room to begin with?"

"You get what I'm saying, though, right? You *knew* what was on the other side, and you opened the door anyway.

That's what Pontius Pilate did. That's what *I* did with that trade. I opened a door, knowing the cliff was on the other side. And out my brother walked."

"That why you picked the name?"

"Philip Parish. Pontius Pilate. Same initials, same fates. Sometimes a thing stares you in the face until you pick it up."

"But you're clean now?"

"Yeah."

"When did that happen?"

"Few years after Abe got hooked. I saw what was happening, how he was changing. It's like that cave, see. Everything dulls around the edges, turns to shadow, stays that way so long you start thinking the shadow is the real thing. I don't know how I did it, but I climbed out of that cave right on up into the blazing sunlight. I tried bringing Abe with me. For years I tried. Figured I'd been there before, knew the way out. He tried a couple times, got clean once. But it didn't last."

"*The sun is too bright.*"

"I found this photo in his nightstand. I don't know when he took it, and I don't know what he planned on doing with it, but . . . anyway."

"The sunlit narrative."

"The what?"

"In my class, you talked about the shaded narrative. How in songwriting, you write the mood of a thing rather than the thing itself. Which seems a little like the 'Allegory of the Cave,' right? Those guys only saw the shadow of things on the wall, not the actual things."

"Sure."

"But that day, you talked about another type of writing."
"Yeah."
"Philip."
"Yeah."
"What happened to your brother?"

58 ➜ and the bird sang

There was a bird in a tree outside the apartment in which Abraham Parish lived, and it would not quit singing, *like birds do*, says Philip, and it was on a Tuesday, he remembers, because Stacy at the Shell station gave him two-for-one jelly doughnuts, and Stacy only works Tuesdays (*she's a student, I think*), and so Philip arrived at his brother's house that morning, an extra jelly doughnut for Abe, and he walked past the tree with that singing bird, *la-la-la, it sang and sang*, and he walked up three flights of stairs, the shirt sticking to his back from the heat of the day, and, reaching the top floor, he knocked on the door of his brother's apartment, *Abe, it's me, you better be up and at 'em*, because Philip had just gotten his brother on with him at Sanders Drywall, and *it was a shit job, but a shit job's a job*, and his brother was *really trying to dig himself out of this hole, see, he needed this job*, but after a few minutes and no answer, Philip pulled a key out of his wallet, one he rarely used, but one that *weighed a brick*, and he opened the door and walked inside, *Abe, where are you?*, and it was a small apartment, not much ground to cover, and Philip was down the hall in no time, *Abe?*, and opened the bedroom door, *Abe?*, and *I saw what I saw, man, I saw him, man, just lying there, my little brother on his bed, on his back, skin as blue as the fucking ocean, just staring at the fucking ceiling like he's waiting on it to collapse on top of him*, and *there are all manner of ways drugs can kill you, but my brother, Abe—in death, just like in life, he followed Jesus, man, choked on his own damn spit*, and *Abe*, and *Abe, my God, don't leave me here alone*, and *Abe, look what I did*, and Philip Parish turned and ran from his brother's room, from the tiny apartment, down three flights of stairs, and he felt blood on his hands, *I'd squeezed the shit outta that doughnut*, and he collapsed on the lawn, to his knees, praying, yelling, *I really don't know which*, crying and crying, *just crying so hard, I am all alone. . . .*

And the bird sang.

59 → hey there, slugger

Penny: One of the French fry eaters has a
        staring problem

Penny: Strange brood, these fried potato people

Penny: That sounded weird

Penny: Okay wait a sec

Penny: The girl with the staring problem is approaching the car

Penny: Actually. I think it's the car she's staring at. Not me

Penny: Okay, um, Noah where are you?

Penny: This girl is literally climbing up on the hood

Penny: Mayday

Penny: Mayday

Penny: SOS

Penny: The French fry eater is ON TOP of the car. Repeat

Penny: ON TOP OF THE CAR

Penny: WHERE ARE YOU???

Penny: Look I know we've had our differences

Penny: But whatever you're doing in there,
COME OUTSIDE NOW

Penny: I've got my pepper spray, but I could use
backup

Penny: OK there you are, thank God

Penny: Wait. Do you know this girl????

Penny: Until further notice, I am shunning you.

Penny: Consider yourself shunned. Starting now.

◀━IIIIIII━▶

No one shuns like Penny when she puts her mind to it. Silent treatment the whole drive back to Iverton, and once we get home, I watch her storm through the yard and sneak inside the house. I sit in the car for a second, reread her texts, pull my phone out of the charger, and lean my head against the seat.

"Well, that was a night."

The smell of Parish's cigarettes linger. Listening to his story felt like holding a vessel and watching the poor guy empty himself into it, and by the time he'd finished, he could barely breathe, he was so exhausted. The way he talked about his brother, even the gentleness with which he spoke the name *Abe*—like if he wasn't careful, it might run off his tongue never to return—reminds me of how I've recently started thinking of Penny:

From his roost in the backseat, Mark Wahlberg yawns audibly.

"Terribly sorry if we interrupted your beauty sleep." I twist around to face him; he looks back at me with that head tilt like he understands every word. "What in the world happened to you, Fluff?"

He sits on those strangely youthful haunches, staring at me like ¯_(ツ)_/¯.

Outside, Mark Wahlberg follows me up the lawn, through the front door, and then scurries off to Penny's room. I take the steps two at a time, extra cautious as I pass the guest bedroom. It's after two a.m., so if Uncle Orville did in fact arrive around one, he's probably asleep, but still—would suck to get caught this late in the game.

Safely in the confines of my own bedroom, it hits me how tired I am. I pull off my jacket, my boots, my Navy Bowie, and crawl into my warm bed.

Very warm. Like, really very warm.

"Hey there, slugger."

Scream my lungs out, and Uncle Orville laughs, and Mark

Wahlberg comes bounding into the room, barking for all the world like a Rottweiler, and my parents are in the room stat, wide-eyed and frizz-haired, and Orville climbs out of my bed in nothing but skintight leopard-print briefs, and Dad whispers, "God, Orville," and my uncle stretches and yawns, all, "Should I put on a pot of coffee, then?"

Without dressing, Uncle Orville makes his way downstairs, presumably to start some coffee, while I have it out with my parents. Much as I hate lying to them, I could hardly tell the truth, that I'd taken their twelve-year-old daughter and the family dog to a bar in Chicago, where I'd left them in the car so I could use a fake ID to track down a local musician about the photograph he dropped in my class at the Magazine Mega Gala, oh, and also, I think I'm in love with this girl who climbed on top of my car.

So I say I couldn't sleep. I say I went to the basement to watch a movie, and that Uncle O must have arrived while I was down there. I ask why he was even in my room to begin with, hadn't Dad cleaned out the guest room for this exact purpose? "Yes, I cleaned out the guest room," says Dad, and then he says Mom just forgot to notify Uncle Orville of the change of plans, to which Mom says she thought Dad was going to let him know. Scratching of heads, non-apology apologies, and we go downstairs to iron things out with Orville (who, gulping the coffee, is either immune to caffeine or in such a constant state of hype it's impossible to tell). "Just a mix-up," we say, "totally our bad," et cetera, and Mom goes to bed, and Dad ushers Uncle Orville to the guest room.

Finally alone, staring down at my bed, all I can see is Uncle Orville in those leopard-print briefs. I strip the sheets, toss them in the hamper, plop down on the bare mattress, and in the darkness of my room I stare up at the ceiling: I think of caves and dogs and Abrahams and Noahs, of birds, of angels in songs and demons in deeds, of shaded and sunlit narratives, of all the doors I've opened for others in full knowledge of the cliff on the other side. And I think of canoes.

Penny must have heard the commotion—but she never left her room.

60 ➜ *fabrics and flapjacks*

Hovering.

Look down at myself in Circuit's bed, on my back, Abraham next to me, barking, total silence, the drenched figure in the corner who will not turn around, the swirling air, a tornado of brilliant colors, letters seeping from walls, floating in complete chaos until some invisible hand reorders them, shoves them across the room, and those two words are so close, I can feel their colors on my face: *STRANGE FASCINATION*. And I am in my body again, eyelids fluttering, and I breathe for the first time in years.

Waking up on a bare mattress is bad enough; waking up on a bare mattress in a cold sweat, having had the same stupid dream every night for months, is the absolute worst.

It's Wednesday, first day of break, and by all accounts I should be enthusiastic about the next couple days. Unfortunately, my uncle's presence in the house combined with the ticking clock of my college deadline makes enthusiasm tough.

I'm about to get up, when I rub my hand across the bare mattress, and it's weird, but I have that sudden sensation like when your left arm falls asleep to the point of total numbness, and you touch it with your right hand, and even though your right hand feels the touch, your left arm feels nothing at all.

It's like touching someone else's arm.

I shake it off, shower, get dressed, head downstairs. "Hey there, slugger." Uncle Orville, still in his robe and little else, is literally flipping pancakes on a griddle. "Saw your dad's cereal options in the pantry, figured I'd take matters into my own hands. Making my world-famous flapjacks. You want some?"

"Thanks," I say, grabbing an apple from a bowl on the counter. "But I have to eat and run."

"School's out, right?" Uncle Orville turns off the stove, pours maple syrup on a tall stack, and digs in.

"I have a chiropractor appointment."

"Oh, right," he says with a mouthful. "The back injury."

On the drive to Dr. Kirby's office, I replay the conversation with my uncle; he didn't put air quotes around "back injury," but it sure sounded like he wanted to.

The thought of returning home after my appointment, of going back to Uncle Orville's half-naked flapjack parade, is downright crushing. Luckily, I hadn't planned on returning home just yet.

"Yo," says Alan, climbing into my car. He grabs my phone from the console, scrolls through my Bowie catalog to find "Space Oddity."

"So how'd it go?" he asks.

I pull out of the Rosa-Haases' driveway. "How'd what go?"

"The chiropractor, dude."

"Oh. Fine." Dr. Kirby did say he saw "a lot of progress," which sort of calls into question the actual state of my back, but maybe also the actual state of his degree. "He says things are looking up."

Alan sighs in that dramatic way he does and looks out the window.

"What," I say.

"Nothing."

"Come on, what."

He shifts in his seat so he's staring at me while I drive. "Just don't treat me like I'm everyone else, okay? That's all. Don't treat me like I'm everyone else."

"What are you talking about?"

"Look, I get it. You felt backed into a corner, all this pressure to be some big swimming stud, and you wanted out."

Verbal denial, at this moment, would only sound like confirmation. So I say nothing.

"Fine," says Alan; he turns back to the window for a second, but thinks twice. "One last thing, and then I'm done, and I'm only saying this now because I'll regret it later if I don't."

"Go on, then."

"You're my best friend, Noah. Since we were twelve and I came out to you, and we whizzed out the window like the tiny bosses we were. You're not everyone else to me. To me, you're you. And I shouldn't be everyone else to you. Four days ago you apologized for not being there for me, and I one hundred percent accept that apology, but part of being there for someone is not bullshitting them. You don't wanna tell me something, fine. Just don't blatantly lie about it and expect me to go along with that, okay?"

"Okay."

"Okay. So. How's your back?"

"There's nothing wrong with my back, and there never has been."

Alan rolls down the car window. "Cool. Now, let's whiz out these windows."

◀▬▬▶

On the way to Ambrosia's Bed & Breakfast, I recount to Alan the details of my conversation with Mr. Elam, and to Alan's credit he never once shifts back to the fact I've been perpetuating a lie since summer. He doesn't care that I don't want to talk about it; he just doesn't want me to lie to him.

"One plus one plus one equals one," Alan says, repeating the last line of my story, about how Mr. Elam's wife loved math, and how it factored into their family motto.

"Yeah."

"But it doesn't."

"Alan."

"What?"

I shake my head. "Almost hard to believe you were in remedial math."

"You're saying one plus—"

"I'm saying *of course* it doesn't equal one. I'm saying if it was a family motto, it probably meant they were a family of three, but still one family."

"Okay, that makes sense. But I'd like to go on record as not appreciating the remedial math dig."

"It is so recorded."

"What happened next?" asks Alan.

"He'd basically given me his whole life story and not once mentioned a kid. So I asked if he had one."

"And?"

"And he showed me the door. That was Monday. Yesterday he was a no-show for the walk."

"Maybe he wasn't feeling well. Maybe his knee gave out or something. That happens sometimes to old people."

"That happens sometimes to any people."

"Wait, isn't that it?" Alan points to the passing AMBROSIA'S BED & BREAKFAST sign in the front yard.

"Yeah, I'm gonna drive his route just in case, see if we can find him that way first."

"Why?"

"Because I don't have the code, Alan, which means we're ringing the doorbell, and I don't know who's going to answer, or if anyone even *will* answer, nor do I know how they'll respond to my request to see one of their tenants because I've never known someone who lived in a bed-and-breakfast, so it's kind of foggy protocol, okay?"

I can almost hear Alan's blink. "It's exhausting, isn't it?" he says.

"What."

"Being you."

"You have no idea."

I follow the route from Mill Grove to Ashbrook, both of us keeping our eyes peeled for Mr. Elam. Even with the heat on, the cold outside is beginning to seep through the windows. I crank it up a notch and zip up my jacket.

"So," I say, eyes on the road. "You seeing anybody?"

"Am I *seeing anybody*? No, I'm not seeing anybody. Why, you looking?"

"You wish." One hand on the steering wheel, I raise the other arm and kiss a bicep. "But seriously, you used to be, like—a serial dater."

"I do love that Cap'n Crunch, though."

"Come on. Talk to me. Let's Dean and Carlo this bitch."

"Noah."

"Alan."

"We're currently freezing our walnuts off inside your fun gay ballsack, driving around the neighborhood, looking for some old guy with a goiter."

"Dude, some respect."

"Sorry. Looking for *Mr. Elam*. Point is, I can't Dean and Carlo under such conditions."

"What about Len?" I ask. "Or was that like a one-time thing?"

"Len who?"

"Kowalski."

"What about him?"

"Len Kowalski."

"Just saying his name over and over isn't really helping, yo."

"You know, your make-out session at the Longmire party. I didn't know if maybe someth—"

"Hold up," says Alan. "Me and Len Kowalski."

"Yeah."

"You saw me and Len Kowalski making out at the end-of-summer party at the Longmires'."

"See, once you start saying his name, it's hard to stop, right?"

"Len Kowalski?"

"Okay, let's not get carried away," I say.

"That little guy used to egg your house, or did you forget?"

"Alan, I'm not mad. People do all sorts of stuff they can't remember when they're high."

"Okay, look. I'm honored to know that in some alternate universe you believe I made out with Len Kowalksi, and you still want to be friends with me. But dude, come on. None out of ten."

"Really?"

"Afraid this falls squarely in the category of one of your changes. Never happened." It's quiet for a second, while Alan blows into his cupped hands. "You ever considered that, though?"

"Considered what."

"An alternate universe."

In the darkness of my desk drawer at home, I imagine an elegant list of four possibilities entitled *WTF HAPPENED*. "Sort of."

"And?"

"I don't think so."

"I mean, I know it's out-there, but—it's a possibility, right?"

Shortly after writing my Concise History on the birth of the word *multiverse*, something had occurred to me that made that particular explanation, while not entirely impossible, highly improbable.

"What year did the Cubs win the World Series?" I ask.

"2016, I think?"

"And how long did they go between World Series wins?"

"I don't know, like three hundred years?"

"And what happened on September eleventh?"

Alan gives me a look like, *Come on*.

I say, "And the President of the United States is . . . ?"

"Please, Noah. Don't make me say his name."

"Exactly."

"What's your point?"

"Point is, all the things that have changed revolve around me. I just can't believe that's how a parallel universe works, that my dog, who could barely walk across the living room without crapping himself, can now leap tall buildings in a single bound, but the Cubs couldn't bring one home for a hundred and eight years."

"I think you're wrong about that."

"It was definitely a hundred and eight."

"Not that," says Alan. "I mean your logic. I don't know much about, you know . . ."

"Quantum theory?"

Alan nods. "But your entire conclusion negates the experience of Mr. Elam, Philip Parish, the Fading Lady—"

"Fading Girl."

"Whatever. You know next to nothing about the origins of your Strange Fascinations. All you're thinking about is how they relate to you and your life, but guess what? They have lives of their own. Maybe they're dealing with similar shit, only you don't know because you don't know *them*."

"Penny hasn't changed. I know her."

Alan takes a beat; then: "Do you?"

I can almost see her drinking that macchiato, claiming to have been born in the wrong decade. "So what, then? Penny, Mr. Elam, the Fading Girl, Philip Parish, the ghost of Mila Henry—you're suggesting all of us, as a group, spontaneously fell into a wormhole and traveled to a parallel universe?"

"What I'm saying is, to *you* the changes revolve around Noah Oakman. But what if they don't?"

Alan was right. How did I know the Fading Girl hadn't changed, or Philip Parish, or Mila Henry? I didn't. I'd taken what I knew of them, how they intersected with *my* life— a video, a photograph, a drawing—and condensed the unknown complexities of human beings down to single-cell organisms.

For all I knew, Mr. Elam once had an urn with the ashes of his pet rhinoceros.

Alan's challenge still hangs in the air when I pull to a stop outside Ambrosia's. Not surprisingly, Mr. Elam wasn't out walking. I shut off the engine, and for a second we just sit there in the silent coldness.

"So." Alan blows into his hands, his teeth a symphonic chatter. "Ringing the doorbell, yeah?"

I don't know if there are other worlds out there, worlds where Alan hooked up with Len Kowalski, where Mr. Elam's wife never got cancer, where I never followed Circuit that night. And while I may never know the possibilities of my many mirrored lives, I know the possibilities of this one.

I open my car door and climb out into the bitter cold. "Well, Alan, don't just stand there."

62 → floods

"Forgot to warn you," I whisper, ringing the doorbell. "He loves bourbon."

"Who?"

"Who do you think? Mr. Elam."

"Conveniently, I, too, love bourbon."

"But seriously, if we get in here today he'll give you bourbon and drink you under the table."

"Sweet. Let's get liquored up and talk more about wormholes. Space-time contingencies, phantom theories and shit."

"Quantum, Alan. It's quantum theory. And space-time continuums. Or *continua*, I suppose."

"Love it when you talk nerdy to me, yo."

The door opens and an older woman with long silvery hair, big bright eyes, and the permanent imprint of a smile says, "May I help you?"

All told, this woman is lit up with more youth than most kids I know put together.

"Yes," I say. "I'm here for— I was wondering about Mr. Elam."

"You're the one he's been walking with every day. Thank you for that." She angles her head up the stairs. *"I don't care what he says, Mr. George needs companionship more than he knows!"* She rolls her eyes, lowers her voice. "He's in a mood. Par for the course this time of year. You two, come in out of the cold and have some tea. I've got everything but those nasty dregs of the devil, Earl Grey."

I recognize her voice as the one who'd greeted us Monday when we'd first walked in. And for the second time I step into the warmth of the entryway, the old rugs and thin-slatted hardwoods and distant crackling hearths of Ambrosia's Bed & Breakfast wrapping me in its arms like a well-worn quilt.

"So he's okay, then?" I ask.

The woman's laugh is as bright as her eyes. "I don't suppose I would go *that* far. But yes, Mr. George is his usual amount of okay. I'm Ambrosia, by the way."

Alan and I take turns introducing ourselves, after which Miss Ambrosia ushers us into a nearby sitting room (the location of that crackling hearth) and then shuffles off to the kitchen for tea.

"This place is like . . ." Alan's eyes rove around the room— the gold-framed pastoral paintings, the dark wood of the coffee table, the grandfather clock, the fizzing flames in the oversized fireplace. I feel it too, a deep and instinctive urge, three words firmly planted in the kid-psyche: *Don't touch anything.*

Miss Ambrosia returns with a tray, which she sets on the coffee table. I have some vague recollection of drinking tea once: a soggy bag on a string, a few bitter sips, and I was out. But this is clearly a different experience altogether, almost ritualistic. There are saucers and strainers and multiple kettles and a little box of leaves (no bags or strings to be found), and just when I begin to wonder if Miss Ambrosia is messing with us, she says, "Four minutes to steep," sets a timer on her wristwatch, and smiles at us over the table.

It's weird for a second until Alan is all, "How 'bout dem Bears, though?"

"Alan."

Miss Ambrosia waves me off. "Big game tomorrow. You give me twenty points, I'll take the under. Best defense since '85, but the offensive line is a sieve, don't you think?"

Alan looks sideways at me, then says, "Ohhh-kay, see, we don't actually speak football? Yeah, I was just being a douche."

"*Alan.*"

"It's quite all right," Miss Ambrosia says. "I enjoy the look on young people's faces when they see I know a thing or two about sports. Football is my favorite, though. Very strategic game. Not to mention all the skull-cracking."

A surprise a minute, this one.

"So no football," she says. "What sports do you like?"

Sometimes you're in a room, talking sports with the elderly owner of a bed-and-breakfast while waiting on your loose-leaf tea to steep, and you wonder if life is inherently this random, or if you are.

"I like baseball," I say.

"Camp Cubbie, yo."

Miss Ambrosia looks from Alan back to me. "Camp Cubbie?"

I completely forgot about Camp Cubbie. "It's nothing. Just this thing my dad put on when we were little kids—like a club—to make sure we grew into good Cubs fans."

"Worked like a charm on that one," says Alan, pointing at me. "Not so much on me. I mean, I get bits and pieces of different sports. Like football, for example. I know what a touchdown is."

"That's a start," says Miss Ambrosia.

"And a down, I think."

"Very astute," she says.

"Also a sack," says Alan, a coy smile growing on his face. "I know all about sacks."

Before he can move on to his go-to sports metaphor about scoring with balls, I say, "Miss Ambrosia—"

"Just Ambrosia is fine," she says.

"Okay. Ambrosia. We really appreciate the tea and whatnot, but we're here to see Mr. Elam. I can't really go into—"

The alarm on Ambrosia's watch goes off, and she's back in action. Before Alan and I know it, we're balancing little saucers on our knees, trying not to clank the teacups around like the complete amateurs we are.

"*Pure,*" says Ambrosia between sips. "That's the one word I use to describe a good cuppa. How do you boys like it?"

I cough, wipe my mouth with my sleeve. "Very pure."

"Pure as the *driven snow,*" says Alan in a low voice.

"Alan."

"Will you please stop saying my name like that?"

"Will you please grow up for like a half hour?" I take a

giant sip for dramatic effect, which ends up scorching my tongue and throat.

Ambrosia smiles warmly over her saucer. "I like you boys. You remind me of my own when they were your age. Not without bickering, but that's to be expected from those you love."

"Makes sense," says Alan. "Noah's basically in love with me, so . . ."

The clinking china gives way to the ticking grandfather clock, which gives way to the popping fire, and even though we're in no real hurry, I'm feeling a pressing sense of urgency. "Ambrosia . . ."

"You would like to see Mr. Elam," she says, sipping her tea.

"If possible, yes."

She nods once—sets her saucer on the coffee table, stands, and leaves the room.

"Dude," says Alan.

"What?"

"You pissed her off."

"I didn't piss her off."

Alan sips his tea with an elevated pinkie. "She gives us tea, pure as a joyous virgin, and this is how you repay her."

"Shut up, Alan."

Ambrosia returns with a manila envelope, hands it to me, her smile gone. "He asked not to see you anymore."

I stand up, take the envelope, try to process how it relates to Mr. Elam not wanting to see me. "Okay. Is it . . . just me?"

"It's got your name on it," says Ambrosia.

"No, I meant—it's just me he doesn't want to see?"

"Yes," she says; it sounds like an apology.

"Okay. Well. Okay, then. Thanks for the tea."

Alan and I head toward the door when Ambrosia says, "'On that day all the springs of the great deep burst forth, and the floodgates of the heavens were opened. And rain fell on the earth forty days and forty nights.' Genesis, chapter seven." The old woman's voice is packed with expectation, like we're both in on the same secret. "You know, in the Bible, Elam was Noah's grandson."

A beat of silence as this information sinks in. "Okay, that's weird," says Alan. "Am I the only one who thinks that's weird?"

Ambrosia puts a hand on my shoulder. "Thank you. For helping him."

"I didn't do anything. We just talked."

"Sometimes talking *is* doing something, Noah. You provided a lonely man with company. And company can be a restorative salve."

When I think about Mr. Elam's room—from the photos with no people, to the uniform leather-bound books, to his dead cat's urn—the entire place radiates loneliness, and I can't help but think the room is a reflection of the man.

"What happened to him?" I ask. "I mean—I know about his wife dying of cancer and all, but . . ."

Ambrosia flinches. "Is that what he told you?"

I nod, and she quietly begins a story, the story of a family on their way to Milwaukee for Thanksgiving, "going to see Mr. George's sister," she says, driving on I-94 when a truck driver heading in the opposite direction fell asleep at the wheel. "That truck drove right through the median and head-on into Mr. George's car, killing Barbara and Matthew on impact, and it's a flat-out miracle Mr. George got out with nothing but a limp. But he doesn't see it that way. He thinks he should have died in their place, as if that's even the way it works."

"Matthew?"

Ambrosia nods. "His son."

I stand there gripping the manila envelope, letting the words of Miss Ambrosia wash over me. "Earlier, when you said Mr. Elam was in a mood. You said it was par for the course this time of year."

"I'm afraid George doesn't feel he has much to be thankful for," says Ambrosia. And even though she's still smiling, she's also crying, the springs of the great deep bursting forth. "Do me a favor," she says. "Check in with him next week? Let's see if we can prove him wrong."

Alan and I walk back to the car in silence, my thoughts stretching to many places: the cold air in my lungs, the pavement beneath my shoes, the wind in my hair; they stretch to the sky, where the winter-gray clouds shift, break apart; they stretch to a room of fragile things, wholly insulated from the tempest outside.

"You gonna open it?"

"What?" I ask, only now realizing we're back inside my car, sitting in its chilly quiet. Alan nods toward the manila envelope in my hands; I look down at my name scrawled the way Mr. Elam walks: methodical, determined, fixed.

This, it seemed to say. I really mean *this*.

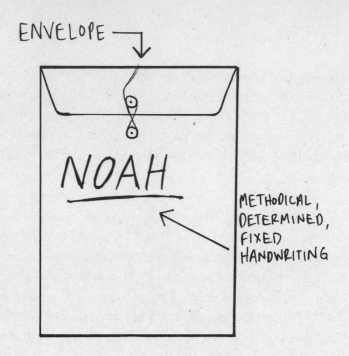

ENVELOPE

NOAH

METHODICAL,
DETERMINED,
FIXED
HANDWRITING

I unwind the string, open the flap, and pull out a box-ing ticket signed by Muhammad Ali, a basketball card signed by Michael Jordan, and the ancient baseball card of a kid named Merkle.

"Holy shit," says Alan, leaning across the console.

Outside snow is falling, heavy now, coming down in those white winter sheets, and I say, "Good thing it's not rain," but Alan isn't listening, he's too busy googling images of Ali's au-tograph to check if it matches.

It will. And so will Jordan's.

I'm not sure Alan even sees the baseball card.

Generally speaking, people are remembered for one of two reasons: a string of successes or a singular failure. After some digging, I'm confident Fred Merkle belongs in neither category, which might explain his relative anonymity.

October 14, 2003. Cubs vs. Marlins, Game 6 of the National League Championship Series (NLCS). The Cubs take a 3–0 lead into the bottom of the eighth inning—five outs away from their first trip to the World Series since 1945—when a fan named Steve Bartman interferes with a possible foul ball catch. The Marlins go on to score eight runs in the inning, winning that game and the next one, and eventually, the World Series. Bartman's interference is widely considered the first domino in the Cubs' 2003 postseason demise, and if you listen closely, lingering echoes of his name can still be heard in the darker corners of Wrigley Field, an edifice haunted by apparitions as thick as the ivy lining its outfield walls.

In the 2015 NLCS, the Mets, led by second baseman Daniel Murphy, sweep the Cubs four games to none. Murphy sets a postseason record for consecutive games with a home run (six), and goes on to be named MVP of the series. Shockingly, he is not the most hated Murphy in Cubs' lore.

Game 4 of the 1945 World Series against the Tigers; local Chicago tavern owner Billy Sianis is asked to leave the stadium due to the stench of his pet goat. As Sianis walks out, he reportedly states, "Them Cubs, they ain't gonna win no more." The Cubs lost that series, and would not play in another one for seventy-one years.

His goat's name was Murphy.

Many Cubs fans attribute the unprecedented misfortune of their club, including the Steve Bartman Incident as it came to be known, to the Curse of the Billy Goat. But I don't think the Cubs' misfortune begins with names like Bartman and Murphy. I think it begins with a lesser-known name.

1908. Final game of the regular season, it's Cubs versus Giants, when a controversial late-inning baserunning error by a nineteen-year-old newcomer named Fred Merkle costs the Giants the game. Cubs fans are ecstatic, hailing the error (dubbed the unfortunate Merkle's Boner) a godsend. The Cubs head into the 1908 World Series with momentum and win the whole thing. Many deem this the dawning of an age in which the Cubs will reign supreme. Words like *dynasty* and *destiny* and *domination* are not uncommon when talk of their future arises. *Merkle's Boner?* say Cubs fans. *More like Merkle's Miracle, amarite? Slap that* MERKLES HAPPEN *bumper sticker on your shiny new Model T and praise the Lord some dumb nineteen-year-old rookie misran the bases.*

False.

In many ways Fred Merkle's baseball career mimicked that of the Cubs. After 1908 his teams reached the World Series in 1911, 1912, 1913, 1916, and 1918, and, just like the Cubbies (and even once *as* a Cubbie), he lost them all.

But here's where things get interesting. Take a look at what happens to those teams that *beat* a Fred Merkle team:

After winning against Merkle in the 1911 and 1913 World

Series, the Philadelphia Athletics lose the 1914 Series in highly suspicious fashion, dismantle the core of their team, and in two years' time, attain the worst winning percentage in modern baseball history.

After winning against Merkle in the 1918 World Series, the Boston Red Sox do not win another World Series for eighty-five years, a losing streak only outmatched by . . .

The Chicago Cubs, coming off a remarkable regular season win over the New York Giants in which a nineteen-year-old newcomer may or may not have committed an error, beat the Detroit Tigers on October 14, 1908, to win their second consecutive World Series championship.

They would not win another for one hundred and eight years.

Generally speaking, people are remembered for one of two reasons: a string of successes or a singular failure. And while some might point to the controversial baserunning error of a nineteen-year-old kid and call it a singular failure, I don't buy it. I don't think Fred Merkle was a failure, and I don't think it was a simple case of one man's shit luck. Call it a curse, call it what you want, I think Merkle figured out a way to pass on that luck to whichever teams were unfortunate enough to beat him.

Fred Merkle died on March 2, 1956, at sixty-seven years of age.

He is buried in an unmarked grave.

In Chapter 17 of *Year of Me*, Cletus says to Nathan, "Sometimes I don't know what I'm writing until it's written. Sometimes I don't know what I'm thinking until I read it. And sometimes I don't know where I'm going until I'm there."

I knew Mr. Elam's gift scared me, but until now I had no idea how much.

I shift the laptop so it lines up evenly with the LED lamp. Across the desk, stacked nice and neat in the opposing corner, printed drafts; my work, my books, my bed, my chair, my room, my body in it, everything in its right place. But whatever comfort I normally glean from the simple order of things escapes me now.

I am thinking: of a man who keeps no pictures of people in his living space, ignores a friendly landlady, and shuns a new kid for getting too close; of a man whose only company is a collection of old memorabilia, his cat's ashes, and his bourbon; of a man whose most frequent motto is *when it's my time, it's my time*, who is fast approaching the anniversary of the day he lost everything, and who is giving away prized possessions. And I am thinking of an unmarked grave.

My phone buzzes. And buzzes again before I can get it out of my pocket. Then again before I can open my texts, and again while I'm reading them.

> Alan: Ali autographed ticket JUST LIKE YOURS
> going for $2200 on ebay

Alan: MJ AUTO GOING BETWEEN $800–1200

Alan: YOU ARE ROLLIN, YO

Alan: totes check out that rando baseball card, I
   bet it's worth bank too

Drop the phone on my desk, google the number for Ambrosia's, and when Ambrosia herself picks up, I tell her what was in the envelope, how I'm concerned for Mr. Elam.

"He's napping at the moment," she says. "Instructed me not to disturb him."

I tell her I'll try again, end the call, stare at the screen— and a thought occurs to me. Across the room I pull my hamper out of the closet, dig through pockets until I find what I'm looking for: the wrinkled-up paper Sara gave me last night.

This Can Only Get Better

Moby Dick Sucks

Alone or Lonely

I consider calling her, but the subject matter seems too sensitive. *Hey, so, about your dad* . . . No, this needs to happen in person.

I spend the next three minutes drafting a text, eventually landing on: Hey, it's Noah. The period, I think, is what really seals the deal with this one. The period says, So I'm not

hyper-anal or anything, but I care enough about you to punctuate this as an official sentence.

A few seconds after sending, I get the panic-inducing ". . ."

. . .

. . .

Just ". . ." for days.
Finally, a response.

   Sara: Noah, Noah, Noah.

I can't help but smile. She used a period.

◀▮▮▮▮▮▶

Sara removes her coat (which is caked in snow) and drops it
onto the floor.

"Did you walk over here?" I resist the urge to pick it up,
hang it neatly in the closet.

"Oh yeah," she says. "I love snow."

"You love snow."

"I adore snow. My love of snow runneth deep." Her eyes
land on the bare mattress. "Laundry day?"

"Something like that."

Sara plops down on my bed, while I sit at my desk and try
not to let my imagination run wild.

"You know those movies where the guy shows up on the
girl's front porch in some grand romantic gesture?" she says.

"Sure. *Say Anything*."

"See, that's a good one. I was thinking *Love Actually*, that bullshit scene where the dude shows up on her front porch with all those giant note cards confessing his love."

"Why is it a bullshit scene?"

"For starters, the girl he's there to woo is *married to his best friend*. Plus, in like the biggest plot hole ever, how does he even know she's answering the door? What's he gonna do if his friend answers?"

"Good point."

Sara nods. "Thing is—and don't think less of me—I could forgive everything if it had been snowing in that scene."

"Wow."

"Well, the way I see it, a guy shows up with note cards and a boom box means he's got some time on his hands. But a guy shows up with snow, that's either destiny or wizardry."

"Or damn fine meteorology."

"Exactly," says Sara. "All of which is hella sexy."

There's always a moment with the girls I've talked to where I see them assess the situation that is Noah Oakman. The extent of cleanliness and organization, the white and pastel, the right angles with which I've aligned my room: I know it's not the usual. And I'm okay with that, because it's how I like things.

But it's not for everyone.

Sara's eyes travel across those angles and colors now. "It's like your bedroom was directed by Wes Anderson," she says.

"I'll take that as a compliment."

"I bet he's super-anal too."

"Too?"

"Noah. Dude. You are clinically anal."

"I prefer lovably particular."

Her phone chimes from her bag, but she ignores it. "Your text said you needed some advice?"

I immediately second-guess my idea. I like Sara, but I don't know her well enough to know how she'll respond to this, and the thing is, I'd really like to get to know her that well, which may or may not happen depending on the outcome of the next few minutes.

I start with Mr. Elam and our walks, and the conversation we'd had earlier this week, and then the conversation Alan and I had with Ambrosia earlier today, and then I get to the contents of the envelope. "He's giving me all this stuff, things that are important to him, or used to be, anyway. And that anniversary is coming up, and Ambrosia said he doesn't think he has anything to be thankful for."

"Yeah."

"You should see his place, Sara. The only thing that even slightly resembles companionship is a jar with his dead cat's ashes. Anyway, I didn't know if . . ."

"My dad, you mean?"

A beat. "Look, I'm sorry. I shouldn't have even brought it up."

"It's okay. He never really . . . There were no specific warning signs with Dad. He never gave stuff away, not that I know of. He was always just . . . sad. As far back as I can remember, he was sad. Sometimes it just happens like that."

It's quiet now, and while part of me is relieved Sara didn't get up and walk out, the other part of me wishes she would so I could go ask Dad if he needs help making carrot butter or something, I mean shit. And this isn't schadenfreude; I feel no joy at Sara's misfortune. This is some other German word we haven't stolen yet, something that expresses a sense of appreciation for what you have when confronted with another person's have-not.

"We should do something, though," Sara says.

"I called over there. Ambrosia says he's napping, asked not to be disturbed."

"Wait." Sara sits up, scoots to the edge of the bed. "You said he had a cat?"

"Yeah. Herman. And judging from the gold-plated plaque, I'd say he *loved* that thing."

And now Sara is off the bed, slipping on her coat. "I'll be right back."

"Where are you going?"

She smiles, says nothing, and she's gone, leaving me to sit alone in my room going over all the ways I scared her off. I reread my history on Merkle, make a few adjustments, and at some point it occurs to me . . . *she'll be right back.*

Her house isn't far.

Shit.

I'm through the door of my bedroom, into the hallway, almost downstairs when I hear, "I'm telling you, Sara, there's nothing quite like jumping out of an airplane."

"No, I'm sure you're right, mister. It's just, we're in kind of a hurry."

"Please, call me Orville."

I take the steps two at a time, join Sara and Uncle Orville in the foyer.

"Well," says Orville, crossing his arms across his very tan, very bare chest. "I'll leave you kids to it, then." He winks at me, all, "Don't do anything I wouldn't do, slugger," and saunters off into the kitchen.

Only now, in the absence of Orville, do I see the cat in Sara's arms.

"Noah, this is Nike," she says. "Nike, Noah."

"We've met, actually." I grab my coat out of the closet. "Let's go."

HERE IS ➼ PART SIX

—Excerpt from Chapter 17 of Mila Henry's Year of Me

'Nowhere to go,' said Nathan.

When they'd first entered the diner, Nathan spoke as if the world was at his feet; now he spoke as someone bearing its weight on his back.

Cletus knew the feeling.

'Look,' Cletus said. 'You are a great artist.'

'Ha.'

'Don't *ha* me. You are. The lofty morons of the world may not see it. You probably won't live to *see* them see it, but believe me, generations from now they'll know.' Cletus held up the small canvas. 'They will see this painting hanging in an art gallery'—

'If galleries are still around by then.'

—'in Paris'—

'If Paris is still around by then.'

—'& they will stand in awe, shaking their heads at the miraculous oeuvre of Nathan . . . uh . . . what's your last name?'

'Brumbleberry.'

Oh boy, thought Cletus. He took a sip of water, cleared his throat, & tried to pick up the pieces of his little motivational speech. 'They'll, um, whisper the name—uh, well. They'll whisper *your* name in, you know, awe & what have you.'

A different waitress stopped by the table to drop off their check. Cletus studied it for a moment. 'How many pancakes did you eat, for crissake?'

'I don't know what I'm doing,' said Nathan. 'I have no one in my life & I have no idea what's next.'

Cletus set down the check, leaned across the table. 'OK, listen. I've had it with the brooding, so I'm going to let you in on two secrets. First, you have no one in your life because you're a miserable git & when you're not a miserable git, you're a completely insufferable git. I know because I'm one too. Guys like us will always be alone, that's fine—the trick is knowing the difference between being alone & being lonely. As for not knowing what's next . . . sometimes I don't know what I'm writing until it's written. Sometimes I don't know what I'm thinking until I read it. And sometimes I don't know where I'm going until I'm there. So I'll tell you what you do. Paint. Forget the lofty morons. Just paint, Nathan.' Cletus glanced at the check on the table. 'Now let's get out of this shithole.'

Together, Cletus & Nathan left the diner without paying.

Covered in snow, standing in front of Mr. Elam's door, I cradle a cat named Nike and consider the wise words of Cletus.

"Mr. Elam! Mr. Elam, open up!"

That Boston brownstone from my childhood vacation lingers, the scent of bookstores and herbal teas, and downstairs I hear the tender reprimands of Ambrosia, "Honey, you can't be up there right now," but I just knock and knock. "Mr. Elam!"

By any practical measure this idea is a long shot—I know that. "Nike likes people that like her," Sara said in the car on the way over. And I recalled a night from months ago, after following her brother home from the Longmire party, how Circuit had called the cat a "little pissant" and then roared in its face like a lion.

"Mr. Elam!"

The loud, satisfying clunk of the door unlocking; it opens a few inches, and Mr. Elam says nothing, just peers into the hallway with dusty red eyes, the eyes of someone with no one, and he looks like he hasn't slept in days.

"I have something for you."

He opens the door a little wider, remains silent.

"Her name is Nike," I say, holding out the cat, and Mr. Elam's eyes turn a little scared, but a little happy, too, and he says, "Okay," and then I hand over the cat, who doesn't make a sound.

"Also"—I pull out the envelope with my name scrawled on it, the boxing ticket and both signed cards inside—"I'm giving these back to you."

Mr. Elam takes them along with the cat and says, "Okay," and there's something about those eyes—like he actually couldn't be more scared, more surprised, more speechless, more content than he is in this moment.

"I don't think you're done with them," I say. "So I'm giving them back."

He nods once, looks at the cat. "Okay."

"Okay, then. That's it, I guess. See you tomorrow, Mr. Elam."

"Tomorrow's Thanksgiving."

"Yeah, I know. I'm thankful for you."

His red eyes well, and he runs a hand through the fur on the top of Nike's back, and that's when I know he'll be okay.

"Noah?"

"Yes."

"Thank you."

From the top of the stairs, I see the white glow of the sun off the snow as it reflects through the foyer window, and it's all so sad and beautiful, and I say, "You're going to be okay," and then I look him in the eye and say it again, willing it true. "You're going to be okay, Mr. Elam. I'll see you tomorrow."

Downstairs I give Ambrosia a quick hug, and I hear her words from earlier today, about Mr. Elam not thinking he had much to be thankful for, how we should try to prove him wrong. "It's a start," I whisper, and I'm out the door, into the cold air, thinking how thankful I am to have found this place even if I didn't know where I was going until I got here.

66 ➔ *moby dick sucks*

In the car on the way home I notice Sara's bag with the Melville patch, which reminds me of our run-in at the library on Halloween, and I don't know why I do it, since I already know the answer, but I ask what book she was there to check out.

"I'd heard about this collector's edition of *This Is Not a Memoir* that had some bonus content," she says. "Why?"

I say, "Nothing," and then, "No reason," but it is something, there is a reason, because the librarian that day told me no one had checked it out for ages, and when I think how timely it was—that Sara happened to be at the library that day at that exact time, that she happened to drop the slip of paper on the ground, that I happened to see it and pick it up—I wonder about those chances.

67 ➔ *alone or lonely*

"Could you please pass the yams?"

My sister must be the only twelve-year-old in the world to utter those six words in that order.

"Certainly," says Uncle Orville, passing an oversized platter of Dad's yams. "There you go, tiger."

Penny looks at me for a split second—I give her the Oakman Roll, a subtle expression of the eye we reserve for when Uncle Orville uses one of his pet names with us. She sees it; she looks away. And that's how I know my sister is still not talking to me. Not a single word since the incident in the Windy City Limits parking lot Tuesday night.

Penny takes the platter from Uncle Orville. "Thank you, Fred, darling."

Uncle O raises an eyebrow, looks around the table. "Who's Fred?"

I swallow a bite of Dad's perennial vegan dressing. "You are."

"I am?"

Penny says, "Yes, darling," and Orville says, "Okay, then," at which point Mom begins telling the table about Penny's obsession with *Breakfast at Tiffany's* until she's interrupted by my three-year-old cousin, Hannah, who decides now is the perfect time to take a poll on who we think would win in a fight between a tiger shark and a gorilla, at which point her little brother, Eli, chucks his dinner right off his high chair tray, points down at the floor, and unleashes a pterodactyl screech as if he hadn't just tossed the damn food himself, and all the while Uncle Orville is like, "Why am I Fred again?" and Dad is punching himself for "under-massaging" the autumn kale salad, and ahhhhh, the whimsical cacophony of the Thanksgiving table, a song of subtlety and refinement.

Also present for the cacophony: Dad's sister, Aunt Becky, and her husband, Uncle Adam, whose combined loins are responsible for Hannah and Eli; Mom and Uncle Orville's considerably younger foster sister, a student at U of C, whom, given our proximity in age, and the fact that she's got this scholarly attractive thing happening—by which I mean she uses words like *mise-en-scène* and *paralipsis* and *petrichor* in a sentence—I somewhat uncomfortably refer to as "Aunt" Jasmine; and Aunt Jasmine's new girlfriend, Noelle.

"It's a meditative sport, at its heart," says Uncle Orville.

Dad, coy smile in place, says, "Is skydiving really a sport, though?"

Uncle O gives him a look, which, if I had to guess, isn't that different from the way he must look at an airplane on the ground.

Even though Orville is Mom's brother, he and Dad have always operated like siblings, knowing just what buttons to push. And listening to them now—as Dad asks Orville about the "subtle strategies" of jumping out of a plane, and Orville asks Dad for the recipe to his *delectable* lentil beet loaf—I wonder about the ins and outs of family.

This morning, Mr. Elam had showed up just on time, our walk beginning with the trademark, "Well, kid, don't just stand there," and ending at the front stoop of Ambrosia's B&B. I'd asked about Nike, if Mr. Elam thought the cat would work out, and got nothing but a quick nod. I couldn't help feeling a little disappointed, not only in his lackluster response, but in my own naivety that a replacement cat would somehow make a dent in Mr. Elam's loneliness. And again I was reminded of my pact with Ambrosia: *It's a start.*

There are eleven of us around this table now, ten of whom are family, and while some of these people annoy the everloving bejeezus out of me, I can't deny their presence is a comfort. Which, so far as I can tell, is the most beneficial quality of family, the assurance that should something happen to one of us, it will happen to each of us.

It's a contract signed in blood at birth: *Do you, Tiny Infant Who Knows Nothing, take these completely random people to be permanent fixtures in your life forever and ever?* We sign that shit on the dotted line, and we do so happily, because it means, for better or worse, we will not be alone.

Thing is, Mr. Elam signed that contract too, and then his family got destroyed—because a truck driver fell asleep. That's it. That's all it took.

That's all it takes, I think, looking around the table.

"I would do it," Noelle says.

Uncle Orville nods and slow claps.

Aunt Becky is all, "I guess I just don't get it."

"Which part?" asks Uncle Orville. "The thrill-of-a-lifetime part, or the part where you have more fun than you even knew was possible?"

"I guess . . ." Aunt Becky looks around the table for help. Finding none, she looks back at Orville. "The part where you jump out of a plane?"

Dad snaps his finger, points at his sister. "It's a basic risk versus reward. One simple malfunction with the rip cord, and it's over. Some guy at the parachute factory forgot his caffeine pills that morning—"

"*Parachute factory?*" says Uncle O, his face like a tightly closed fist.

"And now you're ten thousand feet in the air with nothing between you and the ground but a useless backpack."

Noelle scoops up a bite of something, says, "I'd still do it."

Uncle Orville meows like a cat, at which point Dad says,

"Orville, come on," and Uncle O says, "What? What'd I do?"

Dad folds his napkin, sets it on the table. "Okay, Orville. One sentence. What is it you love about skydiving?"

Uncle Orville's face opens up, and for a second it seems he might cry. "For about ten minutes," he says quietly, "from the time you jump, to the time your feet touch the ground, you're the only person on earth."

I see Mr. Elam alone in that easy chair, drinking bourbon in silence, eating a meal from a plate in his lap; and Ambrosia, sweet Ambrosia, downstairs by the fire, wishing she'd insisted he join her, but knowing what he meant when he shook his head and said, "It's our anniversary." I see Nike at the foot of his chair, and Mr. Elam's weathered hand scratching her back. I see Mr. Elam's eyes, and through them his mind, winding its way back, always back, to the face of that truck driver who had taken his contract and ripped it to shreds. Mr. Elam raises a glass to Barbara and Matthew, to the ashes of Herman the cat; unsure if they can see him, he prays his dwindling faith is faith enough, holds his glass high, and considers the old family motto—*one plus one plus one equals one*—and feels the weight of an equation now riddled with subtraction.

"One," he says to no one.

Uncle Orville got it wrong: the drop lasts a lot longer than ten minutes.

If I were to die this moment, right here in this scalding hot shower, and a few curious scientists cracked open my skull for a peek inside, among the neatly cataloged brain-shelves of Bowie and boots-on-hardwoods, somewhere between the diagrams with little arrows and the Concise Histories of Me, I imagine those scientists digging their forceps down deep and, "Got it!" says one of them, pulling out a butterfly.

I climb out of the shower in a daze, now dry off, now boxer briefs, now mesh shorts, now brush teeth. There's a fluttering going on up there, some sort of pattern that's eluded me for weeks.

Uncle Orville's toiletry bag on the sink: one toothbrush, one electric shaver, one deodorant, one . . .

One.

The butterfly flutters, one synaptic branch to the next.

I step quietly through the hallway, stop in front of the guest room. The door is closed, that blue glow of the TV shining through the crack near the floor. I imagine Uncle Orville sitting up in bed, shirtless, tired eyes glazed over as some late show host carries on with antics aplenty, the same joke on a loop, only my uncle stopped laughing years ago. And I think of him at Uncle Jack's viewing, standing over the dollish corpse of his twin, and I wonder what it must be like to lose the only person who ever really got you, to see your own likeness in an open casket.

I slip into my room, close the door without a sound.

It's probably unfair of me to think this way. Plenty of people go their entire lives single and happy. But it's not just that Uncle Orville is single. It's not just that he sends those pathetic VHS commercials to the family, and it's not just the annoying pet names or the oozing self-confidence.

Standing in the dark, unmoving, I stare at the outline of my bare mattress. Night showers always inject a dose of calmness into the bone, that sort of refreshing lethargy that usually follows a nap.

It's when I do my best thinking.

My thought at this moment: *Uncle Orville has not changed.*

I often think of history as a series of patterns, of historians as pattern-studiers, psychics as pattern-predictors; and the rest of us do what we can to spot the patterns as they come.

Parish, Henry, Mr. Elam, the Fading Girl, Penny, and now Uncle Orville: my constants. Per Alan's suggestion, I investigated each of them, but patterns don't emerge on an individual level; they emerge on a collective one. And when I look at my Strange Fascinations, at Penny and Uncle Orville, not as individual trees but as the proverbial forest, a pattern emerges.

Orville. *From the time you jump, to the time your feet touch the ground, you're the only person on earth.*

Penny. *Grab a paddle, darling.*

Parish. *Abe, my God, don't leave me here alone.*

Henry (via Cletus). *Guys like us will always be alone, that's fine—the trick is knowing the difference between being alone & being lonely.*

The Fading Girl. *One Face, Forty Years.*

Mr. Elam. *One plus one plus one equals one.*

The only people in my life who haven't changed are more than just alone: they're lonely.

Once the dust from Thanksgiving clears, my parents hover over me like a couple of starved Dementors turned loose at a Teletubbies conference.

University of Milwaukee: the front-runner, the obvious choice. Manhattan State is still on the table, but at this point I think my parents would joyously shit themselves if I said, *Hey, let's go check out the University of Alaska Anchorage, I hear they have a top-notch bobsledding program*. I know my options, and I know what I should do, but the chasm between *should* and *want*, as always, looms large.

◄IIIII►

Me: Hey.

Sara: Noah, Noah, Noah.

Me: Sara, Sara, Sara.

Sara: What's up?

Me: I need to get out of the house. Wanna see a movie?

Sara: *blushes* . . . he wants a second date

Me: Did last time count as a date, though?

Sara: All the other guys with whom I've gone
to an old man's house and given away a
family pet have called it a date, sooo . . .

Me: In that case, yes, I would like a second date.

Sara: Okay good. Well. I can't.

Me: Oh. Okay.

Sara: Like, I legit can't. I'm stuck in Elgin until
Sunday. Family T-giving. #blessed

Me: Haha ok. I understand.

◄||||||►

Me: Hey

Alan: WHADDUP, NO?????????????

Me: Wait, are you high?

Alan: No. Val recently accused me of "texting
while apathetic"

Me: Ah

Alan: Trying to right the ship

Me: Good luck with that

Alan: What's up?

Me: Wanna see the new(ish) Spider-Man at the Discount? I've only seen animated Spider-Man. Trying to right the ship.

Alan: Good luck with THAT. You'll need it, considering IT'S NOT SPIDEY

Me: Oh

Alan: It's the new(ish) Superman, and I've heard it sucks kryptonic balls

Me: Well I need something to turn off my brain. Kryptonic balls it is. You in?

Alan: Can't

Me: WTF not?

Alan: What the fuck not?

Me: WHY. WHY the fuck not?

Alan: Not sure you can do that, tho. The W in WTF is historically "What"

Me: OMG

Alan: I can't come because homework

Me: BS

Alan: Beautiful Sunrise?

Me: You forget who you're dealing with here. I know you aren't doing homework because I know you. #joyousvirgins

Alan: Fine. It's not homework. I'm sick. Stomach bug.

Me: You're not sick

Alan: What, you have telepathic thumbs? I AM SICK. PUKING MY GUTS OUT

Me: You would have led with OMG YO VOMIT EVERYWHERE AGHHHHH

Alan: Shit. You're right

Me: Come on, out with it

Alan: OMG YO VOMIT EVERYWHERE AGHHHHH

Me: Too late

Alan: OK, but don't hate me. I'm at the Longmires

Me: Get the fuck out

Alan: Sorry. Guys night

Me: Guys night at the Longmires

Alan: Yeah

Me: What does this entail?

Alan: Video games, vodka, Will asking the ins
        and outs of my "gayness"

Me: God

Alan: Jake punching Will in the shoulder, then
        waiting for me to answer

Me: OK

Alan: Your mad?

Me: You're. You're. You're. You're. You're.

Alan: MY BAD YOU'RE MAD???

Me: No.

Alan: You're something tho?

Me: I'm fine. Imma go watch Spider-Man murder Lex Luthor

Alan: #hopeless

Me: #hopelesslyblessed

I text Val, but no response.

On a whim I decide to nudge the Fading Girl before I leave. She has yet to respond (via YouTube or Gmail), but I remind myself that she owes me nothing, that I am entitled to zilch, and that my right to press send does not supersede her right to ignore. Without even bothering to type a draft, I drop the curser in the box that says Add a public comment, and type the following: Hi. Me again. You don't owe me anything, and I'm sorry if these comments are annoying. For what it's worth, this will be my last attempt: I'd really like to talk to you. Email is twobytwooak@gmail.com if you get a second. Thanks.

No exclamation marks this time.

69 ➡ *attractions, coming and going*

The Discount is the malignant mole on Iverton's upper lip—and I love it. To be more precise: some tycoon built this multiplex cinema without checking the zoning laws, and as it happened, that particular area wasn't zoned for a legit movie theater. And since the whole place was already rigged out, some other (far less successful) tycoon was all, *Let's just show movies, like, a couple months after they're released, mmmmm-kay?*, and then everyone else was all, *Problem solved, I guess*, so now we get these old movies right around the same time they show up on Netflix, but hey, we can see them on a giant screen mere feet away from complete strangers in the dark, so I'm not sweating it.

"One for the new Superman, please."

"Just the one?" asks the kid from behind glass. He's young and squirrely in that way that makes me wonder if he came straight here from middle-school band practice.

"Yeah, guy. It's just me."

"Two bucks," he says.

"Oh."

"Is there a problem?"

"It's always been a buck fifty." I point toward the sign on the door that reads THE PREMIUM CINEMA EXPERIENCE FOR $1.50. "See?"

"We upped the price, bruh."

I hand over two dollars, fairly certain I'm getting taken for fifty cents from a seventh-grade clarinet player, and then head to concessions.

Going solo at the cinema seems like it might be fun. I can just enjoy the movie, laugh at the parts I think are funny, cry if I want without wondering if whoever I'm with is laughing or crying at the same parts.

Just the one?

Fucking kid doesn't know me.

I order a small popcorn and a Coke, assure the cashier that I do in fact just want the small, which is exactly what I ordered, and yes, I say, I know it's not the highest value in the house, but it's all I want, and I'm not one to waste. He hands over the popcorn and Coke, and I make my way over to the guy on the stool who will take my ticket.

This is the way of society.

And for that matter, when did movies become like a social outing? I mean, I get the drive-through thing, or at least back in the fifties and whatnot, with the tops down, chewing gum, drinking beers, making out. *That* kind of social movie experience I can respect.

"Noah!" Val, out of nowhere, runs up and hugs me.

"Hey."

"You here alone?" she asks, and only now do I realize she isn't. Right next to her is Jake Longmire's girlfriend, Taylor Something.

"Yeah," I say. "Seeing movies alone is going to be my new thing, I think." A hard sip of Coke, like that, like I'm owning it.

"How very Noah of you." But she says it with a smile, not in a mean way—I don't think. Taylor Something clears her throat, and I feel bad not including her in the conversation.

"What are you guys here to see?" I ask Taylor Something.

"Just leaving, actually," she says, which explains Val's unanswered text. She refuses to pull out her phone in a movie theater.

"So what did you see?"

"The new Superman," says Val, pointing a finger in her mouth and gagging. "That whole franchise is just intent on circling the drain of suckage until it sinks to the bottom of the sewer where it belongs."

"Ah."

"What about you?" asks Val. "Coming or going?"

"Coming."

"Which movie?"

"The new Superman."

Taylor Something chuckles, all, "I'll meet you at the car, V," like she can't stand being in my presence for one more second, and also, where the fuck does this girl get off calling Val *V*? Val is *Val*, sometimes *Valeria*, but never V. And if she's V to anyone, she's V to Alan and me, which she's not, which brings me back to, *Where the fuck does this girl get off?*

"I didn't know you guys were friends," I say, choosing the far tamer route.

Val looks at the ground, and suddenly the air feels thicker. "We just started hanging out recently."

"Oh." Something in my brain goes off like someone flipped a switch.

"Well, I should probably go," says Val. A sly smirk: "Enjoy the movie."

"Ha. Yeah." I give her a quick hug, and she turns to leave. "Val."

"Yeah."

"Are you dating Will Longmire?"

Her face turns a little red, and at first she doesn't answer.

"I ask because Alan is over there for guys' night right now. And here you are with Jake's girlfriend."

"Yeah." She nods, looks at the ground, then me. "I mean— yes, I am."

"Oh. Okay. I just hadn't seen you two like that around school, so I didn't know."

"It's pretty new, but it's something we've both wanted to try. Plus he was already considering USC, so if it works out, it wouldn't necessarily be long-distance."

"Good," I say. "That's great."

"Yeah."

"Well, I don't want to miss the previews, so—"

She interrupts me with a hug, our third in the last five minutes, and when you've spent as much time with a person as I've spent with Val, you start seeing life in sentences, feel the ebbs and flows of its lyrical current, the pulse of punctuation: I don't care that Val is dating someone, even if it is a Longmire brother, and I don't care if he joins her new life in sunny LA. And if Alan wants to be friends with that crew, fine, but it sure feels like they've built this whole other canoe on the sly, and now they're off into the great unknown, leaving me on the banks of the river, waving good-bye.

"Bye, Noah."

"Bye, Val."

She leaves, and that's the end of the sentence.

The only thing worse than an inevitably shitty movie is the slew of inevitably shitty coming attractions. And the previews are on the Discount timeline so each movie is announced as "coming soon," even though most of them have already come and gone. Eventually the lights dim, and just as the opening credits begin—just as I'm about to switch off my phone—a Gmail notification.

From chewie.elephant57@gmail.com.

Subject line empty.

The slew of elephants in the Fading Girl video, the Chewbacca figurine—it's her, I know, but at first I can't open it. The unread email just sits in my inbox like it owns the place, like it's always been there, like my phone is its home and I'm an intruder. It stares back at me from the screen as if to say, *And you are . . . ?*

Take a breath, click it open, and read: So what's your question?

I spill my popcorn on the way out of the theater.

70 → *(no subject)*

Inside my car in the Discount parking lot, I open the notes app on my phone and draft a response, going through all the various stages of suckery before landing on:

> There's no way for this to not sound weird (and believe me, I've tried all the ways), so I'm just hoping you'll appreciate this message for what it is: an honest plea. Something is happening, and even though we don't know each other, I think you may be able to help. I would like to meet you. I'm tired too.—Noah Oakman.

I read through it a bunch of times, but in the end figure this is my best shot. Honesty, right up front. I copy and paste the message into Gmail and press send, then proceed to stare at my inbox for a solid ten minutes.

(No subject)

(No subject)

(No subject)

I stare at it so long, the words themselves start to look silly, un-word-like: *No. Subject. No. Subject.* It's harsh, really, like saying, *Here's this email with no point whatsoever.* And then (No subject) turns into . . .

(No subject)

That simple transition from plain text to bold sets off an internal twinge of adrenaline that always seems to accompany the almighty Unread Message.

Her response reads:

> Haughty Coffee, Inc.
> 149 Concourse Ave.
> New York, NY 10029
>
> It's in East Harlem, between E 116th and E 117th St.
>
> If you decide to come, just email a day before with what time you want to meet. Flexible schedule. If you're a creep, I'll stab you. For serious.

71 → *there are two kinds of plans*

Some take years to unfold, often requiring massive amounts of preparation and forethought before implementation, at which point those plans may need time to germinate for a while, soak up sun, water, and soil before bringing forth full fruit.

"Okay," says Mom, sitting up in bed. "Okay."

Dad pauses *Seinfeld*. "Okay."

After months of sideways glances and hardcore hovering, I find my parents' reactions lacking. "Yes," I say. "Okay."

"So you've given this a lot of thought, then?"

"Yes," I say, calculating the drive home from the Discount. There was some traffic on North Mill, so we're looking at a full twelve minutes of thought probably. "Understand I haven't made a decision to *attend* Manhattan State University." I clear my throat and carefully recite the lines I'd memorized on the way over. "But I've done some research, and I think the institution has a lot to offer. Coach Tao seems to be taking the program in the right direction, and I'd like to see it for myself before making a decision."

The looks on my parents' faces—both of them nodding their heads off, trying to play it cool, failing miserably—is comically restrained. I leave them like that, knowing full well they'll be up most of the night talking, getting shit in order. My parents are driven, not prone to dally, lifelong subscribers of that other kind of plan, the kind where you get your ass in gear and get a motherfucking move on.

The next day is Saturday.

Dad and I eat breakfast in the airport.

72 ➜ what I think when I look down on the clouds

I think I am small potatoes.

I think small potatoes taste just as good as large ones.

I think I should listen to jazz more often.

There are many places I would like to live, and many times in which I would like to live, and I think listening to music that was composed in a time or place I've never lived is the closest I can get to making that happen.

Stories do that too, I think. Give us new homes.

And if someone were to ask, *Noah, what's the most important aspect of story?* I would most likely answer, *character,* but I'm not sure that's true, because my favorite books contain my favorite places. I do not say, *I love Harry Potter,* or *I love Frodo Baggins*; I say, *I love Hogwarts,* and *I love Middle-earth.* Thoreau's *Walden* is less about the book, more about the pond. The woods.

And so setting, I think, is the secret weapon of storytelling.

I always want to meet new people until I've met them.

I think if I spend enough time with a person so we get woven together like an old basket, eventually we'll think in similar patterns until our various histories are apples and oranges spilling over the edge of the basket, and I think this kind of shared history is dangerous.

I think it's okay to recognize a thing's faults and still like that thing. Because apples and oranges spilling from a basket can be beautiful too.

I think I'm whatever personality hates personality tests.

I think nostalgia is just a soul's way of missing a thing, and like long-distance love, nostalgia grows deeper with time until the reality of what a thing actually was gets blurred to the point you miss the idea of the thing more than the thing itself.

I like the idea of hot cocoa more than drinking hot cocoa.

I like the idea of horror movies more than being frightened.

I like the idea of spontaneity more than being spontaneous, and I like the idea of the outdoors more than being an outdoorsman.

I like the idea of being an ideas guy.

I let the jazz in, forehead against a chilly double-plated window, my thoughts multiplying with abandon—until they stop, condense, like one hundred divided by one hundred.

And I think it took me soaring thirty thousand feet above the earth to finally dig up the root of my problem:

I romanticize my past and I romanticize my future; right now is always the bleakest moment of my life.

"You okay?" asks Dad.

"What? Oh. Yeah."

The two of us hold on to a silver pole in the middle of the packed subway. I'm gripping it a little tighter than Dad, I think.

Last time I was in New York City I was six, and Dad brought the family with him on some catering job, but since Penny was still a baby, Mom never left the room. I have vague memories of going out with Dad once or twice, but I didn't see much, certainly nothing of the subway.

Safe to say, New York City has effectively shorted out the cleanliness circuits in my brain.

The train lurches and rumbles down the tracks; to be honest, the only thing more uncomfortable than the grimes and odors is the fact that no one will look me in the eye, even the people in my immediate circle whom I keep bumping into. It's like we're all in denial of the situation.

Also, a guy in the corner is reciting poetry at the top of his lungs.

Dad looks down at me, smiles with a quick wink, and I feel better; and then I feel silly for feeling better, like I'm six again and all I need to stop the bleeding of the earth is a quick wink from Daddy.

But I mean, yeah, I'm glad he's here.

Last night, after telling my parents I wanted to visit Manhattan State, I went straight to my room and packed a bag: toiletries, clothes, the usual, plus the last few months' allowance. I would need to get around without anyone knowing, which meant no credit cards. I knew full well the chain reaction I'd set off the next room over: Mom, whose work schedule was least flexible, would call Coach Tao to inform her that I would be flying to New York to visit over the weekend, which meant Dad was already packing and would book the earliest possible flight the next morning from Chicago to New York, and that's pretty much exactly what happened. This morning before the sun came up, Dad and I were in the car to O'Hare, reviewing the ins and outs of the itinerary he'd worked up last night. We landed at JFK midmorning, took a cab from the airport to this swanky guesthouse in SoHo owned by some up-and-coming boutique hotel entrepreneur for whom Dad had recently catered some equally swanky event, "but my God," Dad kissed the tips of all five fingers on his hand, then exploded them with a burst of Italian gusto loud enough to make the cabbie give us a look, "my simmered daikon and shiitake was on *point* that night," followed quietly by, "no wonder he comped our rooms."

Once inside, we unpacked while I tried not to have an organizational orgasm at all the right angles, the perfectly symmetrical curtains and pillows, the unclutteredness of it all, the whole place just oozing sleek and sophisticated. Dad said, "Half hour before we need to leave for lunch and catch the train," at which point I got out my computer and got down to business. First order: find a gap in the weekend schedule, a couple of hours where I could get away without Dad interfering. According to his itinerary, our post-lunch activities today included meeting Coach Tao for a tour of the Fighting Gophers' swimming facilities. Their next meet wasn't until December, but the team was back from Thanksgiving for training, which Dad and I would attend. Then, tomorrow at one thirty, we were scheduled for a tour of the campus itself. (Whether it was common practice for college tours to take place on Sunday afternoon, or just my mother's ability to turn up the lawyer voice and get anybody to do what she wanted, I couldn't say.) After the tour tomorrow it was back to the airport for an evening flight home. The only real time gap was tomorrow morning. Knowing Dad, he'd want to get breakfast at some obscure restaurant, but I could get out of that easy enough. I scanned the Fighting Gophers' events calendar. It was Thanksgiving weekend, so there wasn't much, but just when I was about to give up I found something on a community board about a Back to School Sunday Brunch scheduled for ten a.m. Obviously not geared toward prospective students, but no reason Dad needed to know that.

Before mentioning it to him, I needed to make sure the timing would work with the Fading Girl, so I logged in to twobytwooak@gmail.com, opened the ongoing thread, and typed: In New York. Tomorrow morning, Haughty Coffee, 10 a.m.? I'll be in a Bowie T-shirt.

Within minutes, I had a response: Fine, see you then. (And I repeat: I am bringing weaponry. If you're a creep, it's over for you.)

The guy in the corner has progressed from reciting poetry to performing one of the Cabinet Battles from *Hamilton*. He's actually quite good, which I'm about to say out loud when the doors open and Dad leads the way off the train; I follow him through the sea of foot traffic moving as one, a tide rushing onward and upward.

At the base of the narrow cement stairs a man sits on the ground, shoeless, sockless, overgrown hair and beard, holding a glockenspiel in his lap. He doesn't play, just cradles the instrument with both arms, a look of quiet desperation on his face that makes me wonder how long ago he gave up. As we get closer, I imagine this man's beard and hair growing inward, and like the Fading Girl in reverse, I imagine him aging backward, his eyes brightening, shifting from desperation to expectation until he's a small boy with a fresh face, the wide world at his feet. Closer now, and I wonder how it happened—if it was sudden, if it was downsizing, if it was drugs or bad luck, or if the world at his feet just shrank like a helium balloon with a slow leak until it dried up and shriveled into this: a voiceless old man holding a voiceless old glockenspiel.

I don't know if Dad does it because he sees the look on my face, or if he would have done it anyway, but as we pass, he throws a twenty-dollar bill in a cup next to the man, and together we walk up the stairs, and Dad says, "You ready?" and I wonder if such a thing as *being ready* is even possible given the discrepancy between the world we've been promised and the broken instrument we've received.

"Yeah," I say, "I'm ready," but really I'm calculating how many pairs of socks you can buy for twenty bucks.

74 ➜ *Manhattan State University is not in Manhattan, nor is Manhattan a state*

Toss in the visual of a gopher fight, and I have to wonder if the founding fathers of MSU were simply looking to create an educational atmosphere of rampant identity crisis. If so, I'd say mission accomplished.

"So where is it?"

"The Bronx," says Dad; he goes on to explain how the school was originally in Manhattan, but then moved and never changed its name, which makes me wonder what would happen if someplace like the University of Illinois relocated to Michigan but kept its name, and the utter chaos this would entail, and yes, I suppose this is the shit you think about when you visit a school you do not care to attend under the pretense of observing an athletic program for a sport in which you no longer wish to compete in the company of a father who has no idea that the real reason you're here is to make haste to a coffee shop in East Harlem tomorrow morning so you can meet up with a perfect stranger who may or may not be the final piece of the fascinating puzzle that is the disaster of your life lo these past strange months.

Anyway.

Coach Tao is nice. She asks about my back, if I think I'll be able to get into shape again ("When it comes to swimming," she says with a wink and a laugh, "you're never more than a couple Twinkies away from last place"), if I'll be ready to compete, and I tell her, "Yes, it's a lot better," and I tell her, "Yes, Dr. Kirby thinks I should be ready to go soon," and I tell her all the things I know she wants to hear, all the things everyone in my life wants to hear: I'll live the life you've laid out for me; I'll follow the trajectory you set from the beginning, I'll stay inside the robot, be a good boy, do whatever you want; and even though it's a lie, I can't *not* say it.

Because I have socks, and because look: I am not gripping a glockenspiel like it's the entirety of my fucking existence. And so "Yes, I will be ready," and "Yes, I feel good," and "Yes," and "Yes."

But no.

⬅️▭▭▭▭▭➡️

"So what'd you think?" asks Dad. We're underground again, waiting on the train. No glockenspiel this time.

"It was good," I say. "Coach Tao was nice. Guys seemed, you know . . ."

"Nice?"

"Yeah."

Dad clears his throat, and I know what's coming. "Listen, you didn't tell that kid . . . what was his name?"

"Paul," I say.

"You didn't decline Paul's invitation because of me, did you? There's plenty I can do on my own."

This being my first college recruiting visit, I had no idea part of the experience was going out with the team, which I'm sure means one thing in Milwaukee, and something else in Manhattan. (Or the Bronx, or wherever.) After practice one of the guys had come up and introduced himself as "Paul, my official host," and apologized for not having time to plan anything, but if I was up for it, the guys would like to take me out.

"I didn't decline Paul's invitation because of you, Dad."

I leave it at that. I could hardly tell him the truth, that I have no intention of attending Manhattan State, that the whole trip is a ruse, that the last thing I want is a bunch of rando college guys to "take me out."

Dad looks like he's about to say something when our train rumbles from the depths of the tunnel, whizzes by in a breath of cold wind, and screeches to a halt. We climb aboard, and since it's later in the day, there are plenty of seats available, and Dad says nothing the whole ride back to SoHo.

From the train stop, we find this little hole-in-the-wall Korean restaurant where Dad orders a beer and beef bulgogi with red lettuce and another word I can't pronounce.

"What did you get?" I ask, once the waiter is gone.

"Bulgogi. It's Korean barbecue, very delicious. . . ."

Dad talks about the ins and outs of a proper bulgogi, but his words become air and my thoughts drift through them, back to a yard at night, and a bag of takeout, and a feeling of wanting to turn around, knowing that I should, and knowing now that I was right to want that. But also: this dish of marinated red meat is never something Dad would eat. And maybe most kids don't pay attention to their parents' dietary habits, but most kids don't have a celebrated vegan chef for a dad.

Eventually the waiter sets down our plates with some fanfare, and Dad digs in. "You think you could be happy here?" he asks between bites.

"Yeah," I say. "Just need time to think, you know?"

Dad nods, sips his beer. "Hey, what do you call a cow with no front legs?"

"What?" I say, but more as a *Wait, what are you doing?* not as in *I don't know, what* do *you call a cow with no front legs?*

"Lean beef," he says.

"Dad."

"What? No good?"

It's not that Dad is above dad jokes; it's that he's above beef jokes. He shrugs, sips his beer again, snags a large piece of meat between two metal chopsticks. "What do you call a cow with no legs at all?"

"Dad. Please."

"Ground beef."

Later, as we stand to leave, he points out that I barely ate a thing. I tell him I wasn't all that hungry. "Nerves," I say, knowing how he'll take it, that I'm processing our day with Coach Tao, and all the ways it might further the trajectory of Noah Oakman. We step out into the cold pulsing veins of the city, and it's true, I am nervous, but not about the ways in which this day might further that trajectory so much as the ways in which tomorrow morning might.

75 → girl, faded

"If I'm going to live in the city, I need practice navigating the subway on my own," I say, which is not *un*true. Dad agrees under the conditions that I text the minute I get there, and that I meet him at the MSU admissions office at no later than one fifteen. (The Back to School Brunch is at a restaurant close to campus, and our tour is scheduled for one thirty.) I agree, and even though I assure him I know exactly where I'm going, he insists on walking me to the stop.

On the way we pass the Korean restaurant from last night. As if that dinner hadn't been strange enough on its own, later, all tucked away in those boutique bedsheets, I'd had an especially vivid rendering of my recurring dream where the person in the corner finally turned around, only just before I saw his face, the colors in the room went from bright to blinding, like someone turned up a dial.

When I woke up, my retinas were burning.

Dad and I walk down the cement steps, find a map on the wall, and go over the route to the stop nearest the restaurant. Just looking at the map gives me heart palpitations—the letters and colors spidering out into unrestricted chaos. But it does confirm what the map on my phone told me earlier, which is that East Harlem is in between SoHo and the Bronx, leaving me with plenty of time to talk with the Fading Girl and still be at MSU by one fifteen.

Dad hands me a MetroCard, tells me to be careful, and that's that. He's gone.

When my train arrives, I climb on, follow all the rules—*no eye contact, head down, you've done this a hundred times, you are not Macaulay Culkin in that shitty sequel.* At the first stop, I hop off, hustle up the stairs into the light of day, and, like a freaking pro, throw my hand in the air. Being from Chicago I'm not entirely unfamiliar with cabs, but whenever we ventured into the city we usually drove, so this is a first for me. I just stand here, hand in the air with nothing happening, feeling every bit like tiny Macaulay Culkin, imagining the entirety of New York City stopping in its tracks:

tires screeching, helicopters hovering, heads popping out of every high-rise window, as somewhere in the heavens God Almighty pulls the needle off the turntable and as one, everyone points and laughs.

Did you see the way the kid tossed his hand in the air? Like he thought that was how you hailed a cab, baaaahahahahahahahahaha!!!!!

A taxi pulls over. I open the back door, fearing some citywide prank, but nothing.

"You getting in, kid?"

Hop in, slam the door like I've done it a million times, do it every day in fact, *all* day in fact, and *God, another cab, but I guess this is the price you pay for living so large.*

"Kid."

"What."

The cab driver rolls his eyes. "Where we going?"

"One forty-nine Concourse Avenue. In East Harlem."

Baaaahahahahaha, the voices ring, the helicopters hover, the tires screech, *did you hear the kid say, "In East Harlem"? Oh my God, I can't with this kid.*

When debating how best to get to Haughty Coffee, I'd considered taking the subway for about a second before thinking better of it. The decision had nothing to do with glockenspiels and impromptu poetry slams, and everything to do with weekend schedules, and the knowledge that, in choosing a train with my stop on its route, I would no doubt board the *one* train that skipped that particular stop every other Sunday between nine and eleven forty-five a.m., or that was under construction, or that had been closed down last month. I simply didn't trust my underground navigational skills enough to take the chance. My second thought was that I would Lyft to the coffee shop. Last year my parents set up the app on my phone "in case of emergency," which was parent code for "in case you even think about drinking and driving," which okay, smart move, but the app was linked to their bank account, so the minute I used it, they'd know.

So: a taxi, then. And as I'm currently learning, it's a special kind of wonderment that comes from viewing the city through the window of a cab, sort of the inverted version of the view from a plane: you see the ground where a single structure was planted, rather than the sky where a thousand of them blossomed.

And I like that.

Until . . .

I touch the window, my fingers in focus, the street blurred behind them, and even though it's alive now . . . "One day, this will all be at the bottom of the ocean."

Sometimes you don't realize you've said something out loud until the deafening silence that follows.

"The fuck is wrong with you, kid?" The driver eyes me suspiciously in the rearview mirror.

I tell him I'm sorry, and with each passing block, I grow more and more tense, like the pit of my stomach is standing on the edge of a cliff. I pull out my phone, open YouTube, and watch the Fading Girl video on my way to meet the Fading Girl herself, hoping this might calm me, but it only makes things worse. And just then, a text . . .

Alan: Good luck this weekend, yo

Alan: NYC is dope. Have fun!

Me: Thanks, man. So far, so good.

Alan: Play your cards right, you'll be a Fighting
  Skunk next year

Me: Gopher. The MSU Fighting Gophers.

Alan: OMG LMAO

Me: I know.

Alan: Like how is a gopher expected to strike
  fear into the heart of an opponent?

Me: I know.

Alan: Do gophers even fight, WTF? Do they just
  adorable their enemies to death?

Me: Better than a skunk.

Alan: Puh-leez. Mofos weaponized their own urine,
  yo. Skunk > gopher all day, *errrrrrry* day

The cab slows, then stops. "We're here," says the driver. I
pay in cash, then stand on the curb and text Alan good-bye. I
want to include a thank-you for calming me down, but I can't
exactly tell him what it is I'm nervous about, so I leave it at
Gotta go. Love! Next, I send Dad the obligatory "here safe"
text and try not to feel guilty about that word—*here*—and
how different it looks from what he imagines.

Dad: Great! Have fun. ☺

Deep breath now—push down that guilt, the nerves and fear—and open the door.

⬅️▮▮▮▮➡️

Haughty Coffee is a small space, tables and chairs bumped up next to each other, and if the MacBooks and scowls and mason jars are any indication, I'd say the owners had a pretty accurate approximation of their clientele when they named their establishment.

I unzip my coat so Bowie is visible, order an iced coffee (in a mason jar), choose a seat near the back corner, and wait.

Five minutes pass.

Ten.

Fifteen. And just when I start to worry she won't show—in she walks. The Fading Girl in the flesh.

Until now, the feeling in my gut has been one of anxious curiosity—what should I ask, what will she say, where might this conversation go?—but no longer. My gut flips, my breath catches, my toes go numb, and I've never passed out, but I suddenly understand the feeling that must come just before fainting, the mild panic and loss of control, and none of this happens because I'm nervous—it happens because the Fading Girl isn't old. Like, at all. It's not that she looks good for her age; it's that she's not even as old as she was at the *beginning* of the video.

She figured it out, I think, *how to age in reverse, how to go from being the darkened millpond back to the bright young waterfall.*

➤→ 315

It's like she found the remote for the movie of her life and pushed rewind.

The Fading Girl looks around, sees my T-shirt, walks right up to my table, and sits down. She doesn't say anything, just stares at me through slightly glared eyes like I'm a faraway sign she's trying to read.

I'm all, "Um, hi."

Still nothing, still reading me. I'm about to ask if she'd like a coffee when she sets a gloved hand on the table between us and points at me. "I want to know who you are. And I want to know why you came here."

If I wasn't freaking before, I am now. "Those . . . aren't easy questions to answer."

She leans back, crosses her arms. "I have all the time in the world."

"I'm sorry, but . . . how did you—" *Grow young again? Age backward?* I am entirely unequipped to finish this sentence. "How did you do it?"

"Do what?"

Shit. She's going to make me ask it. "I watched you age. Like, a million times, I watched you, but here you are all of twenty-five years old, if that."

"I knew it." She shakes her head. "I knew you were a creeper."

"I'm not a creeper."

"You watched my mom's video a million times, and you're telling me that's not creepy?"

Slowly, it comes together: the grainy scanned-in Polaroids, the distinctive seventies flare . . . "She was your mom."

"Look, I don't really like going"—she moves her arms in a circular motion—"*out*. Like this. So I'm going to ask you

316 ←

some questions, and if you're not straight with me, I'm going to scream."

"You're going to scream."

"You should know I can scream really loud."

"Okay."

"What's your name?"

"Noah Oakman."

"How old are you, Noah Oakman?"

"Sixteen."

"Where are you from, Noah Oakman?"

"You can just call me—"

"*Where are you from, Noah Oakman?*"

"Chicago area."

"Where specifically?"

"Iverton."

This answer seems to give her pause, but she keeps going. "Wren Phoenix."

It doesn't sound like a question. It doesn't really sound like anything at all, so I say nothing.

"Wren Phoenix," she says again.

"I don't know what you're saying."

"Wren. Phoenix. That name mean anything to you?"

"I didn't even know it *was* a name."

"Straight answers, Noah Oakman."

"No, the name means nothing to me."

This disappoints her, which actually gives me a little satisfaction. So far she's owned this very bizarre conversation, and whatever dissatisfaction she might feel at the moment pales in comparison to my confusion.

"Wren Phoenix," I say. "Was . . . that your mom?"

There's that glare again, and just when I'm afraid she

might actually scream, she says, "I'll be right back." She walks to the register, orders something, and waits by the bar while I try to loosen up. When she comes back, she says, "So what's a sixteen-year-old from Iverton, Illinois, doing in Manhattan by himself?"

"I didn't come by myself."

"Explain."

"My dad came too. I'm visiting Manhattan State."

She puts her nose down by the rim of the mug, makes an audible sniffing sound, and it begins to dawn on me why this girl maybe doesn't "like going out."

"I'm Ava," she says, then moves her eyes from her latte to me and offers a gloved hand.

I shake it, try not to stare, but the resemblance is uncanny even for a mother-daughter. I only saw photographs of the Fading Girl—Wren Phoenix, I guess—but the way Ava looks at you like she's looking *inside* you is exactly the same as her mom. "So," I say, "if that's your mother in the video—"

"Why am I here instead of her?" asks Ava.

"Yeah."

"I keep tabs on the comments section."

I nod like this makes total sense. "Okay."

"Don't say 'okay,' like that. You don't have to pretend like it's normal. She's gone. That's why I check the video comments."

"Oh. I'm sorry to hear that. When did she die?"

Ava raises her mug over her head, looks under the bottom like she's trying to find something. "You're not a very good listener, are you, Noah Oakman?"

"What are you doing?"

She lowers the mug, goes back to glaring at me. "It is important to me that I know where things come from. This mug, as expected, is from China. Not that it matters, but now we know."

"Okay."

"I never said Mom died, I said she was gone. Which is why I check that comments section, in case someone knows where she went. I hacked her emails and Facebook account, too. And quit saying 'okay,' like the things I do are normal, it's insulting."

Unhinged, that's the word. Ava Phoenix is unhinged.

"So your mom . . . ?"

"Disappeared. Two years ago."

I don't know what I was expecting, but not this. "I don't know what to say," which is exactly the truth. "Did you, like—"

"Call the cops? Uh, yeah. She's an official 'missing person,' or whatever." Ava sips her latte, and then asks, "Would you like to hear a very sad story, Noah Oakman?" I say, "Yes," but as the daughter of the Fading Girl unfolds her mother's story, I wish I hadn't.

76 ➔ *Ava Phoenix, a conversation*

"We moved here from Vancouver when I was twelve. I didn't want to. Moving across the continent from your friends, your whole life. I pitched a fit, but Mom was resolute."

"Was it for a job?"

"Ha, right. *Job.* That would be the normal adult thing, wouldn't it? No, get this—the two of us moved to New York City so my thirtysomething-year-old divorced single mother could *chase her dream.* Pathetic, right? I mean, she always painted. My earliest memories were of her hanging her own art on the wall, stepping back to admire it in a state of utter serenity like she'd really gotten that one right. That usually lasted a day, two tops, before she'd rip it down and toss it in the trash. I don't know why she thought she could handle New York."

"Maybe she just wanted to see if she had what it took."

"I can tell you she had the drive. Hell, she may have had the talent. But she did not have the constitution. Mom basically crumbled once we got out here."

"And she'd already been taking the pictures at this point? For the video?"

"Yeah, she'd been doing that since before I was born. So far as I know, there were only a handful of days she didn't take a picture—a few vacations, a surgery to remove her gallbladder, I think, and then the few days it took to move out here. Oh, and I guess the day she had me? But mostly, you could set a clock by it."

"But you're not in any of them."

"In Vancouver she always took the photos in our basement, alone. But yeah, once we got out here we lived in this tiny two-room apartment, so I usually watched her do it, but she didn't want me in them. Said it had to be the same room, same items every day to highlight the object of the piece—so, *her*—as the variable. If everything around her changed over time, her own change wouldn't feel as significant."

"*The piece*, you called it."

"Yeah."

"So she thought of it as art."

"Oh, definitely. I don't know what her original concept was, as far as what to *do* with all the photos, but yeah. She thought *One Face, Forty Years* would be, like, this multimedia masterpiece. At the very least she liked that it was *hers*, you know? Just hers, no one else's. You ever do that?"

"Do what?"

"Have an idea, something personal that belongs just to you—and then later on you find a bunch of other schmucks had the exact same idea? When Mom started, she never could have predicted YouTube, or the dozens of others who'd done the same thing. So now here she had this lifelong work, this thing that was *hers*, this extraordinary thing in her hands like some rare bird—and the advancing world made it utterly common. It broke her, I think. And that's when things started to get weird."

"Weird how?"

"She stopped taking care of herself? Like, stopped bathing? Stopped brushing her teeth? At some point—this is going to sound weird, I know, but—at some point I realized she was saying the same things over and over again."

"Like what?"

"Like she had these little phrases she'd use, but she said them every day like she'd *just* thought of them. Like this one, I'll always remember. 'I just want to create,' she'd say. 'Just to create.' Like that, you know? And then something else like, 'It's not enough to put yourself into your art, you have to—"

"'Die to it.'"

"That's right."

"It's Mila Henry."

"Who?"

"The author."

"Oh, right."

"What else did she say?"

"Weird stuff. Some of it, I still don't understand. Something about a new sweater."

"What?"

"Like her life was an old sweater, and she'd outgrown it. Kept saying she needed a new sweater. I told you it was— Hey, are you okay? You're not going to hurl, are you?"

"I'm fine."

"Hang on. I'll get some water."

77 → the advancing world

While Ava is getting water, I leave, just walk out the door, and I think about what she'd said, about holding some extraordinary thing in your hands like a rare bird only to see the advancing world crush it. Aimless walking now, the buzz of traffic, the shoes of strangers, and I half expect Ava to chase me down, but it doesn't happen.

She's probably busy inspecting the bottom of my fucking mason jar.

More walking, more buzz and shoes, and, *If everything*

around her changed over time, Ava said, *her own change wouldn't feel as significant,* and between that and the new sweater thing, it's like one of those charts they give you in elementary school with two columns of seemingly random objects and you're supposed to draw a line from the object in column A that somehow relates to the object in column B: the iron goes with the shirt, the bacon goes with the frying pan, the bird goes with the nest, and the Fading Girl goes with Noah Hypnotik.

I throw my hand in the air, a cab pulls over, and on the drive up to the Bronx, I look out the window and think about this peculiar habit of Ava's. She said she needs to know where things come from, but I don't think that's it. I think when a person loses something, they take what they can get. Ava's mom left, and because Ava can't find the place where lost things go, she finds the place they came from. Ava takes what she can get.

We all do, really.

YES, IT IS TIME FOR ➤➤ PART SEVEN

"You know how many times I've quit? Thousands, just for the good of my own soul. I'll finish a sentence and declare it my last. For me, if it's worth writing, I have to go empty, exit the robot. If it's worth writing, it fucking hurts, is what I'm saying. But—inevitably I write more sentences. So I don't know. Maybe there's something beautiful about it too."

—Mila Henry,
excerpt from the Portland Press Herald *interview, 1959*

Hiding a hard-on in front of your dad feels a little like hiding a golden ticket from Willy Wonka: he had one first, he knows where it came from, and he knows its shape in your pocket.

Thing is, our flight attendant looks exactly like Jyn Erso from *Rogue One* and smells like an amaretto Oreo, so this is basically a dream I've had. She hands Dad and me our ginger ales and moves on down the aisle. Dad's looking at me, I can feel it; I wonder how long I can sit hunched over like this without him asking questions.

"You okay?"

Not long, I guess. "I'm good."

He gestures to my back. "Not the most comfortable seat, I know. How's your back feeling?"

"It's, you know . . . fine. It feels fine."

Dad opens his mouth, and I think I know what's coming—some shit about Manhattan State, how lucky I am to still have opportunities, how proud he is—and then: "You can tell me anything, you know."

Okay, not what I was expecting.

And then he starts in about how when I was born, he was a stay-at-home dad, and we were "dirt poor, but, Noah, I'm telling you, that was the best time of my life," and he goes on about what a unique situation it was, how Mom was studying for the bar, and he was just taking care of me during the day, coming up with creative dinners every night, and he doesn't even know how it happened, but things started to click, and now, "Like that, we're off looking at colleges."

I never know what to say when he talks like this. It's like I was part of this momentous occasion, only I have no memory of it.

"Anyway," he says. "You can always tell me anything."

And I open my mouth to do just that, to tell him I faked this back injury because I was done with the pressure, and I'm not even sure I want to go to college much less swim at one, but instead what comes out is, "Dad, what happened to Mom's face?"

"What?"

The airplane's engine suddenly sounds louder.

"Her scar." I motion down the side of my cheek. "She won't talk about it."

Dad is all, "Oh," in a breath, and in that one word I hear the complexities of family. "You don't . . . remember?"

I want to say, *I never knew to begin with*, but so much has changed these last months, so many familiar things turned foreign, I'm not sure how to separate what I'm supposed to know from actual knowledge. "No, I don't."

Dad clears his throat. "We were always so open and honest with you about this, even when you were a kid. Thought it was for the best, but . . . now I don't know."

"Dad."

"When we get back, I think we need to have a serious discussion about getting you into therapy."

"Dad. What happened?"

"You really don't remember?"

"I really don't. Should I?"

Jyn Erso passes: Dad orders a scotch and tells a story.

◀▦▦▦▶

Once home, it takes all of three minutes to unpack my bag.
I flop down on my bare mattress and try not to think about
the conversation happening in the kitchen right now. The
ride from O'Hare had been painfully silent, and when we got
here, I gave Mom a quick hug and came straight upstairs. Get
in, get out, leave them to talk.

I pull a pillow over my head and scream.

79 ➜ and the ice

It had been an especially snowy November that year, *you
were ten*, says Dad, meaning pre-Iverton, back when we lived
in Ohio, and *your mother's job has always been demanding*,
and Dad pauses, drinks, and the ice shakes in the little plastic cup, and *in the early days she hadn't learned how to cope
with that, with the stress of it*, and the plane bumps around
a second, causing that sudden communal telepathy where
every passenger wonders, as one, *What on God's green earth
are we doing up here anyway?* but it calms, and Dad says, *she
started drinking, like a lot*, and he didn't know what to do with

that, tried to talk her down, talk her out, talk her into AA, but *she wouldn't listen,* and then one day at lunch with a client, Mom came back to the office drunk, and she was put on leave, given severe warnings, but then it happened again, and *they fired her on the spot, right in the middle of the day, and God, I just wish—I wish she would have called me,* and Dad says that again, that he wishes she would have called him, but instead, *with the afternoon off, she decides she'd like to pick up her kids from school for once,* another bump in the sky, communal panic, everything is fine, Dad continues, *so she picks you up at the middle school first, and then on the way to get Penny, she hits a patch of ice,* and again Dad says, *such a snowy November,* and *she overcorrected, hit a telephone pole,* her blood alcohol level off the charts apparently, and *you were fine, thank God, but she sustained pretty severe cuts and bruises to the hands, arms, face,* and here it was, the wake-up call she needed, and she got cleaned up, AA and everything, *but she never forgave herself for putting you in danger like that,* and Dad finishes his scotch, looks at the ice in the glass, and *it's why she's so concerned about your back,* and he holds off tears, *it haunts her that you may have bruised some vertebrae in that car accident,* and he shakes the glass, nothing but ice now, then looks up with wet eyes, *you really don't remember any of this?*

Another patch of turbulence rattles the plane—and the ice.

Downstairs, in the kitchen, the muffled voices of Mom and Dad: they're talking about me. Still.

I don't know.

Maybe I need help. Probably, I do, but right now I have this intense desire to lean in to the familiar, to do something for someone that matters.

I knock lightly on Penny's door. No answer. Very slowly, I twist her handle and open the door a crack. It's dim, the only light coming from the lamp on her bedside table; Penny is fast asleep, a book on her chest rising and falling with each breath. At the foot of her bed, Mark Wahlberg raises his head and looks at me, and I put a finger over my mouth, which— of course—he seems to understand. He puts his head down on his paws and doesn't make a peep.

Back in my room, I dig out that old letter with her *Breakfast at Tiffany's* pros and cons list. At the bottom of the page where it asks, *Will you watch* Breakfast at Tiffany's *with your darling sister? Please check one*, I put a checkmark in the box next to, *Yes, of course I will.*

Down the hall again, in her bedroom, I place the list with my answer on her nightstand, ease into her favorite leopard-print beanbag chair in the corner, and watch the book on her chest rise and fall, rhythmically up, rhythmically down, up, down, like that.

So who's in your canoe, Penn?

"It's useful being top banana in the shock department."

I don't know what that means.

Means grab a paddle, darling.

I sit like that through much of the night, unable to turn my brain off long enough to fall asleep, unable to work up the energy to get up and leave. I just sit in my sister's beanbag and wonder how long she'll offer that paddle before letting it slip into the water.

Best not to find out.

81 → *the herculean curtain call*

"Is this for *real*?" Slowly, Penny's face comes into focus. "This," says the blurred face, "right here," pointing to the bottom of her pros and cons list. I sit up gingerly, rub a massive crick out of my neck. "This checkmark. Do you mean it?"

"God. Penny. Gimme a sec."

It takes a full five count to remember where I am. I can't say for sure when I fell asleep, but my best guess would put it somewhere around three a.m.

"Okay, I just gave you, like, ten seconds," says Penny. "Is this real? You wanna watch *Breakfast at Tiffany's* with me?"

Even in my daze I can't help admiring the life within my sister: the smile in her eyes is like a bubbling volcano, ready to erupt at the first sign of confirmation that yes, in fact, I am agreeing to watch this movie with her.

I clear my throat and rock back to get some momentum to stand. "Yeah."

"Yeah, what?" she says, the two words ending in a sort of hybrid laugh-squeal that only my sister could make cute.

"I checked *yes*, Penn. Don't push it."

I don't know what the right word is for Penny's dance moves. Probably, there isn't one, but it's like if a puppy got drunk at a fifties sock hop and wouldn't stop saying, *Oh yeah! Oh yeah! Uh-huhhhhhhhh.*

I tell her I'm not feeling well at the moment, that we'll watch the movie in the basement after school, and you'd think I'd handed her a blank check and told her to go crazy at the mall.

But I mean, yeah, I feel pretty much golden.

⬤⬤⬤

As it turns out, faking sick to get out of school is a lot easier when your parents are currently walking on eggshells every time you enter a room.

"I don't feel well," I tell them in the kitchen. "I think I'm coming down with something."

"Okay," they say, and within an hour everyone's gone. I switch my phone to silent, toss it on my bare mattress, and open my laptop. Sometimes a thought takes forever to form, moving along at a snail's pace; other times it explodes like a supernova, those precious final moments in a star's life when its true greatness is most terrifying, a herculean curtain call for the ages. And even though I can barely keep my eyes open, I need to get this supernova out of my brain.

2003. Nick Bostrom, a professor at Oxford University, publishes an article presenting the "Simulation Argument," in which he outlines three potential options for the future of the human race, or a "posthuman" stage: a) we go extinct before reaching the posthuman stage; b) having reached the posthuman stage, we are unlikely to run any simulated realities; or c) we are currently living in a simulated reality.

The idea is this: given the trajectory of technological advancement, and under the assumption that this advancement will continue, one might assume a simulated reality will be possible at some point, and given the assumption that those in the simulation will be unaware of their simulated state, it then follows that if our current civilization *were* simulated, we would a) have no way of knowing, and b) swear it was real. Like dancing shadows on the back of the cave wall, or like Neo in the beginning of *The Matrix*, we would accept what's offered, live inside the robot, and do so thankfully. But what if

83 → *the cursor blinks*

But what if . . .
  But what if . . .
  But what if . . .
  I close my document and open Google, type in "Elam"
and "Ambrosia" and "Phoenix," "Ava" and "Wren," and I consider the significance of names, Philip Parish to Pontius
Pilot, Nathan in Jonathan, and of my own name in relation
to Abraham and Elam, and my own name in relation to Neo,
and my own name in relation to NOAA, and my own name. I
stare at the screen for a minute or an hour, and even though
it was a single night's bad sleep, I suddenly feel I haven't slept
in months. Close the computer, stumble to bed, close my eyes,
I let this chilling idea grow, my cheek and hands against the
rough fabric of the bare mattress.
  But what if . . .

84 → *Piedmont*

It's a thick slush of a fog, a ghost town; I walk through it, wondering if someone relocated Iverton to the top of a mountain,
but that's silly—you can't move a whole town, and now I'm on

a street I don't want to be on, and now I'm in his yard. The moon is large and bright and looks like a black-and-white photo of a watermelon.

"The moon looks like a watermelon," I say, but they don't listen.

"You know who I met in that cave?" asks Kurt, rocking in his chair, smoking that cigar.

Abraham Parish says something, but I can't hear.

"Where's your dog, Kurt?" I ask. "Did you lose your dog?"

The old man looks at me, points next door to the Lovelocks' house. "He went back inside. That ol' watermelon got too bright."

I'm on the Lovelocks' porch now, about to open the door, when I feel a hand on my shoulder. "Careful in there," says Abraham Parish. "It gets pretty dark."

I hug him and then step inside, torch in hand, following Bowie's voice to the back of the cave. Moisture gathers and drips from the curved walls and ceilings, hits the rock floor in tempo with the echoing song, Bowie's countdown to takeoff. The flame of my torch flickers, then goes out for a moment before coming back even brighter, and now those letters drip from the cave walls like sap down a tree, pooling on the floor where they come together to spell something entirely new: PECULIAR WAY.

"Don't worry about the vase."

Someone else is in here with me. I hadn't seen him before, but there he is in the far corner. I only see his back; his face must be close to touching the cave wall. He's drenched from head to toe, water dripping from his hair, his clothes and hands, landing on the cave floor, where the drops join and multiply, join and multiply.

"Alan."

My best friend turns around, faces me for the first time. He says nothing, just lip-synchs "Space Oddity." It always was his favorite.

I climb into bed under freshly washed sheets, big fluffy pillows, and I could sleep forever. By the bed, Abraham the Lab barks silently, and as I close my eyes, I think how terrifically odd that it should end now as it began 26,000 years ago: with a boy and a dog in a torch-lit cave.

85 ➜ *the oracle*

"Shit," says a voice. "No, no," and then, "shit," again, and something presses against my face, squeezing my head like an orange in a vise, and my throat is dry, and my whole body aches like I've been running for days, and the voice says, "Shit," and there's typing, typing. I reach a hand up to pry my head loose—whatever it is, it's warm to the touch, and before I can remove it, a sound of something rolling across the floor, and then the voice is close: "Hang on a sec," and I feel a set of hands reach around behind my head, and a soft click and the weight is lifted. The brightness of the room is blinding at first, but as my eyes adjust, I realize it's only bright by comparison to where I've been.

A ceiling: the first thing I see.

And then a face leaning over me. "Hey." Circuit's eyes are red and buggy, and there's an edge in his voice like he's on the brink.

I try to talk, but the only thing that comes out is a cough.

"Take it easy. I'll be right back." He disappears, the rolling sound again, and I hear him leave the room. There's a weight on my hands and feet, but I can't move to see what it is, can't even lift my head. Music plays in the background, the ending of Bowie's "Space Oddity."

What the fuck.

"You've probably got a pretty substantial headache at the moment." The rolling sound again, which I now recognize as the wheels of a desk chair across a wooden floor, and Circuit's face hovers over me. "Also, the apparatus may cause temporary paralysis, but nothing to worry about. I brought aspirin. And water." Circuit grabs me under both arms, hoists me up until I'm propped against the headboard, and assists me with the pills and water.

I get my first full look of his room since the night of the Longmire party.

His desk is still cluttered with textbooks and papers all over the place, a box of brown sugar cinnamon Pop-Tarts, empty bags of Cheetos, and no fewer than a dozen crushed cans of Mountain Dew. A laptop hums with a variety of windows flashing across the screen at rhythmic intervals, charts and long series of unreadable digits; and next to the computer, that set of giant goggles, which Circuit had named, though I can't remember what.

"Easy now," he says, leaning down to remove what looks like a pair of ski boots from my feet. He sets them on the floor, and then unstraps a glove from my left hand, then my right. "As your speech and mobility are currently limited, how about I talk first? I should warn you, though"—Circuit leans forward, rolls his chair right up to the edge of the bed— "you'll probably want to hurt me, Noah. And I mean bad. But understand this, right off the bat. I do not apologize. Not now, not ever. Okay?"

I'm crying, and I don't know when it started, but I know why: I believe him.

Circuit rolls back to his computer, minimizes all screens, and opens YouTube. "Let's start here."

⟨▸IIIIII▸⟩

The video opens with a title card in all caps reading ENVIRONMENT MODIFICATION TRIAL F. It then cuts to footage of a rat in a cage. The cage is oddly decorated: in one corner there's a miniature Statue of Liberty dressed in a tunic and a blue beret; in another, a standard white baseball in a glass case; and covering the floor are green-colored wood chips. A small television facing the cage airs an episode of *Tom and Jerry*. The rat is in its exercise wheel, when a narrator with an Australian accent says, *"Meet Herman. Herman is two years old and has lived in this cage for the duration of his life. From the day he was born, his home has been meticulously kept, every item exactly the same, and in the exact same place."* The narrator goes on to explain that Herman's exercise wheel is hooked up to a device that sprays a puff of the same coconut-scented perfume every tenth rotation, and that this particular episode of *Tom and Jerry* has been on repeat for two years. A variety of cuts show Herman eating, drinking from a bottle hooked up to the side of the cage, sleeping comfortably. *"This is Cage A,"* says the narrator. *"Cage A is Herman's home, the only one he's ever known."* The video cuts to another cage similar in decor, but with a few subtle variations: the Statue of Liberty in this cage wears a toga and a green beret; in the opposite corner, there's a tennis ball in a glass case; and the wood chips are dark blue. *"This is Cage B,"* says the narrator, who then points out the differences between the two cages, including the piney scent emitted every fifth rotation of the exercise wheel, and the recurring episode of Wile E. Coyote and the Road Runner on the television. *"Now let's see what happens when Herman is placed in this new home,"* says the narrator. A gloved hand slowly lowers a wriggling Herman into Cage B. The rat hits the ground running, scurries from one corner to the next, kicking up wood chips and climbing walls. The narrator explains that they left Herman in Cage B for three hours. *"He never calmed."*

Fade to black.

A few seconds pass, and the words ONE MONTH LATER appear; we fade in on Herman in his original home, Cage A. The gloved hand appears again, this time with a syringe, and the narrator explains that Herman will receive a small dose of Telazol before being relocated to Cage B.

Fade to black.

ONE HOUR LATER. Herman wakes up in Cage B. He sniffs around the base of the Statue of Liberty's toga, the tennis ball in the glass case. He watches a few seconds of Coyote and Road Runner, and then ever so calmly climbs inside the exercise wheel—and runs. *"There are two possibilities as to the outcome of this environment modification trial,"* says the narrator. *"The first is that Herman's brain is sim-*

ply more compliant to modification when induced during an unconscious state. The second and far more compelling possibility is that when transferred during an unconscious state, Herman is unable to tell the difference between the two environments."

◄▐▐▐▐▐▐▶

At some point during the video I regain a little feeling, sit up in bed, and while everything hurts, at least I'm mobile.

"Dad once told me about how in the early days of personal computers people were nuts for this program called Paintbrush. One guess what it did." Circuit chuckles. "Our society has been mesmerized by computers like a baby with a rattle—but not Dad. He spent years designing software that runs parallel to, and in conjunction with, the human brain, allowing the subject to live and thrive inside simulation. I watched it happen many times, one of the benefits of being homeschooled. I'd get all my work done in an hour and spend the rest of the day helping him."

For some reason I can't meet Circuit's eyes as he talks, can't bring myself to witness in his face the levels of determination I hear in his voice.

"He built the Oracle." Circuit picks up the binocular-goggles, turns it in his hands. "The headpiece came first, then the sensory boots and gloves. Named it after that character in *The Matrix*. You ever see that movie? Entertaining, albeit antiquated. Anyway, unlike Oculus, Google Cardboard, or that Samsung VR piece of shit—glorified video games one and all—the Oracle operates in tandem with all major search engines, enabling the user to truly experience things, *know* things that they hadn't previously experienced or known. Places, ideas, facts, smells, and tastes, it's all there. But the real beauty of the Oracle is how it responds to what's already in your brain. For example . . ." He swivels back around to face the computer, pulls up one of the previously minimized screens, and says, "Who is Fred Merkle?"

The bottom drops out, and my eyes close like curtains at the end of a play.

◀▥▥▥▶

"There you go."

I open my eyes, cough, and sit up.

"Go easy," says Circuit. "You passed out for a minute, a fairly common aftereffect. Here"—he holds out a granola bar—"this will help."

My mouth waters before it can form the words *fuck off*. I unwrap the bar and shove it in.

"My dad loved scotch," says Circuit. "Now, I don't pretend to know much about the production process, but I get the gist. Distill a spirit, age it in a barrel. Or a *cask*, as the Scots call it. I learned from Dad that not all casks are created equal. Ex-sherry casks, ex-bourbon casks, ex-Chardonnay casks, all of varying qualities, each scotch aged for various lengths of time, and this process plays an enormous role in the final product."

"What's your point?" My first words are raspy, but it feels good to talk.

"Your brain is the raw spirit, Noah. The Oracle is the cask. It takes what's already there—knowledge, life experience, opinions, ideas—and fills in the gaps. Adds flavor. Dad built a masterpiece, no question." Circuit taps the Oracle. "But there was one problem. Do you know what that problem was?"

"Fuck you?"

"Ha. No, the problem with virtual reality has always been infuriatingly simple. *User awareness*. While in simulation, the user has the presence of mind to distinguish between what is real and what is not, reducing the experience to nothing more than masturbatory escapism. Fucking Paintbrush 2.0. Imagine building a fully functioning automobile from the ground up only to have misplaced the ignition. And that user awareness—that was Dad's misplaced ignition. After he died he left me a notebook full of technical theories, instructions, things he'd tried that worked, things that didn't. He *wanted* me to do this, to pick up where he left off. He wanted me to find the ignition. And I did. I found it when I found Environment Modification Trial F. A simulation that begins only when the subject is in an *unconscious state* could, theoretically, allow that person to live in simulated reality without ever knowing it was simulated."

"Hypnosis."

"It had to be more than sleep, but I didn't trust myself to knock someone out cold," says Circuit. "Of course, you'd had quite a bit to drink, which helped."

"You're fucking nuts."

Circuit shrugs. "I could never build what Dad built. But when I found that video, I knew I'd found the ignition. My contribution to changing the world as we know it."

Watching Circuit as he talks feels like watching a child in the cockpit of a plane: I believe *he* believes he knows what he's doing. But Circuit hasn't built this machine; he's done nothing but climb atop the shoulders of its architect to press go. What of its quirks and flaws? How might it operate differently on someone whose state is, to begin with, so radically altered? I've been to enough parties to know people aren't the same when they're drunk, and I've seen the eyes of the hypnotized—but both at once?

"Why me?"

Circuit scrunches up his face, speaks in a mimicking whine. "'I want a new trajectory. Everyone in my life is stagnant. It's like my life is this old sweater, and I've outgrown it.'" He laughs a little, shakes his head. "I mean, seriously, I couldn't have drawn up a more apt subject than you."

I look back down at the sheets, the made bed, the outline of where I've been. "So what then—you lured me into your cage?"

"Well, I had some help."

"You're so full of shit."

He shrugs, says nothing.

"Who?" I ask.

"Not really my place." Circuit rolls back to his desk, scrolls through a playlist on his computer, plays "Life on Mars?" and says, "You know, I was never really into Bowie before, but I made a playlist for our session, and I have to say, he's growing on me."

"You manipulated me."

"It doesn't work that way. It's not a video game, I wasn't controlling your moves, telling you where to go, what to do. The Oracle takes what it finds there"—Circuit points to my head—"and integrates it with what it finds *here*." Circuit points to his computer. "If you can google it, you can live it."

"Physical traits, things people said and did—things were different. You made that happen."

"I didn't."

I point to his computer. "Just like that second cage had all those changes, you rearranged shit in my head."

"It's not an exact science, Noah. Living in simulation is roughly the equivalent of living in fiction. And as with any fiction, variations and flaws are to be expected. That you experienced changes in those around you does not surprise me in the least."

"What about the pattern?"

This gives Circuit pause. "Pattern . . . with the changes?"

It's never been difficult for me to place myself in that diner with Cletus and Nathan. *Guys like us will always be alone, Noah, that's fine—the trick is knowing the difference between being alone & being lonely.*

"Huh." Circuit turns to his computer, opens a document, and types. "Interesting," he says, and I imagine rolling up this bedsheet and cramming it down his throat, smothering his face with one of these pillows, holding it there until his body spasms and goes still. "Fascinating," he says.

"What is?"

"Dad dropped almost a hundred volunteers into simulation, and while all of them reported variations within the Oracle, you're the first one to report a pattern among the variations. I won't lie to you, Noah, I'm a little aroused right now. What was the pattern, if you don't mind my asking?"

Some feeling has returned to my legs, which adds a dash of flight to my daydreams of fight.

"Doesn't matter," says Circuit, seeing in my eyes that he

won't get an answer. He sighs and leans back in his chair, every bit the contented madman. "Think of it. From here on out, there is literally nothing that stays the same. Fired from your job? Ugly divorce? Cancer diagnosis, death in the family, *shitty fucking life*? For the right price, here's a new one. Or you could just take a quick vacation, like you."

Tingling now, in my legs. My blood is running, and I am not far behind. "A quick vacation?"

Circuit's eyes change, and he smiles like he just recognized an old friend, and I think how his teeth would shatter like glass, how his blood would spray across the room and paint the walls red.

"What month is it?" he asks.

Something about the simplicity of the question makes me want to vomit. "November."

Circuit laughs in a spurt, claps his hands together. "Fucking beautiful."

"What."

"The simulation ratio is roughly one hour to every two weeks. It's been just over six hours."

"Since what?"

But the weight falls, and Circuit turns back to his computer as if even he can't face what he's about to tell me, and all the words from tonight break apart into letters now, floating in the air, and the room turns every shade of brightness the world over.

"It's been just over six hours since we left the Longmire party."

Before my Navy Bowie days, I used to go to the mall with Mom near the end of summer for new clothes. We'd walk those white tiled hallways, and I'd say how much I hated the mall—the assertive kiosk employees, the smell of the food court, the synthetic convenience of it all—and Mom would shrug like she agreed, but what did I expect *her* to do about it. "Just pretend you live here," she said once.

I remember looking around, imagining all these store-fronts in the dark after closing when no one else was there, and I found I had amazing aptitude for romanticizing even the most treacherous of settings by simply imagining those places as home.

Just pretend you live here.

I walked those empty hallways in my mind, and moon-light through the windows painted the white tiles blue, and there was no one else around, all the mall bots in bed, and even though this space was dark and empty and slightly off-center, it was home.

Imagine living in such a place.

And that's where I've been.

"Noah," says Circuit, but my legs are back and I've been in this room long enough. At the landing now, down the stairs, and I'm about to open the front door when I hear a rustling from the living room, and there's a lamp on in the corner, and

Sara just waking up on the couch. She yawns and stretches, all, "You know you're tired when you'd rather crash on the couch than climb the stairs to your own room." And then she smiles at me, tilts her head a little. "Noah-with-an-*H*, right?" And Nike the cat hops into her lap, and the fear that's been boiling in my stomach reaches its tipping point.

"Noah, please." Circuit's voice from the top of the stairs is chilling in its normalcy. "Come back. Let's talk."

A last look at Sara—and I'm out the door, through the yard, hit Piedmont running. The sun is just starting to come up, and next door Kurt raises a steaming mug of coffee. "Mornin'," he says, like the whole world is as it should be. And at his feet Abraham the longhaired collie barks once, and it's like this whole night I've been reading the following sentence, and that bark is the period:

My life for the past three months has been erased.

87 → the closest word

Open the front door like a Band-Aid, the alarm goes off, and if Mom and Dad weren't awake already, they are now, but one thing I know: I need my room. I keep my head down, avoid the kitchen, scramble upstairs, lock the door, crash into bed, and let this thing sweep over me. Something between grief and regret and impulsive anger, but all of it and all at once, and because there is no protocol for being told you have to relive a portion of life—no map or outline or anyone who's been there before who can say, *It's going to be okay*—I'm left with a nameless feeling.

A knock on my door. "Noah!" Dad doesn't wait for me to answer before trying to come in. "Noah, open the door."

"I'm okay, Dad. Just need some sleep."

"Noah, let me inside now."

He doesn't get angry often, so when it happens, it's unnerving. I open the door, and the minute I see his face, I know: whatever this is, it's not anger.

"Where have you been?" he asks.

"Sorry. The party went late, I crashed at Alan and Val's. I know I should have texted but—"

His face is unreadable; and for some reason the house suddenly seems quiet.

"Dad."

He swallows, and his eyes go empty, and as Dad talks, that nameless feeling begins to take shape, *Last night Alan hit his head in the Longmires' pool*, begins to come together into something recognizable, *He was without oxygen for a while*, begins to shift into focus, *He's at Chicago Grace now*.

"Is he okay?" I ask; it doesn't sound like my voice.

"He's in the ICU. Stable, but we don't know much. Mom's there now."

"I have to go. I have to be there."

Dad nods. "You ready?"

⟸▦▦▦▦⟹

On the drive in, Dad explains how just after one a.m. Val called, trying to find me, and when she told them what happened, they dropped Penny at the neighbor's so Dad could go out looking for me, and Mom could join the Rosa-Haases at the hospital. "She's been there all night." It's quiet for a second, and then he says, "I went to the Longmires'. To find you, I mean. You weren't there, so I drove the streets to see if you were out walking. I kept calling you, and I was about to call the police."

I am only vaguely aware of the conversation, of Dad's asking where I was without really asking.

I am only vaguely aware of my existence in this car.

I should have been there.

I pull out my phone to call Val—and my stomach turns: five voicemails, a dozen missed calls, a string of texts from Mom and Dad, and a series of texts from Val, the first of which is a single word, time-stamped 1:01 a.m.

Val: Noah

Val: Where are you??

Val: Alan hit his head

The next message is time-stamped 3:22 a.m.

Val: We're at Chicago Grace. He won't wake up

Val: Where the fuck are you

I should have been there, should have been there, should have been there, should have been by the pool to jump in and grab him, should have been at the house to stop him from swimming high in the first place, should be at the hospital right now at the very fucking least.

"It's going to be okay," says Dad, but we both know it means nothing.

Numbness: it's the closest word.

88 → *mirrored lives*

I was twelve the first time I went to Wrigley Field. After watching hundreds of televised games I was all geared up to see the park in person: that Kong-sized marquee, the brick and ivy walls everywhere, the sun shining bright on a big Cubbie win. But it was overcast when we arrived, and the average-sized marquee promoted Budweiser as much as it did the Cubs, and the outfield walls were the only ones covered in ivy, and I saw them for all of twenty minutes before it started pouring.

This was not the Wrigley I knew.

Alan is on his back in bed, not flat, but propped up a little. His eyes are closed, he has a tube down his mouth, a tube in his nose, a neck brace, an IV running into his arm, and when I walked in, my first thought was, *Sorry, wrong room.*

This was not the Alan I knew.

I hug Mom, then Mr. and Mrs. Rosa-Haas, and then Val—this one lasts longer. "I'm sorry, Val. I should have been there.

I'm so sorry." She shakes her head in my neck, and I feel the dampness of her tears, her runny nose, and from here I see Alan's head in the brace, pierced by the tubes, and I just can't fucking believe it. Mr. Rosa-Haas says something about getting coffee, and the adults leave, and now the three of us are alone.

"I told him not to," says Val. "Told him he was being stupid, he should just ignore Jake," and she goes on to explain how at first no one knew what had happened, and by the time someone realized Alan was underwater, it took a while for them to heave him out, at which point he wasn't responding. "We got him in my car and brought him here. I went, like, a hundred the whole way."

"Do they know anything yet?"

Val shakes her head. "They did a CAT scan, I think. MRI, maybe. Said he definitely hit his head, so."

I can see it, all of it: Alan jumping in, wanting to put Jake in his place, swimming right for the wall, misjudging . . .

Val starts crying. "I heard them tell my parents they wouldn't try to wake him up until he could breathe on his own. Until then"—she points to one of the machines next to his bed—"this thing does it for him."

It's quiet as we stand arm in arm over Alan, and I can't stop re-creating what it must have looked like, and how different it would have gone had I been there. But I wasn't, and now Alan is in this bed, hooked up to all these devices, and who knows if he'll ever wake up.

"Just look at him," says Val, and she takes her brother's limp hand, linking the three of us together, the most delicate of triangles.

I stay at the hospital all day. And I don't know when, because time isn't compatible in this room, but at some point Dad leaves to get Penny. It's decided he'll take her home, and Mom will get lunch for the rest of us, and afterward, she'll wait with me here, and I wonder how anyone is capable of making plans right now, or why anyone would ever make a plan, seeing as how everything goes to shit anyway.

Twice—once when Mom was reading a magazine, once when she fell asleep—I found myself staring at the side of her face: that smooth skin, not even the hint of a scar.

I am vaguely aware of a dinner of some kind.

I am vaguely aware that I haven't cried yet.

I am vaguely aware that Val and I have not spoken since I first arrived. But then no one is talking, not really.

A few times I think I see Alan's fingers move, but I can't be sure.

And that night, when they say, "Family only," I tell Mom I'm sleeping in a chair in the general waiting room.

She sleeps in the chair next to me.

89 ➜ *passage of time (III)*

Three days and counting. I visit mornings and nights.

I would stay if they would let me, but they don't.

When not in the ICU, I'm locked in my bedroom with

this numbness, my new shadow. I sleep the hours away, and sketch morose diagrams of failed skydiving attempts, burst goiters, and the face of an old woman whose existence has been made utterly common by the advancing world. And I feel every moment slipping away as it passes, like I boarded some infinite bus, but missed my stop, so now I'm doomed to watch everyone around me get exactly where they're going, knowing I'll never join them. Exiting the robot has never meant death, not to me, but maybe that's what happens when you miss your stop. Maybe you're stuck in this sort of existential purgatory, not quite here, not quite there, not anywhere really.

Nights, Mom sits on the edge of my bed and tells stories like she did when I was little. I lie there while she talks, and when she's done she kisses my forehead, and in those moments I am forced to consider the depths of my own darkness, that in the stage performance of my time Under, my subconscious self would cast my loving mother as an alcoholic who drove her car into a telephone pole with young Noah in the backseat. And when the soft click of the door announces Mom's departure from my room, I am left alone in the dark to think about that; I am left alone to resume my undoing.

I would move into Alan's room if they would let me.

But they won't.

"It puts you behind right out of the gate," Mom says, but I can't quit staring at the side of her face. "I'm not going, Mom," and I roll over in bed, pull the clean white sheets up to my chin; outside my door I hear their muffled argument in the hallway.

After skipping the first two days, my parents have decided it's time for me to go to school. They can say what they want, but my best friend is in a coma that I could have prevented had I not gotten drunk and let a madman drop me in his rat cage for three months (or six hours, whatever), so no, I don't think I'll get up and get dressed and restart a year I've already halfway finished.

I grab my computer, climb back into bed, open my manuscript and stare at the screen. I'd left it open to the last thing I'd written: A Concise History of Me, Part Twenty-Two, about a boy and his dog in Chauvet Cave. Below it, there is nothing. Eighteen Concise Histories, thousands of words—gone. Like they never existed.

They never did, I guess.

⬤▮▮▮▮⬤

Can you burst an eardrum with a finger, or would it take something sharp, say, a pencil? Can you break a kneecap with a hammer, and how long does it take a lighter to burn through skin and muscle before finding bone, and how many stories can a person fall from and survive, and what is the meatiest part of the human anatomy, the place you could really do some damage before ending a person's life?

I don't visit Alan today. Instead I sink into the heaviest of underwaters, my blankets and pillows, and I lie there with the lights out, envisioning creative ways to inflict pain on Circuit. From the outside looking in I imagine one might think, *It was three months—get over it*, but it's not about the time, not really. It's about the Manhattan State trip, and the Wormhole. It's about every story Mr. Elam or Philip Parish told, the thousands of words I'd written that were now erased. It's about how *of course* Sara Lovelock loved what I loved, had the voice of an angel, was obsessed with Mila Henry, and basically embodied everything I'd ever wanted in a girlfriend: she was, quite literally, my Dream Girl.

It's about my best friend who may not wake up.

What you do, what you think, who you do it with—this is your life. So yeah, it was three months, but it's not about the time. It's about the life.

91 ➜ *the contingency of caring*

"Val won't leave." Mom looks like she's been crying; she's wearing the same clothes from yesterday. Dad steps lightly into the room behind her. "She says you didn't visit today, and she's not leaving until she sees you."

I haven't gotten out of bed yet, and unless . . . "Has anything changed? With Alan?"

"No," says Dad.

How such a small word can be so damaging, I'll never know.

I roll over, pull my comforter over my head. "I'm tired. Tell her I'll see her tomorrow."

From under the covers, I hear Dad circle the room until he's standing over me. "You think this isn't hard for the rest of us? Alan is like a second son to me, Noah. And when he wakes up, imagine his disappointment when he finds his best friend out cold. Now Val has absolutely *planted* herself in the kitchen because she cares. You know what that is? That's a friend."

I feel like crying, but can't. Take a deep breath, pull back the comforter: "I should shower first."

Dad's face is pure relief. "We'll sit with her until you're ready."

After they're gone I get out of bed, grab some fresh Navy Bowie, but before I get to the bathroom, Penny walks in.

"Hey, Penn. I can't really talk right now."

She walks over to my desk, sets a piece of paper next to my laptop. "I made something for you."

"Oh. Thanks."

"I miss you, Noah." Fluff emerges out of nowhere. "Right. We *both* do, I guess."

After Penny and Fluff leave, I pick up the folded paper. It has my name drawn in marker across the front: the *O* in *NOAH* is a bright yellow sun, and the *A* is an upside-down heart. I unfold it and cry for the first time in days.

Dear Noah,

"Even the darkest night will end and the sun will rise."

Have you read Les Misérables, darling? Victor Hugo was a freaking genius, IMO. Anyway, you're in the middle of a pretty dark night right now, I think, so I wanted to remind you that the sun will rise. It will! Promise, K?

Love,
Penelope

PS—And maybe after it rises we can watch Breakfast at Tiffany's? Consider it, darling.

◄▐▐▐▐▐▐▶

Val's hair is dirty, she's still wearing the same holey jeans from the hospital, and when she asks, "Where were you today?" the tension in her voice is palpable.

"I don't know, Val. How is he?"

"Same. I don't know."

"But he can't breathe on his own?"

She shrugs. "Soon, they hope."

"They hope."

Val pushes herself up onto the counter. "Noah, I need you right now. My parents are worthless, totally outside themselves. You cannot check out on me again."

"Again?"

"You know what I mean."

"I don't, actually."

Val says, "You've been different for weeks. Distant, or something."

I know what Dad said, that Val is here because she cares, but caring is contingent on the one receiving it. I'm about to say as much, but instead what comes out is, "Val, where are you going to college next year?"

"What?"

"Next year. Where are you going?"

She slowly drops down off the counter, and I can tell she's about to cry. "Who gives a fuck about college right now? Alan is hanging by a thread, and of all the people in his life, No, I cannot fucking *believe* you are as checked out as you are."

"Val, listen. I'm not—I'm not checked out. Something happened to me."

"What does that mean?"

"At the party. Or afterward. I met someone, and I'd had too much to drink, and I shouldn't have been so trusting, but like you said—I've been off for a while, and he said he could help—so I followed him to his house. Val, this kid—he fucked with my brain. I am not right."

The kitchen feels eerily silent for a beat, and then Val says, "Was it Circuit?"

There is this thing, I think, an unnamed thing that lives so deep down inside, we forget it's there; but once in a while something happens to set that unnamed thing on fire. "What?"

"Circuit Lovelock." She steps forward.

"Hold on."

"I have to tell you something, Noah," and that fire inside becomes a flame. "Remember last week when we were all in the pool, and I mentioned how the Lovelocks had come over for dinner? They brought us that giant tin of caramel corn that Alan was going on about. He was at practice the night they came over. Anyway, after dinner, Circuit asked about my photography, so I showed him some of my equipment. And I don't know, we were talking about hobbies, I think, and he mentioned how he was into hypnosis, and—"

"Hang on." I grab Val's hand, lead her down to the confines of the basement, where she continues.

"So Circuit tells me this story about a friend of his who'd busted his knee playing basketball, but apparently all the doctors said this kid was fine. The kid wasn't lying, it was just a psychological thing. So he brings the kid over to his house, puts him under—hypnotizes him, I mean—and afterward the pain is gone. Just like that. Noah, all I could think about was you and your back, how no one could pinpoint what was wrong. So I told him about you."

"Told him what, exactly."

"I told him how one of my friends hurt his back swimming, and how you'd been in like a . . . fog ever since."

"A fog?"

"Circuit said he could help, but it had to be organic. Said it couldn't feel like a blind date, or an official meeting or something. It couldn't feel set up, or else you wouldn't be relaxed enough."

"So what did you do?"

"Nothing, not really. I just had to get you to the party. And then to the library."

And now: I know who Circuit was referring to when he'd said, *I had some help*, and now: I remember it was Val who pointed me in the direction of the library at the Longmire house, and now: standing in this basement, I think back to a time long ago when two friends watched *Across the Universe*, how simple things had been, and how much things had changed since.

"I don't know where he took you or what happened. The deal was one hour in that library, that's it. He said that would be enough."

"He played you, Val."

"What do you mean?"

"Circuit was never interested in helping me. Probably found out about my back injury, then made up some story about a basketball player's knee, knowing you'd bite."

"Why would he do that?" asks Val.

It is time to say this out loud: "Circuit didn't just hypnotize me."

◀▬▬▶

That night, for the first time since waking up in Circuit's room, I have my recurring dream: it's a different room, a different bed, but the same blinding brightness, the same letters floating around in the air coming together to spell PECULIAR WAY, and there's Alan in the corner, dripping wet, and he turns around and lip-synchs "Space Oddity," and beside the bed a dog tries to bark but cannot.

Early the next morning, Mom walks in without knocking. "Rise and shine, Noah. Time to go."

I've been awake for a while, staring at the ceiling. "I'm not going to school."

"I'm not talking about school."

I sit up. "Alan?"

"He's the same. This is something else. We leave in a half hour," she says.

"Mom."

She stops, but doesn't turn around.

"Is Chicago Grace on the way?" I ask.

"It can be."

Half an hour later, I gently place Penny's pink skull suitcase in the backseat of Mom's Land Rover.

"What's that for?"

"Nothing," I say. "Just a bunch of comics Alan left in my room. Figured he might like to see them when he wakes up."

At Chicago Grace, Mom parks in a visitor's spot, says she'll wait for me there. I head inside, suitcase in tow, walking with the confident step of a person who knows where they're going because they've been there before.

Not the kind of confidence you want in the hallways of a hospital.

Only when I get to Alan's room, I find it empty. At a nearby desk I ask a nurse if they moved him, hoping this might indicate some improvement. "Okay," he says, looking Alan up in the computer. "Looks like your friend is under eighteen, which puts him in pediatric ICU. We had limited availability there until last night."

I follow the nurse's instructions to Alan's new room, which is basically a replica of his old one: same machines, same smells, same overall gloom, et cetera. The only real difference is the wallpaper, a rainbow backdrop covered in ABCs.

Inside, Val and her dad sit by his bed in silence.

"Noah, how you holding up?" Mr. Rosa-Haas gets up to hug me; as is the fashion trend at the moment, he's sporting the same clothes he's had on for days, and giant bags under both eyes.

"I'm okay. You guys?" He shrugs, can't seem to get anything out, so I change the subject. "Where's Mrs. Rosa-Haas?"

"Airport to pick up her sister. I told her to go home after. Shower and rest, but we'll see." Mr. Rosa-Haas points to the pink skull suitcase. "You moving in?"

"I brought some of Alan's comics. Thought I might read to him a little bit."

Mr. Rosa-Haas motions around at the rainbow alphabet wallpaper. "Little kid's suitcase for a little kid's room. Fitting."

I can't tell if he's making a joke, or if he really is bitter about Alan being transferred to this room, but he seems pretty unhinged—not that I wouldn't be. "Do you think it would be okay for me to have a few minutes alone with him?"

Val—who hasn't said one word since I got here, much less looked me in the eye, which I am 100 percent okay with—jumps in. "We were just talking about breakfast anyway, right, Dad?"

Mr. Rosa-Haas smiles. "Perfect timing."

After they leave I scoot a chair next to Alan's bed, have a seat, pull my phone from my pocket, and put "Space Oddity" on repeat. Then, unzipping Penny's suitcase, I pull out

Fluffenburger the Freaking Useless. I wasn't sure how he'd respond on the ride over, but he is just too legit senile to give a shit about much of anything, and I have to admit: it's sort of nice having the old grumps back. I set him in my lap, where he might as well be playing dead.

"So, hey," I say. Head down, I gently rub the back of Fluff's neck—and then I look up at Alan. "Hi. Before you say anything, I know—by far our shittiest Dean and Carlo, right? Good news, though. I checked with the cafeteria, and they agreed to cut the pizza into rectangles for you. Something to look forward to. Oh, also. We're taking a basket-weaving class when you wake up, followed by a campfire dinner in iron skillets because I am done talking about that shit. It's high time we took agency in making our dreams come true." It feels silly talking to someone when they almost certainly can't hear a thing, but this morning I woke up with a thought and no matter how crazy it seemed, I couldn't get it out of my head. "Speaking of dreams"—I lean in, lower my voice—"I saw you. In a dream, I mean. You were soaking wet, standing alone in a corner. And there was a dog." I look down at Fluff. "Always a dog, trying to bark, but never could." Now take a deep breath like I'm about to dive, look up, and lean in—and go. "I don't know where you are right now, or if you can hear me, but I'd like to tell you a story if that's okay," and just like my mom has done so many times, I whisper a story by the side of a bed, a story about a kid who was afraid of being alone, who felt nothing would change, who mistreated his friends. "And one night this kid goes to a party," I say, and I give Alan the Concise History of my time Under, and when I'm done, I kiss his motionless hand, and of course it was Alan in my dream: for as long as I'd been Under, he'd been Under too. "I'm so sorry," I say, and now I'm crying all over him, "I'm sorry I wasn't there for you," and that numbness I've felt begins to lift, only the reality of what comes after is even worse.

"Listen, Alan. It's your song, okay?" I turn up the volume as Bowie sings of floating in a most peculiar way. "I woke up to it, and maybe you can too," and I have to believe in the possibility that everything was born for this, that last night's dream, and all those that came before, were more premonitory than hallucinatory, "please, just come out of the cave," and I have to believe there's a moment when you step back and see purpose and design in what was once thought random and accidental.

"It's all set up now, Alan. Just like the dream. Listen," I say, as the song eventually hits its reprise. "Can you hear me?" I ask along with it, and all around us the room comes alive, that alphabet melts off the rainbow wallpaper, those brilliant letters seep and swirl, and all these shattered pieces of my time Under come together right in front of my face: "You're not alone, Alan."

Fluff tries to bark, but nothing comes out.

93 ➜ *the maze*

"I cannot *believe* you rolled him into that hospital in a suitcase," says Mom.

Fluff is either sleeping or passed out in the backseat. Honestly, I'd fear the worst if his labored breathing weren't going toe-to-toe with the Land Rover's prehistoric diesel engine.

"He did great, actually."

"And *why* did you do it again?" asks Mom.

"It's a long story."

"Well, it's a long drive."

"How far are we going?"

"You'll see," says Mom, all coy, but when she pulls onto the highway the GPS on her phone says, *"Starting route to . . . Jasper, Indiana,"* and tells her to turn left in a couple hundred miles. Mom glares at the phone as if it is both sentient and ornery.

"Indiana?" I say.

"What."

"What if Alan wakes up? Or what if—I don't know, what if something goes wrong? And I'm hundreds of miles away?"

"First off, nothing will go wrong. And second, *when* he wakes up, you won't be able to see him immediately anyway."

"Mom."

"This is happening, Noah. It's for you. And this is happening. We'll be back soon enough."

I turn and watch the trees speed by in a blur. "So what's in Jasper, Indiana?"

"Whole lot of wood."

"What?"

"It's the Wood Capital of the World, you know," says Mom.

"Are we in need of wood?"

"Not that I'm aware of, no."

"So . . . why are we going to Jasper, Indiana?"

"Jasper who?"

"Okay, I get it. The mysterious mom routine. I'll let you have this moment."

Two hours later we stop for gas and a bathroom break, and then it's back on the highway. I try to write a Concise History with pen and paper about the evolution of revision and how back in the day writers like Tolstoy and Thoreau and the Brontës had to write everything longhand, which meant every word on the page contained value, as opposed to the writer hacks of today who have the luxury of trying something, failing, deleting, trying something else, failing, deleting until they have a final product. Those old writers had to focus on the front end, had to know where they were going and why.

I thought maybe since I was writing it longhand, the piece would feel sort of meta-in-the-moment, but no, it doesn't, it's just shit writing because I'm a writer hack of today.

━━━▶

We stop for lunch at Wendy's, and Mom is all, "Don't tell your father," and we both order fries, Frosties, and bacon cheeseburgers with extra bacon, which prompts the guy at the counter to ask if we want our hot food first, to which Mom replies, "No, the amount of time it takes to eat a bacon cheeseburger is the exact amount of time a Frosty needs to get melty," which makes me wonder how many times Mom has been to Wendy's without telling anyone.

Sometimes I wonder if I even know my parents at all.

We put a hamburger in the backseat for Fluff, leave the windows cracked, and then choose a table inside. The food is gone in no time, and Mom is right: the Frosties are perfectly melty.

"So how'd the conversation go with Val yesterday?"

"Not good."

She nods, scoops an enormous bite of Frosty onto her spoon. "Not good how?"

"She lied to me? Manipulated a situation?" I push my unfinished Frosty away, lean back in the chair. "Anyway, none of it matters."

"Why's that?"

"Why do you think?"

Mom's spoon freezes in midair. She nods a little, takes a bite, looks at me, another bite, another look, staring and chewing . . .

"What is it, Mom?"

"What?"

"You're looking at me like I'm one of your clients."

"No, I'm not."

"You are."

"Fine," she says. "You know everything, and I know nothing."

"Don't be a dope."

Mom plops her spoon in her empty Frosty cup, sighs heavily. "See, I thought being dope was a good thing."

"Not if it's a noun."

"So it's like the word *ass*?"

"In what way is it like *ass*?"

"You know, like, if you're *being an ass*, that's not good. But if you see, like, a Corvette with those shiny rims on the tires—"

"Oh my God."

"You would say, *That is one cool-ass car*. In that case, *ass* is a good thing."

An elderly couple in the next booth over gets up and leaves.

"I can't believe my mom just said 'ass is a good thing.'"

"What about *AF*?" asks Mom. "What's the skinny on that?"

I slowly drop my head to the table. "Mom, please. I'm begging you."

"Like when someone says *dope AF*, what is that?"

"I cannot believe I'm having this conversation with you in a Wendy's."

"We could relocate. There's a gas station right next door."

Head still down, I say, "*AF* is short for 'as fuck.' So like, *dope as fuck*. Is what that means."

"Ah, okay. So one might say I'm a pretty dope AF mom, right?"

"Are you done?"

"Your mother is never done being dope AF."

"Okay."

"It's more of a lifestyle, really. Dope AF, too legit to quit, party like it's 1999."

I try to hide my smile, but I'm not sure it's working because now Mom is smiling like we're in on some secret together. And then she says, "Honey, I know with Alan in the hospital it might seem like nothing else matters, but I assure you that's not true. If anything, things matter more. I don't know the extent of Val's lie, but I know Val. And your relationship with her is more important now than ever."

"It's complicated, Mom."

She cleans off the table with a napkin, puts all our trash on a tray. "My roommate in college used to piss the bed."

A beat, then: "Okay."

"Have I told you this story?" she asks.

"I don't think so."

Mom shrugs, continues. "Carrie was a big drinker with a tiny bladder. Mornings after parties usually involved a trip to the laundry room. She was a socialite, a serial dater—prettier than me, cooler than me, bigger boobs than me—"

"Mom, gross."

"Seriously though, they were like—" Mom holds both hands out a couple feet from her chest.

"*Mom.*"

"Anyway. I was dating this guy Dalton. Or was it Gordon?"

"Who even are you?"

"I was only with the guy a few weeks, tops. The story isn't really about him, anyway. We'll just say it was Dalton. And Carrie was going out with this guy from the tumbling squad who had these huge muscles. So one night the four of us are at this bar, when I start feeling sick. Like, *really* sick. I tell Dalton I have to go, but he can stay if he wants. Obviously, I'm hoping he'll drive me back to my dorm and dote on me, but he says if I'm sure it's okay, he'd like to stay, and that he can get a ride back to school with Carrie and what's-his-face."

"With the muscles."

Mom nods. "So I leave. Drive back to the dorm and after a few—*episodes*—I'm straight to bed, dead asleep in no time." Even when Mom tells a true story, she does it with the same timing and tone she uses when telling those bedtime stories; I've heard enough of them by now to know when she's ramping up. "At some point in the middle of the night, I wake up to the sound of Carrie having sex. Unfortunately, it wasn't uncommon, and normally I'd just pretend to be asleep, but this time I wake up sick as a dog, and I decide that's it, I've had it. So I flip on the light and I'm about to tell her off when I see Dalton. In bed with her."

"No."

"Yeah."

"*Your* boyfriend."

"Yeah."

"In bed with *your* roommate. While *you* were in the room."

"Dalton's eyes had that total glazed-over look. I mean, he was just *really* drunk—"

"Yeah, I know the one."

Mom pauses, raises an eyebrow.

"I mean, not *personally*, just—movies and whatnot. So what'd you do?"

"Well, I yelled a lot. Broke up with Dalton, obviously, and stopped speaking to Carrie altogether. She felt awful, kept trying to apologize, and I just . . . wouldn't listen. And then two weeks later, she was dead."

Mom and I sit in this sort of weird fast-food silence, and she lets that last line hang in the air.

"What happened?"

"She wrapped her car around a telephone pole. Blood alcohol level off the charts. Plus, we'd had a ton of ice and snow that November. Dalton was in the car with her. He was injured pretty bad, had this horrible scar on his face the rest of his life, but—"

"Oh."

"What?"

"Nothing, it's just"—*disheartening? Exhausting? A giant sigh of relief?*—"I think you have told me about Carrie before."

"See, I thought so."

Okay, yes, some relief. Relief that I hadn't randomly attached my mother to this horrific act, that I now know the origin story of the scar. But it occurs to me now how drastically I was mistaken: the notion that my time Under was orchestrated by Circuit is not the worst-case scenario; the worst-case scenario is that my time Under was, as Circuit implied, orchestrated by me. Stories told when I was a kid, incidents and conversations long buried in my subconscious had been harvested and scattered all over the place like seeds. In the coming days, weeks, months, years, who knew what latent thoughts or fears might rustle up to the surface, or in what scenarios? If it could happen with my mother in a Wendy's, it could happen with anyone anywhere.

"I bring it up for a reason."

I look down at my napkin. "Mom."

"Not forgiving someone is like a growth. Starts off small, harmless enough—but burrowed in. And if you let it, it will consume you from the inside."

"You mean Val."

"I mean you, Noah. I don't know why, but I think you blame yourself for what happened to Alan. And I'd like to be the one to say it's not your fault."

"You don't know that."

Mom sets her hand on top of mine, a new urgency in her voice. "It's like this big maze, see. With fire-breathing dragons and land mines and decoys at every turn. And the maze goes on for hundreds of miles, and just when you think maybe you've gotten through—a dead end. Years of wrong turns and mistakes and battles with those dragons, years of bruises, cuts, and burns, but eventually? You make it. You come out the other end of the maze, and you're a little banged up, but you're okay. And maybe you meet someone else who was in the maze at the same time, only you didn't know it. So you talk to this person, compare notes on the maze, and you hear all the ways they made it through that you never thought of, and you tell them all the ways you made it through that *they* never thought of, and from this shared understanding you grow to love one another. And that love deepens with time. And maybe you and this other person have a child." Mom starts crying, and so do I. "A perfect, lovely little kid, and you swear you'll do everything you can to spare your kid from the fire-breathing dragons and the land mines and the decoys. *I'll draw them a map,* you think, a detailed map of the maze outlining the quickest routes, pitfalls to avoid, shortcuts that took you years to learn, and maybe this way they won't end up with bruises and burns like yours."

I squeeze Mom's hand tighter, let the tears come. "Mom."

She smiles and cries. "You think you have so much time to work on the map, to make it just right. And then one day you wake up to find your perfect, lovely child is already there, right in the thick of the maze. You were so diligent, kept watch every night, and you don't know when or how it happened, but it did. Your kid is in the maze without a map, and there's nothing you can do but watch."

"I love you, Mom," and I think about a conversation that never happened, in the middle of an eighties explosion, where I told my sister that survival was about finding the right friends, and it occurs to me that in a way I was reporting back something I'd learned from the maze—in a way, I was showing up for my sister. And maybe that's something I can do for her more often.

Mom blows her nose into a napkin. "Forgiveness isn't a miracle, Noah. It's not magic. But yes, you should forgive Val. And while you're at it, you should forgive yourself."

"What if I can't?"

Mom's smile is a rainbow after a hard storm. "Yeah, I remember that decoy."

94 → affectionate roots

We reach Jasper, and Mom turns into a small cemetery with a gravel driveway. She navigates between rows of cracked gravestones overgrown with weeds and dried grass, and eventually pulls over the car, cracks the windows for Fluff, shuts off the engine, and opens her door.

"Follow me." She doesn't wait, just gets out and starts walking, and when I finally catch up, she stops between two headstones.

"Mom, what are we doing here?"

She points to the ground.

AND FINALLY ➻ PART EIGHT

THE NEW YORK YEARS

Autumn 1946. At the age of eighteen Henry traded the wilds of her childhood farm life outside Boston for a different kind of wilderness: New York City. It is believed that this move was forever a point of contention between Mila Henry and her father, that Hank Henry resented his daughter for abandoning him as her mother had those many years ago (see: *"FAMILY & EARLY LIFE"*). And when, the following year, Hank Henry fell to his death from the roof of his barn, many speculated that perhaps he hadn't fallen, that perhaps he'd jumped, that the bitter realities of growing old alone—of losing first his wife in childbirth, and then that very child to faraway aspirations—were simply too much for the man.

Whatever the case, her father's death did nothing to quell Mila Henry's writing career. In 1949 she published *Babies on Bombs* to some acclaim, though its harsh rendering of wartime violence, and a particular subplot involving a widow who abandons her only child, made the book far too divisive to be a commercial success. Around this time, Henry had met and married writer Thomas Huston, and together they had one son, Jonathan. Later, Henry would say of having children, "It's rather like getting smacked in the head by your most favorite hammer."

Both Mila Henry and Thomas Huston lived and wrote from their home in Chelsea, but the daily task of raising their son fell to Henry, as Huston commonly referred to child-rearing as "woman's work."

And so Mila Henry did that work, and while doing it, managed to pen what most critics believe to be her finest achievement: *June First, July Second, Augustus Third*. Upon its publication, the *New York Times* called it "a revolution on the page, a creation that will breathe long after its creator has taken her last." This proved quite prophetic, as *June First* has become one of the most successful, widely read books of its time. Seemingly overnight, Mila Henry became a household name.

Thomas Huston was never published.

—*Excerpt from bonus materials of Mila Henry's*
This Is Not a Memoir: A Memoir (Collector's Edition)

Mila Henry's headstone is significantly shorter than those around it, as if through the years it has gradually, but determinedly, sunk into the ground.

My first thought: this is a joke. But the look on Mom's face indicates otherwise. My second thought: it's a different Mila Henry. This actually sticks for a second. There must be other Mila Henrys, maybe dozens or more if you count the ones who've already died. Also, there's no way *the* Mila Henry, *my* Mila Henry is buried in Podunk, Indiana, without my knowledge.

And then I see the inscription under her dates of birth and death: HERE'S TO THE SILENCE BETWEEN THEM.

"It was your father's idea," says Mom. "Coming here. Killed him he had to work today."

"I don't understand," I say, which doesn't really begin to cover the extent of it.

Mom points to a headstone just next to Mila Henry's.

"She never lived here," says Mom. "Mila, I mean. But I'm guessing you knew that already."

How many hours have I spent combing the Internet for articles of her past, her

AFFECTIONATE
ROOTS

HENRY

NATHANIEL
"HANK"
1905-47

MARTHA
1907-28

own favorite writers and muses, her tragedies and successes and relationships? Enough to piece together a map of her life, one that excluded most, if not all, of the Midwest, and one that most *certainly* excluded Jasper, Indiana.

"Mila's maternal grandparents were from Jasper." Mom points to more headstones down the row with other last names, people I've never heard of, so many names through so many years, none of those names remembered, but all of them integral to a name that would never be forgotten, as if they were the affectionate roots of some immortal tree. "When Mila's mother died giving birth to her, Mila's grandmother insisted her daughter be buried here."

I can't stop staring at Mila Henry's name on the stone. And what an odd thing to be so physically near her now. After all these years of *feeling* close, to now *be* close.

"Why did you bring me here?" I ask. It sounds accusatory; I don't mean it to be.

"Your father and I wanted to get you away from things, even for a few hours. We figured it was time you met your hero. But also"—she looks up at the country spread wide in every direction, the symmetrical rows of headstones and flags, fields and fences and scattered oaks, and beyond that a horizon, a beautiful and vast American nothing—"there's something about her being buried here that I like. Not that she cared one way or the other about Jasper, Indiana. But I think she wanted to be near family."

Mom's earlier words of forgiveness are all the more potent over the grave of someone who never could quite grasp those two words—*I'm sorry*—except in the only way she knew how: a story on the page.

I'm sorry, Nathan. I'm just so sorry.

I knew her parents' names were Martha and Hank, I just never knew Hank was a nickname for Nathaniel. Looking at her parents' shared headstone, I have to wonder: Did Mila Henry feel guilty about leaving her father? Did she wish she'd stayed? Did she spend the rest of her life blaming herself for what happened to him?

"It's not your fault," I say aloud.

And standing over the bones of my favorite writer, my immortal tree, I feel its roots beneath my feet, pulsing and even now alive, lifting this short and fractured headstone from soil to sky, and in that blinding blue firmament a thousand forgotten names join in the single, unending chorus of Mila Henry.

"I'd like to be the one to say it's not your fault."

The ride home is quiet. I look out the window and think how sad it is that the only things we know are those things the keepers of history choose to tell us. They could give a shit about heroes once they're dead and used up, apparently. And while this is disappointing, I can't deny the intimacy I felt at Henry's gravesite knowing it wasn't a memorial in some brochure, or even a very public place.

People ruin everything if you let them.

I close my eyes, lean my head against the window, and think of the inscription on Mila Henry's headstone—*Here's to the silence between them*—and I wonder if there is value to be found in other unfilled spaces too. Maybe all the things I'd done while Under, all the conversations and actions, all the life I'd once thought stolen, maybe those things were the words, and now I'd found the silence. Maybe I could take those phantom months, stack them on my desk, and label the pile *First Draft*, knowing it's not my best work, but that's okay. There's always revision.

⬅▨▨▨▨▨➡

I'm jolted awake by the ringing of Mom's phone. She checks the caller ID. "Your dad," she says, and then answers. "Hey. Yeah, we're making good time. Probably home around midnight."

Something about falling asleep while it's bright outside, and then waking up when it's dark is so completely disorienting.

"Okay," says Mom into the phone.

My phone buzzes in my pocket.

"Okay, and?"

Two missed calls from Val, and a text.

> Val: He's awake

96 ➡ *our best lives*

I hadn't expected to see Alan the night we got back from Jasper (though not for lack of trying), but I'd fully expected to see him first thing Friday morning. As it turned out, even though the doctors had confirmed there were no significant brain or spinal injuries, had successfully weaned him off meds, gotten him off the ventilator and breathing on his own—even though he was *awake*—I was not allowed to do what my heart and soul wanted to do, which was burst into his room with cake and flowers, pick him up and spin him around by his waist, laughing and crying and singing selected tunes from *Hamilton* at the top of my lungs.

"So when *can* I see him?"

"Probably tomorrow," says Mom. "They'll be done with the tests, and he should be fairly lucid. But these meds he's been on have amnesic properties, so we don't know what he'll remember. And he may be a little loopy."

Dad says, "Which one is *Hamilton* again?"

Mom points to Dad. "For example."

<hr />

Next day, Val tackle-hugs me the second I walk into Alan's room. "I'm so sorry," she whispers in my ear, and I think about the growth of a grudge, how it had already started to burrow in, and how much further it could have gone had I let it run its course. "It's okay," I say, and I hug her back, "you were trying to help," and like Mom said, it's not a miracle. It's not magic. But it is good.

"You guys have just been waiting for me to slip into a coma so you could start dating again, huh?" Alan smiles weakly from his bed, face flushed, the kind of groggy you can see. He shakes his head, all, "Uncool, yo. Uncool," and even though his voice is raspy, I've maybe never heard anything so clean and beautiful in my life.

I walk over and can't help smiling at the absence of life-saving apparatus. "Feeling pretty good, are we? Well rested?" I look at a fake watch on my wrist. "Had a pretty solid nap there."

"You know I'm naked under all these blankets," says Alan.

"You know I'm straight under all these clothes." I kiss a bicep. "Maybe someday, though. Play your cards right, who knows."

And my hand, which had been on the side of his bed, is now in his, and Alan says, "I missed you," and I start crying.

"I missed you too."

And now Val is with us, and this sterilized room in the pediatric ICU is as good as my room at home: we climb into bed, Val on one side of Alan, me on the other, the equation of our triangle in full form—*one plus one plus one equals one*—and for a while we lie there, content in the shape of us.

◀▥▥▶

Val and I watch *Gilmore Girls* on her phone while Alan falls in and out of sleep between us. Since I was last here, it's like someone tried to see how many flowers they could fit in one room.

"Titi Rosie," says Val, answering my roving gaze. "She doesn't bring flowers, she brings the florist."

"So she made it in okay?"

"Yeah, she's currently holding down the fort at home. And by holding down the fort, I mean cooking enough food to feed the tri-county area."

Alan stirs like he might wake up, but then doesn't.

"Are your parents at home too?" I ask quietly.

"Yes. They left when they found out you were coming."

"Oh. Why?"

"I mean, look at us."

"Right."

"Oh, also." Val points to one of the many bouquets on the table next to the bed. "Guess who those are from?"

"Who?"

"Tyler."

"Tyler . . . Walker?"

"Nope."

"Not Massey."

She nods, explains how apparently Tyler Massey's family had spent the summer somewhere in England, where he had an awakening. "Word has it, he's been going around school, apologizing to everyone for being a douchebag. Anyway, he found out what happened to Alan, sent those over."

"That's nice."

"Maybe more than nice. Read the note."

I pull the little white card off the vase, read Massey's chicken scratch:

Very sorry for the way I treated you. If you can forgive me, I'd love to take you to a movie sometime. Xoxo—TM

"Holy shiznit," I say. "He xoxo'd him."

"Crazy, right?"

"Monumental, more like."

I'm this close to a joke about Tyler's burgeoning film

career, and how this news may or may not shed light on his latest effort, *The Vagina Dialogues*—when I realize *The Vagina Dialogues* only ever existed in my head.

"What's funny?" asks Val.

I hadn't realized I was laughing. "Nothing," I say. "Just glad, I guess."

"Speaking of monumental"—Val points to my shirt and pants—"what happened to Navy Bowie?"

This morning, for the first time in a while, I reached for my Bowie tee and found myself thinking, *Not today.* And so, in keeping with the personal revision idea, I dug to the bottom of my bin and found my only non–Navy Bowie articles of clothing that still fit: an old gray V-neck, some black pants with a tan stripe down the side, and a pair of white high-top Chucks.

"Yeah, I don't know," I say. "Figured it was time for a change. What do you think?"

"In a word?" says Val. "*Funereal.*"

Out of nowhere, Alan says, "I was going to say *zoological.* But funereal is better."

"I didn't know you were awake," Val says.

"I am sneaky," says Alan. "Like a jackrabbit."

"You're on drugs."

"Like a jackrabbit on drugs. But good drugs, yo. Noah, I'm gonna ask the nurse to get you some of this goodness for your back."

I can't tell if Alan is really with us or not, but given the fact that he could fall back asleep at any moment, and I may or may not be able to talk to him again today, I figure now is as good a time as any. "So, about my back."

"Ah." Val pauses the episode on her phone, sits up in bed, and turns to face me. "Is this it?"

"Is this what?"

"The apology," says Alan. "Better make it a good one."

"Wait." Now I sit up, and they're both looking at me, trying to act hard-core, but unable to ward off mild amusement. "How long have you guys known?" I ask.

"Seriously?" says Val. "Since, like, the beginning, dude."

Alan says, "You're literally the worst liar, No."

"In the history of lying liars," says Val. "The literal worst."

"Um, okay."

Val crosses her arms, raises her eyebrows. "Well?"

"What."

"Yo. Just because the lie didn't land," says Alan, "doesn't mean you weren't out there tossing it around on the daily."

"Right. Okay." I clear my throat. "I am truly sorry I lied about my back."

Alan nods at Val, who says, "Apology accepted." She slides down in bed and is about to push play again, but I stop her.

"Wait. You guys are my best friends," I say. "You're not everyone else to me. To me, you're you guys, and I'm sorry for betraying that. Also, Alan, before you fall asleep—"

"Jackrabbits don't need sleep."

"I'm sorry I wasn't there for you. I'm sorry I left the party, sorry I was a dick *at* the party, and I'm sorry I didn't appreciate you the way I should have. Both of you. I'm really sorry, and I hope you guys accept my apology."

Alan puts a hand on mine. "Already forgotten, yo."

"Thanks."

"No, I mean, like, I literally forgot about it. Like I don't re-member any of that."

"Oh."

"They said this might happen," says Val, "with his meds and shit."

"Right."

In the ensuing silence, I stare at the screen on Val's phone, willing her to push play. Because even if Alan doesn't remem-ber those things—including and especially the look on his face when I told him to stay in the kitchen with his friends and get high—I always will.

"Just tell me one thing," says Alan.

"Name it."

"Do Luke and Lorelai *ever* get it on?"

Alan is asleep again, and this one does seem deeper. We stay in bed like that, Val and me on either side of him, the two of us watching Rory Gilmore move into her college dorm room at Yale, which still seems odd after years of her Harvard dream.

"Why SAIC?" I ask.

"What?"

I'm not sure, is the thing. I'm not sure why I asked. "It's al-ways been SAIC for you. Why?"

Quietly, so as not to wake Alan, Val says, "It has one of the best photography programs in the country. Undergrad and graduate, if I decide to go that route. Plus, it's local. Why do you ask?"

Now I know why, and even though part of me wants to say, "No reason," I can't, because along with everything else, Val's feed is back to normal, to her first and true love: movies. Because there's only one city in the world that so perfectly integrates the magic of movies and photography. And because the only thing worse than Val leaving is Val sticking around for second best.

"You should go to LA."

She sits up on her elbows, pauses the episode. "What?"

This is right, an opportunity for revision, I know that—even so, I have to hold back tears. "I read somewhere that UCLA's photography program values narrative aspects over technical ones. Val, that's you. That is *so* you." Swallow—go on. "You're the most talented person I know. And you're the absolute best person to watch movies with. And I think you should be doing more than watching them."

I can't read Val's face. I don't think she's mad, but—I don't know. She puts her head back down on Alan's chest, pushes play on her phone, and after a solid minute, says, "You'd come see me?"

I reach my hand across Alan, and she takes it, and together we feel the rise and fall of his chest as he breathes, hear the rhythmic beating of his heart, let this tangible proof of his life wash over us, each wave a reminder that we are, in fact, living our best lives.

"All the time, Val."

Tuesday after school I knock on my sister's bedroom door.

"Come in!"

Inside, Penn is hunched over her desk with her iPad and four open textbooks; Fluffenburger the Freaking Useless limps toward me, and just when I think maybe he's going in for the snuggle, he fakes right and heads out the door into the hallway.

Yeah, it's good to have him back. Mark Wahlberg was entirely too big for his britches.

"Ready for a change?"

I look back at Penny. "What?"

She motions to my clothes. "Your outfit."

"Oh. Yeah, it was time."

"I agree and approve."

"Well, that's a load off."

"How's Alan?"

"He's good," I say. "Should be home in a few days."

"Good. I like that guy."

I swear. This girl. "Yeah, he's all right. Listen, I was thinking about watching this movie called *Breakfast at Tiffany's*? I've heard good things, didn't know if you'd maybe wanna watch with me."

Whatever reaction I'd imagined this might conjure doesn't happen. Penny squirms in her seat. "That's sweet of you. But no thanks."

"Really?"

"Yeah, I'm—done with that movie now."

"Penn, are you feeling okay?"

She looks up at me over her sea of homework. "This girl in my class, Karen Yi, watched *Breakfast at Tiffany's* on my recommendation. And then yesterday at school she asked me how I could like a racist movie like that. I asked her what she meant, and she said she cried because of how horribly they depicted Mr. Yunioshi. And now she won't even look at me, she's so hurt."

I'm trying to remember the last time I've seen Penny like this, so quietly, deeply shaken. I listen to her tell me she's done with *Breakfast at Tiffany's*, and how she doesn't want to be the kind of person who likes stories like that, and as I listen I find myself sad that her heart is so clearly broken, but happy that her heart is capable of such brokenness.

"Penny."

"The movie really hurt her, Noah. And I told her to watch it."

In the brief silence, I stand there wondering at the ways in which I might protect that heart. "Penn, you are a singular human being. And I love you. And I think I have an idea."

So we watch *Breakfast at Tiffany's*, and since Penny never actually recorded the time stamps of Mr. Yunioshi's scenes, we write them down as they happen. During one of these scenes, Penny actually looks away—from the TV, and from me—and I know she's thinking of her friend from school, and it half-way breaks my heart to see it dawn on her that this most wonderful and cherished of things is not without serious blemish. But I also know that sometimes—not always, but in the best of cases—innocence lost can be knowledge gained, and I think this is one of those times. Because in truth, whatever hurt Penn feels watching this now pales in comparison to the hurt Karen must have felt.

I want to hug Penny, and so I do, and I tell her she can still love this flawed thing. I tell her it will be a different love, a little sadder maybe, but wiser, too. I tell her that if we can't love flawed things, we probably wouldn't love anything at all. And she says that makes sense, because she loves me even though I mostly ignore her, and that pretty much breaks my heart the rest of the way.

Penny falls asleep near the end, and I find myself alone, watching Holly Golightly dump her cat into some rando alleyway, and it's one of those weird moments when you feel a movie is trying to tell you something, but you're not sure what, and so you sit up and take note.

I sit up. I take note.

Earlier in the movie, Holly Golightly adopts this cat as a pet, names it Cat, and now Cat is in all these scenes, just sort of hanging around like a normal cat, but not really part of things until the end when Holly releases it into the alleyway, and of course, it is *pouring* rain, so watching it, you're like, *Wow, Cat's a goner, I guess*, but then, like, five minutes later Holly's love interest—a writer she calls Fred Darling—really gives it to her for acting like a child, and he goes off in search of Cat. At which point Holly sees the error of her ways and joins him, so now she's running around in the alley in the pouring rain, screaming, "Cat! Cat!" like a total nutjob. She finds Cat in between these wooden boxes, picks him up, and then turns to Fred Darling—who's been standing there staring at her the whole time, apparently—and then they sort of stumble into this awkward kiss, but the thing is, Holly is still holding Cat, who winds up smooshed between the two, looking right into the camera like, *Man, you would not* believe *the fucking day I've had*.

And that's it. The End. So yeah, at first I hated the movie. But then I figured out what it was trying to tell me.

98 → the sun will rise

I half expect twobytwooak@gmail.com to be taken. It's not, so I claim it. A minute later, on YouTube, I scroll to the comments section of the Fading Girl video, type in, Hello—I really enjoyed your video, and would like to ask a quick question. If you have a free moment, would you mind emailing me at twobytwooak@gmail.com? Thank you. Not a single exclamation. And I haven't read *Les Misérables*, nor seen any of its theatrical iterations, so I have no context for Penny's advice, but I know truth when I hear it, and I have known a very dark night, and I know how to pick myself up off the ground. So I link my Gmail app to my new account, and because sometimes it feels good to say things out loud, I say, "That's one down."

Five minutes later I have the date and location of Pontius Pilot's next show programmed into my phone calendar. "That's two."

And the bones of Mila Henry may be buried in the ground of the Wood Capital of the World, but I know those bones for what they are. I've seen their roots dug deep in the earth, and I've felt their pulsing aliveness, and some may say she's dead and gone, but I know better: she is with her family; she is forgiven. "And that's three."

I look around my room, revel in its cleanliness, its organization; I listen to Bowie's "Changes" followed by "Space Oddity," and even though it's late, the house long asleep, I say, "Even the darkest night will end," and I think of how my Strange Fascinations are rooted in a single thing: a fear of being alone.

Thing is, I've never been older than sixteen. I can't know what it's like to have lived a whole life only to look back and realize I was truly lonely. But I know the flip side of that coin, what it's like to see my life spread out in front of me as a hundred roads to be traveled, and what if I choose the wrong one? Or worse, what if the wrong one is chosen for me, and I get to the end of this road and no one else is there? That fear I know well. And sometimes I think the potential of loneliness is scarier than actual loneliness.

I grab my phone. Seems a good time for some company.

"Three down, one to go," I say to the empty room.

Me: You up?

Alan: For you? Always

Me: You're texting with Tyler, aren't you?

Alan: ¯_(ツ)_/¯

Me: You know there's an emoji for that now?

Alan: I heard. Kids these days

Me: No sense of work ethic.

Me: So how you feeling?

Alan: Fine. A little better. I mean there's some
improvement, so we'll see.

Me: Wait.

Alan: It's okay. Doc says things are progressing.

Me: ARE YOU BEING ME???

Alan: IT'S A LITTLE TIGHT, BUT GETTING
THERE

Me: Touché.

Alan: Been waiting to do that since I woke up

Me: If you're quite done, I need you to join me on a quest

Alan: Sorry. I thought you just said you needed
me to join you on a quest

Me: I did.

Alan: Sorry. I thought you just said you did

Me: I'm being serious.

Alan: When you say *quest,* you mean like
    NeverEnding Story?

Me: I cannot believe you still reference that movie.

Alan: I mean your dad was HELLA eager to
    show it to us.

Me: Haha and remember he kept calling it "wack"

Alan: OMG YES

Alan: "THIS MOVIE IS A LITTLE MORE WACK
    THAN I REMEMBER"

Me: The cokeheads of the 80s really found a home in children's
    cinema

Alan: No joke, dude. Labyrinth, anyone?

Me: Yeah, but Bowie

Alan: Well yeah, Bowie

Me: Okay, Atreyu. Here's the deal. I wanna take a cat to this old
    dude.

Alan: I don't know what that means

Me: It means I want to take a cat to an old dude

Alan: Hang on, I'll just google it

Me: Dude, it's not a euphemism.

Me: A literal feline.

Me: To a literal man who might actually die soon

Alan: What's wrong with him?

Me: Nothing. He's old. Shit happens

Alan: OK, well, I might sit this one out? No offense. Sounds kinda dumb. Plus Tyler and I are discussing funny sex words

Me: OMG, I didn't mean this very minute.

Me: Also. Which words?

Alan: Lovemaking

Me: Why is that funny?

Alan: Come on. Like it's a pie with an intricate recipe?

Me: Ah. OK. Got it

Alan: Mmmm, honey, this love you made is
        outstanding.

Me: I get the picture

Alan: Could you email me the recipe for that
        love you made last night? DELECTABLE

Me: So are you joining me or not? The QUEST needs you, Atreyu

Alan: On my way

Me: OMG I WISH

Alan: Right?

Me: When do you get out?

Alan: They said Thursday probably

Me: Thursday it is. I'll come over after school.

Alan: The Never-End-ing Stooooo-horrrr-
        eeeeeyyy!

Me: Atreyu out!

Alan: IM ATREYU YO

Me: Whatever. Don't stay up all night sexting

Alan: ¯_(ツ)_/¯

‹‖‖‖‖›

Thursday after school, I drive straight to the Rosa-Haases', which both smells and looks like it's been converted into the basement kitchen from that British show my parents can't get enough of, where like a million people are running around in tuxes, and every meal has seven courses, and for all the "ladyships" and "lordships" around, it sure seems like the flour-faced cook is the one who knows what's what.

"Eight o'clock, nene," says Titi Rosie, dumping some delicious-smelling concoction of oregano and onions and garlic and I don't know what else into a food processor. "At the *latest*, you hear me?"

Before I can assure her that I understand, Mrs. Rosa-Haas walks into the kitchen and literally makes me pinkie promise to have Alan back by eight p.m.

These two basically live on the same page.

"I promise," I say, as solemn as possible. "Back by eight. Got it."

Val walks in, leans over the freshly pureed concoction in the food processor. "Your sofrito smells like heaven, Titi Rosie," to which her aunt shrugs and nods like, *Yeah, it usually does*.

Mrs. Rosa-Haas then reminds me that Alan is not allowed to overexert himself in any way whatsoever. Behind his mother's back, Alan mimes jerking off, which makes me giggle, which Mrs. Rosa-Haas interprets as me not taking her seriously.

"This is a joke to you?"

I shake my head. "No, Mrs. Rosa-Haas. Alan was being super-inappropriate behind your back."

Alan gives his mom the innocent puppy-dog look; she returns it with that smile moms sometimes give where you could swear they're crossing their fingers behind their back. "Love you, mijo," she says. "But back by eight or it's over for you."

"Where're you guys going?" asks Val, grabbing a bottle of water from the fridge.

"Taking a cat to this old dude," says Alan.

"I don't know what that means."

Alan smiles at me. "Told you."

"It's not a euphemism," I say. "We're literally taking a cat to an old guy. You should come with."

Val takes a long swig. "With those skills, Noah, it's shocking you're single."

"The universe is a mysterious place, Val."

Minutes later, the three of us are in my car, scrolling through ads for free cats on Craigslist. "How lucky are we to be alive right now?" says Alan. "Getting ourselves a Craigslist cat."

Val is all, "Wake me up when they deliver."

Alan pretends to be on the phone. "Yes, hi, I'd like one large thin-crust, a tabby cat, and some fucking Fancy Feast, yo."

"May I live to see the day."

We eventually land on a Craigslist cat whose address is only a couple miles away. Alan gently pats the dashboard. "Make haste, ye fun guy ballsack!"

I don't suppose I'll ever feel normal again. Certainly not conversationally. But there's something to be said for knowing things turn out okay in the end. "You know," I say. "I saw this commercial, and it's actually pronounced *hun-day*."

Twenty minutes later Val has a cat named Bonkers in her lap, and we're headed to the gas station on OMG's route, and they never once ask what made me think to do this, never once make a joke about it. And ever since my conversation with Val in the basement—where she confessed to unwittingly assisting Circuit, and I told her the gist of what he'd done to me—she's been nothing but a supportive friend. And even though I'd given all the details to Alan in the ICU, he was in his own Under at the time; I don't know if he heard me, if what I did that day helped bring him back. And I do wonder how things will change with us next year, what other shapes our friendship might take, but I'm hopeful that one day, in the Rosa-Haas pool, maybe, I might come up for air, break the surface, inhale, wet hair in the hot sun . . .

"Dude," Alan might say.

"That was like a record," Val would say. "You okay?"

And I would take a few deep breaths, grateful not to be alone. "I have to tell you something," I might say; and instead I tell them everything. Because really, what else does it mean to share history if not to share a story?

Three days later there's an email in my twobytwooak@
gmail.com inbox from someone with the email address
singthebodyelectric@yahoo.com. The message is brief. Six
words. I read the email twice, set my phone on my desk, and
stare out the window.

⬅▶

"Hi," I said, unsure how else to start.

"Who are you?" he asked, a reasonable question.

"I'm Noah." I held up the cat. "This is Bonkers."

*The man looked anxious, eager to get back to his walk, and
I tried not to think of him as Mr. Elam, tried not to think of all
the ways I thought I'd known this man. "Look," I said. "I know
this is weird, and I don't know you. But I thought maybe you'd
like to have this cat."*

*"I can't carry that cat," he said, as if that were the only thing
stopping him.*

"I'll carry him for you."

*The man nodded once, started walking again, and I fol-
lowed. We passed Alan and Val, who sat on the hood of my car
at the gas station; they sort of smiled, sort of shook their heads,
and I sort of shrugged, as if it were all too random for any of
us to respond with any gesture of certainty. I followed the old
man to a small house a few blocks away—a far cry from a cozy
bed-and-breakfast—and again pushed down the sensation of*

sadness that crept in every time something didn't line up with what it was while Under. The man fumbled in his jacket pocket for a key, unlocked the door, stepped inside. He hung his cane on the wall, and then reached for the cat.

"Thank you," he said.

"You're welcome. Also—if it's okay, I'd like to visit you sometime."

The old man stared for a minute, pointed to his goiter: "I won't talk about this."

"Okay."

He gently stroked Bonkers. "I don't understand."

"It's just—I see you every day. On my way to school, on my way home. I see you out walking. And you're always alone. And I'm not saying that's bad. Maybe you want to be alone. But it also occurred to me that maybe you think no one in the whole world really sees you. I know I feel that way sometimes, like no one really sees me. And I wanted you to know that that wasn't true. That someone else in this world sees you. And if you'd like to tell me your story, or just talk, or whatever . . . I'm here."

Bonkers purred, and the man said, "Okay," and I could tell he was still trying to figure me out, but it also looked like he might cry, so I smiled at him, reached out, and scratched Bonkers on the head.

"Would you like to come by tomorrow?" the old man asked.

"Sure."

Next day after school, I knocked on his door, and he opened it, and the first thing he said was, "What would you like to know?"

I pull Whitman off the shelf, flip to the poem "I Sing the Body Electric," and how perfect that the Fading Girl should use this for her email address, that all this time I've associated her video with the slow deterioration of the body, when perhaps she sings it electric. "O my body! I dare not desert the likes of you," says Whitman, and I'm beginning to suspect a plot wherein my Strange Fascinations have been conspiring together to remind me that this world is both very real and full of very real magic.

I reread the message from singthebodyelectric@yahoo .com: What would you like to know?

100 → *a beautiful piece of land*

"I don't know," I say, and it's true. Mom and Dad don't say anything, just look at me, and I can't meet their eyes so I plow on: "I don't know what I want. Next year, or the next ten, I don't know," and it feels good, this emptying of my head, my heart, "and my back is fine, I'm not injured, I lied about that, and I'm sorry. I wish I hadn't," and still, my parents say nothing. "I'm not even sure I ever loved swimming as much as everyone thought I did. It's like—your yams, Dad. I ate them once when I was a kid without really thinking about it. And then every time after that, you piled them on my plate, all, 'I know how much Noah loves yams,' only I didn't, not really.

So maybe I'll go to college. Maybe I'll swim. Or maybe I won't. I don't know. But swear to God? You *make* me go? And I'm going to Europe. You'll go to sleep one night, wake up the next day, and I'll be gone." Mom and Dad still aren't talking, which I find somewhat disarming, but at least they aren't physically restraining me for basically losing it in the kitchen. "You're always telling me I can tell you anything. So there it is, there you go. That was me telling you anything. Everything, really."

Dad starts crying, because of course.

"I'll make mistakes," I say. "But they're mine to make. Right?"

They both nod, and now all three of us are hugging, and it reminds me of how things once were, years ago when I was little, the pre-Penny days. And while I can't imagine our family without her in it, there was something special about it being just the three of us, something intangible and charmed, and whatever that was, it's here now. The hug ends and on my way out of the kitchen, I take a last look back to find my parents beaming at each other. They're still crying, but they're smiling even more, and I realize that whatever intangible charmed thing we had when it was just the three of us, Mom and Dad had a whole different life before even I came along.

It makes me think of this beautiful, empty piece of land. And maybe people build something on that land, like a barn, and maybe that barn houses all these animals, and it stands strong for years, and then one day a son or a daughter gets married in the barn, and all the old people who built that barn look around at it with loving eyes. Because they remember how this used to be an empty piece of land, and while that was beautiful, they think of all the animals who have called this barn home, and of their children who will always remember being married here, and the old people are happy, so happy they built this barn.

Mom and Dad's smile really is a beautiful piece of land.

The cursor blinks . . .

I write some things. They suck, mostly. But there they are, right there on the screen in front of me, all *existing* and whatnot.

So annoying.

I write some more things, and they suck to even greater degrees. So many words, a parade of progressing suckage: suck, suckier, suckiest.

Mila Henry said she always had difficulty writing the passage-of-time chapters because she "preferred minutiae," and "which detail should I leave out?" I always found it interesting that Henry somehow managed to implement the practice of including everything—right down to which socks were worn on which days by which characters (from *Babies on Bombs*)—while still maintaining the ideal that "writing is less about the words and more about the silence between them." But that's life, I guess. It is complex and nuanced and not one thing any more than it is another.

The cursor blinks . . .

I shut the laptop and it makes that *thop* sound when the screen connects with the base of the computer. On my worst writing days, it sounds less like *thop* and more like *stop*, which I interpret as my computer telling me to just quit already.

Outside, gray clouds loom, looking for all the world like the floodgates of the heavens are about to open, the springs of the great deep bursting forth. And for some reason I think of the smile I just saw in the kitchen.

I open my computer.

"No, I don't think I will stop."

epilogue ➔ *and lo! the world emerges a strange and fascinating place*

January 8, my birthday: the ultimate bookmark in the Passage of Time.

"Noah, it's freezing," says Mom, but she can tell from the look on my face that I'm going out anyway, that when I announced my decision to take "nightly walks," I did not mean, "nightly walks, except during inclement weather." I bundle up—gloves, hoodie, coat, boots, earbuds under double-layered hats—and hit the streets, like that.

It's what I do.

Tonight we had chicken cordon bleu on trays in the basement while watching *Wait Until Dark*, Penny's latest obsession. Family movie nights are like a thing now, and I don't know—I love it, but it also makes me sad, like the four of us are trying to soak up what time we have left together. Penny pretends to be inconsolable about my leaving, but I think deep down she's excited at the prospect of flying alone.

Cold in my bones, Bowie in my ears, I walk the streets of Iverton, and I say, "Happy birthday, buddy," and Bowie says, *Cheers, mate,* and there is nothing like this, like seeing your breath in front of your face as if it's trying to prove your own existence to you, nothing like the rhythm of one foot in front of the other, each step a contract between your mind and the robot that you are, quite literally, in this thing together.

Suddenly, and without meaning to, I'm on Piedmont, pulling my earbuds out from under my hat, letting that salient, immortal voice float up into the winter-black sky.

Next door, an empty porch: Kurt and Abraham are in for the night.

From the curb, I stare up at the Lovelocks' house like it's an off-limits diorama in a museum after closing. There is a form of reverence here, but mostly disgust and fear and a strange sense of connection, and it occurs to me that if I've intentionally avoided Piedmont on my nightly route—and I have—then it's no accident I'm here now.

I step through the yard, up the porch steps, knock on the door now, and there's that violent urge—but that's not why I'm here, not why I knocked, not why I'm ringing the doorbell.

Why am I ringing the doorbell?

The door swings open.

Since last summer, I've seen Circuit once: in his car at a stoplight. I almost vomited on my steering wheel.

"Hey," he says, and behind him there are voices, laughter—as if this were a completely normal house. Circuit says,

"Noah," but I can't talk yet, so I just shake my head once and that seems to be enough.

I focus on Circuit now, on where he has been: the emotional hell he must have gone through with his father's passing, the way his father passed, and the tragedy he endured. I've heard the cultivation of empathy grows stronger with use, and so I try to use it now. Surely, this kid in front of me would be an entirely other person had those things not happened. Surely, it wasn't his fault, not really.

I forgive you.

Difficult enough to think, much less say.

So I stand on the porch in silence, and Circuit waits, and just when I think, *It's no use, just knock his fucking teeth out already*—it begins to snow. Not a dusting, but a heavy, thick-flaked snow. He says, "Come on in, man," but I don't. I let the snow land where it may and wonder at the longevity of its history: its lakes, oceans, and pools; its cave rivers; its underground civilizations. And because *every atom belonging to me as good belongs to you*, I wonder how many bodies this snow has sung electric only now to land on mine. "History is a long time," I say; and that's when I know I will forgive him.

But not until I can mean it.

"Okay," he says, but he's gone now, and Piedmont, too, and Iverton along with it, the whole world consumed, and from way up here I see those subtle connectors stretching through time and space in that most peculiar way, skipping from one snowflake to the next like smooth stones across a pond.

You know those movies where the guy shows up on the girl's front porch in some grand romantic gesture?

And I wonder what truths might be found in a conversation that never happened.

I adore snow. My love of snow runneth deep.

"Noah," says Circuit. "You okay?"

A guy shows up with snow, that's either destiny or wizardry.

"I'm fine," I say, and I don't know if those stones ever land in the same place twice, but I think it's time to find out. "Is your sister home?"

ACKNOWLEDGMENTS

Thanks directed here ➼ Arnolds and Wingates for signing that family contract. Love the whole bunch of you.

Also here ➼ Ken Wright and Alex Ulyett at Viking, I am running out of creative ways to denote your brilliance. So: you guys are brilliant. Same goes for the rest of my Penguin family: Elyse Marshall, Jen Loja, Theresa Evangelista and WBYK (for my gorgeous glam rock cover), Kate Renner (for its equally gorgeous interior design), Dana Leydig, Kaitlin Severini & Janet Pascal (copyeditors extraordinaire), Carmela Iaria, Venessa Carson, Erin Berger, Emily Romero, Felicia Frazier, Rachel Cone-Gorham, Mariam Quraishi, John, Allan, Jill, Colleen, Sheila, Doni Kay, and all those top notch sales and marketing people.

And here, of course ➼ Dan Lazar (Agent Royale), Torie Doherty-Munro, James Munro, Cecilia de la Campa, Natalie Medina, and all at Writers House; and Josie Freeman at ICM.

A hearty "thanks, yo" to ➼ Adam Silvera for being the greatest muse a guy could ask for. It really is sad how much you love me.

Noah and I owe an enormous debt of gratitude to ➼ Courtney Stevens, Becky Albertalli, Jasmine Warga, Nic Stone, Yamile Mendez, Melanie Barbosa, Ellen Oh, Kelly Loy Gilbert, Jeff Zentner, Brendan Kiely, Bill Konigsberg, Blair Setnor (for all things swimming related), Brian Armentrout & Jared Gallaher & Kelly Meyers (for answering my many medical inquiries), Nicola Yoon, Victoria Schwab, Michelle Arnold, Gary Egan, Rebecca Langley, Abby Hendren, Teddy Ray, Michael Waters, Stephanie Appell & the beautiful people at Parnassus Books, Amanda Connor & the beautiful people at Joseph-Beth Booksellers, and all the fabulously smart librarians and booksellers who do truly heroic work on the daily.

But mostly ➻ Stephanie and Wingate, thanks for floating through space with me—even if it is most peculiar.

Turn the page to read deleted texts between Noah and Alan!

Alan: OK

Noah: OK

Alan: We're like . . . shit

Alan: I forget their names. That boy and girl

Alan: From that book

Noah: I'd like to help you, Alan.

Alan: It was a movie too

Noah: Really, I would.

Alan: Teenagers. With cancer. Go to Amsterdam

Noah: The Fault in Our Stars

Alan: Bingo

Noah: How are we like them?

Alan: Remember? One would say okay, then the
other would say okay

Noah: Okay

Alan: Okay

Noah: Promise me something.

Alan: Name it

Noah: If you're thirty. And I'm thirty . . .

Alan: I'VE BEEN WAITING FOR THIS MOMENT
ALL MY LIFE

Noah: . . . and no one's taken us to Amsterdam yet . . .

Alan: Okay not what I was expecting

Noah: . . . we'll go together.

Alan: Fine. I will take you to Amsterdam

Alan: But only if we split a doobie in a gondola
with one of those dudes who sings super
loud

Noah: Your analysis of Holland is both accurate and respectful,
I'm sure.

Alan: What pairs better with weed, champagne
or absinthe?

Alan: Maybe it's a parallel universe???

Noah: Doubtful.

Alan: Not *this* universe. The other one

Alan: The one where I like DC Comics. Maybe *that's* the parallel universe

Noah: Quick question. What do you think "parallel" means?

◄||||||||►

Alan: Deepest desires, go

Noah: You first.

Noah: And my undying love doesn't count.

Alan: Oh

Noah: Nor do my swimmer calves

Alan: YOU ARE MAKING THIS VRY DIFFICULT

Noah: ¯_(ツ)_/¯

Alan: OK fine

Alan: Someday I would like to make a living on my art

Noah: The beat poetry, you mean?

Alan: I do mean that yes

Noah: Are there professional beat poets, tho?

Alan: HOW DARE YOU???

Noah: I just mean, like—is beat poetry something people do for money?

Alan: At least I answered the question

Noah: Fine. I'll answer. But you'll laugh.

Alan: I swear, on behalf of professional beat poets everywhere

Alan: I will not laugh at your dreams

Noah: I would like to make a living by living.

Alan: So like a hunter/gatherer type sitch?

Noah: No.

Noah: Maybe.

Noah: I don't know.

Noah: A job I don't hate. Friends and family I love.

Alan: Ah

Noah: Less concerned with what I do, more concerned with who
I am.

Alan: Like how they do in Spain

Noah: Is that how they do in Spain?

Alan: Dude. They eat dinner at like midnight
over there

Alan: Chill as fuuuuuuck

Noah: OK yes. I would like to be a Spaniard when I grow up.

Alan: Like Javier Whats-his-face, with the tragic
haircut

Noah: Bardem. And that haircut was just the one movie.

Alan: Really?

Noah: I think his hair is pretty okay otherwise.

Alan: How about some beat poetry for Javier
Bardem's hair?

Noah: Do I have an option?

Alan: Bardem was his name

Alan: Acting, his game

Alan: Such a badass, such a great ass, such
range, such range

Alan: But when doors began to shut

Alan: On that handcrafted butt

Alan: People wondered why, how, what?

Noah: (We did wonder why, how, what)

Alan: I'll tell you why, how, what

Alan: It's that fucking bowl cut

Noah: BRAVO

Alan: *takes a bow*

Noah: I especially like the "handcrafted butt"

Alan: I know you do, Noah. I know you do.

◄▮▮▮▮▮▮▮►

Noah: Come over?

Alan: IT'S ALL HAPPENING

Noah: Not a booty call.

Alan: Sorry, can't

Noah: Fine

Noah: I'd rather 'flix and chill with Gilmore Girls anyway.

Alan: Just shortening "Netflix" to "flix" doesn't make it any less sexual

Noah: Just me and Rory

Noah: Jess can come too, I guess

Alan: Noah

Noah: #TeamLogan not invited

Alan: Noah

Noah: And #TeamDean can get the fuck off my lawn

Alan: Keep talking like this and you're going to die alone

Noah: You know what they say

Alan: What's good for the goose is good for the other thing?

Noah: That. Also, hell is other people

Alan: Whoever said that had no friends

Noah: Sartre. No Exit.

Alan: Gesundheit

Noah: Why can't you come over?

Alan: I'm busy.

Noah: Doing?

Alan: I'm vry cozy at the moment

Noah: Are you busy or vry cozy?

Alan: You're like a child who won't quit asking
    why.

Noah: WHY WHY WHY?

Alan: OMG, fine. I'm watching The Great British
    Baking Show while perusing Snapchat.
    Happy?

Noah: From what I hear, those aren't chats being snapped.

Alan: See, this is why I didn't want to tell you

Alan: Anything to do with the Internet and I can count on you turning into an old man

Noah: You just said I was a child.

Alan: You are a childlike old man

Noah: God, I hate his face

Alan: ???

Noah: Sorry. Dean just called himself a saint

Noah: I guess because he's *allowing* Rory a night to herself?

Noah: This guy tho

Alan: Not much better over here.

Alan: Mary Berry about to crack some skulls over these soggy bottoms

Noah: I don't get how we're not the most popular kids in Iverton

Alan: That's what I'm saying, yo

Alan: We are misunderstood in our time

Noah: Every time, really.

Alan: All the times

Noah: What's a soggy bottom??

Alan: When the bottom of a pastry is wet or not
    cooked through

Noah: You must really love this show.

Noah: I said, "What's a soggy bottom," and you answered
    seriously.

Alan: Shit, technical challenge is lit, gotta go

YEAR OF ME

by Mila Henry

CHAPTER 17 →

'Let's order first!'

'You shouldn't exclaim things,' said Cletus. 'It's shit writing.'

'But we aren't writing!' exclaimed Nathan. 'We're having conversation!'

Cletus considered this. 'Shit conversing, then.' As was his custom when feeling he'd driven home a particularly stimulating point, Cletus simultaneously shrugged & sneezed. He unfolded the menu in front of him, his eyes landing on a staged photograph of a humongous plastic-looking burger drenched in melted cheese, when an excessively tall waitress approached. Way up there, *almost near the damn ceiling for crying out loud*, thought Cletus, a nametag on her apron read, *Hi there, I'm Occasionally.*

Occasionally what? wondered Cletus. *Parched? Randy? Bored beyond belief?* Cletus considered the possibility that this woman's name was, in fact, Occasionally. His own last name was a noun; it had served him well enough. However, having never met someone with an adverb for a name & unsure of the proper etiquette Cletus decided against asking the waitress outright.

'Is that your real name?!' exclaimed Nathan.

'*Nathan*,' said Cletus under his breath. 'Are you always such a spurious cur?'

'It is actually,' said the waitress whose real name was apparently, incredibly, Occasionally. She laughed in a terse spurt like a bum car revving its engine & asked, 'What's a spurious cur?'

'No matter,' said Cletus, taking in his first human adverb: she wore a green apron & had brown hair the color of bark. Cletus decided Occasionally resembled a maple tree, specifically one from his bastard of an ex-neighbor's fucking gorgeous backyard.

She stood there smiling, patiently awaiting their orders.

At least she's unassuming, thought Cletus. *Better 'Occasionally' than 'Victoriously' or 'Voraciously.'* If there was one thing Cletus could live without it was pomp. Also, the shingles.

'Well, I like it!' exclaimed Nathan. 'Your name, I mean. Sui generis & all that. Good for you!'

Occasionally the Maple's smile grew like an unruly vine. 'So what can I get for you gentlemen?' she asked.

Recalling a certain pedestrian turn of phrase, something about beating & joining, Cletus held up the menu & pointed to the aforementioned photograph. 'I'll have one of these humongous plastic cheeseburgers!' he exclaimed.

Cletus Foot was, by all accounts, shitty at both writing & conversing.

After taking Nathan's order ('Pancakes! Extra syrup, please!'), Occasionally rumbled off behind the counter, leaving Cletus & Nathan in a cloud of somewhat awkward silence.

The cloud stuck around as it turned out, & before long Occasionally was back with their plates of food.

'These pancakes are the best!' said Nathan, barely having sunk his saffron-colored teeth into one bite.

Oh-me-oh-my, what a goof, thought Cletus. Nathan was a goof, to be sure. What other possible conclusion could be drawn of a person claiming one pancake to be inherently more valuable than all the pancakes griddled the world over? There was a 'best martini,' a 'best concerto,' a 'best lay.' There was no 'best pancake,' & to suggest otherwise was goofy, decidedly so.

Or so decided Cletus.

'How's that burger with cheese treating you?' asked Nathan. 'Looks delish!'

'Just call it a fucking cheeseburger, will you?'

'Right-o!'

'And don't say *right-o*. Or *delish*. While we're at it, don't say anything. I prefer to masticate in silence.'

'Aye-aye, skipper!'

Cletus had had his eye on an especially savory bite, very cheesy, right in the heart of the bun-burger ratio. It was during this bite he paused, looked at Nathan, & asked the question they had both been avoiding. 'What is the meaning of life, do you think?'

Now: true, they'd only met a few hours prior at the singles mixer in the basement of a local Baptist church where they'd both been kicked to the curb for 'conduct unbecoming' (though unbecoming *what* exactly had never been made clear; Cletus secretly suspected his chiseled features & impressive body mass index were simply too much for those weak Baptist knees), but Cletus felt a certain brotherhood with Nathan. He felt he could tell him things.

Nathan, on the other hand, knew exactly why they'd been kicked to the Baptist curb (he had brought one of his paintings to auction off to the highest bidder, while Cletus saw a room full of people & seized the opportunity to read aloud his favorite passages from his latest sci-fi duology; they'd been peddling their goods in God's house for godsake), & while he had no guarantee that Cletus was an honest, working man, he knew they were alike.

Animals usually do.

'I'd like to think it's art,' Nathan said.

'Hmm?'

'You asked about the meaning of life. I'm saying—I'd like to think it's art.'

'Me too.'

'Creation.'

'OK.'

'The creation of art.'

'Yes, that would be nice.'

Nathan mopped up the last bit of syrup & pancake & ate without pleasure. 'I see you met Her too, then.'

'Who's that?'

'God.'

To anyone who happened to be listening the question would have seemed abrupt & outlandish, but Cletus knew better. 'Oh, Her,' he said. 'Yes, we've met.'

Occasionally stopped by—*more frequently than her name might suggest*, thought Cletus—to refill Nathan's coffee. Nathan thanked her & it occurred to Cletus that his new companion had thrown in the towel on his exclamations.

'So, uh,' said Cletus. Unwilling to shed light on his own encounter with the Almighty before hearing Nathan's, he resorted to utterances rather than words, fragments rather than sentences. "Um, huh," he went on, unashamed. Being rotten at conversing often meant leaving little threads of discussion hanging around in your wake. 'Anyway,' he said in a simultaneous shrug & sneeze.

Nathan dropped his head to the table & began rhythmically pounding it against the Formica.

'Stop that,' said Cletus.

Nathan did not.

'Stop it. People are staring.'

This only seemed to strengthen Nathan's resolve. He pounded harder, & with each pound, uttered the words, *'I-don't . . . under . . . stand . . . I-don't . . . under . . . stand . . .'*

'You're brooding,' said Cletus. 'I cannot tolerate brooding.'

This stopped Nathan, if only momentarily. 'I'm a brooder,' he said, forehead still on the table. 'Father was a brooder, Grandfather was a brooder. Brooding is in my bones. I was *born* to brood.'

'Quit saying the word *brood* for crissake.'

Nathan raised his head & the look in his eyes almost broke Cletus's heart. 'Where did you see Her?'

'On the road to Montana,' said Cletus. True, he hadn't planned to speak of it first, but there was such a thing as pity-spurred generosity. 'She parted clouds. You?'

'Cemetery. I was visiting my aunt Ingrid when out of nowhere . . . *bam* . . . there She was right next to me. I poured out my heart. Told Her I was afraid I'd lost my soul. Know what She said?'

'What?'

'She put Her arm on my shoulder & asked where I'd last seen it.'

Cletus considered the day he'd driven his truncated auto

from Arizona to Montana, eating a hot dog, minding his own damn business, when She'd parted the clouds above, Her voice booming down upon him with such force he'd had no choice but to pull over. Her methods had seemed so revelatory at the time, so entirely God-like, but in retrospect, Cletus wondered if they weren't just a touch lazy. Parting the clouds seemed a laughably human idea for the cosmically Divine.

'She doesn't love us, Cletus. Does She?'

Cletus thought about what God had told him, to quit stealing people's mail, & for the love of Herself, do what he'd been created to do: join the Marines. He'd done just that & now here he was, sitting in a diner with a perfect stranger who wouldn't quit banging his head against the goddam table.

'No, I don't think She does,' said Cletus.

Nathan went back to pounding his head.

Cletus took a sip of water & raised two middle fingers to the room.

In time, Nathan stopped. But his forehead was red from where he'd been pounding the table. 'I don't have any money,' he said.

'It's fine, I'll pay for the pancakes.'

'That's not what I meant. I mean—I have nothing. In life. I've wasted my talents & my time & my faith & now there is nothing left of me. I'm a ghost.'

'Nathan.'

Cletus watched his new friend cry. The young man was clearly down on his luck, but there was more to it than that. Truth be told Cletus saw much of himself—much of who he wanted to be, much of who he used to be—in Nathan. For Cletus, the world had stopped letting him down when he'd stopped expecting it not to. But Nathan still felt things &

deeply. Nathan still believed in possibility, still believed there was a chance the world was not in fact a smoking shitball of disappointment.

Which it was, of course. One big stinking, smoking shitball.

Cletus opened his mouth to break this news to his friend, when suddenly he glimpsed a small burst of color protruding from the inside pocket of Nathan's blazer. 'What is that?' asked Cletus.

Nathan pulled out a painting about the size of a pocketbook. 'I thought maybe it would impress someone. At the mixer, I mean. Silly of me.'

'May I?' asked Cletus, taking the canvas in his hands. He turned it, then again, trying to decide if he loved or hated it. The painting seemed both loud & soft, a little presumptuous of its virtue, until Cletus looked closer & decided no, it had just the right account of its own virtue. And then Cletus began to cry (a thing he rarely did), & he was dumbfounded (a thing he rarely was), for he understood that what he held was rare magic, that Nathan had harnessed that magic, had completed the unspoken commission of artists the world over: *Create something* new *for godsake*.

Cletus looked from the art to the artist, this shell of a man sitting across from him, & in a blinding revelatory blaze, he understood. To complete the commission—to create something truly new—it was not enough for the artist to put themselves into their work; they must also die to it.

'I just want to create,' said Nathan, as good as dead. 'Just to create.'

Cletus reached his hand across the table, placed it on Nathan's. 'So did She. And here we are. But you know—I'm not sure Her creation would know what to do with yours.'

Nathan was overcome with emotion at these words & the two men wept openly onto the Formica tabletop. Nearby patrons whispered, eyes darting furtively at these strange men who would dare cry & hold hands in so public a place. Cletus did not care. For in one hand he held magic & in the other the magician.

And Cletus Foot wondered if perhaps the world was not so giant a shitball after all.

'I'm sorry, Nathan. I'm just so sorry.'

It was silent for a while—Cletus was the first to stop crying. But the two held hands like that for some time, content in the simple & silent company afforded by the kindred spirit.

'Let's get out of here.'

'Nowhere to go,' said Nathan.

When they'd first entered the diner, Nathan spoke as if the world was at his feet; now he spoke as someone bearing its weight on his back.

Cletus knew the feeling.

'Look,' Cletus said. 'You are a great artist.'

'Ha.'

'Don't *ha* me. You are. The lofty morons of the world may not see it. You probably won't live to *see* them see it, but believe me, generations from now they'll know.' Cletus held up the small canvas. 'They will see this painting hanging in an art gallery'—

'If galleries are still around by then.'

—'in Paris'—

'If Paris is still around by then.'

—'& they will stand in awe, shaking their heads at the miraculous oeuvre of Nathan . . . uh . . . what's your last name?'

'Brumbleberry.'

Oh boy, thought Cletus. He took a sip of water, cleared his throat, & tried to pick up the pieces of his little motivational speech. 'They'll, um, whisper the name—uh, well. They'll whisper *your* name in, you know, awe & what have you.'

A different waitress stopped by the table to drop off their check. Cletus studied it for a moment. 'How many pancakes did you eat, for crissake?'

'I don't know what I'm doing,' said Nathan. 'I have no one in my life & I have no idea what's next.'

Cletus set down the check, leaned across the table. 'OK, listen. I've had it with the brooding, so I'm going to let you in on two secrets. First, you have no one in your life because you're a miserable git & when you're not a miserable git, you're a completely insufferable git. I know because I'm one too. Guys like us will always be alone, that's fine—the trick is knowing the difference between being alone & being lonely. As for not knowing what's next . . . sometimes I don't know what I'm writing until it's written. Sometimes I don't know what I'm thinking until I read it. And sometimes I don't know where I'm going until I'm there. So I'll tell you what you do. Paint. Forget the lofty morons. Just paint, Nathan.' Cletus glanced at the check on the table. 'Now let's get out of this shithole.'

Together, Cletus & Nathan left the diner without paying. Cletus agreed to follow Nathan to his house, where they would further discuss their artistic endeavors.

On the way there, Cletus got lost.

They never saw each other again.

Keep reading for an excerpt from David Arnold's critically acclaimed novel

The Uncomfortable Nearness of Strangers

September 1—afternoon

Dear Isabel,

As a member of the family, you have a right to know what's going on. Dad agrees but says I should avoid "topics of substance and despair." When I asked how he propose I do this, seeing as our family is prone to substantial desperation, he rolled his eyes and flared his nostrils, like he does. The thing is, I'm incapable of fluff, so here goes. The straight dope, Mim-style. Filled to the brim with "topics of substance and despair."

Just over a month ago, I moved from the greener pastures of Ashland, Ohio, to the dried-up wastelands of Jackson, Mississippi, with Dad and Kathy. During that time, it's possible I've gotten into some trouble at my new school. Not trouble with a capital *T*, you understand, but this is a subtle distinction for adults once they're determined to ruin a kid's youth. My new principal is just such a man. He sched-uled a conference for ten a.m., in which the malfeasance of

Mim Malone would be the only point of order. Kathy switched her day shift at Denny's so she could join Dad as a parental representative. I was in algebra II, watching Mr. Harrow carry on a romantic relationship with his polynomials, when my name echoed down the coral-painted hallways.

"Mim Malone, please report to Principal Schwartz's office. Mim Malone to the principal's office."

(Suffice it to say, I didn't *want* to go, but the Loudspeaker summoned, and the Student responded, and 'twas always thus.)

The foyer leading into the principal's office was dank, a suffocating decor of rusty maroons and browns. Inspirational posters were plastered around the room, boasting one-word encouragements and eagles soaring over purple mountain majesties.

I threw up a little, swallowed it back down.

"You can go on back," said a secretary without looking up. "They're expecting you."

Beyond the secretary's desk, Principal Schwartz's heavy oak door was cracked open an inch. Nearing it, I heard low voices on the other side.

"What's her mother's name again?" asked Schwartz, his timbre muffled by that lustrous seventies mustache, a holdover from the glory days no doubt.

"Eve," said Dad.

Schwartz: "Right, right. What a shame. Well, I hope Mim is grateful for your involvement, Kathy. Heaven knows she needs a mother figure right now."

Kathy: "We all just want Eve to get better, you know? And she will. She'll beat this disease. Eve's a fighter."

Just outside the door, I stood frozen—inside and out. *Disease?*

Schwartz: (Sigh.) "Does Mim know?"

Dad: (Different kind of sigh.) "No. The time just doesn't seem right. New school, new friends, lots of . . . new developments, as you can see."

Schwartz: (Chuckle.) "Quite. Well, hopefully things will come together for Eve in . . . where did you say she was?"

Dad: "Cleveland. And thank you. We're hoping for the best."

(Every great character, Iz, be it on page or screen, is multidimensional. The good guys aren't all good, the bad guys aren't all bad, and any character wholly one or the other shouldn't exist at all. Remember this when I describe the antics that follow, for though I am not a villain, I am not immune to villainy.)

Our Heroine turns from the oak door, calmly exits the office, the school, the grounds. She walks in a daze, trying to put the pieces together. Across the football field, athletic meatheads sneer, but she hears them not. Her trusty Goodwill shoes carry her down the crumbling sidewalk while she considers the three-week drought of letters and phone calls from her mother. Our Heroine takes the shortcut behind the Taco Hole, ignoring its beefy bouquet. She walks the lonely streets of her new neighborhood, rounds the sky-scraping oak, and pauses for a moment in the shade of her new residence. She checks the mailbox—empty. As always. Pulling out her phone, she dials her mother's number for the hundredth time, hears the same robotic lady for the hundredth time, is disheartened for the hundredth time.

We're sorry, this number has been disconnected.

She shuts her phone and looks up at this new house, a house bought for the low, low price of Everything She'd Ever Known to Be True. "*Glass and concrete and stone,*" she whispers, the chorus of one of her favorite songs. She smiles, pulls her hair back into a ponytail, and finishes the lyric. "*It is just a house, not a home.*"

Bursting through the front door, Our Heroine takes the steps three at a time. She ignores the new-house smell—a strange combination of sanitizer, tacos, and pigheaded denial—and sprints to her bedroom. Here, she repacks her trusty JanSport backpack with overnight provisions, a bottle of water, toiletries, extra clothes, meds, war paint, makeup remover, and a bag of potato chips. She dashes into her father and stepmother's bedroom and drops to her knees in front of the feminine dresser. Our Heroine reaches behind a neatly folded stack of Spanx in the bottom drawer and retrieves a coffee can labeled HILLS BROS. ORIGINAL BLEND. Popping the cap, she removes a thick wad of bills and counts by Andrew Jacksons to eight hundred eighty dollars. (Her evil stepmother had overestimated the secrecy of this hiding spot, for Our Heroine sees *all*.)

Adding the can of cash to her backpack, she bolts from her house-not-a-home, jogs a half mile to the bus stop, and catches a metro line to the Jackson Greyhound terminal. She's known the where for a while now: Cleveland, Ohio, 947 miles away. But until today, she wasn't sure of the how or when.

The how: a bus. The when: pronto, posthaste, lickety-split. And . . . scene.

But you're a true Malone, and as such, this won't be enough for you. You'll need more than just wheres, whens, and hows—you'll need whys. You'll think *Why wouldn't Our Heroine just (insert brilliant solution here)?* The truth is, reasons are hard. I'm standing on a whole stack of them right now, with barely a notion of how I got up here.

So maybe that's what this will be, Iz: my Book of Reasons. I'll explain the whys behind my whats, and you can see for yourself how my Reasons stack up. Consider that little clandestine convo between Dad, Kathy, and Schwartz Reason #1. It's a long way to Cleveland, so I'll try and space the rest out, but for now, know this: my Reasons may be hard, but my Objectives are quite simple.

Get to Cleveland, get to Mom.

I salute myself.

I accept my mission.

Signing off,

Mary Iris Malone,

Mother-effing Mother-Saver

RETRACING THE STICK FIGURE on the front of this journal makes little difference. Stick figures are eternally anemic.

I pull my dark hair across one shoulder, slump my forehead against the window, and marvel at the outside world. Before Mississippi had her devilish way, my marvelings were wondrously unique. Recently they've become I-don't-know-what . . . middling. Tragically mediocre. To top it off, a rain of biblical proportions is absolutely punishing the earth right now, and I can't help feeling it deserves it. Stuffing my journal in my backpack, I grab my bottle of Abilitol. Tip, swallow, repeat daily: this is the habit, and habit is king, so says Dad. I swallow the pill, then shove the bottle back in my bag with attitude. Also part of the habit. So says I.

"Th'hell you doing in here, missy?"

I see the tuft first, a tall poke of hair towering over the front two seats. It's dripping wet, and crooked like the Leaning Tower of Pisa. The man—a Greyhound employee named Carl, according to the damp patch on his button-down—is huge. Lumbering, even. Still eyeballing me, he pulls a burrito out of nowhere, unwraps it, digs in.

Enchanté, Carl.

Read the *New York Times* bestseller from David Arnold

"Arnold's funny and touching second novel is about many things: making peace with the past; the families we create; abstract painting; and what it means to be a 'genuine heart-thinker'. . . Arnold has a talent for stringing together words in just the right, jumbled order. His sentences are arrows." **—The New York Times Book Review**

"[In] David Arnold's follow-up to last year's wonderful *Mosquitoland* . . . Arnold continues to show mastery in crafting relatable teens struggling with dark circumstances . . . They're a highly enjoyable bunch of outsiders." **—USA Today**

"Funny, sweet, utterly heart-wrenching." **—Entertainment Weekly**

"A gorgeous, insightful, big-hearted joy of a book. *Kids of Appetite* made me fall in love with the world a little bit more."
—Nicola Yoon, #1 *New York Times* bestselling author of *Everything, Everything*

"*Kids of Appetite* is one of the most honest, emotional, human books I have ever read. You will feel it. This one's a life-changer."
—Becky Albertalli, Morris Award–winning author of *Simon vs. the Homo Sapiens Agenda*